Tales of Fire and Embers

Xandra Noel

This is a work of fiction. References to real people, locations, events, organizations or establishments are intended for the sole purpose to provide authenticity and are used fictitiously. But, if you do happen to walk into a forest and find a fae prince, you need to message me immediately!

Tales of Fire and Embers

-Tales of Earth and Leaves book 2-

"The most powerful weapon on earth is the human soul on fire."

-F.Foch

Summer

Anwen

Chapter One

"Tell me sprout, how would you like to see your princeling again?"

His words made my body stop abruptly. I remained as silent as a marble statue, unable to fill my lungs with air.

See him again. See Ansgar again. The words drilled into me. Their power, a desire ablaze in my heart. My mind. My body. Inside every muscle. *See him again.*

"How?" I whispered, my words as heavy as iron, wanting to shackle the answer from his lips. Rhylan materialised in front of me, jumping the fifty feet that separated us in a split second. His mouth displayed that proud smug smile of his.

"How?" I repeated, demanding, my words catching strength, powered by the roots of hope blooming in my chest. "Tell me!" I shouted, my fists finding their target on his stomach.

I shoved him with all the anger I had, all that remained, but his stature barely moved a muscle. That grin popped over his mouth again, plastering mockery and curiosity.

"You must be desperate…" the bastard purred into my ear, delaying the words I wanted to hear most.

"Rhylan, I swear to god…" An empty threat. Both he and I knew it. There was nothing I could do, nothing in my favour. I had no advantage over him and I remained completely and helplessly at his mercy.

"How can I see him again? How is such a thing possible?" I insisted, my eyes wet with unshed tears of anger and false hope. If he had come here just to tantalize and mock me, I would not give him the satisfaction. He had already done enough.

"It's quite simple, little sprout." I grimaced at the mention of the nickname he gave me long ago. When I was but a silly girl. Now he had found a wounded woman.

"Hush now, tiny sprout. You will give yourself a heart attack. My question is simple." He took the step that separated us, closing in the distance. Rhylan's adamant eyes scanned mine. Reading my thoughts, I understood. He had that power, after all.

He must have not liked what he saw in there, because his upper lip twitched.

"Your mind is so depressing," he pointed a finger at my temple and patted it over my skin, emphasizing his findings.

"I wonder who is at fault for that," I spat. My patience ran thin by the second, and I did not plan on spending any more of my time as the target of amusement of a fireling, no matter how powerful he may be.

He understood my impatience and displayed a proud grin.

"Very well. To business then."

I stepped away, making my way around him, decided on leaving him behind, and returning to the car. But he moved to the side, blocking my way.

"What would you do to see Ansgar again?"

As he said the words, the fireling grabbed my chin, lifting my face slightly to meet his eyes. Just the mention of his name on Rhylan's lips formed another crack in what I thought was an already too broken heart. But what I found on his face was pure interest.

"Everything." I responded in a single breath. The truth. I would do anything to go back in time and see my love again.

"Great." Rhylan smiled with satisfaction. "Let's make a deal."

Ansgar

Chapter Two

"Let's see if you are feeling chatty today, prince."

I heard the voice as he opened the cell door, making the hinges scream in pain. Just as I had been, over and over and over. I could barely remember my own name.

The fireling walked to me, finding my body crouched in a corner, trying to amass whatever coldness I could from the musty stone wall. It did not help much, did not offer any relief for my infected wounds nor the fresh cuts he had come to inflict.

"Come now, you disgusting filth, the commanders wait for no one."

As he finished spitting the demand, I felt my body lifted by the shoulders and dragged outside the cell. I could not see much, between the iron shackles on both my wrists and ankles and the hair running down my face in big lumps of dried blood, I barely distinguished my surroundings.

Throbbing pain squeezed my ankles when the iron chains clattered against the stone floors and bumped back into my legs. I did not know how much time had passed, how long I'd been here.

Tortured day in and day out. Though the concept of sunlight remained relative to this place.

There was no light around, the only vision of its shapes was held by flaming torches planted against the walls and candelabras in the main halls. Like the one I was dragged into. The commander's quarters.

I did not bother to study the halls, nor did I try to form a mapping of the surroundings in my head, like I did when I first arrived here. Plans of escape, of retribution, had kept me hopeful for months, the only nourishment I found in this forgotten chaos.

Dreams of Anwen and reuniting with my family gave me more strength than I could possibly think, judging by the guards' and commander's expressions at the end of every failed torture session.

At first, I even mocked them for using such old techniques on a prince. Treating me like I hadn't been trained in the eventuality of an attack. I even suggested new machinery to them and offered to draw up some plans and wait until they finished building the new torture device. "I can at least take some credit in elevating this place," I'd mocked.

It was not appreciated.

When I offered to trade my life for Anwen's, I did not have any expectations to continue living. Nor did I understand Rhylan's kindness to give us another day together. He could have claimed my energy then and there, instead, he offered us more time. To create memories that helped me remain nourished, even though I was only fed when Marreth happened upon my cell.

In the initial days, all three Fire Kingdom commanders

established a thrusting presence around me, barely abandoning my captured self to replenish their energy or get food. Even that, they did in turns.

Serpium remained through it all, week after week, even month after month if my scabbing and reopened wounds proved an accurate indication of the passage of time. The second commander and master torturer of the Fire Kingdom took delight in surprising me with different techniques, and I reciprocated, with various echoing screams on a daily basis. After a while, I recognised him by the way he walked towards my cell and I could envision his tall, bald and shirtless presence without having to look at him any longer. Serpium took delight in showing his skin and displaying the scars he had accumulated throughout his miserable existence. Judging by the burn scars on his neck and right shoulder, he had been punished in his youth and enjoyed returning pain towards others.

He did not like to talk too much, or at least not directly to me, unless it was to ask the same question, tirelessly, over and over again. When I did not respond, or my answers came with screaming gushes rather than the desired words, Serpium went on talking to his blades instead, telling each and every one of them which body part they would penetrate, at what depth and the angle they would be inserted through. It seemed to offer him a sense of tranquillity since the blades did not respond but only executed his commands without protest. I never saw the second commander without a sharp object by his side, be it to use or just to give him peace at the thought that he could, indeed, inflict pain at any time he desired so.

In time, the commanders became more creative with the torture attempts, even though each passing day added another drop to their failure. The iron shackles held a constant presence, weakening my body with each advancing moment. Unbearable pain held me awake at night, stopping me from the dreams that had kept me alive. Other times, they resorted to serums and potions, making me see things that were not there. They differed on the whim of the commander in charge. At times, they made me see Anwen in my cell, running towards me and hugging me, placing her sweet face on my chest, just like she loved to do. Other times it was father's death. The kingdom covered in flames.

I recognized Crypto's work, he liked psychological torture more than anything. The third commander exchanged roles with Serpium, my daily pain-inflicting companion, every few sessions and experimented with potions and mind-altering elixirs on my already weakened spirit. His approaching presence became noted by the smell of putrid mud. It created a cover over his dark features and heavy brown hair and gave him the distinct aspect of a male who loathed his assignment.

Crypto's visits in my cell did not linger, he either forced liquid down my throat or vaporised it in my cell until I succumbed to the effect he had prepared for me. During the few seconds of lucidity I conserved after his arrival, I heard him complaining about having to dig tunnels towards the other regnums, something he did not appear too keen on. It made sense that he was always grumpy and tired, complaining about dirt to the extent that his body had taken a liking to the bits of ground he had to dig through and made sure to conserve some of it on his clothes or the top of his head and shoulders. The male walked like a princess on a mating day, only he did so leaving dirt in his stead rather than rose petals.

Today, they must have come up with something even better. The commanders liked to announce it personally, yet I did not expect all three of them to gather just for me.

"Greetings, prince," a mocking familiar voice echoed in my head while the doors opened. Two sentinels lifted my arms and proceeded to drag me across the halls. I had been mistaken in thinking they had prepared another visit to the commander's quarters.

The halls we passed penetrated deeper into the core of the earth and wider decorated tunnels opened up in front of us. Red carpets I could stain with my blood and accumulated filth with. Not that I had a long expanse of minutes, the two sentinels dragged me so quickly I barely had time to lift my head and attempt to scan the walls for any clues as to our destination.

Door after door, halls, and stairs, they all formed before our steps and took us through a wide span of the kingdom. I guessed that if I had walked, I would have covered at least five miles since our departure point. Distance during which the iron shackles on my ankles clincked against my skin with each forced movement and I observed, pleased, how tiny drips of my blood left a minuscule stain of those shiny carpets. It formed a reminder that I had been there, that above all odds, I remained alive for this long. I guessed that those stains will live longer than me.

Memories could barely keep the flame of my life burning. Replaced by pain, lack of sleep, and barely any food, I felt my energy fading away, dripping out of me just like the blood smudges that ran away from my body to escape another torture session.

Before I had a moment to react, tall adamant carved doors shifted in front of me and formed a path to a black marble throne room that opened before my eyes.

This is where they hold court. I was to meet their leader. A relieved breath escaped my aching body. It could only mean one thing.

Execution.

Anwen

Chapter Three

Rhylan followed me back to the car as I forced my brain to work quickly, to find a plausible explanation for all of this. How could Ansgar still live? I squeezed back memories of the moment when his entire body vanished right in front of me, of how I'd squeezed the dry leaves he left behind, begging my mind, their goddess, and that energy that connected us to combine them into Ansgar again, to bring him back to me.

This had to be another one of Rhylan's tricks, though I had still to piece together his reasons. And why he felt the need to appear out of thin air after a year, offering me a deal. Whatever that meant.

My attention snapped back when I heard voices. We were approaching the event, and people still lingered for either interviews, celebrations, or photos. And I was bringing back a fae that came out of nowhere.

"Tell me everything, right now!" I stopped and grabbed Rhylan's wrist to force him by my side. During this time, he had frolicked through the woods around me, without a care in the world. He turned to me, slowly, without yanking his arm away, but stepping even closer, shrinking the distance.

"So eager, sprout. So eager…" No grin accompanied his lips

this time, only sheer temptation. He stared at me as though he was the devil, offering me the undeniable promise. If what he said was true, if there was a way for Ansgar to be alive and for me to see him, I would do whatever he asked.

"We'll chat more in the car," he announced and continued walking towards the crowd, dragging me after him since I refused to let him go.

By the time we got out of the woods, we probably looked like a cartoon feature, the average-sized woman struggling to stop a mountain of a man in his tracks. I even had my knees bent and soles jammed in the soil, yet his every step forced me to be dragged after him, towing my arms and my entire body with each determined movement.

The click of the cameras forced me to return to composure and release him abruptly. Probably too late, since reporters and cameras immediately zoomed on him and started questioning. With that, I guessed the titles would change to "Mystery man and heiress alone in the woods" and judging by the ten-questions-per-second round they bombarded us with, the story would not continue as an eco-friendly article. Through it all, Rhylan kept his cool and nodded or smiled charmingly, without releasing a single word. Furthermore, his imposing stance formed a path through the journalists for me to follow back to the car and he even opened the door for me to sneak inside.

As soon as I did, he stepped in after me, without expecting an invitation and pushed me further on the backseat with his hips to make room for himself. Alan, the driver, did not wait for an invitation and ran the engine, taking both me and Rhylan away from the agitation.

We kept silent for a few minutes until the new forest was completely behind us and Alan asked if my guest was coming with us to the airport.

"No," I replied at the same time as Rhylan responded with a "yes."

"I am not taking you to the airport, you will disappear just as you came and stop bothering me with your tricks and lies." I responded abruptly, keeping my vision focused on the driver rather than acknowledging Rhylan's presence, who sat so close to me that our thighs touched from time to time from the car's movement.

"Anwen, we have a lot to discuss and I assure you, what I told you in the forest is completely true," he responded, eyes so focused on me I could practically feel him scanning through my brain.

"Stop that," I demanded and instinctively covered my temple to block his power.

"You are anxious, hopeful, stressed, and emotionally in pain, and I have the answer to all that. It requires a long story, many details you won't like, and it might even tell you a thing or two about your brother."

I turned to him in shock, eyes wide, trying to decipher if he uttered any shred of truth.

The bastard smirked. "Yes, I will join Miss Anwen to the airport," he told Alan without shifting his eyes from mine. Since I did not respond, I heard the driver's voice muttering "very well," then focusing his full attention back to the road.

"What is your plan, Rhylan?" I asked in a low tone, trying to keep the conversation as private as I could with another person seated right next to us.

"I need you, sprout. There is no other plan. Ansgar needs you," he responded in a whispering tone.

"Even if that were true, since when do you care?" I huffed, momentarily forgetting my calmness.

"Since I realized my miscalculations in some steps I took, and ironically, you are the only person who might help put it all back together." His adamant eyes penetrated mine and Rhylan allowed me to scan him, to search every feature on his face and understand that his words spoke the truth.

A small jolt in my stomach flashed at the sight of him, the closeness we experienced. I didn't think I would ever see him again, yet here he was, in the same car as me. Without averting his gaze, Fear Gorta reached into his pocket and after searching for something, he extended his palm to me. I looked down to see a kitkat, then back to Rhylan whose lips curved upwards from the memories we shared with that chocolate bar. The days he visited me back at the mansion and the secrets he revealed while eating full packets of kitkats.

I reached for the chocolate, hands shaking from what it meant. "Is Ansgar truly alive?" my voice trembled with sudden hope, with revived dreams that I thought lost forever.

"He is. I swear it."

Over a dozen journalists waited for us by the time we reached the airport. During the ride, Rhylan did his best to talk about normal things and calm me down, though his presence alone raised palpitations in my chest. He asked cordial questions about the project, how I got the idea — that didn't go too well — how many forests we had regrown and he even gave me some updates on Evigt. The son of a duke had been dispatched in Ansgar's place and managed to restore the energy levels, much to Rhylan's discontent. The fireling hadn't intervened though, and muttered something about staying focused on the main goal.

Hundreds of camera flashes hammered around us, surrounding the car and there was no way to get out and safely into the plane other than through the gathering of press that appeared to be multiplying by the second.

"Is this your everyday life?" Rhylan asked with surprise and no small amount of excitement.

"No," I replied with disgust, "It's all because of you. Because you just had to come out of the forest and make a spectacle."

"So they all gathered to admire me? My handsomeness?" he grinned proudly.

"Urgh, just keep your mouth shut and get in the plane." I ordered him and opened the door on my side, struggling to make way through the cameras and flashes, muttering a 'no comment' from time to time when a mic was shoved into my face and questions about the man accompanying me arose.

To my surprise, Rhylan did as told and remained only a step or two away, copying the 'no comment' formula, though he did stop from time to time to throw a smile for photos. Five seconds after I got into the safety of the jet, he climbed the stairs behind me and flashed a passport and a visa at the customs officer in charge of private departures.

"Mr. Gordon," I heard the man say while returning the passport to Rhylan. After that, he gave the okay to the pilot and headed down the stairs.

"Mister Gordon?" I was surprised. "Do you actually have a surname?" I took my usual seat and continued mocking him.

"To your surprise, sprout, I've had many names for many centuries. The beauty of immortality," he flashed a grin and threw the passport in my lap. Curiosity overwhelmed me and I opened it to discover Rhylan's photo, along with the surname Gordon and a date of birth from thirty-four years ago in Macedonia. I flicked through the pages and stood surprised to discover a generous amount of stamps and visas, all across the globe. It could easily rival my brother's own passport.

"Why Macedonia?" I asked with unsuspected curiosity.

"Long time ago… Elisa," he smiled nostalgically at what I could only suspect were lingering memories of a lover he left behind somewhere in that country.

Before I had time to ask more questions, the pilot welcomed us

19

on board and sealed the safety doors and one of the flight attendants came to make sure our seatbelts were securely fastened before take-off. Rhylan took the seat opposite mine and we remained separated by a small table, throwing each other odd looks throughout the process.

Once we floated safely in the air, both flight attendants came to take our order. Even though they were talking to me, their stares did not leave the sight of Rhylan, who took the opportunity to remove his elegant jacket and remain in a black shirt that hugged his muscles like he was a marble sculpted statue.

"We are fine, thank you." I replied without giving him a chance to add a word. The only thing I wanted was to start the conversation we had been delaying for so long and I really didn't want to eat. My stomach formed a ball of nerves and the half kitkat I had in the car threatened to make its way back up.

"We would like a cheese platter and one of those tapas snack spreads for starters." Rhylan took the lead and smiled at the women. His eyes ran from one face to the other while he made sure to give them both the same amount of attention. "Then we'll have soup, either French onion or pumpkin and filet mignon as an entrée. Something with chocolate for dessert and an extra cold bottle of champagne." By the time he finished his right hand was an inch away from one of the girls' thighs and instead of jerking away, she looked ready to fall into his lap.

I grimaced, aware of the effect Rhylan had on women. I too had almost fallen into that trap before I knew better and I couldn't even imagine what went through those girls' minds. Or whatever thoughts he was putting in there himself. "Miss Anwen here and I would like privacy, so please only return to deliver the food during the flight."

The disappointment in both their faces looked evident, but they nodded and excused themselves, not without taking one last look at him before pulling the curtain.

"You're disgusting." I accused and sat back in my seat.

"Jealous, sprout? There's plenty more of that for you too," he grinned but I immediately cut him off.

"I have no interest in you Rhylan, other than whatever lie you are about to spit out of your wicked mouth. And I don't care what thoughts you put in their heads. I did my studies this time and I know everything about you and your powers." I accused before he even had a chance to speak or spin any part of the story in his favor.

"Did you now?" He looked impressed and copied my gestures, making himself comfortable and lying on the seat. "What exactly do you know, Miss Anwen?" He pressed the last words, spreading them like a whisper in my mind.

"That." I nodded the acknowledgement of his actions. "That you can talk into people's minds. That you can read my thoughts and you—"

"Read your thoughts?" he chuckled at the information. "Is that what the internet says about me?"

"Not everything I learn is from the internet. There are books also," I retorted.

"Little sprout, for this to work, you need to start trusting me. And for you to do that, you need to know some truths. One of them is that I am unable to read minds."

21

"That's a lie and you know it," I accused.

"I do not read minds, but I can sense feelings, which sometimes is the same. If you think of a number or a specific phrase I cannot see it," he explained.

"What is it that you see then?" I demanded.

"Colors, feelings, emotions, whatever you display in a specific moment. For general feelings it's normally colors, like when you are feeling blue, you are not actually blue, you are yellow. I always found that annoying, but hey, who am I to change people's expressions?"

He stopped just as one of the girls returned with the cheese platter, the snacks, and two glasses of champagne along with the bottle. Rhylan snatched one of the glasses and emptied it in a few gulps. "If something specific is happening, like your constant anxiety and abrupt pain stabs, it's different and I can read whatever is happening to your body. But no, I can't read minds," he stopped to throw another seductive smirk at the girl who made her way past him.

"How can you speak inside my head then?" I enquired, remembering how he had done it twice in just a few hours.

"That's a different matter, which we'll need to talk about someday. At the moment, I assume, you have more pressing questions." Rhylan grabbed a slice of cheese and one of the crackers from the other platter and started building himself an impromptu sandwich.

"Tell me what happened in Evigt. Tell me everything."

To my surprise, Rhylan resigned to the order and served himself a full glass of champagne, which he emptied in three gulps this time, preparing for what was to be a long explanation.

"Due to circumstances I do not plan to get into with you at this point in time, I discovered the young prince's assignment in Evigt. Let's just say it was not as fated as the siren made it feel like. As soon as I received said information, I organized a visit to his accommodations and through some kind of calling, you decided to pop out of hiding at a precisely perfect temporal arrangement. I did not know who you were at first," he paused as though there was so much more that needed to be said and he struggled with the timeline and information he planned to give me.

"So you are the one who hurt me that day," I merely stated, even though I already knew the answer. I wanted to see if he had the nerve to deny it, if he actually thought that I would be so naive as to believe his lies again.

"Indeed," he settled for one word. "I threatened with spilling your blood, knowing that it would drive the prince into a dash of panic and he would feel obligated to come to your rescue." He paused just enough to stack a slice of brie onto a tiny piece of toast and adorn it with onion jelly, then shoved it in his mouth and, very unlike his usual elegance, continued speaking as he struggled to chew in between words.

"At first you were just a means to an end, Anwen, I will admit it. I have met tens of thousands of beings throughout my life and I will not waste both our precious time and pretend they meant something or that I ended up caring about either of them, especially humans. Frail, small creatures who live the illusion that they are

23

superior and dominate all others. So yes, until I learnt more about you, you represented a means to an end."

"Do you expect me to believe you care about me now? A frail human?" I retorted. I was not hungry but seeing how Rhylan enjoyed all those dip platters almost made me want to grab a bite. I wouldn't though. Until I heard the whole story or the lie he planned to twist me in, I couldn't release the thousand knots building up in my stomach.

"I do not concern myself with your beliefs, Anwen dear. When one has the absolute truth, he does not need to investigate further."

"Continue with the story," I demanded and without protest, he did.

"When I drew him out in the forest to find you, I did not expect the burst of energy your touch created. I had scheduled an easy death for you, brutal but quick, bloody enough to curse the forest, and expected the prince to fight, hopefully to the death. You touching him both weakened and shocked me, forcing this old plan to be put on hold. I spent my life planning every possible outcome in any given situation, but you two being mates is not something I ever expected."

"What does it have to do with you?" I immediately asked but another thought sparked in my mind and led to a different question. "You knew we were mates?" I did not understand how he could possibly have known when it took us both months to realize. What business had it to do with Rhylan?

"I'm an old fae, Anwen. I have learnt to understand specific things through the years, and mating bonds is one of the least

24

complicated. It doesn't take a genius to distinguish that burst of energy and both of your hearts started shining. It was clearer than pure water."

"What does it have to do with you?" I still didn't understand.

"Trust me, that is something you do not want to know right now and a fairly minor detail in the overall story. After all, you wish me to tell you about Ansgar, do you not?" He stopped and pressed his back deeper into the chair, making his chin raise slightly, just enough to make us reach the same eye level. By the way I was situated, I had a perfect view of his features and those dark eyes that still hid so much from me.

"Tell me about Ansgar," I urged, forcing myself not to blink and held his stare for as long as I could. Luckily, he interrupted the eye contact, probably more to my benefit, and continued.

"He won the fight that day. The smug bastard told the entire forest how he managed to cast me off by sheer force and assured every one of his mighty protection should I come back," he scoffed, laughing at the expense of my boyfriend. My mate. My Ansgar.

"Do not speak ill of him again, or I will open the security door and throw you off this plane. I don't care if we all die in the process," I bluffed. At an extremely bad timing, it seemed, just as the flight attendants arrived with the soups Rhylan had ordered. Both their smiles dropped and they stopped abruptly, unsure if the best process was to interrupt a visibly heated conversation, ignore my outburst, or run and tell the pilot.

"Low blood sugar," Rhylan turned to the girls with a reassuring smile. "This one gets cranky when she's hungry."

25

They instantly relaxed and started serving the dishes, not missing the opportunity to smile or engage in some small talk with the gorgeous man that seemed to adore telling jokes or 'accidentally' touched them inappropriately when trying to help. Two minutes later, they were dismissed and left Rhylan in my company with sorrowful faces.

"You were saying?" I dared him to continue, careful of every word he uttered.

"I was saying that *Prince Ansgar* defeated me that time, so I was forced to retreat and form a new plan. One that involved obtaining what I wanted from him, but also let me get close to you. So I decided to form part of the Forest Guard, seeing how they had free access in the territory and proved an easy and unsuspicious way of being near you."

"How did you manage to do that?"

He huffed. "Faerie rings. Right at the entrance in the forest. I kept them blocked for a few hours and made them think they had already seen you. I took the uniform and food, came to visit and did my job," he smiled with pride.

"What about the emails? How did you know about the door?"

"Oh sprout," he shook his head disapprovingly. "So naive. There are ghost programs that track your every movement online. All your faerie searches? All your brother's travels? Every single email or conversation you had was carefully stored. It's really easy to hack into things," he raised his shoulders like he was describing something as easy as eating chocolate.

"Why? What did you get out of it?" I asked, without giving him

26

time to enjoy the pumpkin soup he struggled to gulp down in between my interrogation. If there was one thing on the very bottom of the list of stuff I cared about, it was Rhylan's stomach.

He stopped and grinned. "More than you could ever imagine. I got to know you." Once again he stopped to stare at me, looking into my eyes as though his long lashes were to turn into curtains and stage his feelings for me. He looked at me with affection. Like he cared.

"Tell me about Ansgar," I demanded, ready to slam my fist onto the improvised table that separated us.

He drew in a breath, apparently displeased that I didn't feel the need to dig deeper into his emotions and enquire his meaning.

"I debated my next move for a long time, ready to abandon my course and find a new plan. But your mate lost track of his royal attributions and behavior when he met you, acting like a youth living his first love. Which I am guessing, in his case, was the truth. You two were flaunting your love in the district for all to see and he made a point in telling everyone about his feelings for you. Even a blind could see that he loved you, so much that he would risk it all for you. So I decided to give you a push. It wasn't your idea to visit the Earth Kingdom, it was mine. You were just a pawn."

Rage flowed through me, forcing my heart to beat at a higher rate and my nostrils to flare with anger. "Why did you pretend to be my friend? Why did you push me to do it?" I barely uttered the words through my teeth, hate towards the man sitting in front of me becoming evident.

"I never pretended to be your friend, Anwen. Those visits we

27

shared, it was real for me," he nodded several times, reaching over the table to grab my hand but I immediately pulled it away. "You served a purpose, I will not deny that, but meeting you, becoming your *friend*," he struggled to release the word, "was one of the most pleasurable moments of the past century for me. You were broken, Anwen. He may have been in pain and drank himself to death, but you were broken. And alone. And I couldn't leave you like that."

"Don't you dare tell me you did all this out of compassion!" Tears formed in my eyes and I realized there was no point keeping them at bay. "You took him from me!" I rose to my feet and launched on Rhylan, unafraid to show him all the pain and hate I had accumulated throughout the past year.

My arms instinctively found his chest and started hitting every surface they could reach. Fingers curled into fists and I found myself punching Rhylan, reaching as high as I could towards his face. He instinctively pushed back into the seat he found himself trapped in and receiving my wrath, protecting his face with a hand while the other blindly tried to reach for me and make me stop.

"Anwen, that's enough," I heard him struggle in between breaths but I could not stop, would not do it. He took everything from me, he interfered with my happiness and killed the man I loved. Out of a stupid game, just to satisfy whatever plan he had formed. *A pawn.* That's what he'd called me. That's what I was to him.

"Stop it!" Rhylan rose from the seat and caught both my arms and twisted them, and me along with the movement, until I found my body trapped and arms forced crossed, squeezed by his strength. Just as Ansgar had done it that first day.

I could not contain it any longer and tears streamed down my face, along with a muffled cry I had struggled to keep in. Not caring anymore, I loosened the tension in my body and allowed my knees to give, making me fall onto the ground, Rhylan's unwelcome embrace the only thing keeping me from collapsing.

He kept a hold on me, squeezing every sigh out with unimaginable patience, waiting for me to recover from the breakdown he had caused and surveying my breathing as I did so.

"It's only a few minutes," I surprised myself with the announcement I involuntarily made, as if I cared about Rhylan's fake concern for me. But seeing how I decided to give out details I didn't plan to, it felt wrong to pause. "I can't stop it," I whispered, "the crying. It comes at weird times and there's nothing I can do but wait it out. It's only a few minutes," I repeated the phrase I kept telling myself whenever accumulated pain or memories burst out of me and forced me to halt for a suffering session in the most inconvenient moments.

"I'm sorry," he replied. He stood so close that his expelled air caressed my ear, and something about his voice toned down my anger. It sounded sincere. My deep breath must have encouraged him because he shifted and sat us both on the floor with a brisk turn, making sure that I laid in a comfortable position, although my arms remained crossed and wrists restrained by him.

"You will see him again, I promise."

If his words were meant to calm me down, they caused the opposite result, forcing a wail to erupt from deep within my throat. I did not know why, but this had a summoning effect on the story and Rhylan chose this as the most opportune moment to continue. Probably because I was already on the floor crying, thus unable to hit him again.

"After you two broke up, I wanted to seek Ansgar and continue the fight. If there is a moment in a male's life when he is at his weakest, it's when he's been rejected by a mate. The cases are so rare, and your connection grew so strong that when he left your side, his energy dropped so low it took part of the forest with it. So I went to that cave he called a home and saw him. He was beaten, dry, small. So easy to kill. But instead of doing it, instead of cutting his head and being done with it," he squeezed me tighter, predicting my reaction to the threat towards Ansgar's life, "I thought of you. How you must be feeling. So I came to find you. I had to know you were alright."

"Just let me go," I whispered but my tone sounded harsh enough to imply a demand.

"Not until you promise to calm down," he breathed into me again, causing my neck to form unsolicited goosebumps.

"We are on a plane and there is nowhere for me to get rid of your presence, but one more second of you touching me will send me into shock. Take your disgusting hands off me!" I raised my voice, loud enough for the two women behind the curtain to hear and come rushing in to find me splayed on the floor in Rhylan's arms. Only then he reluctantly released me, letting go of one wrist first and loosening the other just enough to be able to stop another attack.

Without looking at him, I rose and retook my seat.

"Is everything alright, Miss Anwen?" one of the women voiced.

"Yes, thank you, just a small misunderstanding," I nodded and assured her that we still needed to be left alone.

During the short conversation, Rhylan had kept his distance and remained in the same spot as before, taking the time to brush away dust from his designer black pants and arrange his hair. He copied my movement and retook his seat in front of me, keeping his hands on his knees and away from my personal space. He looked shaken, as though I had hit him with a dagger instead of a demand. I kept silent and the fireling took it as a cue to continue speaking.

"The Cloutie root arrangement was a spur of the moment. I hadn't expected him to make his mark visible in the district until the official ceremony, so I understood he had done it exclusively for you. And your eyes sparkled so brightly at the thought of seeing him. Knowing what happened between you two that night, I consider I even did you a favor. When you returned, the forest brimmed with light, the energy of the place vibrated so much that sooner or later, one of the other kingdoms would have come to investigate. So I took advantage. It was only right for me to be the one to harvest it, seeing how I played a part in its making. I'm not sure you are aware but Cloutie trees are sacred for the earthlings."

"I know everything about them," I spat. "I know how the goddess gave them to her people after her death and how they are used to heal wounds. I also know that damaging one is punishable by death. *One home, one root, one death.* Isn't that the saying?" My rage threatened to burst out again, succumbing to the memories of what I had done, of how stupidly I behaved. "It can also be used as a curse if one damages the tree and passes it to another to use. An exchange method to claim life. I know it all, Rhylan, I've had a lot of time to trace back all my mistakes."

"I didn't expect him to accept the trade so easily," he admitted.

"What happened by the river?" The question he tried to delay for the past two hours, forcing me to hear the story as he wanted me to. He had no escape from it now.

"I expected him to fight, to try to kill me and be free of the debt. But he was too concerned about you, about the repercussions it would have on your life if he were to fail. I asked him to surrender something else and have his life spared, an heirloom of their goddess. The fool chose death." Rhylan raised a hand to stop my protest before I even had time to interject. "I repeat; he is not dead. But he chose to die rather than betray his kin. Out of compassion, for him, for you, I gave him another night. You were just two youths in love, behaving like the world was yours. I needed to give you another few hours of bliss before I took everything away from you."

"That's why he insisted for my dad to pick me up Sunday morning? He knew when he was going to die," I released a breath and the realization with it.

"He thought he was going to die, yes. That is what I told him. That is what I claimed as an exchange," Rhylan explained but I was done with this.

"HE DIED IN MY ARMS!" I shouted, barely keeping the urge to hit him again, to expel all that hate and anguish on him. I felt my heart palpitating so eagerly it almost reached my neck, sheer rage boiling the blood in my veins. The man responsible for Ansgar's death stood right in front of me.

"He is not dead!" Rhylan repeated for what seemed like the millionth time that day, but I would not listen anymore. It was all a plan to torture me, going through the memories and giving me hope, only to make me relive it all again and take sick pleasure from my pain.

"He turned into a pile of leaves in my bed. I saw him release his last breath. How can you tell me he is not dead?" I demanded, wiping tears that blocked my vision of him away.

"Exactly," he responded with unquenching calmness. "He turned into leaves. There is no body to leave behind because he transported that body along with him. The only thing he left was the connection to Evigt. I had to unbind the energy that kept him grounded to the district through his Keeper Oath," he explained with patience, speaking slowly and clearly, guessing that I would need time to process the new information. As he spoke, a ray of hope bloomed into my soul at the thought that maybe, just maybe, I could see Ansgar again.

"Where is he now?" I immediately asked.

"He is in the Fire Kingdom, with King Drahden and Queen Shayeet. You will be able to visit soon," Rhylan reassured.

"How soon?" I jumped from my seat, struggling to bottle up all the reborn feeling inside my chest.

"As soon as you give me what I want," Rhylan purred, his hand leisurely reaching for another glass of champagne.

Chapter Four

There were many things I had to learn as a youth about the Fire Kingdom. I knew their origin, how the spirits first appeared, created by Belgarath, the first god. How they lived banished along with the deity under the surface of the earth when the goddesses united against him, fighting together for a free world of creation. I had to memorise the many wars the firelings had been involved in and knew about their mighty warriors, beasts that resurfaced and were reborn out of pain and torture.

I remembered what kind of attacks they presented the highest vulnerability towards and which kind of blades I had to use for their different species. My oratory tutor even insisted that I memorised the meaning of the few words of their native tongue that had escaped through history, should I ever be trapped in a situation where I needed to understand conversations.

But I never knew their rulers. None of us did. The only firelings we had ever encountered were the warriors they dispatched onto the surface, ready to attack and kill everyone standing in their way, fighting for their land's liberation. For some reason, none of us expected them to have a life underneath there, to organise themselves and build great halls for their leaders to feast and command. Which is why I knew this information would not be permitted to escape their kingdom. Nor I along with it.

As soon as the great doors opened to receive my crouched self, all surrounding noise stopped abruptly, allowing the chains that clinked on my every forced step to make the necessary introductions. I tried to lift my shoulders as much as I could and push my neck back, forcing my eyes to accumulate more information. Through rippling locks of hair, I saw the tall walls, adorned with historical scenes, columns that sustained the high ceiling, filled with black wax candelabras and spotted the gathering crowd.

They did not look like the firelings I had encountered. They had women, young children even, wearing their finery, embellished with crystal jewellery and decorated with pure gold accessories. I never understood why they had to be so connected to gold, but the firelings worshipped the metal above all else. All credit to them, their pure gold daggers proved lethal, though highly difficult to handle.

Some of the children walked close to me, so unafraid, that my two keepers, Serpium and Crypto, had to shove them away from our path with their sword sheath, but the closer I got to the vantablack sculpted podium, the louder the commotion caused by my forced approach. I might have been the only outside-being most of them had seen throughout their lives and they seemed determined to come as close to me as they could to either poke me, spit at me or leave their mark in any other way.

A blow to the back of my knees forced me to fall and bend them. Coincidentally, it had to be only a few feet away from the dais where their leaders sat comfortably in adamant sculpted thrones, embellished with leather and other gems I did not care to observe. Trying to stand proved impossible, even though every nerve in my body urged me to force myself to my feet, but the tip of Serpium's sword rested right above my Achilles' tendon. One move and I would have to give up my right leg forever. I settled for raising my chin, struggling to find the most dignified position I could be allowed into.

A male and a female observed me quietly, so I did the same and analysed every inch of their appearance. He looked old, older than father, with balding patches and ashen skin. He dressed in finery, a bright crimson velvet used for a tunic, and the finest cotton dark trousers. Various gemstone rings shifted along with his fingers, adorned in such a way to make the jewel clink disguise his trembling old hands. His companion, dressed in chiffon black with gold accessories and belt, displayed vicious dark blue eyes and long greying hair, woven into a crown atop her head. The king and queen of the Ash Regnum, the underground city we all suspected existed, yet none of us ever reached within its borders.

"Prince Ansgar," the male took the lead and addressed me first, as per the tradition of a host royal welcoming another. "We finally meet," he nodded towards me, an invitation to take part in the conversation.

"It is not a meeting if one party doesn't know who the other participant is," I pushed my voice through the pain of my sore throat, ignoring the wounds that slid open on my lips. Another present from Serpium, he thoroughly enjoyed my rosy lips and loved to decorate them with my own blood each night.

"That is because the honour of our meeting was not supposed to be granted to you, yet here we are," the male stood, visibly offended by my lack of respect.

"Good to know," I replied but as soon as I did, the hilt of a sword found the back of my head and forced me to fall even lower to the floor.

"The prince must be tired, my King," the female's voice resonated. "Perhaps a conversation over dinner would prove more beneficial? After all, he has been in the cell for the past year, such a long time alienated can make one forget manners."

I raised my head just enough to see her hand falling over his, trying to calm the anger I had awakened.

"He does not deserve it," the king retorted and shook her hand away as though she were a fly settling over a juicy piece of steak. "I am King Drahden, ruler of the Fire Kingdom for the past three hundred years," he made the introduction, his elevated stance clearly meant to showcase his power. The king only nodded towards his companion and said "Queen Shayeet."

The female bowed her head towards me, a small smile appearing on her lips. A year, they'd said. They kept me in a dark mouldy cell for a year.

"We find ourselves at an impasse, prince," the King forced me to avert my eyes from his companion and shift my attention to him. I reluctantly did so, not before taking the time to linger one more second onto that small smile.

"Do we?" I responded, faking confusion.

"You seem to refuse the only request we ever had for you. I am unsure how the other kingdoms train their royals but isn't it bad form to refuse your host's requests after enjoying their hospitality for such a long time?" Even his teeth lost their shine throughout his long life and shone grey like his skin.

I remained silent, refusing to continue the conversation. The King was goading me, the only purpose of this talk, to offer entertainment to his court on my account. I chose to spend my final moments with dignity, if they wanted me dead, they would have to just order it and not blame it on my behaviour. I would not offer the satisfaction.

"My King," Shayeet intervened once again and stood from her designated throne to step closer to her partner, adopting a lazy posture and supporting her head on his shoulder. "Let us invite Prince Ansgar to dine with us, some wine and food in his belly will wear off that condescending attitude. You know kids..." she slowly scratched a nail over his cheek, a light lover's caress.

"You are lucky, Prince," he turned to me and spat. "The Queen seems to take a liking to you, but do not confuse her kindness with salvation." As he finished speaking, he waved a hand, dismissing us.

Almost immediately, strong arms grabbed underneath my shoulder and forced me to my feet.

"Commanders, take the prince to my bathing chambers. The girls will know what to do," the Queen's order stopped the yanking for a second and forced my guards to change direction and drag me towards the left side of the dais instead.

During the walk to the queen's chambers, the two commanders complained about the dinner invitation I had received and their lack of desire to guard me through it all. They executed the orders however and within minutes, I stood in a bathing chamber where two fireling females had a hot bath already prepared and waiting. For me. A spark of relief flooded me and the desire to jump in the warm water overwhelmed my will. The only baths I took during my stay here was when Marreth, the first commander, took pity on my disgusting dirty self and threw a few buckets of water in my cell.

"He stays in chains," Crypto ordered and gave me another push, forcing my body to step closer to the females.

"Unless you pick him up yourself and throw him into the pool, we can't do it," a perky voice echoed from one of the females. "You know how particular the queen is with these things," she added.

Crypto huffed and crouched at my feet to rip the chains that kept me prisoner for months. As soon as the iron left my skin a tang of energy resurfaced from a piece of myself that I had thought I lost forever.

The commander did not waste any time to slide a blade at my throat, cutting just enough to make me tense. "An hour, you disgusting rat. If you try anything, I will make sure you suffer."

He then turned towards the females and continued with the threats. "If he is not ready by the time I return, it will be your blood he will bathe in." The commander threw me another glance to ensure the receipt of the message and exited the bathing chamber, leaving me unaccompanied in the presence of the two females.

My hands remained tied and there were no weapons in sight, so even if I wanted to attempt escape, there was nowhere to go and I barely had enough energy to keep myself standing. Fortunately, I didn't have to do it for very long, as the two females started pulling at my clothes and ripping them apart until I was left bare and pushed in the large bathing tub.

They did not address me, only spoke amongst themselves, and paid no attention to me or my body, although by this time I had lost all bashfulness. I seated myself in the bathtub and kept my arms raised to prevent the iron chains from touching the water.

The sensation warmed my skin, tiny goosebumps evading and enjoying the tingles of the water and soap bubbles. If I closed my eyes and tried to set myself away from the constant burning pain in my wrists, I could pretend to be at home, in my own chambers, after a long day of training.

The blood and dirt immediately mixed with the water and formed a muddy stew, so the women pushed me back up and forced me out of the tub, making me stand, half-dirty and dripping until they cleaned the mess I had made and replaced the swampy water with clean one. To my delight, they added more soap that formed tiny bubbles and without waiting for their invitation, I jumped inside and leaned back again, soaking my hair with delight.

They sighed, obviously displeased with the new dirt and dried blood I released but they did not have time to replace the water yet again so they started pulling at my body parts and scrubbing away the remaining dirt. The rough sponges scratched over every inch of skin and made me suddenly aware of the numerous cuts and wounds I had thought healed. I expelled a harsh breath when one of the females cleaned my back, which made them both pause for a few moments and exchange looks.

"How are you still alive?" a small voice shared the barely audible question. I did not answer. Not because I did not want to have this conversation, but because I did not know what to say. For the first time since I'd been there, another person wanted to open a conversation with me, as normal beings do in everyday situations. It did not present as a threat or interrogation, she simply wanted me to talk to her. Out of curiosity. And I had no answer.

"You arrived just after the Summer Solstice, and everyone thought you would be gone by the Autumn one," the other female took the reins of the conversation, trying to explain their curiosity. "No one has survived Commander Serpium this long," she added.

"I'm not doing it for the sense of achievement," I replied and my throat scratched in pain once again. The conversation with the royals had been the longest I had in months and the lack of food and nourishment converted the back of my throat into a permanent wound. I swallowed my pain, which made one of the females rise from the edge of the bathtub where she was seated by my side and rush towards a table. I heard pouring sounds and shortly after, she returned with a golden goblet full of liquid, offering it to me.

I did not move, keeping my hands close to my chest, so tight that the iron shackles crisped small burns on my chest.

"Drink," she urged, a small encouraging smile painted on her lips.

I did not. Every single potion that was shoved down my throat had been used to hurt, not to heal. I could not trust a good willing gesture, they turned out to be traps in disguise. The worst kind. They would catch one at a vulnerable moment, make one trust the person, and get hurt in the worst ways imaginable. I had survived this long by keeping my mental barriers high and my body alert. I would not fail now.

The other female seemed to understand my hesitation and took the goblet in her hands. Looking into my eyes, she pushed the rim slowly to her mouth and in another gentle movement, drank deeply, making sure that I saw how the liquid dropped down her throat. She did so a few times, then stopped and brought the goblet close to me, placing it at the edge of the bathtub, within my reach if I chose to have a drink.

"It is only wine," she said. "Not the good kind, the one you are probably used to. It's a servant's wine, but you are welcome to have some if you wish."

"Thank you," I responded slowly and they took it as a command to continue washing me, respecting my wish of silence.

"I don't know," I said after about a minute, with a calculated tone. I debated whether to keep my mouth shut or take advantage of possibly the last conversation I would have for the remainder of my existence. After a few seconds of debate, the latter won.

They both turned to me and stopped the scrubbing motion to catch my words. "How I survived this long," I added.

"Because you are strong," the one who offered the wine responded in my stead. "The earth feeds you."

"The sun gives you power," the other added.

It was then that I realised that I must have been the only non-fireling being they had probably met. Judging by the candles situated on every hall and the ashen skin everyone in here seemed to have, they had never seen natural light. Trees growing. Never breathed the wind or seen a rainbow. My world, the one that gave me strength, as they so eloquently put it, lived in a myth to them.

"I do miss the sunshine," I decided to continue while my hands jumped towards the goblet and brought it close to my lips. The first sip flowed slowly, caressing the back of my throat like a much-needed ointment, healing the bruises and wounds. The rest of the liquid dropped in eager gulps, so quick that the female took it from my hands and immediately rushed to refill it.

"How is it?" the female washing my back asked, taking advantage of my newly found desire to share details. "The sun?" she clarified.

"Harsh," the words spurted out of my mouth and took them both by surprise. "It burns, most of the time. Causes wounds on the skin and dries out unwatered roots and barks, makes the leaves scorch out and fall." Clearly, this was not what they expected me to say, because they both looked at me with deep angry frowns, so I allowed myself to remember and spoke again. "It likes to paint colours on the eyes when they are closed. The sun comes and amuses the lashes, creating hues underneath the eyelids. If it's very bright, they are red and ticklish, and dancing blue shadows mix with the colour. At dusk it likes to play with the cheeks, making smiles rise easier."

"And the moon?" they asked, almost in perfect synchrony.

"The moon is for the lips," I immediately said. "Not as bright as the sun, but it makes beings courageous, outspoken. The moon likes to watch kisses flow," I said, remembering Anwen's wide smile underneath the moonlight.

"Is that why you do it?" one of them asked as they pushed me out of the bathtub, concealing me under cotton towels.

"Do what?" I asked, fighting the urge to grab the towels and dry myself off, were it not for the shackles preventing me from moving freely.

"Resist it. Remain alive. For the moon and the sun?"

I smiled at the beautiful way she explained my situation and nodded. "For my mate as well," I added. Anwen's beautiful face had been the most effective balm of them all. They did not reply, expecting more explanation, so I obliged. "I do it so that she can continue to enjoy the sun and the moon, for her to be happy." They did not need to know more. I could not say more without breaking.

"If you ever leave here, can you take us with you?" one of them asked and now that I looked at them I saw the similarities. Sisters, I realised.

"I don't think there will be any sun where I'm going," I smiled bitterly.

Anwen

Chapter Five

"And what is it that you want?" I asked annoyed, ready to give this all up and start punching him again. I knew it was not as effective as I wished, he probably felt tickles instead of pain, but it helped me to know I could physically hit him. Not my proudest moment.

"I need your help," he simply stated, like it was the most obvious thing.

"Spell it out already, Rhylan," I demanded and for the first time since we started talking, I felt the need to snack on something so I grabbed a breadstick from the discarded remains of what Rhylan had eaten.

"It's quite a long story, which you will need to understand before you can accept to work with me. And seeing how your patience is dissipated, I feel disinclined to talk at the moment. Maybe another bottle of champagne would calm you down?"

That was it. I was done. I did not want to take any more of this, the way he was mocking me, lying to me, making fun of my feelings, and torturing me over and over again by telling me his side of the events. I felt sick, impulsive, and hateful.

Through whatever instinct possessed me, I picked up the butter knife and threw myself over the table and over Rhylan, catching his body with my own and trapping him under me. Then I lifted the blade and pointed to his eye, keeping it only an inch away from his eyeball.

Of course, the bastard did not react, looking like he enjoyed the newly found position under me, and relaxed even more, stretching his shoulders to reach the back of his seat.

"I didn't take you for a blade kind of woman, but I like it rough, so go for it," he smirked and licked his lips suggestively.

I pushed my threat, even though I knew at this point, it was only child's play for him.

"Tell me everything right now, or I will gut you like a fish." I said, surprising even myself at my choice of words.

Rhylan snickered, not at all affected by my wannabe violence. "Saw that in a movie, did you?" The prick did not mask his amusement and started to fully laugh underneath me, making his body and face shake with the movements, so much that I had to retrieve the knife to avoid the laughter from piercing his own eyelid.

"Is there no way I can hurt you?" I asked defeated, pulling my body away from his and trying to return to my own seat. By instinct, Rhylan placed a hand over my back, needing to keep me in place, but I immediately jolted at the sudden and uncalled-for touch, so he retracted it and apologised.

I spent the next few minutes trying to clean remnants of food off my jeans, quite ineffectively. Pumpkin soup and chocolate strawberries wouldn't just fade with a tissue, no matter how much I struggled or poured sparkling water over the stains.

"I'll wait here until you change, then we can really talk," Rhylan offered to my surprise. He must have sensed that another breakdown planned to come along because I could barely keep the tears from escaping.

Without another word, I headed towards the back of the jet, where a bathroom and a changing room had been installed for my mother and since I was the one to use the plane, two outfit choices hung prepared for me in case of emergencies.

I assumed that mom probably thought I would find myself in need of a dress for a formal dinner or a suit for an impromptu interview and not because I covered myself in half-eaten food while trying to attack an immortal fae, but judging by the full menu splayed out on my jeans, anything would do.

I took a very quick shower first and discarded my dirty clothes in a wardrobe bag. I wasn't the biggest fan of private jets or showering in one, but under the circumstances, I felt grateful for dad's insistence that I take a jet whenever I travelled overseas. Every single time, I protested and explained how much it increased the carbon footprint when I could have easily travelled in business class, but seeing how Rhylan had decided to join this time, I felt grateful for the privacy.

Ten minutes later, I appeared back in the main cabin wearing a black dress, tighter than I would have liked, and Louboutin heels. It was either this or a wavy cocktail dress. As I appeared from behind the curtains, I made Rhylan paralyse from what he was doing. I did not expect him to be sitting on the floor, along with maps and huge pieces of paper with lots of drawings.

"You look beautiful," he uttered, unable to shift his eyes from me, but I ignored the compliment. It was not needed or desired.

"What are you doing?" I asked and stepped closer to him. It felt weird having him on the floor, almost at my feet in that situation and I could not help a sensation of pride that powdered over my body.

"I am preparing the truth, as it is and as you need to see it," he said. "But first, I am looking at your gratified self. You like seeing me on my knees, don't you?" He threw me that seductive look of his that had everyone falling for him in seconds.

"I do," I admitted. I found no point in lying, especially since he could read my feelings or whatever. "It gives me great satisfaction to see you on your knees. You should try doing that before Ansgar too, seeing how it is your place and all." I took advantage and made him squirm.

"The things you do to me, sprout..." Rhylan sighed and shifted upwards, walking towards the two seats we had occupied and grabbing two pillows.

He then came back and placed them on the ground, making a small nook for me before he pointed to his handiwork and invited me to take a seat.

"Is this really necessary?"

"There are a lot of maps and drawings that you will need to observe as I speak." He pointed towards the huge world map and the other pieces of paper he had marked or drawn on. He'd made himself busy while I was away. "Don't worry, I'll still be on my knees, I know how much you enjoy that," he smirked again.

I sighed and removed my shoes, placing them on the side and

shifted my dress just slightly, so that I could sit on the pillow fort he had made for me. Once I found a comfortable position, I pointed to the map.

"You can start," I said.

"To understand my purpose, and my mission, you will need to know the story of the gods."

"I already know that there are three goddesses and they created the world, I've read that..."

"No, no, no, sprout. For this to work, you have to keep that pretty mouth of yours closed for most of the time." He raised a hand to stop any words from escaping me. "Here," Rhylan reached and found a notepad, or what remained of it since he had ripped more than half the pages to create whatever he was planning and gave it to me along with a pen. "You can write your questions and at the end, we can go over them."

"Seriously?" I sighed, not wanting to deal with another one of his theatrical arrangements.

"Consider this one of your work presentations. I am a new company that wants to tell my story, and you have to listen and not interrupt to understand my policy," he said proudly.

"You mean brand identity," I corrected.

"That too," Rhylan agreed, unwilling to accept his initial error. This male was as vain as Snow White's stepmother.

"What do I do if you say something stupid? Or if I want to comment or protest?" I enquired, more to annoy him than anything else.

"What would you do at work?" he frowned.

49

"Fine, I'll listen to you and write down my questions." I finally agreed and pointed towards the maps again, urging him to start.

We had another four and a half hours of this flight and I was firmly convinced Rhylan would make sure I landed with a full-on headache and a thousand more reasons to be upset and angry with him. But he looked willing to finally tell me whatever it was he needed from me, and I couldn't say no, because all I wanted was a way back to Ansgar.

Even though I wasn't convinced at the beginning of the journey, I understood now that Rhylan wouldn't have wasted so much time if it weren't real. I had done my best to annoy him and stop him in his tracks on every occasion, and he still looked determined to deal with me, for whatever purpose.

It could only mean one thing, that I had some kind of power here, and although I did not understand it, I planned to use it and take back the man I loved.

"Belgarath was the first god," Rhylan started and I settled back, holding my notepad and getting ready to retain any useful information.

"He created the world from nothing, having only *the chaos* as company. For many millennia, he remained alone, crafting and sculpting, modelling his creation. We do not know what made him determined to do so, some of our scholars think it was solitude or the need of a partner, but he searched the earth for something. Something that was missing.

No matter how hard he worked, how ingeniously he created or how thoroughly he planned, the god did not feel the joy of his creation, because part of himself missed."

I remained silent, as Rhylan requested, taking notes on the pad he had provided. None of this was in the books I'd found or the internet pages and videos I had lived to search for. He was telling me the truth, for once. I hoped...

"Years must have passed, another millennium maybe until he discovered what made him so unhappy. The lack of a partner, which he did not think to make. You see, even the mightiest god felt the need for company and did not think to create it for himself. Because what use would it be, to alter another part of yourself, just to have the conversations already happening inside your mind?" He paused for a moment, as though this last phrase described more than the god's life, but his own.

"Not having found what he needed, Belgarath stopped. He stopped and released all his anger, his fears, his desire for company into the world, and along with it, he gave something he did not plan to. A tear."

"A tear? As in, he cried?" I heard myself speak, but Rhylan did not seem to mind.

"He did not cry, the gods do not cry like humans and nowadays faeries do. It was only one tear, a single one that escaped his eye and travelled down to his cheek, to fall on the ground. It was because of this gesture, a symbol of release, of the deepest feeling from his own soul, that it possessed so much power. Belgarath summoned his deepest desire with that tear, the need for companionship."

"What happened?" I asked. Clearly, me staying quiet did not really work.

"A goddess appeared. The first amongst the goddesses. Marynnah, she was called." Rhylan continued to point at the lines he had drawn on paper for me, following a trail that marked the appearance of the goddess.

"The goddess of water," I added.

"She became that, too. But for a long time, she was Belgarath's wife and partner. The gods did everything together and he loved her so much that he created the oceans for her and all the water on the planet. For her delight."

"What about all the other planets? Some of them have water too. Where did that come from?" I asked, struggling to wrap my mind around the science, which I had studied at school and their story of creation, which I would have considered a fairy-tale were it not for the proof of their very existence.

"I do not have all the answers, Anwen," Rhylan responded slightly disappointed. "There are theories in which the god decided to abandon his home and create a brand new one and others that state he received the assignment of earth from his rulers. I do not have the answers to the universe, I wish I did," he sighed. "What I can tell you is what I know. The story of the four gods and how this world came to be."

I nodded, pushing him to tell me more.

"Unfortunately, after a long time, Marynnah started being haunted by the same demons that left her husband. As he busied himself with working on his creation, she felt lonely at times and wished to have someone to converse with. The goddess told her husband this and Belgarath was pained to see his partner suffering, especially since he knew what heavy feelings her heart had to carry. So he created another goddess, a sister for his wife. Zaleen."

"The goddess of wind," I said excitedly, proud that I knew the information.

Rhylan nodded and smiled. "Goddess Zaleen proved good company for a long while and the two sisters enjoyed each other's presence above all else."

"Did Belgarath marry her too?" I asked quickly, ready to experience judgemental feelings towards the maker of the earth.

"No, Belgarath and Zaleen were not very fond of each other. The only reason she existed was to make his wife happy when the god travelled and worked, and the only one he truly loved was Marynnah. Which is why the betrayal hurt so much."

"What betrayal?" I escaped a breath. Clearly, Rhylan had accepted the fact that I would speak as and when I wanted to, because he looked fairly unaffected by my interruptions.

"Even with Zaleen, Marynnah could not find complete happiness. After all, she existed from Belgarath himself and had his powers, so one day, while she and her sister spent the day swimming the waters, Marynnah started crying, releasing all her frustrations into the sea. And an entire world bloomed. Everything there is and has been in the waters appeared from that moment. The creation of living beings."

"Hadn't Belgarath already created beings?" I asked, confused.

"He did not, his sole creation focused around the earth. The waters, the rocks, even gravity and the movement around the sun, the seasons, the moon, you name it. But he never wanted living beings to roam around his work and damage it. So when the two goddesses came to him and dragged him to the waters, to show him what had happened, the god became enraged and destroyed it all. Everything that had been alive till then were all destroyed by Belgarath."

"Oh gods," I said, trying to imagine what that meant.

"As expected, the goddesses did not take his fury lightly and while he was away once more, they developed a plan. To entrap him and rebuild the world. In their perspective, Belgarath stood in the way of his own creation, loving it so much that he proved incapable of letting anyone enjoy it. So while he slept, Marynnah shackled him in iron chains, the only metal that hurt their skin, and along with Zaleen, they trapped him deep under the earth, so close to the centre that the heat alone would cause too much pain and it would make him incapable of finding the strength to escape."

He paused, to my benefit, giving me a minute to collect myself before he continued.

"With Belgarath trapped, the two goddesses ruled the earth. They created water-life and Zaleen played with her powers to create waves, made the birds fly, and blew over the trees to make their roots stronger. But they had been so used to a third god, that at times, loneliness overpowered them. So one day, Zaleen came with the idea and asked Marynnah to use the powers Belgarath gave her to create another sister. A goddess who could rule over the plants and trees. That is how Catalina appeared. The three goddesses created more life, and the humans came to be and everything was happy and peaceful until their final breaths."

"So what does it have to do with the deal that we're supposed to make and Ansgar?" I asked with confusion.

"Everything. We're just about to get into politics now," he pointed.

"Oh goodie," I replied humourlessly.

"Even though it looks like Marynnah was the strongest goddess, Catalina had the highest number of subjects, which is why, today, the Earth Kingdom is the strongest one. The Water Kingdom comes in second, very close to the power, and the Wind Kingdom simply exists, they do not have any real power anymore. They have tried to get alliances for centuries, but the other two kingdoms like to keep everything locked in."

"And the Fire Kingdom?" I questioned.

"Even though we are not a kingdom officially, as per their rules, summits, treaties, and whatnot, my people have always been present, trying to escape into the earth and find a home for ourselves," he explained.

I would not be fooled. I knew how they tried to find homes, how they killed pregnant women and unborn children. Ansgar had told me everything.

"We agreed not to lie to each other," I grunted.

"Our methods are not favoured by the other kingdoms, but we have only one mission in mind, ever since the beginning of time."

"Which is?" I pressed for the truth.

"Avenge our god. Before his death, Belgarath created the firelings, thousands of us, born from his pain and wrath. With the sole purpose to overcome the earth and restore his creation to what it once was."

"Is that why you are not burnt by iron?" My mind jumped from one memory to another, from the image of the god to Rhylan trapping Ansgar in the sitting room of the mansion I used to live in, back in Evigt.

"Not all of us, but yes, we inherited the ability since we grew strength from our god's pain."

"What does it have to do with anything?" I still did not understand my role in this battle that seemed to have gone on for thousands of years.

"The goddesses lived a long and happy life together, but even though they were strong, and loved their creation, they did not have the power to survive Belgarath's death. All three of them had a dash of his power, which received a summoning back into the earth when our god faded, taking the three goddesses along with him and forcing them to give up their eternity. They turned into mortals, each one forced to live her last years on earth powerless. Marynnah chose to return to the waters and lived with the sirens, Zaleen chose a solitary death and Catalina married her mortal lover and lived her last years as a queen in the Earth Kingdom."

"She was smart, I would have done the same," I pointed out.

"When Belgarath's strength left them, so did the power he had placed into them, offering immortality. It escaped their bodies and turned back to what it initially was. A tear. One for each goddess. The last remnants of Belgarath's power. The most protected three objects in the entire world. Together, they can bind the energy of the earth and restore our god's life."

"So where are they?" I asked, starting to become aware of the plan Rhylan had drawn for me.

"With each of the royal families," he expelled defeated.

I took a long minute to digest everything, the story he had told me, the origin of their gods, and the history of hate among their people and kingdoms. Of course, the truth is in the eyes of the beholder and my brain struggled to piece together the conflicting information I had received from Ansgar during his stay in Evigt with what Rhylan told me just then.

I did not understand our place in this and part of me still hoped that I would wake up somehow and all of it, Erik's death and consequently my trip to the earth goddess' burial place could fade away as if nothing ever happened. But that would mean negating my feelings towards Ansgar and everything we had lived together. And also…

"What does this all have to do with my brother?" I suddenly asked, my brain unveiling the information Rhylan dropped in the car.

It might tell you a thing or two about your brother.

"Maybe it's not the best moment to find out more," Rhylan stopped and moved to grab the world map where he had circled specific points with a black marker. "It is something that can affect your senses and we are not done talking yet," he expressed his determination.

"The sole purpose of me being in Evigt was because my brother asked me to," I pressed, tired of the back and forth he seemed to enjoy. I knew he was thousands of years old and felt the need to elongate everything and draw time in his favour, but I stood a mortal, who used social media and had an internet connection, so I wanted all my information within seconds.

"I did wonder how you'd come to be there, mere months after him," Rhylan admitted and my world stopped.

"Erik was in Evigt? Did you meet him?"

I could not take it anymore, bile rose in my throat from the anticipation and I had to sit down again, letting my body fall onto the cushions I had abandoned as soon as he finished talking about the gods.

"Anwen," he made a move to approach me but I raised my hand and flattened my palm on his chest. Instinctively, I found the collar of his shirt and gripped it hard, forcing Rhylan to shake into position by my side.

"Tell me!" I yelled, expelling tiny drips of my spit on his designer clothing.

"Yes, I met Erik. I was the one to tell him about Evigt and the other burial places," he admitted and it felt like my chest turned into a lake and Rhylan had just thrown the biggest stone onto the flat surface.

"How?" my lips trembled, eyes dripping uncontrollably. Yet another lie, another secret he had kept hidden from me all this time.

"I sensed your brother in Mexico, a while back, and approached him, posing as a regular human. I found out more about him and we became friends. Over time, I trusted him with the information about the fae, but he did not believe me. He travelled with a group of other men, friends of his and, as I finished telling him who I was and what

I wanted, he retreated to them, blaming my actions on too much alcohol, as though I indeed was a frail human," Rhylan cursed under his breath.

"A while later, when I accepted the mission to investigate Evigt and prepare for the arrival of the young prince, I met your brother again. I confessed surprise at his new appearance, he looked tired and spent, even so, he threatened me," the faerie said with a dash of pride.

My brother's actions made Rhylan *proud*.

"What did he threaten you with?" I asked, admiring my brother's courage.

"Revealing my identity. Amongst other things."

"Rhylan," I struggled to say, tapping my palm repeatedly over my right knee and trying to keep my nerves as calm as I could, even though tears continued to flow freely on my cheeks.

"I do not know as much as you want me to, Anwen. I am sorry. I found him in Evigt and he knew about the goddesses. I do not know what he did in the forest, I couldn't find out because he made me disappear. Forced me to," Rhylan tried to explain.

"How can you kill a prince but be scared of a mortal?" I demanded, ready to sink my fist into his face yet again.

"I did not kill a prince, I already told you. And your brother knew things. Things I did not want to admit to myself even. He asked me to go and I did. I never knew what happened to him until the mermaids summoned me with payment for their favour."

"What happened to him?" I asked.

"He was murdered. By the sirens," Rhylan sighed heavily.

Chapter Six

It was Marreth who appeared through the door just as the females finished drying me off, finding me struggling to ignore remnants of shyness at two unknown beings of the opposite sex touching every part of my body. The commander wiggled his brows suggestively at the sight of me.

"Looks like the queen wants a new toy." Then he started directing the two servants as to which parts of my body needed applying the ointment he had brought in. The smell resonated unpleasant to all our noses, especially after the nice-smelling bubble bath, but at the immediate contact with my skin, the ointment made the pain disappear. Even the festering cuts on my back found much-needed relief and when they also applied it underneath the chain marks on my wrists, I remembered a feeling long since forgotten. The lack of pain.

"Better?" Marreth asked proudly, expecting praise.

"Thank you, commander," I said, making him relax into a chair to watch the next process of my preparation. Grooming and dressing. While the females brushed my hair and selected black garments, similar to the ones the royal family wore, to dress me in, the first commander poured himself a glass of the servant's wine and sat comfortably in a wooden chair by the door.

He observed me for a while, moving his head into different angles to study my body and the wounds that had been so joyously inflicted by the other two commanders. Marreth hadn't been one to enjoy causing me pain. For most of the time, he took the first position in the interrogation for a few days — or weeks, I didn't really quite know — then passed it onto the other two. I did not know if he'd done it out of spite or because he genuinely did not want to participate in what came next.

Amongst the three commanders, Marreth had been the one to show me kindness, from time to time. Sometimes he brought me food and drink, and a bucket of water on the odd occasion to clean my wounds. Today he had brought the ointment that gave me sweet relief.

"Tonight is a test, prince, don't confuse it with generosity or compassion," the first commander announced from his seat, making sure that I turned in his direction. His golden eyes scanned me attentively, ensuring the message was conveyed correctly.

"Why are you telling me this?" I asked in my newfound tone.

"The hourglass is running against you, and tonight may very well be the end of the road. Know how to play your hand prince, it can be your last."

With this, he rose and signalled the time to the females, making them move quicker, as he exited the bathing rooms.

Within minutes, Crypto returned to collect me, ushering the females away. As they walked out the door, one of them threw me a long stare, a silent request for their freedom, should it ever come to it. I nodded and smiled with gratitude, aware that I would not see them again.

To my surprise, Crypto did not add iron shackles to my ankles and allowed me to have a dignified walk towards the dining room.

A different corridor opened before me, conveying the same decorations as before, the ruby-marked walls and black wax chandeliers that illuminated all the pathways on this side of the building.

The more I walked, the more impressed I became with the firelings' way of life, they had truly created a beautiful place to exist in, even with the lack of basic materials. All my life I was taught to see them as enemies, but being here, in this place that they called home, made me understand their curse.

The dining hall that we stepped in felt similar to the throne room. Instead of the dais hosting the two thrones, large tables were situated along the room, gathering all the court to feast together. Above them all, onto a set of stairs, a smaller table accommodated the king and queen, with a few empty seats on each side, for special guests.

The third commander rushed me through the grand hall, amongst the seats at the long tables, and through the entire length of the room, until we reached the royal table where Marreth already sat next to the queen.

Crypto forced me in the only seat opposite them, facing everyone and keeping my back towards the court before he occupied the chair at the right of the king.

All gazes turned towards me, expectant.

I returned the gesture, scanning each and every one of their faces in turn. I observed the King's crown and forehead wrinkles, the Queen's intricate hairstyle and new jewellery, Marreth's long dark locks that appeared brushed for once, and Crypto's short brown hair that still preserved some grains of dirt.

"My friend is missing, should we wait?" I directed the question to my walker for the day, knowing it will irritate the third commander out of his skin.

"Serpium has plans for you, prince," the King took the reins of the conversation, understanding I would not be the one to cooperate or follow whatever intention they had for me.

"He has delighted me with many of his ideas during this time, King Drahden," I replied nonchalantly. "How long have you been king for?" I asked and grabbed a bun from the table, without invitation, and raised it towards my mouth.

To their surprise, I took a big bite out of it although my teeth barely broke the shell, struggling to interact with solid food after such a long time. Apart from the times when Marreth made sure I was fed, which did not come very often, the most I'd eaten in the past months had been a disgusting oat broth that tasted like slug vomit.

I would not succumb to this; I would not sell the remainder of my energy out of cowardice. I did not know much about these rulers, only heard about their merciless ways but had never seen them in the flesh. Still, they were the ones who directed the wars I had been trapped in, the ones where Vikram nearly lost his life and father lost a brother, where my grandfather could barely protect his own kin and had to form an alliance with Water to get his people out of the battlefield and where many others, thousand others, had perished.

Now they dared treat me with respect for a few hours, as though the long time of torture could be erased with a warm bath and a loaf of bread, expecting me to betray my kingdom for a few days of comfort. If that.

"I have ruled the Fire Kingdom, *boy*, for the past three hundred and twenty-six years," the king spat, throwing my lack of manners a disgusting look.

"Hmm," I nodded and continued to chew on the piece of bread. My stomach immediately rejected the first swallow and struggled to send the food back, but I forced myself to keep it in. After all, I had a part to play.

It seemed interesting to me that they had chosen my execution to be clean and even put on a show for their court, portraying them to be kind and forgiving, and I, the disruptive one who would not give a short answer for peace. *The Tear of the Goddess*. How did they even know about it? How did they even know our customs? Fortunately, they didn't know them that well...

I sensed my answer displeased the king because he tried to remain silent and continue with whatever plan they had for me, but my impertinence annoyed the royal so much he had to stop and demand an explanation.

"What do you mean by *'hmm'*, prince?" he demanded and I had to keep my smile in. It was working.

"Oh, nothing," I waved him off — as much as the iron chains still on my wrists allowed me to — and found some kind of brown sauce to dip my bread into, then continued chewing silently.

No one dared speak while the king slowly boiled with rage.

"I insist that you speak your mind," he murmured through his teeth, anger conquering more territory on his figure with each passing second.

That is when I let my smile show, straightened my back, and put the remaining piece of unchewed bread back, adopting the most royal posture I could find.

"You are not very experienced as a so-called ruler," I said, raising my shoulder as if it was just a minor thing. "That is all," I smiled again, like an amenable and reassuring guest who did not mean to imply anything by such a comment.

"Is three hundred years not enough experience for you, *my prince*?" His displeasure resounded across the hall, making all the glass clinking and chattering halt abruptly.

I raised both my arms and pointed across my shoulder, like I was trying to show him the perfect example of my meaning.

"An experienced ruler never counts years, but decades, or in your case, centuries. The way you are doing it makes it look like an achievement, rather than a birth right. Like you are so proud that you survived this long and wilted on the throne."

Marreth choked on his wine at my phrase and Crypto rose to his feet, ready to execute me then and there. They were both stopped by a hand gesture of Drahden.

"What else?" he demanded and I knew I had him caught by the royal balls. Chances were, the more I irritated the king, the quicker he would order me dead, and with it, lose what they wanted most, so I gave the king exactly what he asked for.

"The way you conduct your court. It's undignifying. Separating yourself and the queen from them on every opportunity, watching your subjects as they eat. Like you expect any of them to jump you and steal your crown." His eyes went wide but before I allowed him to speak I made sure to add, "Which is very old school, by the way. I think one of my great-great-great-grandfathers has a painting somewhere with that style of crown. The pointed edges," a swished a finger to shape it in the air, "They've been out of style since the renaissance, at least."

"You do not deserve our hospitality!" The king rose to his feet and shouted at me across the table, making everyone but the intended recipient shiver. "We offered you clean clothing. We accommodated your grooming and invited you to join our table. All in the hope that we could reach an understanding. Yet you come into my kingdom and spit in my face, mock me in front of my court and expect the right to converse? Have you no gratitude?" His echo expelled the words seconds after the male had done it, forcing the great room to pulsate with his anger and resonate it across all of his subject's ears.

"You are no ruler, and this is no kingdom. You are but a remnant of your god's ambition, sentenced to a life of imprisonment. And instead of words leading towards finding peace, you had been training armies to steal other territories since your very beginnings. And now you think I can be bought with a bath and some clean clothes? I am not one of you, *Drahden*," I knowingly released his name without a title, "I do not settle for nothingness."

It was the wrong thing to say. As soon as the final word left my mouth, a burst of pain hit me straight in the chest, making me flip through the air and fall across the table below, rolling in the remnants of their half-eaten food.

My body was then yanked upwards and thrust into the black wall, scraping my face along the fall. I had managed to irritate him in such a way that the king resorted to using their god's power and plastered me against the wall, over and over until I felt fractions of my bones turn into shards. Until my blood became so hot, it started boiling in my veins, and I stood powerless, trapped in a body that no longer felt my own.

By the time the king was satisfied with the inflicted damage, I remained a pile of wounds and twisted limbs, unable to rise from the floor, feel my legs, or even speak. Breathing seemed the only task my lungs could focus on.

"You are right, prince," the king stepped towards me — or I guessed he did by the approaching sound of his voice — "You do not settle. Your energy is still pure and death would be a too easy task for such strength in spirit."

He lifted me by the hair and dragged my bloody face close to his own, to make sure the venom he prepared to expel found its mark.

"Tell me, prince, have you ever heard of a *changeling*?" The king analysed my features with sheer curiosity, scanning every micro-expression my injured face could possibly make.

But I gave him none, partly because I did not know what he threatened me with, and partly because I could not feel nor control any of the muscles across my body. The blows Drahden had inflicted on my already injured form made me lose the last thread of control I possessed over my spirit. Pain flowed freely around me, signalling body parts that I had thought lost during the fall.

I could not speak or move, the only thing keeping me afloat was the king's will, who, either understanding that I could not physically utter any words or lost the grip on his patience, ended up answering his own question.

"Changelings are a new type of fireling, ones that have been created during my reign," he echoed proudly, making his voice flutter across the room while the rest of the attendees remained as silent as my future grave. "They become a fireling and fight for our cause, even though they were not born in our kingdom. They answer to me," he said proudly.

I did not understand what he tried to tell me, nor could I wrap my mind around it. The only dominating presence was pulsating pain and agonising ache, which kept me from thinking clearly. From thinking at all.

"Do you know where we recruit them from, prince?" Tired of me ignoring his questions, Drahden pulled my hair in such a way to make a negation out of the forced movements of my neck.

"No?" he played his part. "From the battlefield. You see, prince, we find the ones like yourself. Young, strong and stern, loyal to the core. And we turn them. We take that beautiful heart of theirs and putrefy it until they become nothing more than animals. Instinctual beings."

"The core fighters…" I struggled to utter the words, although they probably resounded half a whisper and half his own understanding of muttered sounds.

"Is that what you call them?" Drahden asked with interest.

We never knew how it happened until now, no one guessed why the best warriors of the firelings resembled other species so much. They fought the hardest, the strongest, clashed till their last breath, with no desire to escape or to have their lives spared.

The front line of each fireling attack, created by converted warriors of other races, once fighting for something they believed in. Now turned into nothing but flesh shields. To spare more of their own folk, to give them a better chance at survival.

"Anyhow," the king continued since I proved incapable of handling my side of the conversation, "let me tell you how it's done because it is a whole spectacle." Drahden said excitedly. "Our great explorer of the mind, Commander Serpium along with a team of apothecaries developed a potion that stimulates brain activity according to a specific trigger. It is all very fascinating."

"I don't care…" I forced my lips to pronounce the words in spite of the pain and traces of blood that started flowing again from my mouth.

"Oh, but you will. You need to know what to expect. See, at first, your anger dissipates. That tiny worm which enables you to have a polite conversation when invited to dine with a king? Gone!"

He used a vanishing gesture with one hand, while the other remained plucked inside my hair, pulling my skull upwards.

"Then, part of your memory will fade. Or be replaced and shifted in perspective. Am I correct, Marreth?" He turned towards the commander, who had stepped closer to us at the beginning of the conversation, resting his left hand on the hilt of a sword, ready to defend his ruler.

"Marreth has been through this as well, so he knows the works better than I do," the king clarified for my benefit.

"That is correct, my King," the commander's voice approved. "Afterwards the loyalty fades, the sense of belonging to a specific kingdom. One becomes an empty shell, ready to be filled as my king desires." His eyes turned to me, reminding me of his words in the bathing chamber. Telling me that this is what he wished to prevent.

"And then, I will use the prince as I please, and he will become a loyal subject of the Fire Kingdom," Drahden turned to his court to announce the decision he just seemed to make. "Unless of course, young Prince Ansgar here decides to tell us what we have been wanting to know since the moment he arrived and enjoyed our notorious hospitality."

I waved my head, neck muscles suddenly aware that they had to fulfil their part. I would not do it. I would not tell them.

But Drahden made it crystal clear, he did not plan to end this without one more chance. He wanted to give me the option to either save myself and doom my kingdom or surrender my body, and everything I was along with it.

"Tell us where the tear is hidden!" Drahden demanded.

The same question they had asked me, every hour of every day since my arrival. They wanted the tear of the goddess Catalina, our creator. They wanted to steal it and claim its power, dooming our kingdom along with it. I would rather give up my life a thousand times over, in a thousand different torturing ways than betray my people.

"No," I said, determined, my forever answer.

They had struggled for such a long time to make me surrender the information, one that only royals had the privilege of holding, and every single time I remained strong, unyielding, no matter how great the pain. No matter how much I wanted it to end and prayed to the goddess to take mercy on me and end it before they did.

But every day, that energy beat inside my heart. Every time I woke up, I found a little more strength to carry myself through the day.

This could not be the end. I would not allow it.

"No?" Drahden acted surprised, as though he truly expected that this time, with the new threat, I would suddenly change my mind. "Are you sure prince?" he acted it out, a show for his court.

He was not giving me a chance to reconsider, he wanted to make sure everyone heard my negation, that everyone saw how after an invitation to court and a warm meal, I refused to grant their king a minuscule request. He would spin the story and make me look ungrateful, proving how they had to keep fighting us. Because we did not deserve the place we were granted at the surface of the earth.

"Just kill me," I muttered, half begging for my life to end.

"Kill you?" I will do no such thing, prince. We are not beasts!"

Drahden placed his hand over his chest, acting offended. From far away within his court, echoes and sighs sounded, copying the King's reaction. The only ones not participating were Crypto and the queen, who chose to remain seated at the table.

"I will not kill you, prince. You are our guest after all, and even though you brought an offence to our court, we will not treat royalty in such a way." He pressed the words, forcing them to resonate across the room, dragged to all of his subject's ears. "I have much better plans for you, Ansgar. Remember that name, by the end, it will be the only thing left of you."

Anwen

Chapter Seven

I stopped. And laughed. I laughed fully, until my lungs filled with cheer and my stomach hurt.

"Anwen…" Rhylan wanted to say something but I stopped him.

"You expect me to believe that my brother, who died in a hospital bed right in front of my eyes, had some kind of underwater adventure and was killed by mermaids?" I huffed at him and started laughing again.

"I expect you to understand the truth. And I already told you that you are too emotional to grasp everything that happened. We should take it slower, we still have a few hours of flight," the old fae advised.

"And where, might I ask, is this magical siren place where my brother happened to wander?" I mocked, knowing full well that Rhylan tried to catch me in another one of his tricks. Maybe, he wanted to distract me from demanding to see Ansgar or wanting to know where he was. That is, if he truly lived, which at this point, I seriously doubted. At the thought, another jolt of pain rushed through my veins, forcing my heart to drop.

"In the Philippines, close to Mindanao Island. There is a cave in one of the gulfs that leads underneath the surface and into the Water Kingdom," Rhylan offered a breathless explanation. "It can't be accessed freely by other fae, or humans for that matter, only if one is summoned, taken there or if a solstice is in bloom. That is when the gates to the kingdoms open. Laws of the goddesses."

Mindanao? Erik had been there. I knew he had because I accessed all his travels, jet bookings, and tickets from his card. And he had travelled in all the three places that resonated with Evigt.

"Where are the other entrances into the kingdoms?" I enquired, keeping what I knew to myself and trying to find flaws in Rhylan's spin of the truth.

"Well, you know Evigt, for the Earth Kingdom, and then there's Mindanao for the Water Kingdom, St John's for the Wind Kingdom, and Goa for ours," he explained, pointing at each location on the map.

The way he said *ours*, instead of *his*, truly disgusted me. He was up to something.

"I understand Evigt because it is guarded, but how do the fae prevent people from just walking in? These are public places, full of tourists and humans," I questioned.

"Did the tree princeling not explain appearing to you?" Rhylan asked, surprised.

"Appearing?" I repeated and shook my head no.

Rhylan sighed. "Did the two of you just spend all this time mating and nothing else? Did you not feel curiosity towards his origin, not questioned things?"

He sounded more like my dad than an evil fae who wanted to

74

take over the world, but it still made me blush slightly at the truth of his words. Ansgar and I had truly lost our purposes into one another and the only thing that mattered was to be together. On my end, I felt happy just spending time with him and getting to know him and felt content with whatever information he offered from time to time.

That's what happens when one thinks they have all the time in the world. I could have never imagined that within months of getting to meet the love of my life, he would be taken away so abruptly. My biggest issues consisted of explaining his appearance in my life to my parents, deciding where we would live or if his family accepted me.

"Rhylan, I don't know if you ever had a mate or not, but from your general knowledge, you should know how it feels. How my heart aches for him and how I would give every remaining second to be in his presence. Do you honestly think, that when I had a man like that by my side, I concerned myself with history lessons?" I replied truthfully, not caring of whatever mocking sounds he made.

Very unlike his normal behaviour, he kept silent for a while, taking in my words.

"Male…" he finally said.

"What?"

"It's a *male* like that, not a *man* like that. You should use the correct term for your mate."

I nodded and extended the silence so much that we both relaxed and took the time to gaze at each other. Rhylan took me in with pity, I could even say slight regret, as though what I had gone through this past year pained him.

I did not want his regret; it came too late.

"So… appearing?" I reopened the conversation, not wanting to fall into the depths of pain yet again, especially not in front of Rhylan. I had cried too many times already.

"It's when one uses energy to jump through matter. One moment you are in one place and the next you are in another," Rhylan explained and memories of Ansgar appearing and disappearing in the woods, sometimes with me in his arms made me understand. "There is no entrance per se, like a door or whatever you are imagining. A mortal could just walk through and never realise. But a faerie will appear from the portal into a specific point in their kingdom."

I nodded. Taking the path down my memories and remembering how I had appeared in a forest in the Earth Kingdom when Rhylan made me drink the Cloutie tea and how, even with Ansgar by my side, we had to travel the same route in the morning, to be able to get home.

"How is one killed by mermaids? Sirens? Is there a difference?" I went back to what interested me, taking advantage that Rhylan seemed to be dropping truths within his words.

"The sirens used to be the royals, direct descendants of their goddess and mermaids used to be weaker, since they did not receive the blessing of creation, but were born instead. Come to think of it, everyone is a mermaid nowadays, but when speaking to the royals, they liked to be acknowledged," he explained.

"Noted, if I ever go for a stroll underwater and discover an actual mermaid, I will make sure to ask about her origin so I can address her correctly," I huffed.

"It may happen sooner than you think, sprout."

"Stop calling me that," I demanded for the hundredth time that day.

Rhylan smirked. "Do you prefer fahrenor?"

I froze in place. How could he know that? How did he know that? Ansgar had been very particular about calling me his starlight only when we were alone, using it as a prayer to our love rather than a pet name. There was no way Rhylan could know...unless...

"Yes, he is alive, I already told you that," the old fae insisted.

"You said you do not know what I am thinking, that you can't read minds?" I questioned, hoping to catch him in his own lies.

"I don't have to read your mind. You're pink and green. You have hope and love pouring out of you," he raised his shoulder to say that it was not his fault my thoughts became so obvious.

"How can you prove to me that Ansgar is alive? How can you prove that you met my brother?"

"Here," Rhylan said and stood slightly, finding support on his knees, and started searching for something in his right pocket. Seconds later, he pulled out a white silk handkerchief and handed it to me.

"I don't plan on crying again," I said when he forced it into my hand.

"Open it," the faerie urged and when I did, it proved impossible to keep my eyes from tearing up again. Inside the fabric, a lock of braided hair rested in my hand and it looked extremely similar to Ansgar's golden-brown hair. I had admired it so many times in the woods, I instantly recognised it. The way the sun weaved into his hair, making it look like the top of his head wore a crown made of light. It had to be his.

"That doesn't prove anything," I said, struggling to contain my emotions and keep Rhylan from discovering any more feelings I did not plan to reveal. This was it, the round of negotiations. And I had to be the one winning.

"It proves that your mate still lives," Rhylan frowned.

"It doesn't," I replied. "You could have taken this from him any time before killing him," my tone sounded accusatory and full of unresolved hatred.

Rhylan sighed, defeated, or tired of this back and forth, I did not know.

"Young girl, I have lived for many years and played my part in many events, but never once have I met someone as distrusting as yourself."

"I'm just stating the facts here," I defended myself. "And I will not make the mistake of trusting you so easily in the future."

"You can send a message to the royal family and have them confirm. Better?" Rhylan asked exasperated.

"That's better. And what is my part in this deal you want to make?"

"The young prince seems disinclined to give us the information about the location of their goddess's tear. I will need you to accompany me into the Fire Kingdom when the time comes and help persuade him." Rhylan released the words quickly and settled to wait for my answer. His face looked stressed and not very hopeful, as though what he had just told me wasn't the best news he could give me.

"So you want me to come with you, to your kingdom under the world and see Ansgar?" I asked while shock and disbelief portrayed on my face.

Rhylan nodded.

"Couldn't you have just said that from the beginning? Of course I will!"

The next hour found me in my allocated seat, scanning the clouds and thinking about what Rhylan had told me, while he took the time to enjoy the air hostesses. I didn't even want to think what they were doing in the changing room, especially since one of the women came out to make sure I didn't need anything until we landed.

Go Rhylan, I huffed. At least someone was having fun.

I did not care what he did back there, although it did irritate me that he suddenly started to give orders and act like the plane belonged to him. But, according to the deal he proposed, it would, if I was to accept.

I had less than ninety minutes until landing, to make a life-changing decision, and even though I already had the answer, it proved difficult to make the deal and I wanted to take advantage of my time until the last possible second.

Turns out a deal with a fireling is life binding, that is if either of us don't keep our end of the bargain, the energy that inhabits us fades away and we die. Apparently, that is what happened to my brother. What we call a soul left his body, summoned by a siren called Muhryn and Rhylan had been there to witness it.

So many thoughts invaded my mind and no matter how hard I struggled to piece them together, I could not. I wanted to cry, to shout, to kick something, to go back in time and keep Ansgar safe, to ask Erik why he wanted me to go to Evigt.

According to Rhylan, my brother knew about the tears of the goddesses and that Catalina's held the most power since she lived the purest life and did not rebel against Belgarath. The one that would help the owner find the others. And Erik had sent me to Evigt to find it.

I did not know what to believe, confusion roamed over me like a never-ending dark cloud that I had no power to escape.

And Rhylan needed an answer by the time we landed.

His deal did not only consist of me leaving with him and finding Ansgar. The bastard had a list of claims, which he presented to me on a parchment of some sort. I caressed Ansgar's lock of hair, then read Rhylan's demands yet again.

In the present note, Fear Gorta of the Fire Kingdom, also known as Rhylan Gordon is listing the terms of the proposal to Miss Anwen Odstar, mortal of origin and resident of the Human Realm.

For the terms to be met by both parties, the undersigned and holder of the deal offering will provide the below:
1. Safe passage into the Fire Kingdom, as dictated by laws and timings, to be granted to one traveller - signed below - only in the company of the

aforementioned

2. *Safe stay within the Fire Kingdom and protection from all residents and inhabitants, consisting but not restricted to royals, commanders, soldiers, court members, slaves*

3. *The opportunity to engage in conversation and/or other activities as seen fit by the aforementioned with a forced resident of the Fire Kingdom known as Prince Ansgar of the Earth Kingdom*

4. *Any other requests need to be presented in writing and in advance. These will only be granted if the deal holder will note a positive representation of their party*

In exchange, Miss Anwen Odstar will need to fulfil the below requests in a timely manner and towards the favour of the deal offerer.

1. *To not engage in harmful activities towards the aforementioned at any point from the acceptance of this contract until its nullity.*

2. *To receive the aforementioned into her human life and grant him family treatment until the visit into the Fire Kingdom is arranged*

3. *To protect and mentor the aforementioned in any required activities that involved human customs and rights and to accompany them until the travel into the Fire Kingdom is organised*

4. *To protect the aforementioned's privacy and identity*

5. *To not rebel or plan to break the contract without the aforementioned's permission. This involves but is not limited to plotting, trapping, shaming, lying, weapon or verbal violence, potions, alliances, etc.*

The breach of the contract will lead to the guilty party's complete loss of energy by the end of a moon cycle. This deal is irreversible and cannot be claimed by a third party unless agreed beforehand by both parties involved.

I remembered how, just a year ago, I found myself signing another binding document that granted me access into Evigt and the queen's mansion and how my hand shook while doing so. The determination towards finding Erik's reasons and discovering why he had sent me into such a place overpowered reason, all I wanted to do was sign and teleport myself there. Be close to my brother and find that missing piece of him.

Rhylan's story about Erik did not offer a clearer resolution, and even though it did make sense for my brother to want me to find the tear of the goddess — and it was not just another one of Rhylan's machinations to complete his deal — I could not be convinced.

The contract I held did acknowledge the presence of energy in a human, Rhylan had explained that it is what we call a soul and once it disappears, the body will go along with it. Scientifically, we are made of matter and energy. But Vikram had told me I couldn't be Ansgar's mate *because* I did not have energy of my own so it couldn't bind us.

I massaged my temples with my fingers and leaned my elbow against the small window, trying to calm my mind enough and be able to see with clarity.

No matter how much I fought or hated the fact that Rhylan wanted to live it up on my family's fortune and enjoy life, while I boiled with anger and expectation until he decided he had enough and took me to see my mate, I knew I had no choice.

Since the moment I lost him, my life hadn't been the same. Each day that passed held me in place like a marble statue, unaware of wind, sun or the passage of time. I only existed and hurt.

I wouldn't lose Ansgar too. I wouldn't make the same mistakes I made with my brother. The one who was supposedly murdered by a siren. The brother who had been by my side, who had protected me and been there all my life, teaching me everything he knew.

I lost him.

But I still had a chance to bring Ansgar back, and by all the gods, goddesses, and powerful spirits of this earth, I would not miss the opportunity.

A dishevelled Rhylan returned just before the prepare for landing message sounded in the jet speakers and retook his seat right in front of me.

"Did your girls have to go back to work and actually earn their wages?" I faked a pitying voice.

"Trust me, they earned them. They even deserve a bonus," he smiled and started to tuck this shirt back in his pants.

I grimaced in disgust, watching him turn his shirt wrinkles into an impeccable, recently ironed garment just by willing it.

"Jealous, sprout? Did you want some attention too?" he mimicked my voice, which made me pout even more.

"Not a chance, buddy. You are not my type."

"I am everyone's type," he smiled proudly and I knew that if he had a mirror at that moment, he would kiss his own reflection.

"If I didn't want you in Evigt, I sure as hell don't want you now," I reminded him, which made him finally stay in his seat without fidgeting. "I have Ansgar," it was my turn to display pride. "Who can compete?" I took the chance to grin at him for a long beat, while he adjusted his seat belt and reminded me to do the same.

"Speaking of Ansgar, did you reach a decision, or should I return to Mia and Glenda for another couple of hours?"

"I can see Mia and Glenda made an impression on you," I tried to stall, not ready to place a binding signature on a piece of paper that meant signing my soul away to the man who killed my boyfriend.

I did not care what Rhylan said, he had left me covered in grief for an entire year, even mocked me when sending that shirt, instead of telling me the truth. For me, it still meant killing my boyfriend. He couldn't just take away all the pain and suffering, the nights I cried myself to sleep missing Ansgar. Not with a piece of paper.

"Oh, yes," he found a more comfortable position in his seat and started daydreaming about what he had just done with the women. "They are brilliant employees, Mia is so flexible and Glenda's lack of gag reflex is just—"

"Urgh, stop disgusting me, I need to get ready for dinner," I said and urged him to stop talking with vigorous waves of my hands.

"I already had dessert several times, but I can be ready for dinner again whenever you wish."

There it was, that smug smirk of his, as though he knew how gorgeous he looked in every single situation, no matter what stupidity came out of his mouth.

"If I am to accept this, when can we go?"

He didn't need more explanation, knowing perfectly well what the question was.

"Autumn solstice. That is when all the portals open and you can enter without invitation, as long as it's in my presence."

I grabbed my phone and quickly googled the date. Twenty-second of September. Six weeks away.

I could do this. What was six weeks compared to a year? What was Rhylan pissing me off every day when in six weeks' time, I could see Ansgar?

"I need to add another claim to this," I said and passed the parchment back to him. "The lock of hair you gave me needs to be verified by the Earth Kingdom royal family before the six weeks are done and we go anywhere," I demanded, and as soon as I said the words, Rhylan did his magic and the writing readjusted before my eyes, containing my requirement.

5. Proof of Prince Ansgar of the Earth Kingdom safe confinement to be confirmed with a member of the Earth Kingdom royal family. No passage outside of the Human Realm will be accepted by the mortal of origin until such claims are to be verified

I took the piece of paper to read and reread it once again, making sure that nothing else had been changed without my knowledge. My hand shook while my fingers felt the smoothness of the parchment. A thousand doubts entered my body and I knew, even then, I knew that he kept lying to me. About Erik, about his intentions, possibly about Ansgar. Was I really agreeing to deal with the man who had tricked me once already, and in such a costly manner?

"Now or never, sprout," I heard that sweet damned voice of his, honeyed wine and bitterness, challenging me, pushing to the extent where I might give in.

"Stop calling me that," I raised my eyes from the paper just for an instant, enough to meet his dark unshakable gaze.

"You should be delighted by the acknowledgement of your love for the prince but well...who am I to judge the lack of a mortal brain?" Rhylan stretched wider on his seat and adjusted his shoulder blades in between the tall pillows.

"Explain," I demanded, aware of taking the bait but he was too eager to share whatever information this was that he ignored my lack of pleading phrases.

"When did I start calling you sprout?" he tilted his head to the side, offering me his full attention.

"The very first time we met, and I told you I hated it," I replied with a pointed finger.

"We met in the forest, when I attacked you. Did I call you sprout then?"

"No…" I hesitated.

With a sexy raised brow, Rhylan continued. "No, I started doing it after the visit at the mansion, when you were pulsating so much green light around, you looked like a leprechaun chasing a rainbow."

"Rhylan, I don't care about your pretentious wannabe funny jokes," I sighed and wanted to turn my attention back to the so-called contract, but his voice made me turn back to him in an instant.

"When I first saw you at the mansion, dearest Anwen, you had already met the prince. And green is the colour of love." He let his eyes follow mine for a second, making sure I understood his meaning, then returned to positioning himself in his seat.

One of the women came out to make sure our seatbelts were

fastened and stayed a while to linger by Rhylan's side, offering me enough time to grab a pen and mark my name in the empty space, just by Rhylan's cursive writing. Because he was right. I started loving Ansgar from the first time I saw him, from the moment he threw himself in front of Rhylan's power to save me. Now it was my turn to do everything I could to get him back.

I returned the parchment, which the faerie took and spread out slowly, checking for a signature.

Once he found it, his face relaxed and he urgently crinkled the paper back into his pocket.

"Splendid," Rhylan smiled in delight.

Ansgar

Chapter Eight

I didn't remember the amount of times I'd been to Serpium's workshop. There was no point in trying to, there had been so many and each time they ended painfully. According to the king, this would be my final one, the worst of all the torture sessions I had been through in the past year.

Once Drahden finished his speech and threats in front of the entire court, he ordered the two commanders to escort me back to Serpium. Not because I had any ability to resist or fight back, but because my body remained so beaten after I'd been squashed against the marble walls like an unwelcome bug, that I physically could not stand.

The king proved his power, I could not deny that and all my intimidation tactics failed miserably. Not that I had time to execute too many, in between insolence and instigating anger, Drahden lost control and everything I had planned for the evening crumbled into nothing, just like my wounded body.

I was escorted out of the room and back into the dark tunnel in between cheers for the ruler and heckles for me. The court members spat on me, threw food in my direction, or insulted everything I stood for. The only positive side to all of this were the food scraps slowly accumulating on Crypto's shiny armour as he and Marreth flanked me and dragged me away.

I sensed the anger rising in the third commander and how he hated me for ruining his one night in their great hall when he had finally escaped tunnel digging.

Too bad for him, but I was about to lose everything if the king spoke true. I did not believe it at first, did not understand how they could just change someone, make them forget, and realign their loyalties in such a way.

"Is it true?" I pushed my throat into speaking and tried to turn my head towards Marreth, who held the left side of my body, with more gentleness than his companion.

I did not know if he truly heard me or if he anticipated the question, but the first commander started speaking, much to his companion's contempt.

"It will hurt." He took another breath and pushed me a few steps, then added. "A lot. The more you fight it, the more damaging it is. You just have to let the poison run its course, prince. There is nothing else to do beyond this point."

His words sounded heavy. As though he still remembered what his transformation felt like and struggled to see me go through whatever waited for me beyond those tunnels, deep into Serpium's workshop.

I did wonder many times about Marreth, but everything became clearer once I learnt about his origin. He had been a soldier in the

Wind Kingdom, and by Drahden's words, he must have been amongst the bravest ones, to be chosen for such an ordeal. It surprised me to learn that a fae that did not hold origin in this court became the first commander, the strongest and most powerful one amongst all three, the right hand of the king. He must have earned the right through sweat and blood, but during all this time, he kept an innate kindness.

That meant hope. It signified that whatever they put inside me, I could still keep a part of myself, just as Marreth had maintained part of his good heart. I would fight it with every shred of power remaining. They would not make me forget. They would not take my memories away.

I would not betray my family and my kingdom, not again.

"Change of plans, Serpium," Crypto kicked the door open and announced our presence with an annoyed huff. "The king wants you to put the worm in this one."

The second commander and my designated torturer frowned and immediately started protesting.

"We agreed that we will chop him up! I spent the entire day sharpening my hunting knives." His voice sounded gruff and tired, annoyance resonating across the dark room.

"What can I say, he was idiot enough to piss off the king," Crypto raised his shoulders and released my body abruptly, making my right half splatter on the floor, barely held in place by Marreth's firm hold.

"Easy now prince, things are hard enough as they are, no need to add more injuries," he murmured softly.

"What happened to him?" Serpium asked with newly discovered interest, enjoying my gory state. He truly loved blood, this one.

"The king made him fly across the walls, you should have heard the bones cracking. Over and over, squashed like the dirty bug that he is," Crypto's voice glittered with satisfaction.

I hadn't realised my bones were broken, I only felt sharp and pinging pain, but it made sense, considering I could not move a muscle and had to be dragged back. They hadn't even bothered with iron chains, which proved the pinnacle of my weakness.

"Damn, I missed all the fun," Serpium growled in annoyance and started putting his knives away with deep sighs.

Meanwhile, I remained on the floor, bleeding all over the dark and stained carpet, among what seemed to be a conglomerate of dried blood stains.

Trying to move or shift into a more comfortable position turned out to be only a blissful wish, every time I tried to send commands to my body parts, they did not create any connections, and when Marreth placed the side of me that he had dragged on the floor, I remained a pile of limbs.

Unmoving. Unable. Waiting for the end.

"Anything else you need from us? I want to get some wine in this belly and some cunt around this cock before I have to return to digging again. Maybe the queen will have me, she clearly had plans with this one," Crypto kicked my body for emphasis, just out of pleasure and because he could. "Got him all shiny and clean, she wanted to learn how the tree people do it, ha?"

He kicked me again, which caused Serpium joy and they both started laughing at my expense.

Not that I cared, I barely kept any awareness at this point and struggled to gather all the beautiful memories I ever experienced before they were gone, turned into a pile of smoke.

I wished my life flashed before my eyes, it would have been much easier to see all the people I loved at once. Instead, I had to think of every one, barely having the energy to remember and focus on what we had lived together instead of the gripping pain that grew with each passing second. Probably the last drop of adrenaline decided to leave my body too before Serpium had a chance to start playing.

"Nah, go dig into something warm brother, I'll deal with this," the second commander's voice sounded from far away.

I felt a pat on my back and a voice that whispered a last encouragement. "Don't fight it, prince. There is no use."

Moments later, the door creaked and a slamming sound spun across the room, announcing the departure of the two males. For a long while, the second commander continued putting his knives away and taking a long time to clean each one, to show me what he had preferred to do to me instead of what had been demanded to.

Through it all, I remained on the ground, thinking about my family and my mate, the sunlight and the breeze, the tower where we hid before dinner, and father's forgiveness.

All things that I tried to keep locked inside my mind, trying to find a corner or some kind of synapsis that would prove stronger than whatever they wanted to do to me. There had to be a way.

"Right, let's get you situated, dear guest," Serpium turned to me and gave me his full attention, once his knives found their home inside drawers and shelves. "I don't know how much they told you, but we're going to be buddies after this. The best of buddies," he mocked with an excited smile and grabbed my body off the ground to place me in a leather elongated chair that looked more like a sofa with straps.

He connected each one with minutious patience until my body remained fixated in place and I couldn't even move my neck. I had become a stretch of nothing and Serpium had the power to do whatever he pleased with my body.

"Please..." All of a sudden I felt scared. Terrified of what could happen to me and any dash of pride vanished from mind, forcing me to beg to a fireling.

His expression dropped at the word, the one he struggled to hear from my mouth for months and his features adopted a pleased movement, as though what I had just said felt like divine music to his ears. Serpium inhaled deeply and absorbed the plea, wanting to keep this moment stored in the drawers of his memories, to be able to retrieve and enjoy at a later date.

"Say it again, prince," he whispered as to a lover, since the sound I had released probably felt like a joyous mating moment to his sick mind. "Beg me again."

I did not hold pride or ego any longer, so I did. I begged. A prince of the Earth Kingdom, trained in enduring pain and torture of any kind, pleading for his end. Pleading for his memories. I begged and cried, releasing tears that shed the last remnants of my identity and for a few moments, Serpium only looked at me, surprise and shock covering his face, expression changing along with my words.

For a moment, there was hope, or at least I tried to force it into me, hoping that my words would touch something inside him and make him have mercy.

"Thank you, your highness," the commander said reverently and his voice truly echoed gratitude.

He had struggled to have this effect on me since he started the torture sessions shortly after my arrival and not once had I given him the satisfaction of begging, of pleading, or trying to make things better for myself.

"Are you going to kill me?" I used the last strands of energy to ask.

"Orders are orders, my prince," Serpium suddenly found his respect for me. As though proving that I could be broken had connected us somehow.

"Please kill me, Serpium. Don't let them turn me into something I am not. It is much worse than death," I started pleading again. Wanting to have it all over with, fearing a life without memories, where I could be used to attack and kill innocent females and children.

"Please!" I began again.

"You see, prince, this is why I can't do it. This is what the king himself wants, that honour of yours." He stopped and threw me a proud and slightly empathic smile. "How many males would beg for death, in a position like yours, do you think?"

"All," I said without a second thought. "Every sane male would gladly give up their life instead of being turned into an executioner," I heard my voice resonate with a decision I did not know I still had.

"None," Serpium retorted. "All males would choose life. It is only the ones with kind hearts and loyalty towards life that would beg for their own end. And that unquenchable allegiance is worth more to the king than a thousand lives. Maybe one day you will even take my job," he huffed and turned back towards the drawers to find whatever tools he needed for what he was about to do to my body.

"No! Stop!" I demanded and tried to jerk from the tight leather bonds that kept me strapped to the chair, but they had been fastened so tightly it made it impossible for me to move an inch.

No amount of begging or threatening proved fruitful as Serpium grabbed vials of potions and prepared syringes of different colours and shapes, to be inserted into me. I tried to escape again, but by that time my mind was the only one left to fight since my body had faded into the chair and proved impossible to control any longer.

With the amount of broken bones and throbbing pain, my muscles decided to stop fighting and surrendered to whatever may come.

"Just chop me up in front of the court," I tried one last time, appealing to the commander's love for blood and gory scenarios. "Have them play *moonlight* with my severed head," I urged, remembering the game we used to play as youths when he would find objects and tried to throw them as high as the moon.

"There is no moonlight in here, prince, and your head is more valuable on your shoulders," Serpium answered and approached with a tray full of syringes and needles, each containing different colour elixirs. He started with my legs and implanted smaller needles into the muscles, pushing a blue liquid from time to time and stopping to see how my body accepted it.

Within seconds, the pain vanished and I started recovering strength in parts of my body I had taken for lost. I regained sense of my toes and could even wiggle them inside the straps.

Serpium smiled. "Works fast, doesn't it?"

"Are you healing me?" I asked incredulously, but even as I said it and he kept poking me with the blue liquid, my body started to feel refreshed, like it belonged to me once again.

"We don't need a broken soldier," he uttered and proceeded to continue the healing with precision.

I could do it. I could wait until he healed my entire body. Until I regained all feeling and then try to escape. The leather straps that kept me in place only worked because I was so weak, but once my muscles regenerated and my bones resealed, I could easily break them and fight for my life.

Confidence resonated across my entire body, with tiny specks of hope that appeared abruptly, as my mind urged me to devise a plan. I watched Serpium with newly found determination, trying to grasp where he would point the needle next, trying to find a specific movement or a weakness to take advantage of once I broke free.

My eyes scanned the room, measuring the knives and blades that rested across the various wooden supports, in so many different places and I started calculating the distance and the movements I had to make to get myself free and armed.

I scanned and measured, scheming and planning, until a needle pumped in my chest and took everything away.

"Take deep breaths and try not to fight it, prince, there is no use," Serpium repeated the same words Marreth had advised, as he stuck the long needle deeper into my chest until it reached my beating heart.

I felt it pulsating away from the sting, trying to make itself smaller and avoid the pain, but with another deep push, Serpium found it and made it stop in place. And me along with it.

Slowly, so agonisingly slowly, the commander pressed on the gigantic syringe, which made the liquid be released inside my beating heart.

That was it, I understood. Once the poison reached my system, it would be streamed to the rest of my body within seconds, and whatever plans I had, whatever I was before this, would change forever.

The commander gave me the poison, aware of every breath I took and every excruciating beat my heart still made, even though it stood poked in metal.

I swallowed sharply, probably the only gesture I would make for myself, which caused Serpium to nod encouragingly.

With that, I expelled. A single breath that became the catalyser of change.

Suddenly, my heart resumed its regular beating, which allowed for more liquid to be sucked into me at a velocious pace, mixing with my blood and every single cell that had to feed on it.

And I felt it. All over, spreading across my chest, invading my lungs and my stomach, at the back of my throat and inside my arms.

It possessed me like a parasite, one that I had absolutely no way of fighting back or expelling out.

Serpium retrieved the syringe once all its contents poured into me. The accumulation of liquid left me in a hazy state, as though a veil of blurriness poured over my eyes the instant the last drop entered my bloodstream.

I remained quiet, relaxed, and breathing more calmly. My body accepted the elixir so easily and I would not deny it, it felt good. Pain started fading away as soon as the substance reached a specific part of my body and I was grateful for it. Happy to have the pain finally disappear.

For so long I had been trapped in it, but I did not remember why. I only felt it vanishing.

And I felt relief.

"That's it, prince." A hand reached my face and opened my eyes wider, scanning my pupils. I blinked a few times to show them that I felt good, that whatever was happening to me, I enjoyed it.

I did not want them to take the sensation away. It felt too good now, I had grown used to it and it offered tranquillity, like the days when I used to sneak out in the garden and hide in the hollow of the big orange tree with an entire plate of peach-filled seed cakes.

Why was I in a tree? I struggled to remember, the memory hazy and fading away, like I had just woken up from a dream and the images decomposed right in front of my eyes.

"Don't fight it," the voice by my side said. "It will get easier in a few hours."

Fight it? Fight what? I only felt bliss.

Anwen

Chapter Nine

Day 1

Rhylan did not make a sound during the car journey from the airport. Apparently, he had decided to give me even more space after we landed, and occupied his time with checking my phone and scanning the apps. I did not know or care how he got hold of it, but it was keeping him occupied, with his mouth shut. I especially loved the second part.

The only time we spoke during the landing was to devise a plan, which apparently he had already taken care of and I only had to be instructed as to how to act and what lies to tell my family.

I had to present Rhylan Gordon as a big investor I met during my travels, whom I invited to talk through my business plans and strategy, but he had always been so busy. Until he found himself suddenly in need of a vacation, which I was more than glad to provide for him. In my own home. With my family.

Even though I tried to tell him repeatedly that it would not go well with my parents and the plan was not believable, he was obstinate to such a level that I gave up trying to convince him. I knew for a fact that my dad would not believe anything that came out of his mouth, especially that I invited someone to spend time with us without consulting with him first. Also, that someone was a sexy dark haired gorgeous man.

It would definitely not go well with my dad.

I sighed, knowing that after a long flight, I had to expect an even longer evening. The only good part of all this was that, soon it would be nightfall and I could go to sleep and wake up to only forty-three days of Rhylan's company. I had already counted and recounted, even set one of those countdown timers on my phone and set several daily alerts to issue notifications at specific times throughout the day. I had to focus on the bigger goal here, and if seeing Ansgar again would cost me forty-four miserable days, it meant nothing compared to the happiness I would finally feel after holding him again.

"There's that hope shining in you," Rhylan decided to analyse my feelings. Or better said, the colour of them. Right.

"Can you just shut up for the rest of the journey, please?" I sighed noisily, tired of Rhylan's perpetual desire to hear his own voice.

"You are distracted and probably have lots of ideas going through your head, but even I know that we have arrived."

As soon as he said it, I realised the car just pulled into the patio and started circling the fountain, bringing us only a few feet from the entrance door, which had already opened and some of the staff prepared to welcome me and carry my bags back to my room.

"Are you sure I can't convince you to stay at a hotel? I'll get you the best one in the city," I pleaded one last time, even though all my requests for Rhylan to find a different home ended up in rejections. He had an unshakable determination to live in our house, and no matter what I proposed, he did not give up.

"And miss all the fun? I want a room next to yours," the faerie said with a smile and opened the car door to exit on his side.

I took a deep breath but before I could expel it back, the door opened and Rhylan was the one to offer me his hand and help me out of the car. A true gentleman, I huffed, understanding that he had already adopted his new role.

I wondered if he could actually pull this off. After all, he convinced me that he was a guard back in Evigt, so playing a classy gentleman in front of my parents shouldn't be as difficult.

"No, thank you," I replied and helped myself out of the car.

Albert, one of the older members of staff came by my side to welcome me as soon as he spotted me.

"Welcome back, miss Anwen. Dinner is half an hour away should you wish to freshen up after your travels. And welcome, mister…" he stopped, awaiting the necessary introduction.

I remained silent and forced Rhylan to introduce himself. The deal did not consist of me playing his puppet with every single person we met.

"Thank you, Albert," I said, ignoring Rhylan and making my way inside. Unfortunately, the man was too kind and Albert's voice stopped me in my tracks.

"Will Mister Gordon require accommodation?"

I should have said no, I should have ignored the question, but after all the dismissals my pleas had received, I knew negating his visit would only waste more time.

"Yes, please find him a room on the second floor, it can be the one between mine and Erik's if it's not occupied."

I knew it wouldn't be, no one had set foot on the second floor apart from me and Marissa, the woman who used to babysit us, who was the only one allowed to wander through my wardrobe and bathroom. Since Erik passed, the room between ours, the one we had used as neutral territory during our childhood fights, remained unoccupied, since Erik's room turned into a mausoleum of his memories.

"O...of course," Albert couldn't contain his surprise and immediately rushed back inside, almost knocking me over to make the arrangements.

If Rhylan was surprised, he did not show it and only made a hand gesture to signal me to enter first. I knew dad had to be in some sort of meeting in his study and mom either entertained or relaxed in her room with a glass of wine, so there was no use hunting them around the house when I would see them in thirty minutes.

I started climbing the stairs and pushed Rhylan to do the same until we reached the second floor. He could get the tour tomorrow after I slept and lost at least some part of the urging desire to kill him for forcing me into this.

"Your room," I pointed to the door. "Erik's is down the hall, mine is that way," I signalled with lazy hand gestures. "You are not allowed in either," I demanded sharply, to which he nodded.

Leaving him to his own company, I turned and opened the door to my own room. As soon as I did, I heard music and knew Cressida had to accompany the sound.

"Bestie!" I heard her snicker.

She lay splayed out on the bed, surrounded by electronics and jiggling her toes to the beat. Around her, several pillows, a laptop, a tablet, and two phones either buzzed or displayed a light-up screen.

"Cressi!" I jumped on the bed and straight in her arms, holding onto her for dear life. She did not react for a second, probably surprised by my rush, but then her arms curled around me and pulled me in tight, making our chests connect for a few seconds.

"What are you doing here?" I asked as I released her, wiping my watery eyes.

"I have a few days off and your mom said you were coming back tonight, so I decided to pop in for a sleepover," she smiled and as soon as I saw her lips form the gesture, I felt a rush of relief flood through me. I could do this, with Cressi by my side. She could guide me through it all, offer me support and help me find a way to get Rhylan away from here until the time came.

"I brought a man home," I said quickly, aware of the time and the fact that I had to give her a year's worth of explanations in twenty minutes.

Cressi's face dropped and her eyes grew so wide, that for a second she looked like the big bad wolf. I saw her struggling to take the information in, to understand what I had just said as a river of expressions flowed onto her face within a split second.

"Who is he?" she settled for an easy question, or she must have thought so.

"It's complicated, and I need you to help me get rid of him

without being too obvious because I need him back in exactly forty-three days and a half."

Cressi laughed and laid back on the bed, arranging two big pillows under her neck, then grabbed her laptop again and pressed play on the music, making the room turn into a disco.

"I'm serious!" I said but her muttered "aha" did not sound very impressed with what must have sounded like a terrible joke.

"As you wish, just remember my words when we go down for dinner," I raised my shoulders in defeat and headed to the bathroom. I still had time for a quick shower and the attire and high heels I wore on the plane did not feel comfy at all, so I couldn't wait to change into some jeans and trainers.

Ten minutes later, with my wet hair pulled up in a messy bun, I returned to the room in a white t-shirt and a pair of jeggings, along with green Converse and of course, clean underwear.

"Ready for dinner?" I asked my friend, who had started editing one of her videos about a fashion parade she attended.

"Let's go," Cressi replied and stood from bed.

That was the only thing my gorgeous sister had to do to get ready, stand up, and go. Unlike the rest of us mortals, who actually had to put in some effort to look presentable enough for the people we had to break bread with.

She did not wait for me to lead and opened the door, knowing her way to the dining hall perfectly well, since she practically grew up in this house too.

As we reached the doors, we heard dad talking to another man and I recognised Rhylan's voice immediately. He had already come down without telling me. That bastard.

I sighed again — it seemed to be my favourite pastime lately— and opened the door to the dining hall, where indeed, my dad and Rhylan stood by the bar, each holding a glass of something amber.

Dad looked relaxed and Rhylan was smiling, but by my side, Cressida froze. Her muscles flexed and her entire body stopped in place, unable to move or help me hold the door that we had pushed in together.

"You brought a man home," she spoke slowly, only for me to hear.

"No kidding," I huffed and made my way into the room.

As soon as we entered, dad turned to us and stepped closer to me, then opened his arms to let me slide inside his embrace for a long hug. All the while Cressida remained paralysed by the door and Rhylan casually sipped his liquor, enjoying the stunned look on my face. "I like him," dad whispered into the shell of my ear, an approval I did not understand at first.

"And who is this beautiful lady?" Rhylan interrupted and stepped closer to a stunned Cressi, who did not move or react to what developed before her eyes. I understood her amazement. She had been by my side in the past year, seeing me cry for Ansgar day after day, so it must have truly shocked her to see me bring home someone else so suddenly and unexpectedly, without her having any prior warning.

"Cressida Thompson," I announced and escaped my father's arms to approach the two. Rhylan had that look on his face and I had to take my friend away before she became his new prey. "You might have seen her on magazine covers and on TV, she is very famous around these parts," I tried to paint a picture that clearly stated Cressi was out of his reach and she had so much coverage that his presence alongside her would not pass as anonymous. Especially since he needed to keep his identity hidden, without having proof of his existence all over the printed press and socials.

"I have no doubt that she is, her beauty is beyond anything I've seen in recent history," Rhylan pursed his lips after he finished speaking and grabbed Cressi's right hand to lift it to his lips. A soft, very long kiss remained planted on my friend's skin, who, to my surprise, smiled so widely, as though she just won a beauty award.

"I don't believe we have been introduced," Cressi spoke without breaking eye contact or removing her hand from his.

Oh no, no, no, no! I knew that look. God damn it, I knew that look and did not like it one bit. Cressi showed interest. Hell, she looked like she might just plan an escape with Rhylan and travel across the globe for a honeymoon. No, this could not be happening, I would not let it happen. I had to snap her out of it and I had to make it clear to Rhylan that touching my friend would break the contract we had. I did not trust the man with a butter knife, let alone with the heart of my sister.

"Rhylan Gordon, but you can call me Rhy, all my friends do," he purred and continued caressing her hand.

"There is no need for that, Cressi has too many friends as it is. Men friends." I clarified, which caused Cressi to frown and finally remove her eyes from his, breaking the trance she had been caught in.

She showed her discontent with a grimace and I widened my eyes to her, trying to communicate that whatever her plans with Rhylan, they were out of bounds.

Fortunately, my mom arrived and once the introductions were made, during which Rhylan posed as a famous investor on his travels around the US and he made sure to flatter mine and my family's hospitality and offer his gratitude, we headed to the dining table where several platters waited, releasing mouth-watering scents.

To my surprise and annoyance, neither of my parents even thought to question the fact that I had brought a man home and seemed pretty content to chat away and make small talk, ensuring to slide one or two interrogation questions from time to time. 'How did we meet?' Rhylan gave a long speech about his closeness to the Swedish royal family and Evigt Forest, how he happened to be strolling in the woods and found me in need of assistance and how we would meet and spend time together. Not entirely a lie but my version of the truth had a lot more to add.

'How did we reconnect since I never mentioned him before?' To this, Rhylan responded that since our initial meeting and several contacts did not particularly follow the rules imposed by my NDA agreement, he thought it best to maintain distance for a while and take care of some other projects while I settled back home. But that we had casually met during my last visit to Europe and since he had a bit of time on his hands, he was very excited to accept my insistent invitations and discover new investment opportunities overseas.

I watched him respond and remained filled with amazement. He looked gorgeous in the Boss suit he just happened to find for dinner, and talked with elegance and charm, responding to the questions just enough to avoid dominating the conversation but get his point across and prevent further questions on the same subject from surfacing. He maintained some things vague, as one should when meeting a possible business partner, but let slide important details that 'accidentally' gave away part of his intentions.

He ate slowly, chewed with his mouth closed, and listened to the conversation before stuffing his mouth with food in case he would have to provide an unexpected answer while found in the precarious situation of chewing. He was perfect, simply put.

Mom adored him and made several faces and pleased smiles towards me whenever she could, to let me know how happy she felt with our guest and dad became involved in conversation and acted towards Rhylan as he used to when Jonathan, my ex, received a dinner invitation. Basically, both of them showed readiness to welcome him to the family.

Fortunately, Cressi was the only one to keep some distance, even though I felt her attention on him for long periods of time, especially since he did not look at her or address her directly. From time to time, Rhylan — who just happened to be seated next to me, while mom and dad sat at each head of the table and Cressi remained parallel to us— made specific gestures towards me, like grab me an extra bun from the basket and place it on my small empty plate or refill my wine glass even after I had just taken two sips. All this theatre to showcase his closeness to me and display his honourable intentions.

I hated him.

"So how long are you planning to stay, Rhy?" Don't mind Cressi already adopting his nickname and going with the flow. She smiled widely at him and her blue eyes shone brighter.

"Forty-four days," I heard myself reply instead of giving Rhylan the chance. "I'll book him a nice hotel soon," I added, more to my parents' benefit. I needed them to know that he would not be staying in our house for long and that I would get rid of him as soon as possible.

"That is very specific," my dad said. "We must insist that you do not find a hotel though, you are more than welcome into our home and I am sure Anwen will love having you close."

Before I opened my mouth to protest, it was Rhylan's turn to respond. "That would be very much appreciated, Mr. Odstar. I generally would not like to trouble you, but I have no family of my own left, and staying in a place where the entire family meets for dinner and casually chats about their day is worth more to me than a stay at the best hotel in the world," he nodded in gratitude and dad followed his gesture.

"It is settled then," mom added and raised her hand to order the dessert.

While assorted plates of chocolate truffles, tiramisu, cakes, scones, and fruit tarts were arranged at the table, Rhylan turned to me and displayed a victorious smirk. He then served himself a cup of coffee from the French pot and did the same for me, even though I had already told him I didn't want any.

"I presume you will have a lot to chat about with your friend tonight. And you didn't have a chance to rest on the plane," he pointed, serving me, then bringing the almond milk closer and dropping two cubes of sugar in the hot cup.

"Why is your stay so exact, Rhylan?" dad enquired.

"Autumn solstice is a very important celebration where I'm from and I invited Anwen to accompany me. This way she can see my origin and the way business is conducted in my lands. I hope it will offer her a fresh perspective," he smiled to my dad's delight. "If you don't mind me asking, Mr Odstar, you have some European ties of your own, am I correct?"

"Please, call me Jason," dad smiled, delighted to have a reason to tell the family story again. "Indeed, I do, and ever since they were kids, I made sure that Anwen and Erik both knew where they came from and how important their origin is."

We all paused at the casual mention of my brother's name and even my dad looked shocked at how easily it had escaped his mouth. Although almost two years had passed, sometimes we still forgot that he was no longer with us, and dad's genuine reaction showcased this fact.

Realising the situation, Rhylan jumped in and for the first time since he reappeared in my life, I felt grateful to have him there.

"I am terribly sorry to hear about your son, he had a brilliant mind and I'm sure he would have had many wonderful plans for the future. I have met him a couple of times and each one proved to be memorable."

Dad smiled and mom barely contained her tears, while Cressi looked at Rhylan with newly found interest.

Without a second push, dad started talking again. "It was my great-great-great-grandfather a few generations ago who decided to make his way to America before it became the promised land of all opportunities. No one knew his reasons, but he must have had a privileged life back in Sweden, since he established a very profitable soap business in New York, when the big city was only a pile of rubble instead of what can be seen now. Ludvig, his name was. Ludvig Odstar.

At the mention of the name of my relative, Rhylan drew a sharp breath, which made me turn to him, but he blatantly ignored my reaction and focused all his attention on my dad, who continued speaking.

"A brilliant young man with a lot of courage. Within years, he became so successful that he opened a second shop with one of his friends, and so, the family business came to be. My grandfather decided to make the change from the classic *Odstar Soaps* to *Odstar Cosmetics* since they had started to produce many beauty products back in the thirties. But we always took pride in keeping the family name and our origin well known. I'm sure Anwen must have told you that I like to visit Sweden regularly and maintain a close connection with important figures back there, even some members of the royal family," dad grinned proudly, just as he did every time he talked about Sweden and where he came from.

Unfortunately, I never knew my grandfather, but he must have instated very strong roots in the family because dad still insisted that we had Swedish princess cake at least once a month for dessert and hired a tutor for us to learn Norse mythology. He also tried to teach us Swedish but neither Erik or I were good with languages.

Rhylan kept an interest in the topic and asked my dad follow-up questions about Sweden, his connection to the royal family, and stuff about the older generations of the family that I hadn't even considered in my twenty-six years of life. He looked very interested in Ludvig and even asked to see the portrait dad had mentioned he kept in the studio. I remained convinced it was all a ruse to strengthen his position in the family and find more connections, to help with whatever plans he had during his stay.

As for me, all I wanted to do was to escape back to my room with Cressida and tell her everything about Rhylan, though I did not exactly know how to do that considering I couldn't really tell her the truth without sounding crazy or scaring my friend.

I resisted another half an hour through dessert chat, during which it came my mom's turn to brag about all the wonderful events she had to organise during the year and tell him, not very subtly, about my involvement and showcase every single quality she thought I had. During that time, I rubbed my head and nursed a headache that took control over the right side of my head and pinched at the back of my eye. I was exhausted, and ever since I had seen Rhylan again, I couldn't take a single moment to relax and settle. My brain must have been overcharged and I felt the veins inside my head pumping with a newly found anxiety at the thought of having to spend this much time alongside a dark magical person.

"Anwen and I will retire for the evening, if you'll excuse us," Cressi sensed my need and placed her dessert fork onto the tiny empty plate with enough noise to draw attention. "It was a wonderful surprise to meet you, Rhy," she snickered in delight, "I can't wait for breakfast." With a wide smile, she stood and urged me to do the same.

Gladly, I mimicked her gesture and stepped quickly to give my dad a kiss on the cheek, then smiled at mom and wished everyone a good night. I didn't look at Rhylan when I said it, making sure he knew my messages did not include him. I did not give a damn how well he rested.

Cressi and I kept silent while we left the dining table and headed toward the stairs and up to my room. It was only when the door sealed shut that my friend started a fit that I could barely follow. In between a lot of 'oh my god, and 'how could you?' served with a side of reproaches for not keeping her in the loop with the current events in my life, I barely managed to utter a word. I let her expulse the feelings she kept so well hidden during the meal. After all, she was a professional and knew how to deal with most situations. Fortunately.

Barely a few minutes later the earthquake that was my best friend settled enough for me to start having a conversation with her, as she found her already-claimed spot on the bed and settled comfortably in a relaxed yoga stance with a pillow between her legs and prepared for the receipt of an explanation.

"Is it my turn now?" I wanted to double-check before I started speaking, though I truly had no idea what to say to her, apart from the plain old message, 'keep away from him.'

"I am eagerly awaiting," she gestured as though to give the flag wave in one of those movies where two cars raced and a hot girl had to give them the go-ahead.

"For this to work, you will need to listen and not freak out. The only thing that is of utmost importance right now is for you to know that Rhylan is not charming or good," I started to explain but understood it wasn't the best thing to say when Cressi immediately replied.

"Is he bad? Bad boy Rhy?" she joked though her tongue involuntarily started licking her lower lip.

"Cressi, no, it's not like that. You need to stay away from him," I tried again in a more decisive tone, forcing the message across.

"Why did you bring him home then?" she asked with frustration, crossing her arms.

"I didn't have a choice" I said and took a seat on the other side of the bed, coming closer to her, but far enough to still be able to catch and analyse her expressions. "He blackmailed me into bringing him here and I don't know why. But I am trapped in a contract and I don't know what to do. I need him to keep his end, yet I don't trust him and I want him out of the house."

"He can't be blackmailing you, he is a perfect gentleman. He's so gorgeous and charming, and amazing, and knowledgeable and interested in you. You should see the way he looks at you! So protective with those big dark eyes of his. I'm in love with him. If you don't want him, I will!"

"Cressi, stop!" I said but my friend grabbed my hands and cupped them to her chest to continue speaking. "Anwen, I know you've been through so much. I know you lost so much and you are probably not even thinking about falling in love again. But it is okay, you can be happy. You have the right to search for your happiness and move on. It's been a year and Ansgar is gone," my friend murmured the words slowly, trying to pierce them inside my head. And I loved her for it. Even though she had no idea what was happening, she showed so much support.

"Cressi, there are so many things I kept from you, so many things you don't understand," I shook my head, not even knowing where to begin.

"Tell me, Anwen. Tell me what is happening to you. Make me understand and I promise I will help," she replied with a soft voice, which told me she would truly try her best to help me. I only had to trust her.

So I grabbed the laptop she had left on the bed and minimised all the screens and programs the influencer in Cressi left open until I found Google. I figured I could use the same method I found out with her, since I wasn't very sure if the deal I signed earlier that day would keep me from saying specific things. But not even the strongest magic in the world could work against the internet. Or so I hoped.

In a new tab, I typed the two words I needed her to learn. 'Fear Gorta', and to my relief, hundreds of results invaded the screen in a millisecond. I opened the one I knew had the best description from my numerous searches in the past year and turned the screen to her.

"Take a few minutes to read this," I said as I planted the laptop in her lap and over the pillow she had placed by her side.

"Seriously? Do I need to grab a pen and paper for you to dictate notes into my blonde brain or are you alright with the internet telling me how stupid I am?" Cressi huffed in disbelief.

"Please, Cressi," I urged and my voice must have shown enough urgency that she accepted the device and lowered her eyes to the information.

While she read, I heard footsteps on the corridor and a sudden knock on the door came accompanied by Rhylan's voice. "Have a good night, ladies," his words arrived cheering and slightly mocking.

Cressi did not answer immediately but looked at me, so I replied. "Go away!"

A playful laughter ticked our ears and the footsteps travelled down the hall until we heard his door open and close back again.

Silently, I urged Cressi to keep reading while placing a finger over my lips, signalling to her that we had to keep our voices low.

"Why are you showing me this?" Cressi asked as her attention rose back to me and I hoped she read at least a few paragraphs of the information on the screen.

"Because that is what he is!" I said with relief, happy to take part of the burden off my chest. "Rhylan is Fear Gorta. And you need to help me get rid of him."

Chapter Ten

My body took me on a psychedelic journey, where every part of my being made its presence known and sent signals back to my brain. I felt my lungs inflate as a stream of fresh air invaded them and forced their expanse, then followed the air to my throat and let it release through my nose. All the while the lungs contracted back again, taking my rib cage muscles along.

I was aware of the skin behind my fingernails, pumping slowly and filling with sweet relaxation as the capillary veins brought the oxygen to them. The back of my throat felt more relaxed than ever before and every time I swallowed, it was like a cold drink poured down it and left a sweet tingling behind. I laughed and wiggled my toes, trying to mentally send more air downwards and carry the rest of my body into this relaxed state I had suddenly been trapped in.

I could not recall what happened before all this started, and the tingling sensation in my cheekbones made me feel so content that it did not even matter. Something in my body told me that I had been waiting a long while for this floating state to overpower me, and it seemed to have decided to take full advantage of the perception.

Even my mind went blank and swam into a lake of faded memories, where nothing I had lived in the past could make its way and disturb the silence of the present. It was like a veil of nothing fell onto my senses and took me on a path where there was only me, and what I felt that mattered.

I did not think about before, a time when I was brought into the world to fulfil a purpose or have an idea to live by. I did not care to know who I was, what I wanted, or what motives made me reach this place, where I was so eager to dive in and take all the suffering away.

"He's deep into it, I'll go to dinner and take a nap afterward, I don't expect him to become aware anytime soon," a voice sounded from very far away.

"'I'll stay with him till morning," another responded, a different side of the ethereal place I found myself in. This one seemed more benevolent and shadowed specks of compassion, whereas the first one echoed tired and unwilling like it had lived on repetition and barely now, could it escape for a short while.

I did not want to think about it, did not want to know and every impulse in me vibrated with the desire to return to the white veil of nothingness, but parts of my body had become aware and muscles started jolting at hearing the two voices.

Why wasn't I alone? Why couldn't I turn into nothing and fade away? Why couldn't I just exist as a dash of air, so light and never-ending? They had been talking about me, I knew it deep down and they had used masculine pronouns. Making me a male. Strange, I did not feel like a male. I felt like a blob of ink pouring down a goose feather, here one moment and vanished in the next, with no purpose or higher goal than to just be.

Why did I have to be a male? It meant I had things to do, responsibilities to attain, and a moral code to follow. It meant I belonged to something, or someone, maybe even had a family, that I had existed through generations in the blood of my ancestors, and my turn to come to life had been decided for the present day.

"No…" I grunted, supplicating my body and mind to return to that time when we just were. I did not want to wake up and face the world, understand what came around me, and be forced to move towards my death.

"Ansgar?" that second voice called, from deep down a cloud of wondering and perdition. It called again and again, the same name resounded until it came closer and closer to where I was. Until I understood it was what defined me.

A name. My name. I was Ansgar.

"I am Ansgar," I said to the voice and a dash of a smile poured through me, even though I did not yet have eyes to see it.

"You need to wake up," it told me and as soon as it spoke, an earthquake of sensation overcame my muscles, forcing them to jolt up and down, disturbing the sweet bliss that kept distributing across me.

"Go away, voice, do not drag me with you," I murmured, even though I did not know which direction it came from or if it had the power to hear me. If I had arms and a body I could have found it and shoved it away, making it fly outside of my white veil, the nest of my bliss.

"You are prince Ansgar of the Earth Kingdom, third son of Farryn and Bathysia, you have two older brothers, Vikram and Damaris. Do not forget them, do not forget who you are. You must fight this, do not let the serum drag them away."

It continued to repeat the same information, over and over, and every time I heard those names, my name, a part of the veil shrank away, leaving me on my own to face reality. To become that Ansgar the voice called for and search through painful memories I needed to forget. There was a reason I had chosen to forget them, to move on and become someone else, something else, but no matter how much I struggled, my synapses snapped and images flooded my mind like erupting damnation, releasing everything at once.

"You are prince Ansgar of the Earth kingdom," the voice pressed needles into my senses. Vivid images pierced through me, but each one came with pain.

A garden full of orange trees appeared. They were in bloom and I had just snapped one of the branches, releasing a soft rain of rosy petals over me. A huge library filled with leather-bound books and a massive rounded skylight with decorated branches adorned the ceiling. I loved to sneak in there before Damaris came home, with a generous portion of his seed cakes, and watch the craters of the moon, thinking they were the footsteps of giants.

"Bathysia," the voice said and the image of a woman with dark skin and beads of stars in her hair caught me and spun me around, making some of the cakes fall on the floor. She would kiss my forehead and each of my cheeks, she always loved to give me three kisses.

"My mother..." I said to no one in particular, except the memories that forced the recognition.

"Yes, your mother. The queen is your mother, do not forget her," the voice pushed. "Hang onto her memory and fight this. If anyone can do it, it's you."

"No," I heard myself interacting with the voice without my consent or realisation. "I will not let the woman with stars in her hair bring the pain back. I will not let you do it either," I urged and went beyond my mental barriers to keep the recurring memories at bay.

I did not want to do this, I could not do this, and every time a new one resurfaced so did the pain. So sharp and poignant, that I could not face it again, I did not have the strength to do so. There was no fight in me and I did not want to go back to whatever I had been before this, before the veil covered me. I would not.

Diving deeper, I surrounded myself with nothingness, I let it fill my body and cleanse those memories away, like a blood-stained shirt in cold water. Slowly, they disappeared down the stream and once again, I remained floating and alone.

I would not fight this, I had no strength left in me and I did not understand why I had to, why the voice insisted so much that I did, instead of allowing me to enjoy a sentiment where I just was, without anyone or anything beyond what I sensed and felt. My mind dominated everything and I struggled to turn into a floating mass yet again, leave my body behind and travel along the routes of the blissful liquid that gave me so much peace.

"Rhylan said you are mated to a human. Sometimes you call her name when you think no one can hear you. You call her Anwen," the voice echoed with desperation, as though this new information was kept in a precious spot, to be used as a last resort.

A halt. Everything came to a stop, even my organs stopped drinking the liquid that had already become thickened with my blood. I knew that name, I loved that name and its bearer. Anwen. It came crashing at once, like I was a fallen leaf on a lake and a waterfall of emotion had just been dropped with the force of a hurricane. I remembered her.

She was my mate. A part of me that I had waited to meet for so long. I responded to her touch, it bound me to her. A connection impossible to break, part of me became her, and part of her would always carry something of mine. As mates.

I remembered a sweet smile and a dimple shining in the sunset, making my heart flutter like no other female had ever managed to do. She fed me and cried at my side, and I kept apologising. I did not recall, but it seemed important. I had hurt her somehow.

So much that she wrote to me. I felt excited and hopped to her door like a fidgeting pixie who had swum in lavender wine, but she asked me to stay away. A piece of wood carried the message, and I had to obey. I recalled the hurt and knew I deserved it. I understood.

But then she came back into my arms and kissed me. Chains. Did she want to hurt me, same as all these other beings? No, her soft hand caressed my cheek while I slept. The iron did not burn; she wrapped it in fabric. Why? Why did she want to restrain me so?

I had kissed her so many times that her taste inundated the roof of my mouth and flowed on my tongue like sweet nectar, the only aliment to give me relief. I knew every part of her body and had been inside of her. Many times.

I remembered her splayed out on a desk, in an opulent room somewhere, her naked back completely at my mercy. I remember slamming into her so hard that the wooden desk moved and dragged her further towards the wall, where she remained captive to me, with no space left to escape. She moaned my name, overcome by pleasure, and my hands had drafted over every single inch of her sweaty body, grabbing and teasing, incapacitated by her sweet release on me. I felt her core clenching me tighter, begging for more, and I gave her every part of me, unrelenting and obsessed until I too had fallen trapped in my pleasure.

I remember how wide my eyes had been when she turned and started giggling, still prisoner to my body. "We just damaged a historical piece," she had said, her melodious voice sounding raspy since her throat had worked overtime, expelling moan after moan.

I loved to see her laugh, to finally see her happy and unburdened. Why had she been so sad before? I did not know, but every part of me needed to go back to that desk and repeat the session an infinite amount of times. It felt better than the white veil of nothing, better than breathing.

"Where is she?" I asked the voice, decided to leave that place and follow wherever I might find her. I did not care about the pain this time. Even though it came in substantial thrusts into every vein of my body, she was worth it. Being with her trumped suffering.

"Tell me where she is," I asked the voice again and struggled to move my head and find its direction. My eyes wouldn't open, or if they did, they could only spot darkness. I did not know. I jerked my muscles awake, they needed to shift out of this sensation. They needed to take me back to Anwen.

"You remember her?" the voice asked. It felt happier, lighter somehow, as though a shrivel of hope had just flown over it.

"Anwen is my mate." I replied. "I need to go back to her. Where is she?"

A thousand questions flooded me. I did not know where I was, my senses became numb and thrashing pain overpowered my body every time I even sketched a thought or tried to recall more of those sweet moments where we joined in pleasure.

I needed them, I needed to transport myself there and be with her again, relive them until I found a way out and back to her. She proved to be the only thing stronger than the pain.

"Remember her," the voice said again and a hand touched my right arm. Which felt trapped, tied to something. I commanded the muscles to move and raise the hand, the arm, a finger even, to no avail. With every inch, a heavy pressure forced it in place. I did the same with my left arm and my legs, then with my chest and neck, but every part became pierced by the pressure. I was strapped, the voice did not want me to move.

"Why?" I asked, demanded from the voice. Why had it made me remember, only to keep me prisoner? Prisoner. That is what I was. *Fire Kingdom. The king.*

"Marreth?" I asked. Suddenly everything fit into place, and I realised where I was, and what had happened. The king broke my bones and I had to suffer punishment. They wanted to kill me.

"I can't believe you remember! How is this even possible?" the commander said. He was the voice. The one who forced me back.

"What is happening to me?" I did not understand why he stood by my side instead of following orders.

"I don't have much time, you've been out of it all night and Serpium will come in soon enough. Just listen. I can't release you or even give you a sip of water, he would know. And it would hurt the serum," he explained.

"When are they giving it to me?" I remembered the purpose of said poison. To make me one of them. As they had done to Marreth and many others, to later be sacrificed in battle. It mustn't work so well, since here Marreth stood, by my side, working against his king.

"They already have; this is your first dose. Listen, prince, there will be more. Many more, until you become one of them. Us," he stopped to correct himself. "I am told I needed ten doses, for you it might be more. Think of it like a drug, once you have a taste there is no turning back. You have to fight it, as it will become stronger. It will take everything away."

"I remember white and nothing. I didn't even have a body anymore. Are my eyes covered?" I asked, suddenly afraid of what Serpium might have done while I drifted off.

A small scratch on my cheek revealed candlelight and Marreth's face close to mine. He pulled the blindfold just enough so I could see slithers of my surroundings.

"You still have both eyes, prince." I didn't even need to tell him my worry, he immediately understood. After all, we both knew what

Serpium was capable of. His head turned a few times and pinched several parts of my body.

"Feel that?" he asked quickly.

"Yes," I replied with slight excitement, happy that all my body parts remained intact.

"Now listen, Serpium is pissed. He wanted to make a show of killing you. So if this doesn't work, he might still suggest it to the king. I heard you begged for death," he stopped and threw me a pitying look.

"A better option than this." I did not shy, there was no point anymore. I had been trapped in a chair all night after being slammed repeatedly against marble walls and tortured for an entire year. My life prospects did not sound too good.

"In that case, you have to fight it. If your transition proves unsuccessful, there is nothing else they can do, but kill you. At least you'll be free to dine with your goddess," Marreth replied with admiration and longing. He too had wanted to dine with his goddess, I came to understand.

Our ancestors believed that once the three goddesses left their mortal form, they departed, to another planet or galaxy, maybe to start it all over again. To create another world. The energy that we held in life bound us to them, and at the time of our death, we would be transported into their new kingdoms and welcomed by the goddess to her new creation, where life started all over again. The goddesses dined with each one of the arrivals, to welcome and embrace them, before assigning them a role in their new life. It was something we all longed for.

"How do I fight it?" I immediately asked, eager to learn.

"Think about whatever keeps you grounded. Your mother seemed to bring you back for a while but pain took you back again. Your mate's memory woke you up. Think about them all the time. Find moments to keep you centred. Every time a memory resurfaces, it will be painful, every dose makes it more so. To the point where you become so afraid of the pain that you give up. That is when they change you. Don't let them," he urged.

Footsteps resonated behind the door causing Marreth to pull the blindfold down onto my face and step away from me.

"Why are you helping me?" I didn't hesitate to ask.

"I was once a commander in the Wind Kingdom. I know how it feels to lose everything you love," he sighed.

Anwen

Chapter Eleven

"Anwen, what are you trying to tell me?" Cressida's eyes widened at my announcement.

"I know it sounds crazy," I repeated. If the roles were reversed and I sat in bed where you are, hearing me say what I am about to, I would also think me crazy. I just want you to know that I am perfectly aware of that," I tried to justify the fantastical explanation I planned to blurt out in the following minutes.

"Okay..." Cressi dragged her shoulders back and settled in a more comfortable position on her side of the bed, readying herself for the conversation. Her expression looked weary, as though she just saw me for the first time and did not recognise her friend in the frantic woman in front of her.

"Right," I paused to scratch my forehead, not knowing where to start. "Remember all the research I did before going to Evigt? How Erik had told me to go there, or at least so I thought?"

"Of course I do, I was the one to plan your big speech to convince your parents," she nodded.

I imitated her gesture, relieved that at least this bit of information sounded reliable in her head.

"I did find some things in the forest, not exactly what Erik wanted me to, or at least I don't think so. But I did find something. I found Ansgar," I said as a tremor sank into my heart again. It had become a tradition that appeared every time I thought about him.

"Anwen, is this one of those things where you feel guilty for moving on?" Cressi asked in confusion.

"Just stay with me," I raised my hands and extended my palms wide, acting like a birthday party magician who needed to capture a young audience. "Ansgar never told me he was a biologist, it is something he let me assume. He only said he came to the forest to care for the plants. Because that is what he was assigned to do." Cressi frowned, but let me continue.

"By the royal family, of which he belongs to," I added quickly, feeding her bits of information.

"From the Earth Kingdom." This time my friend's frown lowered so deep, it created an upward reflection of her nose.

"Of the faeries," I finally added and waited for the volcano that was my friend to erupt.

"As in Ansgar is a faerie?" Cressi asked carefully.

"He is a fae," I corrected but it felt totally beyond the point.

"What's the difference?" Cressi continued to display her frown.

"I don't really know, from what I've seen, the fae look like humans." I raised my shoulders, surprised that I hadn't investigated the minor thing further, yet here my friend was, questioning everything from the first note.

Cressi stopped for a while to analyse what I had just said, then grabbed the laptop and read the description again, shifting her gaze to me from time to time, then back to the screen and continued to do so for a few minutes.

"And Rhy is this kind of fae. A Fear Gorta?" she asked finally.

I nodded and waited for her to have a laughing fit or to blatantly get out of my room screaming. Instead, she remained seated on the bed, the only proof of her shock the fact that she extended her hand to grab the cucumber water bottle from the nightstand and took a few big sips.

"Let me see if I get this straight," Cressi said and started gesturing with her hands, placing people and specific points in time, as though she displayed products or talked about something eventful on a video to her followers. "Erik told you to go to Evigt, which you did. And you found Ansgar there, who is a faerie of some kind, and fell in love with him in what people think is a magical forest."

I nodded, allowing her to continue. "And then Rhy met you in Evigt and you became friends and he is also a faerie of some kind, but from another place of fire. And then the first faerie, which is Ansgar, disappeared from the magical forest?"

I nodded again, tears forming in my eyes. I realised how crazy it sounded and that I had absolutely no proof apart from her physically seeing Ansgar during our video chats and whatever articles I found on the internet. I had no photos, no proof of me visiting Earth Kingdom, and especially no method to show how a body can just turn into leaves. And I was sure as hell Rhylan would deny everything if I confronted him.

"He died," I finally said. "Or so I thought. Apparently, Rhylan took him to their kingdom to find out some information Ansgar refuses to give them," I added.

"So Ansgar is alive, in a faerie kingdom, where I am guessing you and Rhy will travel to on..." she paused for emphasis, "Autumn Solstice, which I am also guessing is a big thing in the faerie world or something," Cressi finished with a smile.

There it was, she was either preparing to mock me, laugh in my face or think all this to be a prank and completely dismiss it. I wondered what my reaction would be if my best friend came to me and said such things, after bringing a sexy stranger home.

Cressi sighed and looked at me in disbelief, but what her lips pronounced next was nothing I could have prepared myself for in a million years.

"I still don't understand why I can't fuck him," she contested, offended by the situation.

My eyes went wide and I wanted to drop to the floor from the relief that overpowered my entire body.

"Seriously?" I breathed, having no clue as to how to react.

"No, I get it. You go to a magical world and find yourself the sexiest guy ever, and then bring another one home for me. I like it," she smiled like a cat preparing to get an exquisite salmon serving.

"Are you not freaking out about this?" I asked with amazement and no small amount of surprise but Cressi waved me off. "Honey, I've seen crazier things at some of the parties I get invited to. It makes sense. It's like The Lord of the Rings just dropped in your life or whatever, but it makes sense. All the secrets, all the sneaking around, your sudden obsession with the forest, this guy coming out of nowhere, and you never mentioning him. Makes sense," she nodded again to calm me down.

Instinctively, I jumped in her arms and made her fall back on the bed, sighing in relief and crying tears of joy at the same time. I had an ally, someone I could talk to, someone to ask for help. I was not alone in this anymore, and who better than my best friend to share it all with?

She hugged me tightly and let me settle my emotions, then we stayed in bed and turned the TV on with a high volume, enough to cover our long conversation. I told her everything. How I met Ansgar, how he lived in a cave and how I found out about him, how Rhylan infiltrated the guard, how I met Vikram and visited their kingdom, and finally, how Ansgar died.

We stopped to cry and to laugh, we hugged some more, and Cressi absorbed every piece of information I fed her. I started telling her about how Rhylan popped out of nowhere with this contract and how he told me about Ansgar being alive, how he followed me and gave me no option but to accept whatever he asked for.

Through it all, Cressi stopped to ask questions or made me explain things better, trying to understand every aspect and angle of the events.

We must have stayed up for hours, but all the stress and anxiety I accumulated throughout the day faded away with her by my side, finally being able to tell someone what I lived and experienced. She did not seem to believe Erik's death either, I think both our brains reached a point where the fantastical elements became too much, and that point was the mention of mermaids. I don't know why, but it proved easier to accept men caring for a forest or fighting each other for territory —albeit supernatural— but the half-women-half-fish part made us both lose the mark.

"First of all, we need to check if Ansgar is truly alive," Cressi initiated the plan. "And then you need to get a copy of that contract. Tell him you are entitled to one," she advised.

"And then what?" I asked dumbfounded. Even though I was the one who had actually met faeries and lived through unbelievable experiences, Cressi turned out to be the mastermind of it all.

"We have to entertain Rhylan," she smiled eagerly, excitement illuminating her beautiful features.

Day 2

"Of course we missed breakfast!" Cressi sighed, shifting in bed. We'd gone to bed late last night. Rays of sunlight creaked between the sealed curtains by the time we stopped planning and finally had enough peace of mind to relax and fall to sleep.

Thanks to Cressi's eventful life and abilities to manage whatever situation came before her, we devised a plan: she would keep Rhylan entertained and take him to expos, a movie premiere, and two fashion shows, while I stayed home and rummaged through his room, phone, and his earthly possessions to discover why he needed to stay in New York and what his plan comprised of.

But of course, we didn't take into account how tired we'd be and the fact that we woke up at two in the afternoon, totally unready for the day and with absolutely no idea as to where Rhylan might be.

A leg kicked me out of the bed as Cressi pushed me to wake up and go get him, while she got ready. But all I could think about was how badly I needed to pee. I sighed, understanding priorities, and sneaked out of the room to walk the twenty feet towards the door separating me from the old fae.

I knocked to no answer. Then knocked again and insisted a few times, until finally, I mustered the courage to go in. After all, he stayed in my family's home, so it wasn't like I intruded —too much.

I found a perfectly made bed with extra pillows arranged on the side. Did he do this himself? I stopped for a second to admire the neatly folded sheets and duvet arrangements, it looked like the welcoming room in a five-star hotel, and I couldn't help but smile at the thought of Rhylan struggling to set a fitted sheet, jumping from one side of the bed to another and wrestling with the corners.

My bladder screamed in urgency, reminding me that we snuck two bottles of champagne in the room late last night and none of it had come down yet. I really needed to pee, and Cressi must already be showering and taking ownership of my own bathroom. Rhylan wasn't even in the room, so a quick two-minute escape to his ensuite wouldn't change anything. Except for my own desire to explode from within.

I reached for the door and found the bathroom empty. Relief inundated me as I planted my behind on the toilet and exhaled deeply, enjoying the pleasure of a good morning pee. I only found a second of quiet when Rhylan's sudden appearance from the bathtub made me almost fall off the toilet seat.

"Busy night?" he blurted out of nowhere in between ragged

breaths. His face had been completely submerged, so a bit of extra credit to me, I couldn't have seen his body in that massive tub, especially not since he was fully underwater and no steam escaped from his location.

"Why am I not surprised? Of course, I can't even pee in peace without you nagging me," I sighed and continued to release the flow, which I couldn't stop by this point even if I wanted to. I would mark this as one of those moments one remembers and mentally cringes for the rest of their life.

"Don't mind me, princess, just here practicing my breathing," he wiped his face from the stream of water flowing from his wet hair and rose slightly into the tub, displaying sculpted muscles and all-over tattoos.

"Don't you dare!" I immediately raised my hands and placed them in front of my face to block my vision in case he wanted to stand. God, I hoped not.

"What, haven't you seen a naked fae before?" he smirked and leaned his back against the tub, spreading each of his biceps onto the sides to give me a better view.

"You don't make the list of the ones I want to see naked, thank you," I blurted out as I struggled to plan my next move. I needed toilet paper, I needed to raise from the toilet and wash my hands, all with Rhylan watching me.

He must have realised and, I did not know if out of compassion or to have another reason to rub it in my face later on, he spared me the humiliation and submerged again, becoming invisible in the tub, giving me the opportunity to quickly do what I needed and escape.

Twenty minutes later, a glamorous Cressi came out of the bathroom to find me snacking on a banana, laptop in hand. I remained in my pyjamas as I needed a reason to avoid whatever insistence Rhylan might suggest when we'd tell him he would be spending the day with Cressi.

"I just peed in front of him," I sighed, fighting the need to cover my face with the nearby pillow.

Cressi choked on a laugh. "You need to learn manners, my girl," she mocked and asked for details while she moved towards the vanity, displaying her extended makeup collection and starting to arrange her face, as my friend called it. I didn't understand why Cressi had to go through so much trouble every day when she looked absolutely stunning, but she loved doing it and even took a few photos for her Instagram, making sure to capture my rugged self in a corner and tag me. *Anwen still recovering after a crazy night of champagne and plotting to conquer the world*, she posted and by the time I grabbed my phone there were over three thousand likes.

Surprisingly, Rhylan was the one to knock on our door and as soon as I heard his voice, I shoved Cressi towards it and jumped in bed to cover myself with pillows and blankets.

"Good morning," Cressi opened the door wider and adopted a sexy pose.

"Good afternoon," Rhylan grinned and stopped to admire her from head to toe. "You look ravishing," he purred and leaned against the door frame, only inches from her.

"And what do you normally do with a ravishing woman, Rhy?" Cressi's fingers hung over the curve of his bicep in a way too comfortable position.

"Whatever she asks me to," Rhylan smirked and placed his hand nonchalantly on her hip, like it was the most normal thing to do under a door frame.

"She is very hungry at the moment, and knows a place where they make the best avo burgers," my friend replied.

I would not invite people to something like that, I couldn't even imagine what an avocado burger must be like. Is it a half an avocado with a patty? Sounded gross. But effective, as my sister continued. "Good company is scarce around here…"

With that, she had a very old fae male on his knees. Even I could see, from far away in the bed, that Rhylan's pupils dilated and were it not for her occupying most of my field of vision, I knew the bulge in his pants must be higher than a kite right now.

He didn't even say anything, he just removed his hand from her hip to grab her own and practically dragged her out of the room. Avocado burgers it is then.

I remained in bed, cuddled in blankets until Cressi's message arrived.

I think I forgot my pink lipstick and we are already in the car. Can you check?

Signal received, path clear, let's go.

I leaped out of bed and ran to Rhylan's room, opening the door abruptly. It looked the same as in the morning, as though no one had even stepped foot inside, no sign of someone occupying the space or personal things on the shelves. Nor in the wardrobe. Or the dresser. No shower gels in the bathroom, no toothbrush, no shoes.

I forced my mind to remember whether he carried any luggage in the forest, but I just couldn't think. I had been too shocked and distracted to even think about Rhylan's wardrobe or needs.

An hour later, I had scanned every inch of the room to no avail. I checked the nightstands, under the bed, even behind the headboard for some kind of secret compartment but found nothing. The fae changed three different designer outfits in a day and didn't even have laundry.

I sighed and returned to my room, disappointed and feeling the failure.

The first item of our plan, *finding Rhylan's secret and blackmailing him into releasing Ansgar* had been a bust.

I texted Cressi back to let her know I couldn't find her lipstick or any of her cosmetics no matter how hard I tried and went to the kitchen to search for something to eat and wait for my friend to be back with the fae.

A few hours passed and I still heard nothing, even though I messaged her three times by the evening.

Day 3

Cressi arrived home at four in the morning, after ignoring all the texts and DM's I'd sent throughout that day. I went crazy thinking the worst, not knowing if Rhylan had done something to my friend and hating myself for throwing her in the deep end of the situation.

To my surprise, as soon as she opened the door, she jumped into bed and started telling me everything they'd done throughout the day and how amazing and knowledgeable Rhylan turned out to be.

A thousand internal alarms started sounding all at once, and the more my friend told me about the fae bastard, the more I panicked.

"Cressi, all this was supposed to be for his distraction, please do not get too excited about the guy," I tried to warn my friend but she ignored me.

Part of me relaxed at seeing Cressi safe, and I knew she understood the danger, she was the smartest woman I knew, so I decided to relax and let her have an adventure. After all, how many people could say they met a faerie and went clubbing together.

Rhylan wanted a distraction for whatever reason, and Cressi turned out to be just that, his entry ticket to the most exclusive venues in the entire city. As long as she didn't mind babysitting him and enjoyed the company, and she remained safe, I couldn't protest too much considering I had brought the male home without second-guessing.

Day 4

Rhylan, Cressi, and I enjoyed a late breakfast in the garden. Well, they enjoyed it, I bitterly chewed on my food and stared at Rhylan with a threatening gaze, communicating to him that my friend was off-limits.

Not that Cressi did anything on her part to reinforce the message, her hands were all over him and she even served him orange juice while he buttered her toast. All this back and forth flirting made me sick to my stomach, so I kept my serving to a bowl of granola and some pecan nuts, chewing slowly and struggling to swallow the crunchy bits.

Neither seemed to mind and Rhylan even cracked a few jokes about my behaviour and tense state. Fortunately, Cressi immediately defended me and retorted.

"That's because you've been a bad boy Rhy, or so I hear," my sister started mixing sugar in her coffee with a provocative grin.

"You haven't seen anything yet," Rhylan replied and shifted his attention back to her. "If you'll let me, I can show you all the various ways I can be bad. I assure you, you'll like them." He threw her that piercing gaze that would freeze the desert. "A lot," he added as if Cressi's panties hadn't already reacted to his voice.

"Urgh, are you going to be like this every time, Rhy?" I mocked his nickname. "Does your small ego need self-inflating every day so it grows just a tiny bit bigger?" I asked and squeezed a granola flake in between my fingernails for emphasis.

"Don't provoke me, princess," he retorted and turned his attention to the orange juice.

"Princess?" I huffed. "What happened to sprout?" I always hated Rhylan's need for nicknames but I'd much preferred his original one than this princess business.

"You don't like to be called a princess?" he raised his gaze at me again, curiosity piquing through his adamant coldness.

"I do," Cressi beamed and shimmied in her chair with excitement.

"Not particularly, and especially not from you," I retorted, ignoring my friend. "I don't see myself as a princess."

"If you play your cards right, you can become a queen," Rhylan replied and proceeded to take a bite out of his toast.

Day 7

I sat at the laptop in my cosy nook in the garden through the afternoon, organising the association and passing workload, responsibilities, arranged payrolls and extra capital, readying for my departure on Autumn Solstice.

I did not know how long it would take me to return, and if Ansgar could return with me, but I had to keep the organisation alive. I still didn't trust Rhylan and tried to search his room and every location of the house that he occupied for longer than an hour every time Cressi took him places. No sign of anything, no clothes, no phone, not even a strand of hair out of place, even his bed covers remained spotless, as if he took all traces with him when he departed.

On the positive side, Cressi gave the impression she was starting to get bored with playing the tour guide and taking him sightseeing. When she called me with updates, she did not talk about him for hours on end or even with the same excitement. I felt relieved. Guilty that I wasted her time in such a way when all my searches and investigation lead nowhere, but happy she did not find the fire fae as charming as she initially did.

Mom, on the other hand, did not waste an opportunity to arrange plans for me and Rhylan to spend time together without Cressida, but I escaped most of them with any kind of excuse I could find. I faked period pains for the past three days, just to avoid garden walks with Rhylan. She kept insisting that Rhylan was such a good man and that I shouldn't offer him on a silver plate to Cressida, making arguments in favour of me keeping him and pinpointing relationship steps I didn't plan on having.

There was no use explaining to her that I didn't feel romantically inclined towards the man and it was just a business partnership between us, she kept insisting that a mother knows best and arguing the way he looked at me. "So protective and loving, like he would give you the world if you only asked."

I only want him to give me my boyfriend back, I wanted to retort but didn't want to get into a story about a man who disappeared but didn't, whom I loved with all my heart.

"Working hard, princess?" Rhylan's voice startled me from the financial report I double-checked before approving a couple million to excavate new ground.

"Stuck with that, are we?" I replied begrudgingly and slammed the laptop shut, preventing him from eyeing the screen.

"Keeping something from me?" the fae retorted but took the seat opposite mine, with the wooden carved table separating us. He grabbed a glass and served himself some of the mocktail I had in a jug full of ice.

"I hope you do not expect me to ever trust you again," I retorted and refilled my empty glass as well.

Rhylan took a generous sip then grimaced at the taste, struggling to hold it down and swallow.

"What on earth is this disgusting mixture?" he asked after the big gulp struggled down his throat.

"Kale, cucumber, some mint, and lime, I think," I stopped to mentally check the ingredient list. "And seltzer. You know, plants that are good for you. Plants that are protected by the earthlings and without whom no life on earth would exist?"

We hadn't talked about it in a week, hiding behind dinners, events and Cressida, but I could not hold it down anymore. I had no reason to.

"Earthlings, yes, I believe you are very acquainted with some of them. One especially," he grinned and tantalised me further.

"I need a copy of my contract," I demanded plainly, keeping my voice in tone. One of the things Cressi initially advised me was to get a copy for myself.

With a wave of a hand, the parchment I signed a week ago appeared on the table. "It's the only copy, but you are welcome to keep it," Rhylan responded nonchalantly and made a gesture to grab the glass for another sip, then thought better of it.

"Aren't you supposed to go places and enjoy life? Isn't that what you wanted?"

"Among all the things I want, princess, enjoying life is very low on the list. I've had many years to do it, and humans aren't as inventive as you might think. It's always the same things that keep you entertained, scandal, drugs, and sex, in no particular order," he sighed with disappointment, like he had expected the journey to be different from what it turned out to be.

"I would say I'm sorry to disappoint, but I am actually glad you are not having as much fun as you might have wanted. Join in the misery," I smiled sarcastically and reopened the laptop, silently dismissing him.

"Is this all you have to say to me?" Rhylan sounded disappointed, like he'd come to find me expecting a fight or something more entertaining.

"Unless you want to talk more about how much I hate you and the things I would do to try to end your life if we weren't in a contract, then please, make yourself comfortable," I snarled.

"You say that, but every time you see me, princess, your hate and distaste grow a little weaker. Remember, I can spot those things," he replied with a small grin. "Although, there is something I want to talk about, something more important."

"Surprise me," I replied without raising my gaze from the screen.

"Cressida," he replied plainly and settled in the chair, preparing his body for a long conversation.

Ansgar

Chapter Twelve

I didn't know how much time passed since the second dose and I lived in terror of the pain starting again. I knew it had to be soon, my muscles jolted with the energy of whatever they had injected but surprisingly, my mind remained clear.

I remembered my family, my kingdom and childhood, that time Vikram wanted to catch a mermaid and populate the nearby lake or when Takara kicked Damaris out of their chambers and left him completely naked on the stairwell because he had said something stupid during their mating.

My head flooded with memories, of us, of Anwen, of her sweet giggles or her frown when she tried to teach me how to use technology and my blunt head didn't understand what needed to be done. I still existed as myself and gained sensation over my limbs, I could even wiggle my toes and smell the musty air around.

I did not know if I remained unattended yet again or if Serpium was taking a nap somewhere in the room, but I did not plan to discover more. I must have spent hours just sitting and waiting, for whatever they planned to do to me next.

Marreth warned about the pain, about clinging to my memories and how hard it would be to hang on. Part of me remained petrified of any changes my body made, thinking it would start any second.

It did not.

Nor did it start with the third dose.

I had probably stayed tied up for a few days, soiled in my own dirt, with no drink or food. Only with constant injections. In my muscles, my heart, and more recently my temples. Those I hated most because they tensed my jaw in such a way, I could barely swallow or drag air into my lungs and my teeth crackled worse than burning logs.

"The king wants to know the progress," a voice sounded as soon as the hinges of the door squeaked to announce its entry.

It took Serpium a moment to react and wake up from the numbness of the past few days, where the only words he had uttered were insults I did not respond to and pretended not to hear, playing my role of a dozy numb prince trapped in the veil of nothingness.

"He's taking it all without protest, the poor bastard must have been too weak to fight back," the commander replied with a pleased tone.

"The king wants it done tonight then, no more wasting time," the voice replied, forcing Serpium's hand, who sounded like he wanted to protest and didn't seem too eager to give up his daily routine.

"Why does he need it done so soon?" Serpium voiced, out of concern or unwillingness to give up his task, I could not tell.

"The general will come down soon and wants to see results, you know how he is," the voice, probably Crypto, trembled at the thought. "Give him the big one in the back of the neck, king's orders." With this, the door shook again and a hard slam announced the departure along with fulfilled orders.

A couple of sighs, a few protests, and lots of swearing accompanied the commander's steps in the small dark room he had tortured so many before me. Jars clicked and drawers snapped shut, then opened again and through it all, Serpium maintained his foul attitude.

Suddenly, the binding over my eyes was removed, allowing me to see light for the first time in what seemed like forever. Until then, I had relied on the few senses I had left to guess the world around me, but now I proved deserving of vision. Something important must be happening. And it didn't seem good.

Serpium's eyes scanned mine, analysing my tired features and the movement of my eyelids, breathing heavily over my face. I remained quiet and adopted an innocent figure, faking entrapment in the mind.

"Who are you?" he asked through gritted teeth, ready for an attack.

I remained silent and blinked a couple of times, occupying my interest with the nearby candle and forcing my head in its direction, even though the straps stopped my weak movements.

"You're done prince; this is the last memory you will ever possess as a free male. Any final words? If we're quick about it, I can maybe still chop you up and call it an accident. What say you? Ready to give up?" His face nearly touched mine. Serpium bent over me so low, as though if he tried hard enough, he could blend with my own skin and become a part of me.

"I don't think I've seen it before," I replied, faking lack of emotion. "Is it new?" I asked, looking beyond interested in the flame. "So warm, like a ray of sunlight made into a ball." I even smiled idiotically, like a youth chasing butterflies in some meadow.

The commander shook his head in disappointment. He must have expected another fight, maybe craved for it. After all, I was the project he couldn't crack for so long, he had experimented many new techniques on me over the past months, each time snapping more pleasure out of my torture. But now I had become a limp body and a trapped mind, following him with no protest towards my impending doom.

A portrait of disappointment, Serpium started the painstaking job of unstrapping me from the table. Every single tie, every muscle, every inch of my body until I remained free, splayed out on the wide chair. It looked more like a settee, I realised once I could move my head freely.

Either way, it bared marks of blood, as many before me who had been through the same fate and ended up losing themselves. It would not happen to me. I could conquer this.

"Stand," Serpium commanded and I did so without protest, but as soon as I ordered my muscles to perform the action, I fell on the ground, unable to move or stand on my own.

"Here," he said and crouched low enough to direct a cup near my head and shake it so I reacted to the liquid.

I eagerly accepted and drank deeply, struggling to swallow and choking more than actually hydrating myself after such a long time without nourishment. It tasted bitter, some kind of wine left out for far too long, but it was a lot better than nothing.

It took me a couple of minutes to stabilise my breaths so I was able to drink like a being again, then to stop while I took a small sip and followed its way down my stomach, where it filled the emptiness.

Serpium took a seat on a nearby chair and waited patiently until I recovered enough to stand and receive his orders. All of it looked planned, my release, my gratitude, the drink, and me following orders. The first step in a new life of obeying a damned king. One I hoped to escape soon enough.

As long as I pretended to be one of them, train and act like them, drink and follow orders, I would soon enough have my chance to be released on the surface with whatever mission, and with Marreth's help, escape. The next time I saw him I planned to offer him refuge in the Earth Kingdom, he looked as eager to leave this place as I was.

When I finally stood, Serpium shifted and moved towards the table, allowing me to find my own strength and follow him. He did not look alarmed to have me freed nor concerned with the multitude of knives around us, which I could easily grab and cause him damage.

"Repeat after me," Serpium commanded and started speaking slowly, allowing me to understand and memorise the words. "I am born from fire and recognize the one true king, Drahden."

I cringed internally, hating myself for having to swear an oath to a ruler that was not father, even though my heart would not truly grasp the words.

"I have found a new kingdom, a new family, that I swear to serve and protect with my energy."

I uttered the words slowly, marking every syllable that came out of my mouth, hating myself for what I was saying. Fuck it, I didn't care about resurfacing anymore as much as I did about killing their king. The miserable bastard who stole beings away from their families and kingdoms, forcing them to fight their own and used their bodies as shields. They all needed to pay.

"How are you feeling?" Serpium carefully asked, commencing his analysis yet again. He scanned my body, my limbs, and muscles, kicking from time to time to study reflexes and pushing me from one point to another to study my reactions.

"Looks good," he remarked proudly. "Time for the last one, it's gonna be painful prince, I am not gonna lie to you."

He turned to one of the cupboards and crouched low enough to reach the back of the wall, where the potion must have been stored. It was different from the ones he had injected me with so far, I could tell by texture alone.

It shone a dark black colour with waves and shimmers like the blackest part of the ocean had been trapped inside. The syringe he grabbed looked small, and the needle just big enough to prick a finger. I hadn't witnessed the application of the other serums, since I remained trapped and blindfolded, but now I had become deserving of my own stance, especially since Serpium believed I was trapped inside a mind not of my own making.

"This is the most important part," he said to no one in particular but felt the need to accentuate his actions by detailing his every move. "This is what will make you one of ours, it will penetrate the tissue deeper than the first one, that was merely to make you addicted. Which, by that dumb look on your face prince, you don't even remember your own mother, am I right?" he cracked a joke only his laughter reacted to.

I kept my face blank, looking at nothing in particular and staring deeper into the wall, as though I had been awakened from a dream and the memories still dripped over my hazy eyes.

"Right, off we go," he said and urged me to step closer to him. With a confident movement, he caught my jaw in between his fingers and turned my head to the side, exposing my neck, while his other hand held the tiny syringe with only a few drops of the potion. I did not understand how such a tiny thing could alter the lives of so many beings and how the firelings concocted it in the first place, but the only thing I could do was trust Marreth.

I had awoken, I was myself and remembered everything, so if the first potion lost its effect, the logical step was for this one to follow and enable me to walk out of here pretending to have become a fireling. Then I would kill the king and break them from the inside. I did not know if there was any chance of me ever escaping this place, I had begged for death numerous times already and only held a very small strand of hope of seeing my family again. What I could do, what I would probably die doing, was to spare anyone else from going through the same fate they pushed me into. Prevent them from being repeatedly tortured and turned into something they would rather die than become.

I would get my revenge.

The needle pinched my jugular artery and expelled the substance in a second, allowing it to flow into my body, carried by my blood and through every tissue, just like Serpium had said.

"You are home, you belong here, this is who you are," he ordered me to repeat, over and over while tingles shimmied inside my bones, my arteries, my liver.

An oath my brain struggled to reject, as the words echoed, forcing me to believe them. This was it, Marreth's warning. Think of them. Repeat the words but think of them. Do not embrace the firelings, *this is not who you are.*

Serpium repeated the words on a loop, forcing me to follow his lead as I pushed memories from back home into my vision. My mother, my father, my brothers. Anwen. I loved them, they made me a better male, they were part of me and I could not forget them. Would not forget them. Farryn, Bathysia, Damaris, Vikram, Takara. Anwen.

"I am home," I forced my tongue to form the words.

Anwen.

"I belong here."

Vikram.

"This is who I am."

Mother. Anwen, Vikram, Takara, Damaris… who else? Someone was missing. Deep relaxation entered my body. It felt like my muscles were formed of air and any memories I had, needed to be dispersed into those vapours. No, I would not allow this, it would not take me. Not now. Not after fighting for so long.

I started counting again.

"I am home."

Anwen.

"I belong here."

Mother.

"I…" Who was I forgetting? It was on the tip of my tongue, but I didn't remember.

Why?

Why?

Come on Ansgar, you can do this. Just like in the training ring. Breathing is everything. Focus on the small details, focus on the opponent's body language. Simply react to their movements. This needed to be the same. Wait, and react.

Let's start again.

Mother…

And… someone. Someone I forgot. Why did I forget? What was the name? It sounded nice, it made me happy to say it, I remembered an overall sense of joy caused by that word. Like being in love. My mind went blank. Suddenly there was no ring, no opponent. Just me. Alone on a field, somewhere. With only my breathing and a sensation of calmness. Something was telling me to fight it, but I was left wondering why. Was it truly worth it? Why not just give in?

What was I saying?

Oh yes.

"I am home, I belong here, this is who I am."

I smiled proudly, content with myself for remembering the words which I could now repeat just like the male wanted me to. He did it with me, these words connected us somehow. He stood there, right in front of me, hands on my shoulders, holding me steady as his eyes scanned me.

I smiled even wider and gleefully repeated, feeling a sense of joy for making him proud. I felt grateful for the support, for the way he cared for me, holding me in place like that, making sure I could hold my own.

"Where are you?" he stopped the chanting repetition and asked.

"Home," I replied gladly, which caused him to exhale. It looked like he had kept it in for a long while.

"What are you feeling right now?"

"Relaxed," I answered immediately, without having to think twice.

"Thank the god, this initial state of mind will form your entire personality. I wish the general were here to see you. To see this," he added with a bit of regret.

"He is not here?" I wanted to make my new friend happy and if he wanted to go and see the general, I would follow. Before I had a chance to offer, he continued.

"He's with that pretty cunt you always cry about. Well, used to cry, we'll get you a few nice fireling females to warm you up. Maybe even the queen will take a spin, she looked interested enough," the male smiled and his eyes sparkled.

"The queen is my cunt?" I frowned in confusion. My mind felt blank and unable to put his words together.

He laughed, amused. "Don't let the king hear you say that. No, the general is with someone else. Someone who doesn't matter to you anymore," he replied with surprising content.

I wanted to please him, and he kept repeating about this general. I wanted to insist, to go find him and show him whatever it was that I needed to.

"I don't understand," I insisted, but instead of keeping the joy on his face, my words brought a frown.

"I hate it when you are like this. It's worse than having younglings around," he sighed and sensed that I wanted to keep asking more questions because he explained. "Our general, Rhylan, is with your human, doing whatever he wants, as the general does."

"I have a human?" my turn to frown came.

"You used to, now you will have a fireling. You can still call her Anwen if you wish, the whores don't care," he raised his shoulders. "You won't get a wife yet; you will need to earn some levels but considering you are recovering—"

My neurons snapped, convulsing in pain and I fell to the ground like a rock had hit the back of my neck. I breathed quickly, pain gushing through my skin and pumping into every part of my body. A surge of agony floated around, engulfing everything inside and my brain howled from the pain.

I felt anger, rage, the impulse to hurt. To kill.

Conducted by the urge, I jumped the male who had crouched next to me and caught his chest under my knees, pumping fist after fist into his head, over his mouth, across his nose, I did not care. All I needed was to unload this wrath upon him. For something he had done, something he had said, I did not know. It did not matter, as long as I kept hitting him.

My knuckles broke from the force of so many blows and I did not feel my fingers anymore. The face of the male looked so mangled, I could not distinguish where his nose or forehead had been. But it was not enough.

He needed to die, he needed to suffer. I grabbed a black bar situated by the nearby table. It was crystal made, adamant or obsidian, and started hitting the male across every part of his remaining body until his screams turned music to my ears. I repeated the brutal dance, hitting and shifting to find a new spot, then hitting that again and stepping onto the next, until he finally stopped.

Until I could no longer hear his pulsations.

By the time I finished, drops of meat hung from the walls, the only proof that the male had once existed.

And I felt joy.

Anwen

Chapter Thirteen

Day 13

Ever since I had the conversation with Rhylan, during which he asked me a million questions about my best friend, he had kept himself occupied with her company. For some reason, he thought Cressi to actually be my sister since she kept referring to me that way, but I quickly clarified and explained how we'd met at a young age and how we connected so well we'd basically spent all our lives together.

I did not want to risk him devising whatever plan and using her against me, Ansgar told me about blood sacrifices and blood connections and I wanted to keep Cressi as far away from all this. She did not seem to mind his company either, though every time they met I received fewer details, and she would go to sleep at her apartment instead of returning together, to avoid spending even more time with him.

Rhylan knocked on my door and made his presence known. If there was one thing I appreciated about him was the respect towards my privacy. He never entered my room or tried to get himself invited in and every time he was supposed to accompany me downstairs for dinner, he knocked and patiently waited in the hallway until I came out.

"Evening princess," he greeted me with a smile when I appeared in the doorway, wearing a white dress. Dad already announced this to be a business dinner, which meant I had to look good, smile politely, and act my part.

"Are you ever going to stop with that?" the only greeting on my end.

"Admit it, you love it," he snarled and offered me his arm, just like he did every evening. Which I ignored, and made my own way through, just like every evening. I did not understand why he became so polite all of a sudden, like he had turned into a respectful gentleman who wanted to preserve my honour or something. I did not trust it one bit and counted the days until this damned deal between us came to an end. I was already sick of it.

I soon realised my mistake, there was something I was even sicker of, and that was the constant presence of my ex, Jonathan, who occupied a seat at the dinner table, right next mine.

"God, kill me now," I said slowly, but enough for Rhylan to hear it.

"What is it?" he asked, alarmed.

"You know what's worse than you?" I turned to him swiftly to scan his face, without halting my walk towards the dinner table. "Him."

As soon as I exhaled the words, the fae's body language shifted, his muscles becoming tense, as though he prepared to run into battle.

"Good evening Anwen, you look beautiful," Jonathan rose from his chair when he saw me and stepped in my direction, trapping me in a hug which I begrudgingly returned. He also placed two unnecessary kisses on my cheek, keeping his lips on my skin for longer than needed.

"Hello, Jonathan," I replied with a forced smile and shimmied away from his arms, making an excuse about my dress getting wrinkled.

He stepped away, returning to the table and holding the chair next to him for me to have a seat. Rhylan occupied the chair opposite Jonathan, with a perfect view of the two of us. There were five other men and two women invited tonight, most of whom I had met and done business with throughout the year. This looked like a launch party or a new marketing campaign and I really didn't fancy having a business chat at the table.

I always hated business lunches, dinners, or whatever involved food, because there was always that awkward moment when I thought no one would talk to me so I shoved a big bite in my mouth, and just then, someone suddenly asked me a question. Or when the business partner would talk on and on and on without eating, until all plates went cold. Add Jonathan's innuendos and inappropriate touches and the evening was set to suck.

"Please allow me to introduce mister Rhylan Gordon, an investor in Anwen's business and personal guest." My dad went along the table and introduced each member of the team to Rhylan, who nodded politely and asked a few perfectly placed questions.

I did not know how old this guy was, but he mastered conversation, ethics and could be just perfect when he wanted to.

"And Jonathan Morris, Head of Marketing, following the proud footsteps of his father and my good friend Louis Paul Morris. You might have heard of him actually, he has a few advertising agencies across Europe," dad said.

Rhylan smiled politely and nodded in Jonathan's direction. "Morris is such a big name in the advertising industry, how could I not? The man is a legend," he replied then quickly added. "The father, of course."

I did not know if Jonathan felt attacked because of this or held a dash of jealousy at Rhylan's invitation to stay with us, because he quickly retorted. "At least you have heard of us, which is something I cannot say about you." Satisfied, he grabbed his wine glass and took a victory sip.

Looking back, I could not understand how I'd possibly been with him. We met when I visited their firm at my father's suggestion to get more acquainted with the team and brainstorm a few ideas, which he blatantly rejected and made me feel incompetent and awkward. Only to then stop me on my way to the elevator and ask me out for coffee, to discuss more about those dreadful ideas. One coffee led to another, then to dinner and when dad found out we'd had dinner together, he insisted on inviting him over to the house. He got along with Erik so he kept coming and all of a sudden we were dating. I'm still not sure if the double dates we kept having with my brother and whatever girl he invited that particular day kept us together, because as soon as Erik passed, I realised I felt nothing towards my wannabe fiancée.

When I broke things off, he made a huge scandal about a wedding ring he had prepared and how he asked my father's hand in marriage, how both our families loved our union, and urged me to think of the damage I was causing to an already damaged family.

Then I went to Evigt, met Ansgar, and never thought about him again. He still popped in from time to time with business excuses, but I almost always made sure to make my presence scarce when he was around.

"I do not feel the need to prove my manhood by shouting my name every time I do business," Rhylan's words pulled me to the present. He also added, "Nor do I own a brand that requires me to do so." And I knew that was to my dad's benefit.

"Really?" Jonathan asked. "Is that what your vast experience taught you? How many businesses do you own, Rhylan?"

My dad wanted to interject, but Rhylan made a gesture to tell him there was no need and continued. "At the moment, I own five, though after investing in Anwen's, it would be my honour to add a sixth."

"Are they small shops in Europe we haven't heard of?" My ex grinned like an idiot, but the entire table quieted and I realised everyone was curious about Rhylan's business. Even I had an interest to know what lies he would spin this time.

"I own Meldan's, Harriet's, and TGX," he said and all our jaws dropped. They were huge stock companies that made millions a day and were famous all around the world for their immense growth and acquisition techniques. "If you want something more generic, then

Larry Mex and Bretnum," Rhylan raised his shoulders as though owning a huge fashion enterprise and an automobile manufacturer was as easy as a stroll in the park.

Even dad struggled to swallow his drink. "We are very proud of our daughter for finding such a diverse investor, I am sure she will benefit from your knowledge, " he finally said.

Jonathan kept his mouth shut for the remainder of the evening and only spoke when needed to or when someone asked him a direct question.

As soon as Rhylan mentioned all his companies, which probably made him a thousand times wealthier than anyone sitting at the table, the entire mood shifted and everyone was ready to bow to his will. A lot of unnecessary flattering, silly questions to boost his ego and appraisals of his business model replaced what was supposed to be a formal dinner.

I was glad that I did not have to speak too much since Rhylan enjoyed the attention and answered all kinds of questions about how we met and what our plans for the future involved. While he bragged about his imaginary life, I enjoyed two courses and a dessert, along with two glasses of wine.

The evening lasted longer than any of us had planned, everyone remained delighted by Rhylan's presence and they kept asking him questions and talking until the late hours of the night. I couldn't take it any longer and faked a few yawns, preparing an excuse to get back to my room at the earliest opportunity.

Finally, when mom and dad were busy sharing a honeymoon story, I excused myself and headed to the door, but Jonathan stood as well and intercepted me on my way out.

"Anwen, wait," I heard his voice and stopped, even though I really wanted to ignore him and move on.

"Yes, Jonathan?" I said with a tired tone of voice, trying to relate my sleepiness to him.

"I just—" he paused, surprised by my attitude, "wanted to know how you were," he stopped and looked at me questioningly.

"I'm fine," I replied quickly. "Thank you for asking," and headed towards the stairs. Jonathan hurried his step and grabbed my wrist, much to my annoyance. I pulled back and snatched it away, making my bones crack with the sudden movement.

"You said you weren't ready, you said you didn't want to date and now I find you bringing a guy here?"

He didn't have a long time to huff his discontent, because Rhylan appeared through the door and shoved my ex out of the way and into the nearby wall. "If you ever lay a hand on her again, I will cut it off," he threatened and I realised he had seen Jonathan grab me.

"It's fine." It was my turn to grab something, in this case, Rhylan's hand to stop him from harming Jonathan or do something crazy, like reveal his power.

"I'm fine," I repeated and he finally turned from my ex towards me. The rage piercing through his gaze dissipated into softness at the sight of me.

"Please, let's go upstairs," he pleaded and I did not protest, only turned and started climbing the stairs. His steps followed behind, letting me know he was guarding my back. They followed slowly, giving me space but close enough to know he was there. Rhylan trailed me until we reached my room and I turned to him. I didn't know what to say, what to do, so I mumbled a thank you.

"You didn't have to fake all that, but thank you for the business slap show you offered tonight," I said sincerely, struggling to catch a few strands that escaped my bun and arrange them somewhere behind my ear, hoping they would find their own way.

"I didn't," he replied, blinking slowly while his gaze extended across my body.

"Do you really expect me to believe you own all those companies when you forced me to bring you to my house so you can enjoy a certain lifestyle?" I huffed.

"Princess, daddy's been busy in the past seventy years and I got bored, so I made sure I lived comfortably whenever I actually got the time to go on holiday," Rhylan smirked proudly and those eyes—nope, Anwen, focus.

"I hate myself for saying this, but Ansgar is a big improvement on this guy," I heard him speak all of a sudden.

My eyes widened, I expected him to say anything but that. It was the first time he spoke about Ansgar without a mocking attitude or an insulting nickname for him or his kind. I nodded again, unable to find a reply.

Of course he was, of course Ansgar wouldn't even have to compete with Jonathan, the race was already won before even starting. A heaviness possessed my chest at the thought, sudden images of Ansgar being the one by my side tonight, of him being the one chatting to my dad and casually sipping wine like he belonged there inundated me.

I couldn't explain it, but Rhylan's kindness tonight, the way he protected me and kept returning every single snap Jonathan had intended made things even worse. So, of course, I started crying. Big surprise, by this point I could probably win a *Highest number of tears per minute* competition or something like that.

"What is it?" Rhylan asked, making a gesture to come closer and touch my face, probably to wipe the tears away, but thought better of it and remained grounded.

"Nothing," I waved my head and quickly dried my tears with the back of my hand. I would not give him the satisfaction.

"Tell me," he murmured, barely audible, like having a conversation with a sleeping baby in the room. His eyes remained focused on mine, staring intently, trying to understand my emotions. Not that he couldn't probably read them all over me.

"I just…" tears flooded my face again and I couldn't do anything to stop them, "I miss him so much. Every day." I stopped, struggling to calm myself and prepare for whatever retort or mockery he had in mind.

To my surprise, he remained silent and looked at me with understanding.

"Go to sleep princess, tomorrow will be better." With this, he took a step towards me and reached for my face. I stopped a breath, thinking he would go for my cheek or my eyes, but he placed a finger on my forehead and pressed gently, leaving an invisible mark.

Then, without saying anything else, Rhylan turned and headed to his room, shutting the door after him without another gaze in my direction. He could be a strange man when he wanted to.

I continued my routine, shower, skincare, hair up, comfy pyjamas, and popped a series on the laptop, just long enough to make my eyes tired and allow me to go to sleep. Wrapped in my comfortable blanket and surrounded by so many pillows they could easily build a fort, I let myself fall into sleep, thinking about dinner, about Jonathan and the discovery that Rhylan had feelings when he wanted to. Or he could fake it really well.

The one thing I did not expect was to dream about Ansgar. I struggled so much to find him in my dreams again those first months that I must have exhausted all my imagination and the memories of him. Because no matter how much I tried, no matter how many videos on hypnosis and REM cycles I watched to try to bring him back, I did not have the ability to do it. I had gotten used to going to bed knowing that memories of him will not visit me, that I had potentially seen the last of him, or maybe my brain strained so much it had completely forgotten what Ansgar looked like.

I held vivid memories of him, of his lips, his laughter, the muscles on his back when he positioned himself over me to bite my neck, his arms and how his fingers interlocked with mine, but I didn't seem to be able to see the entirety of him anymore. Except for tonight.

When I dreamt of him, those first months, it was always in the forest or the mansion. I saw him in my bedroom, in the kitchen, or the forest, but this night, Ansgar opened the door to my room and woke me up.

He was wearing his uniform, the loose pants he usually strolled in across the forest and the set of knives I loved seeing displayed across his bare chest, but none of it fit with the surroundings. Even Ansgar seemed different, his hair arranged very regally, like the night of his marking. He just stood there, watching me, looking at me like he hadn't seen me in forever.

"Ansgar?" I stood from bed and spoke, trying to get away from the pillows and closer to him.

"Fahrenor?" he replied in disbelief, looking at me like I was a ghost.

He immediately hurried by my side and cupped my face in his palms, checking my skin, feeling me, wanting to make sure I was real. Wasn't that my job? It was my dream after all. He just had to appear and interact with me. Keep my heart company.

"What is happening?" I asked with concern. I couldn't believe that the one time I was dreaming about him in months, he had to act weird and ruin the fun.

"I don't know, I tried to come back to you for such a long time. I don't know what is happening. I feel like my mind was blocked until now, that I couldn't find you anymore," he said, voice like a whisper.

I felt the warmth of his skin on mine, the way he squeezed my face, hard enough to make sure I was truly there.

"Ansgar, is this a dream?" I asked quickly, disbelief coming over me. Was he truly here, in my room?

"I don't know fahrenor," he shook his head, eyes still locked with mine. "I do not know where I am," he stopped just for a mere second to check his surroundings, then his gaze came back to mine.

"I love you," he whispered and without a second thought, he placed his lips on mine, kissing me eagerly. The taste of him overpowered me, a taste I had thought forgotten.

"Ansgar!" I broke our connection. "This is real. I can feel you, I can touch you, you are here!" I cried and jumped into his arms, touching as much of him as I could, joining my body with his to feel the heart beating in his chest.

"This is real, this is real, you are here," I kept repeating over and over, stroking his hair, touching his face, caressing his skin. I felt him, I tasted and sensed him. By some kind of miracle or spell, Ansgar was in my room. I even stood from bed to check the time and mirrored my face on the screen while I did so. It definitely wasn't a dream.

"I don't know how long it will last," Ansgar said, putting his face behind mine in the camera reflection. Instinctively, I pressed the small circle and snapped a photo. The noise of the blip and the tiny image being dragged downwards let me know that I finally had a picture of him, something to remember him by.

"Let's not waste it," I replied and turned to him, joining my lips with his again. Even the smell of orange and fresh earth came along with him, inundating the fabric of my bedsheets as I pulled Ansgar towards me, positioning his body over my own on the mattress. If what he said was true, if we didn't have much time, I did not want to waste it. I wanted to be with him every second of this blessed magical moment. I would not cry, I would not talk about missing him and the suffering I'd been through. I would taste, caress and possess his body, make him feel loved and appreciated, and show him how much he's been missed.

"Are you alright? Are you safe?" The only question that mattered before I continued, the only thing I wanted to know.

"I don't know where I am, this dream doesn't let me see. I only know I am here with you. I remember the cabin; I remember you caring for me. There is so much space in between that my mind cannot follow. I remember looking for you, trying to get to you. Now I'm here," he said and smiled.

"I'm here," Ansgar murmured, as though he could not believe it himself.

"You're here," I repeated and laughed. I actually laughed with a heart full of joy. The immense joy I felt at having him with me again. I placed my palm on his cheek, the same gesture I had done before our first kiss and Ansgar rested his own palm over it, trapping it in a loving conjunction. I approached his face again, slowly, gently, taking it all in, studying every detail of his face, his jawline, his shadow-grey eyes.

"Hie vaedrum teim," I repeated the words I always told him in my dreams. The same words he woke me up with in the mornings after spending the whole night wrapped in blankets and orgasms.

They unleashed him. With one swift movement, Ansgar pulled my body even closer to his, if such a thing was possible, and pressed me under him, making me feel all of him, along with his desire. And I wanted him inside of me, with desperate need.

Our lips clashed, a battle of tongues and teeth, biting, licking, caressing until they combined taste and smell. Until my mouth belonged solely to him. Ansgar's hands grabbed my shirt and pulled it quickly over my head, unveiling my breasts.

I mimicked the movement, focusing my attention on those sculpted abs I missed so much, and united my skin to his, my chest to his own, needing to feel the skin-to-skin contact. Our beating hearts recognised each other and started pumping with joy, making our bodies more relentless.

Ansgar's lips parted from mine and explored the territory he already knew so well. From the shell of my ear to my neck, down to the valley of my breasts where his hands pulled and squeezed and tantalised, his teeth biting softly until I remained a mess under him. The pleasure was too much, feeling him by my side was so good that I almost came then and there. And he hadn't even pulled my pants off.

"Baby," I pleaded, unable to contain this, needing him so much it hurt.

I didn't even have to say it; he knew what I wanted. He stopped paying attention to my left breast, which casually rested in his mouth, just long enough to pull down my pants. My panties went along with a brutal motion and I remained bare under him.

He smiled and looked at my lower parts with hunger, as though he hadn't enjoyed a meal in the year we'd been apart and I was the main course. I couldn't take it any longer, seeing him like that, on top of me, made me desire him with a passion, so I stood just enough to grab the waist of his pants and make a downward motion, ordering him to pull them down immediately.

Ansgar wiggled his legs out of his pants while he returned his full attention to my breasts and as he did, his length sprang free.

Hard, thick, and ready for me. Oh god, I wanted him now.

I positioned myself under him, pushing my pelvis to his own and feeling his desire onto mine. I made a motion to grab him, but he shifted away, continuing to play with my breasts.

"Ansgar," I moaned in a threatening tone. I couldn't understand why he was taking so long when I would have jumped him in a second.

"Don't rush fahrenor, we have all night," he replied from the valley of my breasts, but shifted one of his hands and trailed slowly, so torturously slowly in between my legs. The movement of his fingers immediately appeased me and I let myself feel.

Feel him, feel everything he was doing to me, the way his fingers penetrated my core and expertly found that spot that had me forget my name or what planet I lived on. By the time I came back to reality, Ansgar's lips had replaced his fingers and my lover pushed his tongue inside me, sucking and flicking just the way he knew I liked it. Needless to say, a second orgasm burst through me before I even had a chance to say his name.

"Just fuck me already," I couldn't contain myself. I needed to feel him. To have him. Now. "Please," I added and looked at him with a pleading gaze while I grabbed his face and pulled just enough to detach his lips from my slits and force him to look at me.

He grinned, but did not protest, only shifted in bed and placed himself on top of me again, pushing at my entrance for confirmation. "Please," I whimpered again, grabbing his shoulders and bracing myself.

Ansgar did as asked and entered me so abruptly that I felt every inch, every thick vein pushing into me, forcing me to split wider for him, urging me to scream at the sheer force that suddenly possessed him. He did not stop, did not let me adjust like he normally did, but continued thrusting. Deeper, harder, until I was screaming, until I dug my fingers so deep into his skin that I drew blood. He rammed into me, impatient and abrupt, ripping every inhibition away. There was only him, the sensation of him, I could not think beyond where we united, nothing else mattered. I felt him so deep that I thought I would split apart, but the pleasure was so intense it would not matter. I would gladly die having sex with Ansgar.

Orgasm after orgasm burst out of me until the pleasure and pain changed their meaning and I did not know what to feel anymore. Still, he would not stop, would not slow down. I moved a hand from his shoulder to his face, touching the strands of sweat curtained on his skin, and forced his gaze to join mine.

His eyes shifted, awakened from trance and moved just a little bit slower, decreasing his rhythm just enough to give me his full attention.

"Feel good?" he smirked, a proud lover's grin, knowing full well what he had done to me, that I would probably be unable to walk straight tomorrow.

"Yes, it was amazing," I replied in between pants, hoping that my answer would calm him enough and allow him to concentrate on finding his own pleasure.

"Good, I'm getting tired," Ansgar replied. Only it was not Ansgar, his tone of voice sounded different and his expression taut, not the sweet man I had come to know and love.

Before I had time to respond, he stopped abruptly, releasing his length from inside of me and rising from bed.

"Ansgar?" I questioned the man in front of me, who all of a sudden became very different and changed his attitude in a mere second. Had I done something to offend him?

"Go to sleep sprout, you have a big day tomorrow." With that, Ansgar's body vanished right in front of my eyes.

Day 14

The knock on the door came later than expected, but I was ready for it. I had an anger fit last night, after realising what had happened and wanted to run across the hall to Rhylan's room. Until I realised that I was naked. And my insides ached from the hard-core sex I just had with my imaginary boyfriend. I barely turned the pillow and placed my head over the silk fabric that I immediately fell asleep.

But this morning I was ready and opened the door wide, preparing the blow I had wanted to plant on his face since last night. Rhylan's cheek turned from the speed of my palm, twisting to the side along with the force I had put into that stroke.

"What was that last night?" I accused and raised my hand again, only this time his instincts kicked in and he caught my wrist. I tried to jiggle it away to no avail.

"Is this the thank you I get for giving you a night with your princeling?" Rhylan huffed, looking at me in amazement, as though he could not believe I had the nerve to be angry about it.

"You forced him in my mind. You made me believe he was real!" I shouted, still trying to escape his grab.

"Princess, judging by your screams, he was very real," Rhylan replied while finally releasing me.

"What did you do?" I questioned, rubbing the wrist he had kept trapped.

"I just planted the image in your mind, it was very easy and you were crying because you missed him. Consider it a favour," he said and made a motion to silently invite me downstairs for breakfast. When I didn't follow, he went ahead towards the stairs.

"You told me you couldn't read minds!" I accused, trailing after him.

Rhylan stopped mid-step and turned to me. "Read them? No. Play with them? Yes," he responded with a wicked grin.

Day 15

I didn't see Rhylan for the day and I felt relieved to be away from him. On the short journey to the breakfast room, he had argued that there was no point being upset about the mind games he played on me since he had offered me time with my mate. "Real-time," he pointed out and my insides twitched at the memories of Ansgar pumping into me with desperation.

Apparently, he had used Ansgar's desires and emotions from when he last saw my boyfriend and combined them with my own memories, then implanted the situation in my mind and made my brain believe what was happening was real. When I argued that I took an actual photo of Ansgar, Rhylan asked me to check my phone and reluctantly, I did so. I found a selfie of me with a surprised face, as if I had woken up on Christmas morning. Just me.

I remained quiet for the rest of the meal and took a car out to the park, needing to be alone and feel closer to nature.

It never was highly important for me to be close to nature before all this. I loved technology and busy areas, I liked going into crowds and being surrounded by people, and never felt bothered by the cement and polluted air around.

That is, until visiting Evigt and discovering how amazing fresh air can feel in my lungs, like taking a big sip of river water to calm the thirst of one's soul. I loved the soft aromas in the air, the smell of pine or the blooming flowers, hearing the wrestling of the leaves or the clink of the river. I loved the quiet, sometimes the forest made it so that I could hear my own breathing, my own heart beating in my chest because there was nothing and no one miles around. Just me and the birdsong.

Since returning, I felt trapped, I hated going to massive gatherings and found myself needing personal space. The only thing that calmed me was being alone and staying in closed spaces, where I could filter air. Sometimes it felt like I stuck my head in a chimney. I missed the forest so, so much.

"Thinking about me?"

"No!" I automatically stumbled on the words as soon as I recognised Rhylan's voice and turned to find him sitting on a nearby bench in his usual Boss attire, looking like a male model ready to shoot a commercial.

"Do you ever not look like that?" I sighed, making my way to him, aware that I unwillingly elicited one of those proud grins he liked to showcase so much.

"Like what, sprout?" he responded, knowing full well what I meant. "Do you not enjoy this connection between us?"

I stopped in my tracks, my body forgetting to take the necessary step, leaving my foot mid-air for a short while, until my knee gave out and I almost tumbled to the ground, were it not for Rhylan's quick reaction. And of course, he had to trap me in his arms, like one of those rom-com horrid scenes.

Fortunately, I recovered quickly enough to separate myself from him and take a seat on the bench, putting a healthy distance between us.

We spent a few minutes in silence, gulping the fresh air and watching the wind dust away fallen leaves. It felt weird, having him there, by my side and through some weird connection that we both had probably shared with Evigt, I knew he was also enjoying the breaths of green air.

"Feels very different here, doesn't it?" I was the first to break the silence.

"Indeed," he agreed, for once not turning to me, somewhat lost in thought.

"Is this connection one of your powers then?" I didn't know why I was pressing on this, why even open a conversation I did not want to have. Maybe because part of me wanted to blame whatever I felt when Rhylan was close to his faerie powers. Because I loved Ansgar, and this weird attraction towards Rhylan had to be just that, one of those tricks he always used to rope innocent people in.

"That's part of a longer conversation, princess, one that we'll have need to have soon," he turned his head slightly to the side, just enough to see me, then redirected his attention to the trees in front of us.

Day 16

@anwenodstar: Cressi, what the hell?

I couldn't say anything else, there were no words to be uttered. The late afternoon found me working on a report, trying to settle all the financial aspects of the foundation, which seemed to take the rest of my life, when the notification buzzing on my phone distracted me. I only turned my head enough to see the screen, but as soon as Instagram told me that @cressidaofficial tagged me in a photo, my curiosity spiked and I allowed myself to stop just for a few minutes and check it out. Since Evigt, social media did not occupy a high place in the necessities of my life, I kept my platforms open for marketing purposes and the odd event that even I had to post.

That photo, however, almost gave me a heart attack. There Cressi was, stunningly gorgeous as always, her golden locks flowing dramatically from under a big sunhat. A huge cocktail with lots of colours and fruit decoration covered almost a third of the photo, which is where I got tagged in. What I did not expect to see, on the left side of the screen was Rhylan. A shirtless Rhylan holding a similar drink, casually resting his chin on my friend's shoulder.

They were on a beach. In Hawaii!

@cressidaofficial: It does feel like hell, but the icy drinks keep us alive. So hot in here.

@anwenodstar: Cressi what in the name of all the living things? What are you doing in Hawaii? Why are you with that bastard?

@cressidaofficial: Oh don't worry about him, he is harmless

@anwenodstar: Allow me to not believe you. Why are you in Hawaii?

@cressidaofficial: Rhy got bored of New York and said you were angry with him, so we got away for a few days. He gets to stay entertained and you get a much-needed break

@anwenodstar: Cressi no! That is not what I need at all. I need the guy to be here, I need to keep an eye on him so he doesn't do anything stupid

@cressidaofficial: He won't, I'll make sure of it. See you Tuesday sexy!

@anwenodstar: Cressi!!!!

@cressidaofficial: Let the guy have some fun, enjoy a few drinks and we'll be on our way :) We need to go, they are organising a luau party and we need to get ready. Love you!!

@anwenodstar: Take care Cressi, don't trust anything he says!!!

@cressidaofficial: Stop worrying so much, we're fiiiiiiine

I tried to write a few more times but she did not answer. Because Cressi was probably dancing with Rhylan and sharing coconut drinks with him, while they laid almost naked on a beach. I could not bear the thought, it made me so angry that I barely contained myself from smashing something. Instead, I went to the gym and trained for hours, consuming my energy and rage until I couldn't physically move anymore. Rhylan was with Cressida, my brain reminded me constantly.

Rhylan was with Cressida.

Day 20

"Please excuse me," I said to mum and dad as soon as Cressi strolled in the dining room, without a care in the world and with a tan that made her look like a Roman goddess.

Without uttering another word, I grabbed her hand and dragged her up the stairs and into my room, pushing her forward to force her to take a seat on the bed.

She even had the nerve to look surprised.

"What the hell are you thinking?" I adopted a mother-like posture and acted as though Cressi just turned fifteen and arrived home at three in the morning.

"What?" she arranged her slightly dishevelled hair with her fingers, using her nails like a comb.

"You go away with him? Alone? Without telling me?" I let my rage blow, along with my raised voice. I did not know where Rhylan was, and honestly, I did not care if he already reached his room and heard my screams from next door. They both deserved it.

"Anwen, it's not like that," my sister tried to defend herself but I did not want to hear it. I couldn't bear hearing her lips say "Rhy" with that sweetness she always accompanied the sound. I would not give her a chance to speak.

"I told you numerous times not to trust that guy. I told you how he tricked me, how he tricked Ansgar, how he played both of us for months, just to win whatever the hell he needed to. He is a bastard, a conniving, deceitful son of a bitch. He is hatred personified, he is anger and destruction, all the bad things in the world combined in a single person."

Cressi did not let me finish and to my dissatisfaction, started defending Rhylan.

"But he is also kind when he wants to be, interesting, respectful and loyal, honest and so, so hot." She uttered the last word with her eyes closed and a small contort of her face, like she could taste that hotness while thinking about it.

"Because he had hundreds of years to practice it!" I could not believe I had to explain this to her. "Maybe thousands. Do you know anything personal about him? Has he told you about his family? About his life? Or did he spin you the stories about how rich he is and how amazing he can act within a short timeframe? Because let me tell you, he was amazing when he wanted to be with me too, back in Sweden. He was as charming and as caring as he is with you, maybe even more. He came to visit me with cake and we sat on the sofa and chatted for hours, have debates about how to break a kitkat or if chewing a square of dark chocolate or letting it melt in your mouth brought out more flavour," I finished speaking breathlessly.

"Anwen, there are things you don't know yet, things that he needs to tell you. He has his reasons," Cressi started defending him but I was on fire, burning my rage with the sharp use of my tongue.

"Stop defending him!" I shouted, maybe for the first time in my life at Cressi. The woman who was like my own sister. "He killed Ansgar! He took him away from me! He has no excuse, he is a bastard, a man who deserves nothing good in his life, only suffering and pain."

"Anwen…" Cressi stood from the bed and made a gesture to come closer to me but I backed away. I couldn't believe she was defending him, that she would risk my anger and our friendship, the entire life we spent together on him.

"Why?" I couldn't understand, so I had to ask. "Why are you on his side instead of mine?"

"There are things you don't know—" Cressi started explaining, but I would not have it. I would not listen.

"Why?" I repeated again, this time shouting, tears sprinting from my eyes. From hurt, from anger, from pain. I did not know.

My friend returned to her initial position on the bed and shifted her gaze downwards, taking a minute to find her composure. When she looked at me, I realised that she, too, was crying.

I made Cressi cry. The strongest woman I knew, the one who had always been by my side, unshattered by anything life threw in her direction.

"Because I love him," she barely voiced the words and her heart along with them.

Chapter Fourteen

I did not stop, could not stop. The hate, the rage, it flowed through me. I became the tool of the power rather than the controlling source. All I wanted, all I needed was to eliminate this hate from inside of me, to cascade the rage onto someone else. And I only knew a way to do it. Blood.

Kicking the door open, I escaped from the mouldy room, leaving a trail of that male's blood and parts of his skin which stuck to the soles of my feet and with every few steps, left a piece of evidence of the being they once belonged to. I did not care, I did not know where I was going, only that I needed to advance and satiate the rage ripping at my insides. It beat within my flesh like a primordial feeling, one that demanded satiation or my own dismay.

I wandered around the dark corridors, scanning the field, not knowing which way to go or even understanding the need to progress. Yet there it was, eating at me, demanding violence and sacrifice. Following the corridors and torches, the only sign of light this place displayed, I found more soldiers who appeased my hunger for blood. I massacred them quickly, in a few swift movements, grabbing the dagger one of them carried and slitting throat after throat until the hand movement became second nature.

Blood covered most of me, I barely kept my eyes open from all the dripping mess that piled across my face and all the rest of my body, yet I continued, feeling even thirstier for the kill than before. It was the dominant sentiment that pierced inside of my mind so fiercely, nothing else mattered. I wanted nothing but to satiate the hatred, and I would use any means to do so. If it would cost me my life, I would happily honour it.

"What are you..." the soldier's voice extinguished as soon as it came. I did not allow him enough time to finish the sentence before stabbing him in the back of the head, without even allowing him the honour of self-defence. He deserved none. He needed to pay.

Pay for what? A voice wanted to ask, yet the rage shoved it away. I did not care. I didn't know what happened before, how I got in this state, but I was sure that whatever it was, the sentiment arrived at request. Something made me become like this, and I needed to listen to my instinct.

Kill, kill, kill, it shouted from deep inside of me, my chest craving the sensation of blood spilling over skin. So I continued. By the time I reached a royal-looking corridor, I had dispatched over twenty males, all of them dismissed to dine with whatever goddess they worshipped.

The sensation of finally getting closer to what I had been looking for all this time leaned heavier as I reached the royal corridors and stepped on the soft carpet. Even the illumination system changed in these parts, another evidence that higher members of court lived in the surroundings. Instead of the barely glimmering torches that accompanied me in the killing spree, these corridors laid ornate with intricate black wax chandeliers, hanging onto the long path at a perfectly calculated distance in order to mimic sunlight.

It did feel strange that the light of day hadn't cropped up throughout my journey, even though I sensed it was sometime in the afternoon. The guards looked too alert in the morning, with high energy levels, like they had just started their shift, and as I went along, I heard talks about upcoming meals, before I jumped them to make sure they would have none.

I had accumulated several weapons and armour during my sprint, so, were it not for the blood piling up on my newly acquired suit, I would look like one of them. I only had to stay in the darkness long enough to approach.

Huge black doors planted in front of me as soon as I finished strolling under the chandeliers. This was it, whatever I was looking for, it had to be inside. My instinct screamed, pushing, urging to kick them open and be done with it, to kill and destroy everyone in sight without caring about the consequences. So I did just that.

I did not expect to find a dining room with hundreds of small tables arranged neatly, close enough to one another to generate a community feeling, allowing beings to converse with the nearby table without having to rise or move from their designated seats. Tall archways reflecting firelight and just a glint of silver protected them from the roof. A roof carved from stone. I was in the Fire Kingdom,

I realised and immediately raised my guard, the possessive killing urge throbbing inside of me. From all across the room, guards immediately sensed my presence and shifted closer, smelling the blood of their brothers dripping from my armour.

I did not wait to be discovered, I had to claim my position and destroy as many as I could before being eliminated myself. I ran to the closest table and started shoving dagger in flesh. I did not care who they were, did not care if they were old or young, if they attacked or not. Male after male, I piled them at my feet while females and younglings ran away in desperation.

I could not stop, would not stop until I destroyed them all. Until I aligned their bodies into a footpath towards that grand table, where their leaders remained as still as trees, not even reacting to give attack orders.

Pathetic, I thought to myself as I shoved a sword into a soldier that must not have been older than me, barely a male coming of age, with no experiences in life. Nor would he have any, I understood as my blade cut across his lungs and let him fall to the floor, only mangled limbs and a pool of blood left of his life.

They could not stop me, no matter how much they tried. Soldier after soldier met my force, and even though I was one male, I fought like an entire platoon, able to take three or four at a time, carefully shifting directions and working my feet in training positions that emerged instinctively. Not settling for a stop.

A moving victim takes less arrows. The advice sounded in my head. I did not know who had told me that, but I felt grateful for the advice. It now proved useful.

"Ansgar, stop!" a voice sounded from far away, barely audible in between the screaming. Yet it caught my attention, and only for a second, I stopped to find its source. A male who rose from the leader's table and tried to move closer to my position, struggling to approach through the swarming of running females and males readying to attack.

That was all it took, a second to receive a sword tackle, the blade piercing at the back of my knee and incapacitating my right leg. It flushed through my system, begging to stop, the tiredness and effort of the day falling heavily and suddenly over my form. I felt like I had been carrying a mountain on my back, the pressure crushing my lungs. I heard my ribs squeaking, begging for a halt.

The hatred urged me on, forcing me to continue, to push the remaining strength until the end goal was achieved. So I did, I ignored the pain, the blood spurting from me, and shifted both my hands, turning them into killing blows. I did not have the time to enjoy the blood from now on, nor to fight in more steps than required, so I settled for quick killing blows. Throat, eye, head, stomach, kidney. Wherever I had a chance, I splintered flesh and bone in my path, forcing my leg to follow towards the opposite side of the room, closer to their leader.

"Ansgar," the male made his way across and stood next to me, two swords in hand, ready to attack. "You need to stop this," he tried to urge but I did not listen. Another one of his distracting techniques.

I slit another throat while turning to him, yet instead of attacking, he raised a hand to silently command the soldiers to move away from us. He wanted this battle to be fair. Just him and I.

Quickly, I turned my gaze to the leader's table. Only an old male and a female remained there, but more and more soldiers hurried to their side to create a protective wall around, blocking their faces from view.

"Ansgar," the male repeated, forcing me to turn to him yet again. "Your name is Ansgar, do you remember that?" he spoke as though he needed to convince me of my own origin.

"You are confused," I spat the blood accumulating in my mouth. I did not know if it was mine, due to some internal wound I could not feel just yet, or piled up from all the soldiers who squirted their remains towards me as they died.

"My name is Death." With that, I attacked.

Anwen

Chapter Fifteen

Day 21

I kicked open Rhylan's door, making the hinges shatter from the blow. I had no idea how I managed to do such a thing since my frail bones did not prove very reliable throughout my life and broke several times, forcing me to spend an entire summer in a cast when I was eleven.

Somehow, the rage boiling in my blood gave me the physical strength I needed to knock it down and find Rhylan splayed out on bed, typing frantically on his phone.

"Son of a bitch!" The words came out on their own accord and the instinct to harm him overpowered me, making me throw myself in the bed on top of him and start blowing hits across his face. Unprepared for the sudden attack, the faerie remained seated for a few seconds, trying to understand what was happening, then with a hasty movement, he turned me in bed and blocked my attack from above, catching both my wrists in one hand while I shook and struggled to escape like a caged animal.

"I guess you know," he only said, shifting his attention to Cressi, who had just walked into the room.

"Rhy…" Only one word from her broken voice and he froze, releasing me immediately and abandoning the bed to walk by her side. I remained puzzled and panting, struggling to escape from the duvet and blankets I had trapped myself in from so much wiggling.

By the time I got myself free, Rhylan and Cressi sat by the door, both looking at me with concern, as though they had suddenly become the parents and me, the kid who just discovered Santa isn't real.

"This ends now," I recovered my composure, understanding that I made a fool of myself but not particularly giving a damn, especially not when my best friend threatened to fall into whatever trap he had set out for her. "You will not see Cressi again, or I will break the contract and remove you from this house."

"Anwen, there are things you don't understand," Cressi took the blow for both of them, protecting the fae from my rage and slowly shifting her body in front of his, to become a shield against my hate.

"You cannot break the contract, you already signed it," Rhylan tried to protest from behind her but I would not hear it.

"You haven't proved Ansgar is alive."

"You saw him a few days ago," Rhylan replied in disbelief.

Bastard, I mentally swore as I remembered what he had done to me. "I saw an image that you projected into my head, that doesn't prove anything. You said the Earth Kingdom royal family needs to verify that the lock of hair you've shown me belongs to him. Instead of doing that, you proceeded to keep yourself occupied with fucking my sister!"

I did not have any mirrors close by but I was sure I probably turned crimson from all the shouting and rage and I was surprised that no one else came to witness the spectacle.

"We will get to that, but first I think it would be a better idea for the three of us to talk. Without hitting each other ideally," he suggested and Cressi nodded, pleased with the quick solution he found. Gods, I hated this, I hated seeing my friend like this, wiggling her tail like an idiot puppy at everything this prick said. He might as well suggest we all throw ourselves off a cliff and she would not object.

"No, you will do it now. We will go to the Earth Kingdom, now," I accentuated the last word to make my point.

"We'll need to get to Evigt first, that would take us an entire day," Rhylan objected but I caught onto the lie.

"Or you do the appear-through-matter thing and we're there in a minute."

His eyes widened in surprise. Or maybe it was panic. I was forcing his hand and he had no escape. The bastard had enjoyed the life here, had done whatever the hell he pleased and now he was forced to fulfil his part of the deal.

"Tomorrow morning," he offered while his hand instinctively pushed towards Cressi's, catching it in his.

"Now," I repeated for a third time. I did not know if he could jump so much, for such a long time and I had no idea what could happen to my body in the process. I'd only seen Ansgar doing it in the forest and Rhylan did it only once, for a few feet, but seeing as he did not object, I must have hit the mark.

"Now," he nodded and took my hand, without shifting his gaze

190

from my friend.

The next second, a deep line of trees surrounded us.

I struggled for a reaction, part of me wanted to jump up with joy at the sight of the forest I had spent so much time in. The other part became weary and guarded, expecting something to pop out of the trees and eviscerate both of us within a split second. I felt guilty for how everything ended, about the fact that Ansgar chose to put my life over the district's and didn't even want to imagine how everything must have struggled after his death. His passing. I didn't even know how to name it anymore, but the hope that Ansgar's family would confirm Rhylan's promises burst through me higher than fireworks on the fourth of July.

My fears immediately materialised as, within a few moments, several faeries and sjorkas came to investigate, and as soon as their eyes spotted Rhylan, weapons were drawn. Instinctively, I shifted close to a Cloutie tree, blending my body within the trunk, hoping that they would not risk hurting it by attacking me.

"Faelar," I exclaimed with relief as soon as my eyes landed on my friend. She looked so different from what I remembered, so much taller, and the beading around her neck, which she once explained to me symbolised her status within the forest had doubled in size.

"Anwen?" she asked with a whisper, finding it hard to believe that I had returned, and with Fear Gorta nonetheless.

I swallowed dryly, observing the hatred in her eyes, the way she kept shifting from me to Rhylan and back again, judging my presence in his company.

"I'm back," I stated the obvious, trying to appease the situation as much as I could. It didn't really matter, because I could not find a trace of my friend left in her and I knew that no matter what I said, the sentence was already decided.

Without waiting for the exchange to end, Rhylan stepped closer to me and the tree, he was trying to shield me in between his body and the trunk should they attack at any minute. Which, judging by the looks on their faces, they planned to.

"I can get Ansgar back," I uttered another attempt, hoping that his memory might re-jiggle the friendship we once shared. "That's why we're here, we need to speak to the royal family."

"And what business does the cursed one have with the Fear Gorta?" a voice echoed distant, forcing the close-by branches to shatter with contempt.

I turned to find its origin and my heart dropped in my stomach. Approaching us, I found a man who looked so much like Ansgar that I had to blink a few times and settle myself, forcing my mind to understand the similarities. The same golden-brown locks, almost the same height, though Ansgar might be an inch or two taller, the same bandolier across a bare chest and grey trousers, the bronze skin gleaming in the sunset. Even the jawline resembled that of my mate, with harsh cheekbones to elongate his features.

"Are you the new keeper?" I immediately asked, disregarding his question.

"Matthyaz," the male introduced himself while stepping closer to us. By the time he reached Rhylan, his hand moved speedily to his bandolier and grabbed a knife, placing it to Rhylan's heart so smoothly, that he made the threat look like a dance.

"I am Anwen," I replied, introducing myself and showing no consideration towards Rhylan's situation. The fucker deserved it and I encountered joy at the sight of the frozen old fae, standing threatened by an earthling.

"I am aware of who you are, mortal," he replied with a speck of loathing, though his eyes did not shift from the main target. "Mistake me not for my cousin, you will not find any amiable being in my district."

Before I found time to respond, he continued. "If you value your life, I suggest you leave in the next second. I find myself disinclined to give you any longer."

"Cousin? You are Ansgar's cousin?" It made so much sense, the similarities between the two and his stance. Close to royalty. His chin remained parallel to the ground at all times, a perfect commanding posture and he did not sketch a movement out of place, nothing that was not probably calculated a hundred times before being made.

Matthyaz risked a quick glance towards me, showing a dash of surprise towards my inability to understand or accept his warning. I had met my fair share of fae and faeries of all kinds and a few intimidating words would not dissuade me from my mission.

"Matthyaz, I need your help. You might not know who I am, but I lived here when—"

"Spare me your dramatics, human." I did not have a chance to explain when his voice cut me off without a second thought. Clearly, what I had to say did not matter to him. "I know who you are, what you did, and what you are now planning. So let me feed you a piece of information you clearly have no idea about since you dare show your face in this district."

If his tone of voice turned into a weapon, I would be long dead. Even Rhylan sensed it and tried to take a step back, to get closer to me but the keeper's dagger must have pierced his chest because I heard a distinct groan coming out from Rhylan's throat. And he stopped shifting, keeping his position intact.

"I know all about your little adventure with my cousin, how you managed to sneak in the kingdom and tricked him into betraying his kin, offering his life for *you*." He pronounced the words slowly, looking me up and down, scanning every part of me and surely finding it lacking. His eyes said what his lips did not. That Ansgar had been a fool to get involved with me when they probably had so much prettier girls back at home. It made me feel small, unworthy and brought out every insecurity I ever had. If a guy like him looked at me with such disgust, what did Ansgar initially think of me? Did he also see me as a worthless human?

"Anwen..." Rhylan's voice shook me from thought, probably sensing my dismay. "There is no need to be disrespectful," he said to Matthyaz, who disregarded him and continued.

"The queen has issued a curse order on you. If you even make contact with a being from the Earth Kingdom, they have the right to kill you and claim the murder as payment from the prince's dissipated energy. Not that it would do any good..." he groaned, reminding me again of my worth.

"Take me to see the queen." The words sounded like an order

194

and even my eyes widened in surprise at the strength I released them with.

It was Faelar who replied this time, her tone pitiful. "Anwen, the only reason you are not dead is because I ordered them to stand down. You are in no position to request anything. The best thing would be to leave," she nodded, expecting me to copy her movement and do exactly what she asked.

"You ordered them?"

I must have had such a puzzled face that she allowed the explanation. "I am part of the sjorka elders now."

Within the year, she changed from the young female I giggled and took strolls in the forest with, into a leader. Her appearance made so much more sense now, the extra beading on her neck, used not for decoration, but for marking rank.

"What happened to Karem?" I remembered the grumpy voice of her grandfather every time he saw us together. He had been the one who wanted to force me out of the forest, Ansgar once told me, warning me to be mindful when visiting Faelar's cabin.

"He dines with the goddess," the keeper replied in her stead. "Along with thousands of others who died because of the decrepit state of this district," he added. Matthyaz did not say the words but I understood them nonetheless. *All to save me.*

"I am so sorry—" I wanted to say so much more, I wanted to cry, to scream, to apologise, to stand there and receive all the hate I deserved. I did none of that, just remained paralysed, shifting my head from Ansgar's cousin to Faelar and back again.

"Rhylan," I called for the fae standing in front of me, who had kept so surprisingly quiet during this exchange. "Give me the pouch," I ordered.

If he wanted to object, he kept it well hidden and slowly, so slowly, weary of the dagger keeping him in place, moved a hand to reach his jacket pocket and took out the pouch containing Ansgar's hair. The one I begged him over and over to let me keep, yet he rejected my every offer on each occasion.

I eagerly snatched it from his hands and took the three steps separating me from Matthyaz, and at the sight of Rhylan's bleeding chest, something in me broke. Even though he had been a bastard who enchanted my best friend, even though he took my love away from me, I could not see him suffering. I don't know what possessed me to do so, but I shoved the keeper's hand away, forcing him to release Rhylan's chest. It must have left a big scratch across his torso, because the old fae's hands immediately went to cover the wound, but at least I knew he healed quickly. A stabbing to the heart on the other hand might not have been such a walk in the park.

Without giving Matthyaz a chance to protest, I shoved the pouch in his hand, forcing him to shift his attention from the bloody dagger to the offering, and pierced him with my gaze until he opened it.

"What is this?" he asked, even though the answer looked evident.

"Your cousin's hair, apparently," I replied and urged Faelar to come closer and take a look. To my surprise and gratitude, she hurried to do so. I did not give them time to ask questions, I wanted to offer them all the answers and try to bring them on my side. While I did so, Rhylan stood behind me, accepting his role as a secondary player in this discourse. Even though I could not see him, I felt him behind me, guarding my back and knew that if it came to it, he would protect me with his life, even though I was the one managing the situation. A wave of pride echoed through me, I could not help to hope that he shared the feeling.

"Up until three weeks ago, I also thought Ansgar to be dead. That is until Fear Gorta came to me and offered me this proof that Ansgar is alive. He is in the Fire Kingdom." As soon as I said the words both their faces turned as white as paper, but I disregarded the million questions they had, deciding it was not the best time to think about how Ansgar was faring there. Part of me already knew that he must not be in great shape considering he was forced to live in an enemy kingdom. "Rhylan and I made a deal that he would take me to the Fire Kingdom to see Ansgar, but I asked for proof that your prince is alive and received this."

They stared at the locks of hair, then at me, then at each other in complete silence.

"Only the Queen would know how to read this," Matthyaz responded.

"Which is why I need to see her," I pushed.

Faelar replied, "You will be executed on sight, you cannot go there."

I wanted to say that I didn't care, that this was worth the sacrifice, and I would gladly risk it, but thought better of it. I did not fool myself with dreams of bravery and always took pride in my realism. If I died, who would go into the Fire Kingdom? I was convinced Rhylan wouldn't take any of them, so they needed me alive. Maybe there was some room for negotiation.

"There must be a solution to all this, Faelar," I pleaded to the friendship we once shared, to the memories I hoped she still possessed of the smiles and good times we had together. Even though now, the hardness on her cheek made her a completely different person, I hoped that my friend, the sweet girl I'd come to meet still lurked somewhere inside.

"You can call the barren one." It was Rhylan who voiced the idea, despite our surprise. "He is only a few territories away, he can appear within minutes," he offered. How he knew all this was something we would be left to wonder and an answer he clearly did not plan on sharing.

"You do not give me orders," Matthyaz's voice sounded rasp, slicing hatred in its path, eyes piercing Rhylan's like a million blades ready to attack. The old fae kept his mouth shut, something unusual for him and I could not avoid thinking he did it for my benefit. Because he wanted to help me and offer me the hope I needed, to verify the truth of his promises.

"Maybe summoning Prince Vikram is not the worst idea in the world," it was Faelar who said it, making the armed faeries turn their heads slowly towards their leader, disbelief marked in their action.

"I will not risk bringing a member of the royal family in the presence of Fear Gorta!" Matthyaz raised his tone, making us all shake along with his words.

"Of course not, he was just leaving," I heard myself say, without even throwing a gaze in Rhylan's direction. In the next instant, I felt him move behind me, my words causing distressing shifts in his posture.

"I am not leaving you alone with them," his words sounded sharp and determined, his body now moving towards me in an attempt to protect but I raised my hand and placed it on his chest, over the wound now barely visible through the cut across his shirt, stopping him from advancing further.

The familiarity surprised not only the faeries around, but me along with it. In these three weeks, Rhylan and I became close, we created some kind of relationship, and even though I could not pinpoint the sentiment connecting my end of the link, I knew I had the power to make him listen. I had power over the most ancient fae known to man.

"Vikram is the one who guided me through the kingdom that time you *helped* me pass," I pierced the words, making him understand that he had absolutely no right of decision in this case, that he owed me for his past actions. "We get along, so I will be fine by his side," I insisted, pushing slowly in his chest. I felt his heart beat faster over my palm and sensed nervousness flushing through his body.

Rhylan was terrified to leave me alone with Ansgar's cousin, terrified that something would happen to me. Because he cared for me or because it ruined his plan, I did not know. I could not think past the present, past the hope that Ansgar might truly be alive somewhere and that I would see him soon.

"Turn around slowly and look closer at the trees, there are forty-one faeries hidden in the barks and branches. All armed." He shifted closer to me, enough to whisper the words in my ear, but I only heard half of what he said, my brain much too focused on the trail his warm breath left on my neck. I did not understand why it caused me to feel this intensely, made me focus so much on the tiny drop of sweat falling from the shell of his ear onto his neck and down on his skin. He stood so close to me that I could lick it if I wanted to, and damn, that thought really wanted to make its way on my priority list.

"I'll be fine, Rhylan, you can go now." I forced myself to wake up from the trance his closeness provoked in me and stepped back, distancing myself from his scent, from his presence, from that wonderful perfume emanating from a single drop of sweat. He smelled of wildflowers and pepper, and oh my god, I wanted to bask in his aroma.

"Anwen…" his warning sounded more like a plea rather than the usual smirking of a request, yet his desperation to leave me alone pushed through his usual calm demeanour.

"Dark one, I will not say it again, nor will I waste more of our time with you. Prince Vikram will not be summoned in your presence, and should you not leave immediately, this conversation will reach an abrupt ending," Ansgar cousin pressed with an evident loss of patience which forced me to look at Rhylan with the biggest pleading and desperate eyes I had probably made in my life.

"I'll pick you up at midnight, princess," he forced the words through gritted teeth, making a display of how much he hated leaving me there. Before he vanished, he turned to Matthyaz. Within the two steps he had to make to reach the new keeper, Rhylan's composure shifted into what I saw, for the first time, as the Fear Gorta. Dark smoke discharged through his body and the

200

surroundings and his eyes had shifted from adamant to scorching crimson, as though his orbits had been replaced by embers. Even the visible tattoos on his forearms turned a dark shade of scarlet and I knew then, that no matter how many weapons or forces they used, it would have no effect on Rhylan. I finally saw him in his true form, the immortal being who could last through centuries, the one who could break empires if he wanted to, and I realised, that the calm and understanding fae I had come to know and live with, was something that existed for my benefit, and no other being had ever been a part of it.

"If I see a hair out of place when I collect her, I will burn down everything you care about. I will make you witness it and howl in pain while your loved ones bleed to death and once I am done with you, I will bathe in their remains." He did not say the words like a promise, more like a guarantee and by the quivering look on Matthyaz's face, Rhylan could easily do that and more with a simple flick of his finger.

He then turned to me and grabbed my hand in his, a gesture meant not to soothe my nerves, but to make it clear for everyone that I was under his protection and the threat he had made to the keeper applied to everyone who dared think about touching me. "Midnight," Rhylan whispered and quickly lifted my hand to kiss it, his adamant eyes locking with mine.

In the next second, Fear Gorta vanished, leaving my hand limp in the air and my chest beating harder.

.

Chapter Sixteen

"What the fuck happened here?" A different voice, more commanding, sounded from the other side of the iron box I had been shoved in.

During the encounter with the male from the leader's table, something had snapped inside of me, the thirst for blood doubling up and engorging every state of my body, forcing me to push beyond the limit I had reached many kills back. With it, I lost focus, my concentration and strategy fading in the presence of the male — probably a general by his fighting stance — who used every trick and tactic in the book to put a halt to my mission, stopping my advancement with a blow to my other knee, which forced my legs to give out and with it, all the territory I had gained.

The next memory was of the box my body had been shoved in, barely wide enough to allow my wounded legs to stretch but not tall enough to let me stand or take a step in either direction. Not that I wanted to, every time I came close to one of the sides of the box, iron scorched my skin, provoking burning injuries I was unable to heal because of the high amount of the metal surrounding me.

The leader hadn't shown mercy, as I so stupidly believed initially, but had sentenced me to a slow and painful death instead, forced to spend the remainder of my time killing myself slowly in this iron coffin.

I did not have long to wait, probably a few more hours or less than a day. Both my legs bled profusely, pus formed at the back of my knee, and several iron injuries marked my skin and would infect in no time if they hadn't already.

Which meant I had to perish in a sarcophagus of hatred and despair, unable to understand the reason for such feelings.

Several other voices explained my situation to the male in charge, though I only heard fragments of what they said. Either way, whatever the explanation, it caused the male fury because he erupted in a series of curses and accusations, constantly referring to a plan that had been settled long ago.

I came to understand that my outburst ruined this male's vacation, which I didn't particularly care about.

"Ansgar?" His voice rasped the same name I had heard before, coming from the mouth of the leader who defeated me. My name.

I tried to answer but my throat remained covered in wounds, making it impossible to utter a thought, let alone respond to the calling.

The male tried a couple more times and understanding overpowered his determination because the next words did not come addressed to me.

"Open the cage and let him out," he demanded, in spite of the obvious discontent of the nearby guards, whom I had heard mocking and swearing at me, calling me names and curses throughout the time these iron walls parched my strength.

"He could be dead already, you blithering idiot." The order came accompanied with protest and the words 'general' attached to each one, revealing the source of his power and might.

This male, whoever he may be, held the second position in the kingdom, after the king himself, yet judging by the decrepit state of the pale old man I had seen running scared from the dining room, this general would soon become the heir to a scorching empire.

Which made him the one I needed to end.

And the fool had just made his plans known.

As soon as the entrance to the small box they had kept me in cracked open, I charged with all the strength I had left, summoning my remaining demons to possess my body long enough to complete the goal. To kill the general and rid the realm of the putrid ramifications of the firelings.

I charged like a beast on last reserves and shoved the male under me, pushing fists and knees in his mouth and cheek, forcing his adamant eyes to bleed and his teeth to shatter. Blow after blow, I damaged him, pounded into him until his injuries shone crimson over broken skin, the mark of my revenge evident and heavy.

Several arms grabbed me, by my hair, back of the neck, and arms, and in the next second, iron shackles thrusted heavily onto every part of my skin that had remained untouched.

"Should we decapitate him, general?" One of them requested

orders while I struggled to jiggle free from the iron they had ensnared me with, to no avail.

"We still don't have the information we need," the male stood from the floor, leaving behind a puddle of blood, yet his face healed so fast that no evidence of prior blows I had snapped onto him remained.

He threw me a smirk, urging me to try it again. To test his patience. And I realised. *I knew him.* I knew that male.

"Shove him in the iron cell," he ordered while fixing his jacket and banishing away bits of dust from his shoulder, completely unaffected by the fact that I had tried to kill him barely a minute ago. "Bring him food and tend to him but keep the chains until I return."

I jiggled again, my last attempt to break free and finish what I started but with a barely perceptible wave of his finger, the male made me fly into a wall, crushing me with the pressure of a mountain until blood gushed through my nose and mouth and I barely saw through the red puddle forming on my face.

"Let's see how the honourable prince can live with the memories of his victims," he added and grinned widely, announcing the trap he had just set out for my conscience.

"General," one of the guards behind me dared protest, though his voice sounded barely audible and shaking, "He killed all the soldiers he encountered after the treatment, there is no one who could survive him."

A plea, a request for mercy, a petition to save the soldiers who would be sent to my cell, ones that I had no control over and no choice but to end their lives. A petition the general easily dismissed with another wave of hand which released the pressure and allowed me to fall on the damp bloody floor.

"I can think of at least *one*," he smirked again, pride evaporating through his form and over his glazy eyes.

Anwen

Chapter Seventeen

"Hello, Vikram." I mumbled at the sight of the middle prince of the Earth Kingdom. His eyes scanned me for several moments, the sight convincing the other senses that what he witnessed was indeed, real. That I had returned to Evigt and stood in front of him, holding a lock of his brother's hair. The only thing remaining of the young prince. Of my mate.

His lips moved, with the uttering of a greeting, or a curse, I could not tell because no sounds escaped his mouth. Vikram seemed to realise this and forced himself to repeat his thoughts, this time making his discontent clear for everyone present to witness.

"What in the name of the goddess are you doing here?" his voice flushed with wrath and the lines on his brows furrowed deeper than I had thought possible. I'd been wrong to think there could be a speck of friendship left between the middle prince and me, his features and body language only portrayed wrath and annoyance, as though my presence was the last thing he expected — or wanted — to see that particular evening.

"I need to speak to the queen," I pressed my words while mentally preparing to shoot arguments in his direction before he had a chance to protest and hoped some of them would attract his interest and understanding. But they were not needed, because Vikram's huff dispersed every intention I had.

"You have reached a limit, *girl*, which you do not seem to understand. And our patience is running thinner than a silk thread." He uttered the words in disgust, forcing me to understand that I meant nothing. I was no one for him. Long gone were the days when he'd snuck me inside the castle and offered me to his brother. He probably regretted that decision every day and I could not blame him. There were nights when I hated myself for going there, for making stupid choices, and not understanding Rhylan's trickery.

Rhylan, who'd brought me there, jumped in front of a blade for me and kissed my hand for everyone to see, baring our relationship to all the faeries and marking his territory, threatening the keeper and all in sight, just to make sure I would remain unharmed. Of course, Vikram must have hated me. I just showed up with the male who stole his brother's energy in their district, the entrance to their kingdom without a care in the world, demanding to speak to their queen. They must have branded me a traitor as soon as Rhylan stepped less than two feet by my side.

"I need to know if this belongs to your brother," I showed him the locks of golden-brown hair which I pressed tight in the palm of my hand, protecting it like a valuable treasure. "I need to know if Ansgar is still alive," I pleaded with him, piercing him with my eyes and hoping he would see the truth in their stare.

"My brother's energy vanished, there is nothing remaining of him," Vikram clarified and each of his words shoved a dagger in my heart. He also made sure to expel them slowly, forcing me to grasp each one and enjoyed the harm they did to me. The prince crossed his arms over his silver breastplate, covering the reflection I cast onto his commander uniform.

"That's what I thought too." I did not know where the strength to protest came from, if not from the desperation to keep hoping, from my sheer need to keep Ansgar alive just a bit longer, to postpone the reality that could come hit me like a freight train within the next second. "I saw him go, I held the stack of leaves he left behind, I was there when the last breath came out of his body." Tears streamed down my face at the memory, at the fact that I had seen the two men I loved most in my life, my brother and my mate, vanish in front of me in such a short amount of time. Loss had become a ghost to accompany me, tied to my heart like an unbreakable thread.

I did not know if the description of what I had witnessed, the new information I gave him —that I was there with his brother, that I had been the one to see him go— or his mere pity for a woman crying made him relax and step closer to me, abandoning the formal stance he adopted at his arrival.

"What happened?" Vikram approached and without caring or realising that we offered a spectacle to all the faeries around, that Faelar and Matthyaz remained in their original position, holding the army that had been threatening me since I had arrived, took a seat on the ground, shifting enough to make himself comfortable as though we could be there a long time. I wanted to do the same and come close to him, but before I had a chance to crouch, Vikram lifted his arms to his shoulders and undid the cape that usually accompanied his armour and folded it like a blanket, then placed it on the ground. For me to sit on. Even now, the prince showed kindness.

I could not contain it any longer and let myself fall on my knees, hands instinctively arching over his shoulders, my face pressed to the side of his cheek, and wept. I cuddled myself in his long dark hair, the scent of earth that seemed to accompany the royal family, and allowed myself to cry, to release all the tension and loss, knowing that, for the first time ever, the person next to me completely understood my emotions. Because he felt the same.

I stayed there for minutes, hugging the brother that had shown me kindness, the one that broke and remade our relationship, and the one who joked and laughed at our union. One who missed Ansgar as much as I did.

To my surprise, his hands wrapped around my body and pressed onto me, at first gently and reassuring, then tighter and more determined, my feelings flowing through him. We could somehow relate better, the tighter the embrace.

By the time I finished sobbing, his shoulder armour full of tears and snot, which I tried to discreetly clean with my sleeve, we had been left alone. Probably a silent order Vikram gave while holding the weeping pile of mess I had turned into. Only he remained, with his dark features shining in the sunset and eyes more understanding than a few minutes ago.

"Can you tell me what happened?" he asked slowly, gently, with all the compassion he could muster, afraid that the question would ruin the calmer state of me.

I nodded and wiped my nose, then cleaned more of his armour as best as I could and sat on the cloak he arranged for me. I could not look at him, could not face what I'd done, knowing that his eyes would question every stupid decision I had made, so I pointed my gaze towards the grass, towards my shoes, anywhere except his direction.

"The tea I drank to come into the kingdom, it was Cloutie root." I sighed and expected a wave of curses or Vikram asking me how could I'd been so stupid. But he did not show any surprise, only asked, "How did you know it would bring you to the kingdom?"

"I didn't," I quickly added. "It was Rhylan who told me so. He infiltrated the forest guard, the men who kept bringing me food and cared for me while I stayed in the forest," I clarified, unsure if he had the details already. "He said his grandmother's sister mated a fae and gave her the tea to come visit. I believed him," I stopped to draw a breath, wishing to go back in time and stop myself from committing such foolishness.

"A few days later, Rhylan came in and Ansgar attacked him. Then he demanded payment and they both went away to sort it out without me being present. By the time he came back, Ansgar became sick, he vomited and then had a fever the next day. I called for help and one of the elders told me what had happened. I came back to see him barely alive. He—" I waved my head, forcing the new tears away, and swallowed hard at the dry lump in my throat. "He died minutes later and his body turned into dry leaves within the next instant."

It came Vikram's turn to swallow hard, so hard that his gulp could be heard from a mile away.

"Where did you get the hair?" he asked.

"From Rhylan," I replied and at the portrait of shock on his face, I started explaining how I created the foundation and how Rhylan had shown up after a year, trying to convince me that Ansgar was still alive, how he asked to live in my house and about the contract, the scheduled visit to the Fire Kingdom and why we'd come to the forest that particular night.

Through it all, the colours on Vikram's face shifted so abruptly that even a disco ball would be jealous. Red with anger, green with disgust, and yellow with shock just to name a few.

The prince had to stand and take a few steps to arrange his thoughts, only then did he speak.

"Allow me to ensure I grasp full understanding. Fear Gorta wants to spend time with you, and take you to the Fire Kingdom after he made you sign a deal?"

I nodded and wished I had the contract to show him until I realised I'd taken a picture on my phone, so I found it in my jean pocket and zoomed the photo enough for Vikram to see. Thank god for no restrictions this time and for Vikram knowing how to handle a smartphone.

"And the bait he is using is Ansgar. The promise that my brother is alive?" The prince wanted to make sure he understood correctly.

"Yes," I quickly added while he returned the phone to me.

"We definitely need the queen for this," he said and as he did, he started dragging me towards the trees.

I followed and watched in surprise as Vikram removed his shoes and pointed me to do the same, then, from a small satchel tied to his waist, which I didn't even notice before, he grabbed some kind of white powder which he started rubbing onto the soles of his feet. Once he finished, the prince grabbed some more and passed it to me, a silent order to do the same.

One would be scared to go into the kingdom again, especially after what happened the first time, but this was Vikram — I calmed my nerves and savagely beating heart — and I had to trust him. Even if the queen ordered to kill me, I had to risk it. Part of me hoped that she would have the same reaction as her son, and help me find out the truth and bring Ansgar back.

I did as requested and rubbed the white powder onto my feet, with Vikram watching my every move. It must have been valuable because I dropped half of it on the ground while rubbing my right foot and he growled in annoyance, just as he took out a bit more powder and placed it gently in my hand, his dark gaze the only warning to be more careful this time.

Once my soles were so full that white marks remained behind my step, the commander grabbed my hand and urged me to walk and follow him.

For the next two minutes, the middle prince and I spun around the trunk of a huge Cloutie tree until the powder on our feet created a white circle around the roots. Part of me wanted to laugh at the ridicule of the situation, the fact that if someone saw us, they must think us crazy. Walking in circles, barefoot, around a big tree.

"It's ready," Vikram stopped abruptly but did not let go of my hand. "Step inside and don't let go," he instructed and I did as directed, holding his hand tightly while his fingers wrapped around me in a firm grip.

A gush of light branded me and forced my eyelids to move rapidly and clear out the pain. The next time I opened my eyes, the trees looked different and Vikram let go. We had arrived in the Earth Kingdom.

Memories of the first time I'd been here came rushing back, my mind inundated with the excitement and need to find my prince. A very different sentiment from what I was experiencing now, which was dread, a panic swirling in my stomach at the fear that the queen might reveal a lie. That she would give me no hope.

I didn't have time to recover from the shock of being transported into the unknown twice in one evening when Vikram's hand grabbed mine and squeezed it tightly once again.

I looked at him, but instead of finding relief and hope, tension sculpted his dark features. He looked like a warrior preparing to go into battle, with not much hope of returning.

"Are you okay?" I asked in a low tone, afraid that the trees surrounding us might discover my presence earlier than needed. The last thing I wanted was to get him in trouble.

He looked at me for the first time, like he just remembered I stood by his side and grabbed my hand even tighter in his. Not in a pleasant, friendly greeting but a desperate and hurtful connection.

I grimaced and wanted to retract my palm from his, but as soon as I made my intention known he jerked me closer to him, making the right side of his body press into mine.

"They will not dare harm you if you are by my side," he

214

muttered. Yet, as he did so, his left hand grabbed the hilt of his sword in preparation for a possible attack.

"Okay," I murmured, coming to realise my precarious condition. He had brought me into a kingdom that branded me an enemy, that blamed me for their young prince's passing, and who would not hesitate to kill me and claim revenge for the loss they had suffered.

The fact that Vikram willingly put himself in the position of having to defend me and fight his people if it came to it, both shocked me and gave me hope. I did not want to cause any more trouble and least of all, I did not want him —or anyone else for that matter — to get injured. But he was willing to do it, which made me realise that Rhylan's words had to be true. That he would not risk it lest he thought Ansgar could truly be alive. And I was the way to get to him.

To my surprise, Vikram did not hide me as we walked into the kingdom. Coward that I was, I thought he would disguise me and take me through some kind of corridor or secret passageway to avoid all the staring and threats. Instead, the commander adopted his usual royal stance and kept me so close to his chest that I could barely walk without stepping on his feet or stumbling across the stone-paved patio.

Thankfully, after about forty minutes into the mini-marathon, we made it out of the forest, across a town square with various imposing buildings and an array of market stalls, where people snarled and cursed at me. We made it through the palace doors and passed the garden where Ansgar's party had been held.

It looked so much bigger now, without the space being crammed with thousands of people and tables, it might have been the size of an entire football stadium including the stands, shops, and parking. It plastered the way to the palace entrance and the huge carved wooden doors I passed through during my first visit.

The castle was built of some kind of shining stone, which made it gleam in the moonlight and the floors and columns wore marble decorations.

Several faeries came to meet Vikram and stopped paralysed when they saw their prince holding me just as tightly as he did when we arrived. Which meant the danger hadn't passed.

"The Queen?" he asked abruptly and harshly, without offering the staff a minute longer to gaze at me.

"In the Western Dining Room, my prince," a tall dark-haired male quickly responded, just as he bowed low for Vikram, who only nodded and proceeded to push me towards what I could only imagine to be the dining hall.

Still holding my hand in his, the prince dragged me along, without looking back or preparing me for what was to be a very graceless encounter. We strolled past rooms and draped corridors, climbed stairs, and passed several halls until we reached another set of wooden carved doors. Only this time, the markings evoked grapes, platters of fruit, and several other types of food that I quickly recognised. We had arrived.

It was only then that Vikram turned to me, slight anguish in his eyes. "If the queen orders you harmed, there is nothing I can do." He pointed his stare to mine, making sure I understood that entering that room meant risking my life.

I nodded, struggling to swallow a massive lump in my throat, then ushered him to open. I had come so far, there was no turning back.

"Mother, father," the prince greeted as he stepped inside the room, his body blocking my presence entirely, a deliberate move I understood and appreciated. "Damaris, sister," he added to the list. The following name made me shudder. "Ansgar," he greeted and my bones chipped away inside my body from the emotion that rushed through me.

I could not contain myself and had to see, I had to know. So I shifted from my hiding place and made my silhouette appear from behind the prince's heavy armour.

To see a child, no older than a few months in the loving embrace of his mother, the kingdom healer. They had chosen to honour the name for another generation, not ready to let their young prince go. Realising what I'd done and judging by the reaction on their faces, I had to do something to turn away their anger and desire for revenge.

So I took the hint from the staff member who received Vikram in the castle and bowed as low as I could, reciting their titles and shifting direction as I spoke, in such a way that my lowered head reached all of them. "King Farryn," I shifted towards the mountain of a male sitting at the head of the table, "Queen Bathysia," I turned my head towards the other end and bowed even lower for the queen and then proceeded to greet the heir and his family, sitting on the right side of the table. "Prince Damaris, Princess Takara, Prince

Ansgar," I muttered but as I said it, the emotion threatened to run through me.

"What is this human doing here, son?" the Queen pressed the words through her tight jaw, without shifting from her seat at the table while the King remained silent, awaiting an explanation.

"She has new information about Ansgar, and willingly risked her life to come see you and ask for council," the prince explained, his tone royal and determined, without stumbling on a single sound. It only made me nod quickly, in support of what he had just said.

"We are not interested in whatever it is she has to say," the female responded, her adamant features darkening like a storm covering a sea at night. Impossible to counteract and lethal. The Queen looked different to the proud mother I had last seen at her son's marking celebration, all of them did. Faces grimmer, eyes that did not embrace smiles to their fullest any longer, because, just like me, they had lost a part of that joy.

I knew the sentiment very well, to spend each day with a person you would always think would be there, only to lose them so abruptly. I had gone through it with Erik, and just when I thought my heart could never recover or I could never truly smile again, there Ansgar came.

"Please, my queen," I wanted to speak but the king's voice quickly dismissed me.

"She is not your queen, she is only queen of the earthlings, a race you do not belong to." His words cut through me like a hot knife through butter, his intent clear and unmistakable. My last chance to leave before the order would be given. The chance to escape a traitor's fate.

"As your son's mate, I consider both of you my king and queen," I replied. I did not know how the words came to me nor how I gathered the courage to respond to the king, knowing full well what happened the last time someone contradicted him. But I had to try.

They both remained silent, mesmerised by the sheer nerve I had, so I took it as my cue to continue before either of them had the chance to give an order I was not very fond of.

"My Queen, my King, I came here seeking your help. Ansgar is still alive in the Fire Kingdom and I have the chance to go to him." I said the words quickly, barely intelligible but they both grasped the meaning, since their faces shifted slightly. Damaris and Takara exchanged puzzled looks, then pointed their gazes at me once more. Baby Ansgar was the only one who looked at me curiously, though I couldn't tell for sure if because he was actually curious or if the position his mother held him made the baby rest his eyes in my direction.

"Congratulations on the birth of your baby boy," I said without thinking, remembering the ritual and what Ansgar told me about his brother wanting a male heir.

"Thank you, Anwen, that is very thoughtful of you," Takara answered with a small smile, genuinely proud of her son while Damaris tensed his jaw but struggled to mutter a thank you.

"He has a beautiful name…"

Damaris huffed in anger, but Takara stood from her seat, claiming everyone's attention. Silently, she walked to me, slowly and decidedly, the silk of her gown creating a shadow of dense colour behind her steps.

"Would you like to hold him?" The kindness in her voice made my knees buckle and my eyes automatically shot to her.

"Are you sure?" I heard my voice tremble, but the healer nodded and passed baby Ansgar to my chest. I initially didn't know how to react, didn't know how to hold him, but once his mother placed him in my arms, the baby settled himself and looked at me with big and curious green eyes.

I chuckled, a tear making its way down my cheek. A happy tear, for once, and somehow, I felt it. That rumble, that connection that made my heart race.

"Ansgar gave quite a bit of his energy that night," Takara answered, as though she could read my mind. "He will always be present," she spoke again, making the baby turn his head towards his mother's voice.

Vikram cleared his throat and took it upon himself to tell the story. Of how he'd been summoned by Matthyaz, how he found me in Evigt, and what I had told him. Through it all, they asked questions and made me clarify the moment of Ansgar's death with as many details as I could over and over again.

We must have stayed there for an hour or two, in the meantime, the youngest member of the family was put to sleep for the night, while I remained standing by the door and going over the details until my knees gave out and I made a falling motion before I rapidly forced myself to recover.

"You can take a seat," the king finally spoke and took away a heaviness from my heart, knowing he did not plan to harm me and accepted me in their company.

I pulled a chair on the left side of the table and only when I accommodated myself, did Vikram make his way across and took the seat next to mine.

Then he approached and whispered softly into my ear, "That's where Ansgar used to sit too." When I turned to him, he looked at me with pride and a dash of understanding, admiring whatever had made me pick that seat. And I allowed myself to move my lips just a millimetre or two, trying to form a smile.

The chair suddenly became a lot more interesting to me and I relaxed, feeling the back support and imagining Ansgar's muscles casually resting on the same wood, like he had all the time in the world to do it over and over again.

"I have this," I remembered the initial reason for my visit, the one that with all the events, memories and explanations had remained sealed in my jeans pocket. "Rhylan gave it to me," I said as I opened the small pouch and placed it on the table, displaying the golden locks hidden inside.

Both the Queen and Takara gasped as they jumped to grab a few strands of hair and analyse it by whatever means they had. While they did so, I explained how Rhylan gave it to me as proof of Ansgar being alive and his suggestion to have it verified by the royal family. By them.

I waited patiently while the females analysed the structure and the queen shed some kind of magic that made the hair float and illuminate the air, then Takara burnt a few strands using the dining table candle and read the echoes of smoke coming out of them. Until

I could not take it anymore and had to ask.

"So?" My heart beat fast, a hummingbird catching wings inside it and struggled to escape. The blood in my veins boiled from the anxiety.

"It's his," the Queen replied and I spotted tears in her eyes, which she rapidly blinked away. Then, her entire attention turned to me.

"Are you willing?" she asked hopeful, a dash of understanding and compassion illuminated her harsh features.

"Yes," I replied without hesitation, not fully understanding what she referred to but knowing that I would do everything to see Ansgar again. And she had just ignited my hope.

"You will not be able to leave easily, maybe not at all." It was Damaris who voiced it, speaking for the first time since I'd arrived. He had kept quiet, analysing and envisioning everything we had said, forming plans and understanding rather than questioning.

"Rhylan can bring me back," I replied, even though concern already started to form. Nothing in my contract stated our release once I got into their kingdom.

"You need to learn some spells," Takara offered with an encouraging smile.

"She needs to be back by midnight," Vikram reminded me. "Fear Gorta is picking her up. And we do not want him rattled just yet."

"We must make haste then." It was the queen who spoke.

Two hours later, I found myself in Ansgar's room, sitting on his bed, which he had last touched when I'd been there and relished in the orange and fresh earth scent he had left on the pillow.

Meanwhile, Vikram and Damaris searched through the adjacent room for a labradorite dagger that belonged to the young prince, repeating its properties for a third time. Labradorite was Ansgar's birthstone, which meant his energy could connect to the crystal and enhance his natural capabilities. I did not know what they meant by that, but we did not have much time and I wasn't ready to give up the bed that held so many memories, that brought me closer to him.

When the clock dinged to announce half-past eleven, Vikram made his way into the bedroom and told me with an apologetic gaze that it was time to go. I barely untangled myself from the sheets but followed the middle prince out the door and down the stairs, where the entire royal family awaited.

I was surprised to be hugged by both the Queen and Takara and be patted on the shoulder by the king, while Damaris shook my hand. They offered some last-minute advice about Rhylan and his trickery, about the Fire Kingdom and deals with the fae, then allowed Vikram to escort me out the door, where a black horse already waited.

"Not again," I muttered through my teeth but did as instructed and once Vikram saddled me in, I held tightly to him and counted the minutes until we were back in the forest.

When we dismantled, the prince made sure I had the dagger well-hidden and gave me a last hug.

"Anwen, don't expect to find my brother in pristine condition. They did not keep him under earth just for the fun of it," were the last words I heard before he shoved me through the portal he had opened into Evigt.

I found Rhylan leaning nonchalantly against the bark of a Cloutie tree, with Matthyaz, Faelar and an entire army studying his every move.

"Nice evening with the in-laws?" he mocked the greeting as soon as I appeared through the gateway, dizzy and ready to be sick.

Everything they said struck me at the sight of him. He wasn't keeping Ansgar safe. Which meant that while Rhylan lived the life with my best friend and my family, my mate must have been struggling under earth, in god knows what kind of conditions.

"Take me home," I said to Rhylan and grabbed onto him while waving a thank you to my faerie friend and the new keeper.

Within an instant, we returned to the summer bar, at the back of the garden, illuminated by fairy lights and ready for cocktails.

"You were right about Ansgar," I stated, breaking my body away from Rhylan. "I believe you now and I want to thank you for taking me to see him."

I did as advised, I did not protest anymore, trying to keep Rhylan as happy as he could be. I needed him on my side so I could ask for a change of contract that marked our safe return. The Queen's suggestion.

"About that, there's been a little change of plans," Rhylan said as he shifted to pour himself a tall glass of scotch.

"Oh?"

"We're going to have to visit a little earlier than expected," he offered.

"How much earlier?" I could not contain the excitement in my voice.

"Three days. It will give me more time with Cressida and you, enough to arrange your business and say goodbye to your parents." He took a long sip, avoiding looking at me, to even acknowledge my presence next to him. Something must had happened because Rhylan looked *worried*.

"What about the Autumn Solstice?" I questioned, remembering what Rhylan explained about portals and energies.

"Sprout," I couldn't but observe how he had reverted back to my original nickname, "As many other things that I've said to you during our time together, *I lied*," he replied, then finished the drink he had served himself and walked away.

Ansgar

Chapter Eighteen

I killed them all. Still, it was not enough.

The wrath forcing me to harm, the reward of each blow and strike did not satisfy the need eating my insides.

I fought the iron chains.

They barely allowed air into my lungs and I struggled to keep alive but every time someone came close to the cell, I jumped and attacked, catching strength from that place that had become putrid with the urge to kill.

To damage.

To stop them all from existing.

They started coming in groups and using only one victim to bring food and water.

One that I would kill in an instant. The food always remained stained with blood, but I enjoyed it more this way.

It meant I earned it. I remained in the dark cell until the next time, until they sent someone new for me to enjoy, the scribble of cracking light when the cell door opened my signal to attack.

The last set of guards made the idiotic decision to bring a dagger with them, thinking it would aid their life.

A nice souvenir I kept after breaking his neck.

The pile of victims and discarded limbs started to grow by the entrance door and the stench made even the putrid scent of my infected wounds seem like a breeze.

I tried shoving the pieces away in the corners and rid myself of them through the cracks, but they did not fit and soon enough, discarded faerie carcasses formed a wall around the dark surroundings, bringing a curtain of death around me.

I wanted to die, my body was ready for it, my mind had given up long ago, yet there was something that did not allow it, something that burst out of me as soon as that cell door opened.

The need to kill, to hurt, to damage.

It felt uncontainable, pushing my body to new limits and tapping into whatever source of energy it found.

So I continued to listen and did as ordered.

Killed, killed, killed.

I was done. I had enough. The bodies formed a wall around me, piled up to the ceiling. My throat bled, the chains pulled tighter, squeezing my veins along with it. The muscles on my arms and legs faded and chunks of flesh hung from the chains, denouncing what was once an athletic male form. I felt as useless as those bodily remains, only that, through some will of the goddesses, my spirit glued together the remaining pieces of me.

I wanted to fade away, for the pain to stop, for the urge to destroy to give out. I had nothing left to give. I was no one. And I wanted to be gone. Various steps approached, hurried, and I hoped this time they would be the ones to take a life. My life.

But I was wrong. The instinct returned, the need to hurt.

I didn't know how I could stand; I didn't understand it. But I pushed on and limped closer to the door, hiding behind the pile of bodies to make myself scarce.

Dagger in hand, I waited for the crack of the hinges to attack, knowing exactly how far my new opponent needed to step away from life and into my death lair.

One step, two, and three. There it was, I had him. I would rip the male apart. I'd do it quickly, one slide across his throat should be enough. So I pointed my dagger and waited.

Only a female walked in, looking disgusted and scared. Her eyes fell on me and widened, her face the embodiment of shock.

She remained paralysed at the sight of me.

"Ansgar," she spoke.

Autumn

TALES OF FIRE AND EMBERS

Anwen

Chapter Nineteen

I spent the next three days with my parents. I did not miss a single meal and even accompanied mom for cocktail dress shopping one afternoon. I did not want to know how Cressi was spending this time, cooped up somewhere with Rhylan, but he would not be a threat once we left. I hoped that he would remain just an interesting guy my friend remembered and joked about when we were old and bragged about 'the olden days'.

As for me, I barely slept, counting the seconds until I saw Ansgar again and worried about Rhylan's open admission of his lies and wondering what I was getting myself into.

But I did as instructed, kept my calm and tried not to show fear, organised the next year for the association and finances, and read as much about the firelings as I could find online.

I knew nothing could really prepare me for what I was about to witness and Vikram's last words did everything but settle my emotions. What if Ansgar was hurt? What if they'd done something to him? What if— No. I paused my thoughts, trying to keep everything as positive as possible.

After all, I was going to see my prince again, alive. What more could I ask for?

"Ready, sprout?" The usual knock on my door announced the fireling's presence, making me run to open it wide.

Rhylan and Cressi stood in the doorway, wrapped in an embrace and my friend's eyes were red and teary. I wanted to jump in and hug her, reassure her that I would be okay, that I would return soon and everything would be as it was. Until I understood I was not the reason for her tears, just as her arms wrapped themselves even tighter around Rhylan's waist. And he planted a kiss on her hair.

I had never seen Cressi like this, except that month when her parents passed and did not know how to react or what to say. If she really loved Rhylan, if this wasn't just one of the hot-guy-flings my friend so often entertained herself with, I had to be the one held accountable for her tears. Because I was the reason Rhylan came here, I asked her to keep him company, so basically, I threw her in his arms and now I was taking him away. Trading her boyfriend for my own.

"I love you, Cressi," I whispered as I stepped closer to her, planting a soft kiss on her cheek and she unwrapped herself from Rhylan just enough to give me a short hug.

"Take care, I'm sure we'll see each other soon," she replied with a quick smile, though her eyes reflected sadness.

I made my way downstairs to find mom and dad in the living room and hugged them both as tightly as I could, going over everything once again and reminding them that we would be remote for a while and that I wasn't sure how long until I could call them.

"Ready to go?" Rhylan's voice announced his presence once again, catching me trapped in another hug offered by my father.

"Yes, I'm ready," I said as I untangled myself from dad, stamped another kiss on mom's cheek, and shared a quick hug with Cressi. Then we headed to the car where a few bags of luggage had been stored in the trunk and the driver passed Rhylan the keys.

We insisted on driving ourselves to the airport, more to avoid suspicion than the actual willingness to spend extra time in each other's proximity.

I lowered the window and waved at them some more, remembering the moment I got in the plane to go to Evigt and how different the feeling resounded right now. If back then I had been hopeful and curious, now I felt resentful and weary.

I was a completely different person, ready to visit another faerie kingdom.

For the following twenty minutes, we both remained silent while Rhylan followed the GPS instructions to the parking we had booked, a quiet one where we could easily fade away without too many security cameras witnessing our disappearance.

My heart beat a thousand times per minute and I knew he could sense it, I knew I showed evidence of my nerves and anxiety, but I could barely keep it together as it was. I would soon see Ansgar. The thought made my pulse jump so rapidly I could easily have a heart attack right there in the car.

"Excited much?" Rhylan broke the silence and forced me to focus on the present. I turned to him for the first time since we departed and studied his features, the tight jaw and lack of amusement he usually displayed. Rhylan was not having a good time. His eyes kept dropping to his hands rather than the road and out of curiosity I did the same. I spotted nothing in particular, except for a black bracelet, elegant and perfectly fitting his style, hanging from his left wrist. It must have been important because he kept staring at it with longing.

"Someone needs to be, you look like your dog died," I replied, careful not to mention or even hint to my friend. I knew Cressi took the separation hard, but by Rhylan's tight jaw and the anxious grip on the steering wheel, I could tell he wasn't having fun either.

Did he care about her this much?

No, I could not think about it. I had one single goal to focus on that day and it was to see Ansgar. Anything else would have to be postponed until I was once again in his arms and found him safe and sound.

So I kept quiet and did not comment on his snarky response, sending a few more emails and scheduling the pick-up for the car. Minutes later, we were underground, trying to find a spot far away and as dark as possible. When he finally found one to his liking, Rhylan parked and took the key out of the ignition, shifting his glazy adamant eyes on me.

"There's no point in taking luggage, you'll receive suitable clothes when you get there," he said while unstrapping his seat belt and clicking the button to do the same to mine.

"Okay," I nodded and shifted in my seat, fully turning to him.

"Leave your phone in the glove compartment, there's no use for it where we're going," Rhylan commanded.

"It worked fine in Evigt," I protested. I planned to take my phone and grab as many photos and videos as possible, hoping to show the royal family and help them discover a bit more about the territory. No one had been invited there, they all said, so they had absolutely no idea what to expect or what to advise me.

"Where we're going sprout, it will burst in flames and burn your sweet little thighs," he moved his eyes quickly towards where the phone sat in my jean pocket then reverted them back to me.

I huffed and went to settings, pressed the factory reset option and shoved the phone in the glove compartment, as he'd asked. The last thing I needed was someone finding the phone and accessing my socials or bank accounts.

"Happy now?" I made a face that caused Rhylan to allow a shade of his usual smirk to pop out.

"Come on top of me."

"What?" I asked with wide eyes, unable to believe the nerve on this guy. He had just been brooding about my friend and now he wanted me to make a move on him. Was he crazy?

"We need to be close to appear and we agreed not to leave the car. If I only take you by the hand, your particles may not transport as well. Do you want to risk it?" he looked at me as if to say that it would be idiotic to even consider it.

"Urgh," I could not hold my frustration in and snarled at Rhylan, just as I moved from my seat and tried to get my legs on either side of his hips, ending up straddling him.

Another smirk, this time a complete and satisfied one illuminated his face while his hands grabbed me and pulled me even tighter. I was physically sitting on Rhylan, our breaths connected, faces inches away.

"Hold on, princess," he whispered and placed his head on my shoulder and a hand over my head, to protect me from injury.

I did as instructed and held him as tightly as I could, closing my eyes and allowing his body to transport mine.

"You can open now," Rhylan said as the hand he had placed over my head started moving up and down, in a soft caress.

Struck by a sudden wave of heat, I shifted in Rhylan's arms, realising we landed in the sand, right in front of a wide entrance to a cave.

I disentangled my limbs from his and jolted away from his touch, yet as soon as I did my skin urged to seek the broken contact again. I waved away the silly thoughts and pushed myself farther back, allowing the fireling to rise and shake off the sand from his jacket and pants.

"Where are we?" I asked looking around to see people gathering their belongings after a hot beach day.

"Goa," he replied. "India," as he continued to recover his impeccable stance by brushing every grain of sand away.

"Oh my god," I looked around like a drunkard, moving from side to side and spinning in circles, unable to grasp what had just happened. That in less than a minute, he moved us from a parking spot in New York to a beach in India.

"I've never even been to India," I said, struggling to keep the panic inside. "I don't have any documents on me, what if the police—"

"Anwen," Rhylan's fingers danced across my face in a soothing motion, forcing my eyes to meet his stare. "We will not stay here long. No one will find you. You are safe," he uttered slowly, trying to make my brain listen.

It worked. Trapped inside Rhylan's gaze and slowing my breathing, I calmed myself enough to stop shaking. Only then, did the faerie release me, but not before placing his lips on my forehead and trailing behind a small kiss. My entire body swirled with electricity at the contact. What had he done?

"Is Coke your poison?" he asked before I had time to move away or even protest.

"What?" I asked incredulously, unsure what he meant.

"We are not progressing until your sugar levels spike higher than a six-year-old's on Halloween. A Halloween with the good kind of candy," he smiled sweetly and I could not contain a choking laugh.

"Are you going to magic a can of coke for me with your shifting powers?" I questioned, half hoping that it would be the case.

"No, I'm going to buy it from that man over there," Rhylan replied with a raised eyebrow, as though the answer was obvious, and pointed to a stall on the beach.

I nodded at the ridiculousness of the situation and took a seat on the sand, quietly waiting for him to bring me the promised drink. He gave me a final scan to make sure I would be alright on my own, then nodded to himself and headed towards the man. My eyes followed him all the way, not having anything else to do. Or at least that's what I told myself.

I enjoyed watching him move, following the imperial stance of his body, the way his muscles stretched any kind of clothing he wore, not enough to make him look too muscular, but enough to make him a gods damned sexy man. The way he shifted, the way he walked and talked when he threw those grins and his snarky remarks, all of it made me like Rhylan. I had gotten used to him, to his presence around me, to his mood swings and mockery, the teasing and the protection I had not expected on his end.

I cared about Rhylan.

"Coke, kitkat, some kind of sugar cookies and a coconut," he displayed his purchases in front of me with pride.

"Do you want me to become diabetic?" I giggled but grabbed both the coke and the chocolate with a quick thank you smile and started chipping away at the dark cubes.

"I want you to be healthy and keep you from fainting when you see lover boy. That would be too dramatic, even for me," he grinned theatrically and took a seat on the sand by my side. Which went against all his struggles to clean himself when we first arrived, but he did not seem to mind.

Bumping my shoulder to his affectionately, I extended a line of kitkat that was already broken in the wrapper, inviting him to have a taste. Just like all those weeks back in Evigt.

"Are you excited to go back home?" I don't know why I asked but he seemed content to take the lead and chat while I ate.

"It's like every other trip. After years of being away from home, you start to discover that you don't know where you belong anymore. The beings left behind remain the same while you change and evolve, but the moment you come back, it's to realise they are the ones who evolved and continued without you."

"I'm sorry," I murmured and opened the bag of sugar cookies, offering him the first pick.

"Don't be," he said, grabbing the smallest cookie he could find in that huge bag and shoving it in his mouth. "Immortality sucks," Rhylan said bitterly.

I felt sorry for him and kept away the need to hug him, so I grabbed a few more cookies and shoved them in my mouth, keeping myself busy with the sugar and cleaning my fingers by sucking and licking the remaining icing, just like a small child would.

Rhylan studied my movements and silently approved every piece that went into my mouth and only when he seemed satisfied with how much I'd consumed did he ask if I felt better and strong enough to continue our journey.

The appearing magical power they possessed was called 'matter jumping,' he explained and all those who had a direct line to the gods and the matter composing the earth could do it. It consisted of splitting atoms and forcing them to reappear in quick succession to a specific place, but they needed to have walked in that particular spot at least once throughout their life, so the connection could be established.

I thought of it as one of those PlayStation games my brother loved to play when he was younger, where he had to discover a map and moved his character from one place to another with the press of a button, once he conquered the territory. One of the many magnificent things the fae could do. Though it consumed a lot of their energy very rapidly, so they avoided taking advantage of the ability.

After I finished the last drop of coke, and Rhylan took it from my hand to place it in the nearest recycling bin, he stepped dangerously close to me and grabbed me in his arms, tightly and assuringly. Words did not seem necessary, we both knew the purpose of the embrace, but my heart started racing and pounding out of my chest, accelerating my breathing and forcing me to put my hands on Rhylan and grab tightly onto him, relishing in the touch. My hands splayed themselves onto his back, feeling those tight muscles and the arch of his shoulders, the way the tension burst at the touch and emanated heat onto my palm.

"Sprout, you are no longer home," I heard Rhylan's voice announcing our arrival and as I unplugged myself from him — even though I had to force my hands to let him go — I scanned the surroundings to find ourselves inside a cave.

Only it did not look like a cave, there was no water carving it and my breath drew dust. It looked like an underground tunnel.

"Are we there?" I asked incredulously, scanning the fae with weariness, afraid that this would turn into one of those tricks where he is nice one moment and a cunning liar the next.

"Yes," he said with a small smirk, regaining his general composure, "and no," he added with a wicked grin, which I knew came into place only to piss me off.

"What does that mean?" I questioned, unsure and unwilling to play this game right now, not when we found ourselves somewhere underground. He might as well disappear and leave me there to turn into a dried mummified body.

"It means that this is as far as we can appear. The rest we'll have to walk." Announcing the itinerary, Rhylan proceeded to remove his designer black jacket and fold it carefully to rest on his left forearm. His right hand shifted to me, an offering to grab it.

"I'll manage on my own," I replied curtly and crossed my arms to point out that I would not be willingly touching him any longer. Not that my body didn't crave it.

Just like with Ansgar, I felt a connection every time he was near me or when our bodies touched. But when I was with Ansgar, I felt warm and eager to touch his body, to reduce the space between us and situate myself as close to him as I could, with Rhylan I felt need and urgency. To connect to him, to forge his skin and mine together and craved that closeness.

"Very well," he said with a perverted grin. "I would follow closely if I were you. Soldiers lurk about these corridors and may stab you before I even have a chance to speak."

Saying this, he turned and started walking towards a very dark corridor, without waiting for me to follow or even caring if I started trailing him or not. I didn't know if he was joking so I chose the safe option and followed Rhylan so closely that if he stopped for a mere second, I would have bumped into his large muscled back.

I did however admire how his deltoids stretched the black shirt he wore, forcing it to fall perfectly moulded to his sculpted back and I did not mind that view one bit.

"These tunnels are millennia old, they won't fall on you so stop fidgeting," he finally spoke after a long silent journey, through which I kept crouching and placing a hand over the top of my head to keep anything from falling on me.

"Why are we here?" I asked, more to keep him talking, because at that moment, his voice was the only familiar thing I had and I needed to hold onto it.

"Many years ago, about ten kings back, they had an idea to try and carve into the southern parts to find another exit. The work took centuries, only to find that the other end led straight to the sea."

"Why did the king want to carve tunnels?" I questioned, curious.

"In case you haven't realised, sprout, my people cannot leave this place, and when they manage to do so, they are brutally murdered. So carving tunnels was seen as the only chance they had to freedom," he explained with a bitter voice.

That meant that his people lived underground. And had always done so.

"What about the sun?" It was a silly question but the first one that popped into my mind. If they were forced to live underground, how could they see the sun? Cultivate crops?

"You might want to say goodbye to that thought during your stay. Only the soldiers meet the sun during battle, and it usually turns out to be the last thing they see."

"But—" I wanted to ask yet Rhylan stole the words from my mouth with his answer.

"How do these people live? How do they raise their children? How do they see the stars and the rainbows? I'll make it simple for you, princess, they don't. So while you're here, you might wanna keep your stories about flying through clouds or taking photos in a bathing suit to a minimum."

Rhylan continued to head downwards, following intricate tunnels and shifting quickly to the left or right, the fact that he'd done this a million times before poignantly obvious.

"You said there'll be soldiers," I questioned while struggling to follow his rapidly increasing pace.

"Did you not see enough of them?" he huffed.

"I didn't see any," I replied with a pant, struggling to follow him when thankfully, Rhylan stopped and turned, giving me a chance to breathe.

"We've passed about a hundred so far," he took the time to look at me and scan me from head to toe, to make sure I wasn't having another low blood sugar crisis.

"Where? We've only passed corridors with statues and torches, I protested.

Rhylan grinned abruptly, all his worry dissipating in a second. "Those were the soldiers," he offered with an understanding smile.

"What?" I replied in shock. "No, those were statues, they were white!" To get technical, the statues we passed looked more on the grey colour scheme than pure white but I attributed that to the darkness and settled dust.

"Most beings have ashen skin here. There is no sun, princess," he spoke as though he'd received the gold medal and I, only an award for participating, but he did manage to make my mouth drop slightly.

Of course. If the people didn't see the sun, their skin could not produce melanin. And if they were born inside this place, they would lose their skin colour through generations. Rhylan must have seen the realisation on my face because he asked, "Ready to meet the king?"

"What? No!" I stopped and grabbed Rhylan's wrist, making him turn to me once again and capturing his attention. "You said you are going to take me to see Ansgar. That's why I'm here. I'm not interested in meeting any kings or visiting this god's forsaken place. Take me to Ansgar, now!" I adopted my most fearsome tone and hoped it would have the desired effect.

What I saw in Rhylan at that moment made me realise every shred of control I thought I had in this relationship had only been a ruse to keep me in line and possibly, keep him entertained. His pupils widened and stretched out the darkness of his eyes, so bleak that it might have enveloped the entire passageway and sucked out the light. His generally snarky smirk turned into a grim curl of his lips, teeth bared. The exact embodiment of that I had first come to know in the forest, the deep voice that attacked me with no mercy and showed no sign of compassion. A being forged by fire and pain, with no remorse.

"Princess, you and I need to have a very serious talk and we need to have it quickly." To my surprise, Rhylan abandoned his elegant composure and grabbed both my shoulders, sliding me onto the tunnel wall and sticking me into the mud as if I were an unwanted portrait. His hands grabbed at my skin, reached within my bones, and kept me from moving, forcing my full attention to stagnate on his face.

"You have entered the oldest faerie kingdom, the most

dangerous and ruthless one, where the beings will show you no mercy or give you a chance to rectify even a glint of those silly things you constantly do or say. And I will not be able to protect you all the time." He stopped and looked at my trembling lips, my shaking features, and the tears that suddenly felt the need to sprout from my eyes. "Nor will I want to," he added.

I forced myself to calm down, urging my body not to show him that I was scared, that he had that power over me. It must have been useless because he looked at me with pitiful eyes and continued my induction. "The king and queen decide everyone's fate, and if they give you an order, you will not remain alive unless fulfilled. There is no room for negotiation, talks, or more time, you will do as commanded and speak with the utmost respect your vocabulary is capable of. Otherwise, you will not reach Ansgar, because you will be long dead."

My body did not pick a worse moment to start shivering. I did not know if caused only by his words or by the accumulation of cold damp seeping into my skin, but one thing was clear, my muscles could not hold the tension any longer, and decided to release it at the exact moment Rhylan finished his threat. I wondered what had I gotten myself into and more importantly, how could I get out, because this new Rhylan, this Fear Gorta, the embodiment of pain and suffering, as he liked to describe himself, was a completely new character who did not understand reason and did not seem to want to accommodate any feelings of friendship towards me.

"You are in my home now, and you will play your part," Rhylan finished speaking and removed his hands from me, wiping a bit of mud from his finger on my jacket. Rhylan casually continued walking down the corridors, without acknowledging my presence or uttering a single word, so the only choice I had was to follow him and see where this road lead me.

I did not have much choice, did not know how to get out of there nor knew anyone who could help, so my safest bet was to continue with Rhylan until I found Ansgar to pass him the dagger I kept hidden in the very uncomfortable corset I wore underneath my white t-shirt. White with specks of mud, thanks to Rhylan's new design.

My steps followed in place and I remained close to Rhylan. This time I kept my distance, wanting to avoid another one of these abrupt anger fits and I kept my mouth shut, not wanting to provoke him further. He did not seem to mind and continued walking, though I spotted him stopping or turning from time to time to ensure I caught up or that I remained safe behind him.

Now that I became aware of their existence, I took longer to study the soldiers we passed, their ashen skin and rough features, the leather armour and iron spikes they wore at specific parts of the suit. Armour designed specifically to wound the other faeries, I'd come to realise by the seventh soldier we passed. The iron spikes on their forearms, elbows, shoulders, and knees had been added to give the fire soldiers easy weapon access in an encounter with the other kinds of fae, who would burn and bleed at the touch.

Initially, I experienced a sentiment of pity towards them, at the understanding that they lacked the beauty of the outside world, that they had been banished generation after generation and their bodies had to develop accordingly to live underground. I felt sad to think about people who would not see the sun or a flower throughout their lives, that they would not have picnics or see fireworks or look at the moon at night, but watching these soldiers, the sheer strength and brutality their stance carried, sadness made way for terror.

They had taken the time to evolve into killing machines, trained for war with the sole purpose of revenge. And judging by their armour and the death glares they shared with me, the word 'compassion' did not exist in their vocabulary.

"The king?" I heard Rhylan's voice about thirty feet in front of me, talking to one of the soldiers.

"In the throne room, general." The man answered quickly and shifted in position, adopting a salute towards Rhylan. *General*, he had said. I stepped closer to be able to hear what they were discussing but suddenly, Rhylan started whispering and the soldier replied in the same tone. The only thing I heard was that the cell had been cleared, something about an underground something and a crypto being no more.

"Of course he did," Rhylan huffed and I reached his position close enough to be able to read the anger on his face. May all the gods save whoever had to be on the receiving end.

"Come, Anwen," he addressed me for the first time after shoving me into the wall and made a gesture as if calling his dog, which I did not appreciate and I added it to the list of things I needed to hate Rhylan for.

He walked me through a few more tunnels until the passageways changed to mimic the inside of a palace, with dark marble columns and adorned carpets to mark the way ahead. Even the light source had changed from sporadic torches to huge candelabras that hung from the dark ceiling in precise positioning and made the corridor look very similar to a red carpet event, classy and cold.

"I apologise for not showing you to your rooms and giving you the option to change before meeting the royal family, but we are a bit pressed with time," Rhylan spoke without looking back, as per the new personality he had adopted since stepping inside this place. I did not know or understood why the abrupt shift, but I assumed some of it related to that word the soldier used to address him. General. I did not know much about military rankings, but Ansgar had told me about his brother's titles and 'general' sounded as high as the commander roles Vikram and Damaris held.

"It's alright," I responded quickly. The last thing I needed was for someone to undress me and wrap me in fabric like they'd done in the Earth Kingdom and I was definitely not ready to part with the dagger that probably left a mark by now on the side of my breasts.

"I'll meet the king first," I said and tried to put a bit more excitement into my voice, though I wasn't sure if he could see through it.

"Remember what I said," Rhylan responded as he stopped in front of a huge set of adamant doors with four soldiers on each side of them. The throne room.

I nodded eagerly and took a deep breath, preparing myself for whatever I had to say or do to be allowed to see my prince.

"King Drahden," Rhylan's voice resounded through the walls and into the massive throne room that opened for us. With this, he stepped forth and hurried to his king, whereas I remained step back, amazed by the grandeur of the hall. They called it a throne room but it looked like one of those huge ballrooms where Victorian families used to gather for dances at the Queen's palace.

It looked enormous and stunning, adorned with golden motives and black chandeliers that followed us, grand pillars at the sides sustaining a tall painted ceiling and lots of benches and tables, protected by the archway of the pillars where other faeries gathered.

They looked very different from the soldiers but wore the same ashen skin. The court members adorned their ears and hair, making the grey a canvas for the beauty of all the other elements. The females wore tall hairdos and pompous dresses while the males wore velvet tunics of varying dark colours and black boots, displaying shiny weapons like daggers or swords.

As soon as the general's voice pierced through the crowd, they remained paralysed. Eyes shifted towards Rhylan and the entryway, where I slowly trailed along after him. He stepped with determination, a glorious soldier returning home victorious, chin raised and shoulders back, elongating his tall posture even more, if such a thing was possible.

The respect Fear Gorta commanded in their eyes evident. The way all the faeries turned towards him and followed his movements like drying plants following a cloud of rain, with the hope that salvation might have just walked through the door.

I, on the other hand, looked small and insignificant beside him, a human who had no purpose stepping inside their kingdom and judging by their frowning and distaste towards me, the only reason

251

I remained inside the room was because of my closeness to Rhylan and the fact that we had clearly arrived together.

"Rhylan," the king responded and stood from his throne on the dais to welcome the general inside a hug. With a smile. A genuine smile. He must have been the first person I saw in my life that looked truly happy to see Rhylan appear out of nowhere.

I remained back, not daring to step on the crimson carpet leading to the king's dark sculpted throne or even set foot on the stairs that lead closer to where the two faeries remained in an embrace, whispering greetings and words of encouragement to one another.

I took the time to scan my surroundings and try to get acquainted with the arrangements of the throne, the new kind of faeries and their garments, and the fact that everything here looked to be displaying dark shades of barely visible colours. Next to the king's imposing throne that could probably seat three people and had such a tall backrest that easily reached ten feet in height, I spotted another throne, a smaller one, if it could be named so, with the same sculpted adornments and a few pillows to make the stay more comfortable. It led me to think the king had another companion on that dais, overlooking his people.

My heart jumped out of my chest, hoping that Ansgar had been sitting there, that they arranged a throne befitting a prince and that he could walk in any second and take his usual seat, without expecting me to jump into his arms.

"What is a human doing here?" I heard the king's voice and the mention of the word *human* brought me back from my wishful thinking since it could clearly only refer to me.

I shifted to the king and saw the older man penetrate me with a questioning gaze. He looked very different from Ansgar's father. Where King Farryn had an imposing stance and a wide torso, making him look like he would everlast the toughest winds, just like the strong roots of a tree, this king barely stood, his grey hair shining through overly adorned garments, meant to distract the eyes of the beholder from old age towards the display of power.

"This is Anwen Odstar, the human we discussed," Rhylan dismissed it and tried to shift the king's attention from me by placing a hand on his shoulder and making a move to shift him towards the throne. But the king remained in place, his eyes persisting on me.

"She displays sentiments of passion."

Before Rhylan could dismiss me again, I took the chance to speak.

"I am here to see Prince Ansgar," I said. "I am his mate." Not sure if that made it a good or a bad thing, since Vikram and the royal family warned me of possible repercussions, but I wanted to be truthful and hoped he understood our connection and how much I wanted to see my prince.

Apparently not, because as soon as I spoke the words, Rhylan's face turned white. White as snow, all colour abandoning his features as he remained immobilised, his jaw moving slowly, barely perceptible, up and down, as though he was trying to speak yet no words could be released from his mouth.

"Are you now?" If Rhylan's face showed terror, the king looked like I just brought in a ten-tier red velvet cake.

"My king, the human is confused from the travel," Rhylan finally spoke and moved from his position on the dais, sliding downwards, slowly stepping towards me, to cover me from the king's field of vision. I sensed his desperation, his dire need to take me away and keep me hidden. But I could not understand why. That was the sole reason for my visit, our deal, everything he had promised.

"Allow me to discover that for myself," the king spoke and with a single eye gesture, shifted Rhylan out of the way, displaying me fully to him.

"Tell me, human. What is your connection to the prince?" He looked intrigued and ready to devour my words. This was my opportunity, I realised. I had the king's ear and I could make him understand, we could reach a bargain or some kind of a contract in exchange for Ansgar.

"It is true; I am Ansgar's mate. It can be confirmed by the royal family in Sylvan Regnum. I saw them only three days ago and they send their kindest regards." I did not know if that was something expected of me to say, but I thought it would look good and as my entire body shook under the sole attention of the king and the entire hall, I didn't really know what the best dialogue response would be.

"So you're here to see the prince and make him whole again?" his eyes sparkled with delight.

"My king, the human doesn't understand the situation and we should first—"

"Yes, indeed. I am here to see Ansgar," I replied before Rhylan had a chance to speak and mess this whole thing up. What was the point in bringing me here if he was now trying to keep me from seeing Ansgar? I hoped the king was more sensible and helped me get to my prince.

"Wonderful," the king rubbed both his hands together, mimicking a warming up by the fire gesture, and sat on his throne, more relaxed and joyful than before. Meanwhile, Rhylan looked like someone was cutting his leg off and didn't have the ability to scream.

"My king, we had an understanding," he uttered, the words slitting from him in an eruption of anger.

"I am merely fulfilling the human's wish, general. Wasn't that the understanding?" King Drahden looked the face of innocence, which made me realise that whatever this was, I had played right into his hand.

"Yet she does not know the terms, doesn't understand the situation. Allow me to instruct the human first and then we can have a discussion," Rhylan insisted, almost pleading with the king, yet his eyes remained fixed on me, wide and scared as if trying to convince me, to communicate with me and stop me from asking for Ansgar.

"You should have instructed her better, dearest Fear Gorta. The human has chosen," he said with a cunning smile. "Alas, to prove my generosity to my trusted general, I will allow her to ask again," the king nodded, making his crown shake in between his locks of silver hair.

"Gratitude," Rhylan released a breath and a bit of colour came back into his eyes until the king's words made us all shift to him.

"Now." King Drahden gestured towards me, a command to step closer and on the dais, where both of them stood. I hesitated for about three seconds, debating what to do next and looking scared at Rhylan's reaction. I had never seen him like that, so terrorised, like his life was in immediate danger, but before I could decide, a group of soldiers appeared out of nowhere and circled me, making me understand that I had no choice but to follow the king's command.

So I climbed the five stairs separating us and reached the throne, bowing with a small curtsy.

He looked pleased, so he settled more comfortably in his throne and voiced one question.

"What do you wish from me, human?"

I slowly turned my gaze to Rhylan, who urged me with pleading eyes before I said, "I wish to see prince Ansgar, immediately."

"Of course," the king smiled, whereas Rhylan looked like he was going to faint. "Marreth, please do the honours," the royal spoke again and another soldier appeared out of nowhere and stepped on the dais, beside me, with a long bow to the king.

"This is my commander, Marreth. He used to be my *first* commander, but your mate didn't feel too comfortable with that arrangement so he made some changes of his own," the king smiled. Not knowing what to do, I smiled back. "He will escort you to your mate."

With a nod, we were both dismissed and the soldier made a full 180, so I had no choice but to do the same and follow him.

"My king, I beg of you, this cannot be done. It cannot happen." I heard Rhylan's voice and turned to see him being restrained by several guards while trying to get to us.

"You can see her again tomorrow, general. That is if her mate doesn't snatch her from you first," the king's content tone of voice was the last thing I heard before being pushed away by the soldiers.

When I saw Rhylan in such a state, my first instinct was to turn and go back to him, but the six soldiers surrounding me became violent and grabbed at me, pushing me out of the throne room. It was only when the doors closed that the commander ordered them to release me and grabbed me by the arm to silently lead me through a vast chain of narrowing hallways.

When I realised that they led back to the way we came from, the nice candelabras and adorned carpets replaced by mud and dirt, I started arguing and asking questions, demanding answers, shaking and protesting, but it was no use. The male's grip on my arm didn't loosen one bit and the soldiers trailing us did not stop, not even when I threw myself to the ground and refused to continue walking.

One of them made a move to hit me with the hilt of his sword in an attempt to force me to stand, but the commander stopped them with the threat of not wanting to be the one to mark the general's guest. He then grabbed me in his arms and continued to walk with me until I saw no point in struggling or resisting and relaxed, as much as one can in those conditions.

I took a moment to analyse the commander, his rough features, and the scars on his neck. They looked like someone had tried to stab his jugular, but even so, he seemed softer than the others. Not in stance or body, because he was as strong as any warrior and probably wore a ton of muscles underneath that armour, but something about him made me ease into his touch, knowing that he would not hurt me, that some part of him was not as dark as the rest of the firelings accompanying me.

"Lean on my shoulder," I heard him utter through his teeth, making it sound like a huff from the extra weight he had to carry.

I looked at him with a questionable gaze and a raised eyebrow, telling the fireling that there was no way in hell I would sit in a lover's embrace with him, but his eyes shifted abruptly from me towards his shoulder and back again, a silent command that I had no choice but obey.

When I did, he shifted his right hand to push my body in an upward position, forcing my chin to stick to his neck, but before I could object, he started whispering into my ear.

"Ansgar is not alright, they tortured him for a long time then drugged him. He lost his mind and he is killing everyone. Going inside his cage is suicide."

I didn't have time to comment, because he shifted me back and continued walking with me as though nothing had happened. I struggled to find myself, to reach for a reaction, to understand what was happening and what he had just told me. Ansgar's cage. *Cage.*

That Ansgar, *my Ansgar* had been tortured. Tortured! And drugged. And now he had lost his mind. What had they done to him? He had suffered for so long while that bastard Rhylan was living the life, having cocktails on the beach and fucking my friend. A burst of rage came onto me and I knew that the next time I saw Fear Gorta I would make him pay. All the attention, all the niceties and friendship had been a ruse to waste time and keep me away from Ansgar. Who was being kept in a cage. A cage!

I asked the fireling to put me down and hurried my step. I started running and forcing all of them to come along with me. I didn't know the way but I kept moving, only to hear some left or right indication when I reached crossroads. I needed to see Ansgar, needed to hold him and tell him everything would be alright. That I would do anything to get him out.

"It's just here on the left," the commander said and I rushed towards the corridor where an entire army stood waiting, swords in hand, their gazes pinned to a metal door.

Iron, I realised. They were keeping him hostage with iron.

I passed them all, forcing them to move out of the way, and banged on the door, screaming Ansgar's name.

"Open the god's damned door," I demanded while shouting at the soldiers, kicking the door with my feet as hard as I could.

"Open it," Marreth's voice came from behind, making all the soldiers stand abruptly and turn to him, some wearing shocked faces. "King's orders," he added when no soldier made a gesture to move.

Some of them nodded and braced themselves, adopting an attack stance, as though an entire army would come rushing through those doors.

"Human," the commander called me to him. "I don't have orders to risk any of the soldiers, so you are on your own. No one who walked through those doors came out alive," he said with a pitying tone, understanding that no matter what he told me, I would go in.

"Open the doors," I confirmed and started walking to the heavy iron gate-like opening.

"Stop right there," a voice I had come to loathe shattered the already darkened walls, leaving small dust vibrations in its wake. Before I had a chance to turn, Rhylan had already caught me by the arm, an unclenching decision preventing me from taking that final step. The doors came to an immediate close and with it, my chance to return to Ansgar.

I became enraged, forgetting everything I was, everything I wanted, and all the times he had recently made me smile, made me feel protected and safe. It was all a ruse, all some mischievous plan of his. I should have known better.

"You do not get to touch me," I roared, withdrawing my skin from his grip as if a venomous bite possessed it. "You do not get to speak to me," I echoed, so decidedly that tiny particles of spit landed on my chin. "You do not get to lie to me again."

"Anwen, please," desperation crumbled in Rhylan's eyes while the soldiers shivered at the words. At their general, begging, pleading in front of a mortal. I did not care, did not have another fragment of patience or understanding towards this man.

"What have you done to him, you bastard?" I accused, watching Rhylan's gaze averting from mine and scanning the soldiers who remained shaking in front of the massive doors.

"He's been tortured for information," I heard the voice of the commander who brought me in and before Rhylan had a chance to interrupt, I shifted to him, placing my hands on his shoulders. Even though I barely reached him, the man being as tall as the nearby columns, I did my best to hold him in a threatening stance, using the remainder of my strength to shake him.

"What else? Why is he locked away like this? Why are these men pissing themselves at the thought of opening those doors?"

The guy who carried me looked at Rhylan first, fearing how he would be made to pay for this information, but decided against it and took pity on me.

"When torture did not work, the king commanded to turn him." Reading my frown, he explained. "A serum is forcefully applied to the body over a duration of time, to make one forget. By the end of the treatment course, the skills remain but the mind vanishes. The final dose drives a primordial feeling, which will overpower the rest and remain for the future. The sentiment created needs to be loyalty, towards the kingdom. So one becomes a soldier."

"You—you want to use Ansgar as a soldier? For the firelings?" My hands started shaking uncontrollably, forcing me to release the man's garments and unpin him from the column he had been situated against. "You want to make Ansgar kill people?" I continued shaking, the muscles in my cheeks forming a vortex of tears and trembling.

"It is done only with the strongest males, they become the best soldiers. They know their army's tactics and can strike with the force of an entire legion if trained properly," the commander explained.

"Something went wrong," it came Rhylan's turn to speak. When I took you to Evigt, I received notification of the events. Which is why I brought you here sooner than arranged." He looked at me as though I would perfectly understand his reasons and even give him a hug for it. What he received was the opposite.

A garland of swearing and filthy words gathered at my mouth, along with fists splaying in his direction. He docked and spared his face from each one, yet the heaviness of the words found their mark. His face said that, at least.

"What went wrong?" I murmured to no one in particular.

"The final dose," Rhylan said. "We don't know why, the commander who administered it had done so hundreds of times."

My stomach jerked. They took away hundreds of men from their homes, doing gods know what to them and then making them crazy, returning them to fight against their kingdoms, their families. Whatever compassion I had felt for these people living underground turned into a loathing puddle and I knew I would never find it in me to understand their reasoning. They were monsters.

"After the final dose, Ansgar came overpowered by revenge. What is clear is that he killed two commanders and over a hundred and fifty soldiers, in the most gruesome ways. He is taking pleasure in it, playing with his prey, like a wounded beast. That's the reason he is in there, Anwen," Rhylan made a gesture to step closer to me but I immediately backed away, rejecting his closeness. He understood and respected my space.

"The reason why he is in there is because no one managed to kill him yet. Every single soldier or troop dispatched inside did not come back. He is somehow keeping his strength even though he has lived in an iron cage since he was changed. It took a day to capture him but the king made a misjudgement in thinking the error can be amended with iron, thinking that a soldier like this cannot be put to waste. He reconsidered shortly," Rhylan sighed.

"What you are telling me is that Ansgar is trapped in there and someone is going to kill him?" my voice trembled, my body finding more resources to summon shaking.

"He cannot be redeemed, Anwen. And he cannot be let loose either. The king allowed you here because he knew you would not survive, he knew how much you mean—" he stopped, not allowing the words. And I did not want to think about what he was going to say.

"Unless provided with proper stimuli, there have been cases," the commander intervened with a tone that announced he clearly knew what he was talking about.

"That is out of the question. Those cases were not as severe as this one," Rhylan retorted.

"But there is hope," my eyes sparkled at the thought, heart becoming steadier. "There is a way to bring him back?" I asked the man.

"If there is, I do not know it," he admitted, and I read a dash of sadness in his voice.

"Open the doors," I repeated.

"I cannot let you do this, Anwen," Rhylan's eyes pleaded, looking at me as though I had become a butterfly that just got out of the shell and was ready to fly away forever. The loss and panic in his eyes were enough to make anyone halt their decision, but not me. I would not lose the man I loved yet again.

I would not lose anyone I loved again.

I could not save my brother. I had to watch the light vanish from his eyes and witnessed how Ansgar turned into dried leaves in my arms. I had been through hell, suffered more than I could gather and

I would not give up this last chance, this crumb of hope, because of fear.

"The only way I'm leaving here, Rhylan, is either dead or through those doors. Your choice," I inclined my head and pinned him with the strongest gaze I could muster, forcing him to understand the truth in my decision.

He exhaled a breath I did not realise he had been holding and blinked once. His eyelashes fell heavy, defeated, dragging surrender across his face.

"I'll reopen them at dawn. Either you come out alive with your fuckboy in check, or I will wipe away your remains when I drag out his dead body."

Darkness pulverised across his features, making him become that feared ancient fire spirit, one that accepted defeat but had still won the battle.

"Open the doors," commanding darkness roared through him as he spoke.

Ansgar

Chapter Twenty

Light crept across my eyelashes, awakening sharp pain. I hadn't seen light for some time, and my eyes took a moment to react. The iron hinges squeaked like a harpies' yawn, allowing a silhouette to form. Another soldier walking to his death.

I felt sick, tired, and wanting for it to be all over yet part of me pushed forward, urging to find and dispose of another kill. Blood, the pinnacle of all my cravings and the only reason I remained alive. To draw more of it.

Surprisingly, this soldier had preferred to bring a torch and slowly walked inside my cell with minuscule footsteps, looking more concerned with the environment and the piling dead bodies than with a swift attack. He must be a youth, no experienced soldier would choose the comfort of the battle environment rather than a quick attack, especially since I proved I could take anyone and leave no survivors.

I wanted to creep out of the shadows and snap his neck in the next second, but since they had resumed to inexperienced soldiers, the battle options must have proven limited and I did not know when I would get my next victim.

At the thought, my heart plummeted, squeezing away that urge to hurt, the desire for vengeance and blood. Panic bloomed through my entire being. What would happen to me once this was over? Will I finally find peace?

I didn't have more than a few moments to think about it, because I had to act. I decided to play with this soldier like a lynx with a freshly caught salmon and draw as much pleasure as I could from this catch, not knowing when I would get the next one.

And pleasure I would take indeed, I thought to myself as the soldier took another step and allowed the light from the torch to shed some luminescence over his features. Better said, over her features. They had sent a female.

Blood boiled inside of me, rage and abhorrence filling up in my veins. The sick bastards had no more soldiers to spare and decided to appeal to whatever mercy they thought I would find.

Hoping that I would not kill a female.

I shifted and my movement must have attracted her attention towards the corner of the cell, where I'd remained hidden, next to the iron bars. I welcomed the touch, the pain, and I'd gone and found the biggest amount of iron and laid myself next to it. In my moments of loneliness, I hoped it killed me and allowed this misery to end, but the arrival of every new soldier had abruptly healed the wounds and pushed me into another killing spree.

"Ansgar?" her voice pierced the darkness, forcing the clouds of nothingness apart, just enough to make herself heard deep within my mind.

"Ansgar, my love, are you here?" The voice continued, stunning me with the calling and dash of affection that came along with that name.

One thing I was certain of, I could be no one's *love*, nor was I deserving of such a title. I understood their plan and hatred flourished like a night's queen flower inside of me, quick and deadly. I would not allow myself to fall victim to a female, one that was sent to lure me into surrendering, appeal to whatever gentle part she hoped to dig out of me, and then kill me in my sleep. I had come too far to let the beautiful voice of such a beast destroy everything.

I jerked away from the approaching light and stepped aside, moving swiftly and silently around her, allowing her to walk around the cell and search for me until I stood behind her, in the perfect position to snap that pretty neck.

I would not deny it, the female's presence stirred something inside of me. Her scent and the way her wavy hair fell on her shoulder, the aspect of her light skin that had the potential to become the softest thing I would touch. Part of me felt ready to connect with the female, to at least have some fun and saturate innate manly urges, but I forced myself contained. Best to be done with it quickly and not allow enough time to feel remorse. Treat her like the enemy that she was.

My hand caught her by the neck so abruptly that she did not have time to squeal. The female paralysed at my touch, dropping the torch she had been carrying and adopting a statuesque demeanour. Even though her body struggled to emanate calm, her heart did not lie. She must have been terrified, that piteous heart racing like a new-born siren towards the first scent of blood.

"Ansgar," she murmured again, only this time the sentiment I expected to find did not come. Even though my fingers pierced both sides of her neck and pressed on her jugular, able to bend her bones in the simplest of twists without fully moving my fingers, she did not look frightened at all. Her body relaxed into mine, back touching my chest as she let herself fall onto me, connecting to my body as much as she could.

"Make another move and I'll snap your neck. I'll kill you where you stand, spawn of evil," I threatened, taking a step back to remove myself from her touch. My chest did not like losing contact with her warm back, protesting through each of the senses and I struggled to keep a clear mind. I did not understand why, but every part of me called to connect with this female.

Struggling to detach myself from her while trapping her neck, I decided to allow her to twist towards me, to face me fully, so I could take a better look. The last thing I wanted to do was press on the wrong bone and rip her jaw, I did not fancy making her die slowly and painfully. So I shifted my fingers towards her jaw, pressing tightly, and forced her to turn, following the hand that held her captive like a rabbit in a snare, until she faced me fully.

At the sight of me, her eyes widened, forcing my fingers to press tightly onto her, which she did not seem to mind or be scared of. For whatever reason, seeing me had the opposite of my intended effect, and the female looked joyful and relieved, rather than fearful for her abruptly shortening life.

"Ansgar…"

She kept repeating that name, over and over, as though she needed to convince herself of what she was seeing, what she was experiencing in my presence.

"It's really you…" she barely murmured in between sobs, her voice broken and shaking, just like the rest of her body.

I continued to hold her by the neck, feeling like a youngling who'd caught a chicken but could not force myself to make that life-ending twist. All the while, the female kept trying to reach more of me, and when she understood that my fully extended arm wanted to prevent exactly that, she went on to catch my wrist and *caress* it with both her hands, crying louder at the contact with my skin, worshipping every part of me that I allowed her to reach.

My heart pumped louder, overpowering my mind and demanding more of her touch, forcing me to close the distance between us. I could not deny it, the female was good, *too good*. Whatever her purpose, she avoided a quick death, entangled me in whatever her ruse was and made me curious enough to follow through.

Her utter joy at discovering me, the reverence with which she regarded me and the building sensation in my chest forced me to allow this to play out. To let the woman have her fun and try whatever it was that she came to do. For that, I had to make sure she did not carry any weapons, and to achieve this quickly, without her realising my intention until after its completion, I removed my hand from her neck and took a step towards the female, situating myself right in front of her, only a few inches separating our breaths.

"Baby," she whispered and plastered herself across my chest, *hugging* me. Hugging me like her life depended on it, like she wanted to press onto my chest so tightly that her own heart would pierce into mine to adopt the same beat. As though she had waited for this moment a long while.

Instinctively, I placed my arms around her and caught her in an embrace, both because that damned feeling in my chest demanded me to and out of necessity to feel for daggers. I traced my fingers across her skin, across her body, from her shoulders to her back, to her rear, and down her hips in long and soothing strokes. Through it all, she exhaled and only held me tighter, if such a thing was possible.

Her head remained buried in my chest, her tiny arms splayed across my torso, clinging to me without a speck of fear or intranquility. This female was completely trusting me with her life. And I didn't know what I'd done to deserve it.

"Why are you doing this?" I questioned, carefully sliding a finger across her cheek and caressing the soft skin. It felt wet and velvety, the contact managing to rise a long dash of goose bumps across my back. "Why are you here?" I asked again when I received no other answer than a continuously tight embrace and deep inhales into my chest. The female did not seem to care that I was covered in festering wounds and dried blood and breathed me in with the angst of a long-awaited reunion.

Had I known her before all this?

It could be the only reasonable explanation, seeing as she did not look like a fireling. Even though her skin was pale, it didn't look ashen and a few sun-kissed dashes across her cheekbones suggested she had recently seen natural light.

Aware that I would receive no reply nor would I have a chance to talk to the female until she had her full in sniffing and hugging me, I allowed her to continue and relaxed inside her embrace, for whatever unknown reason. My initial reaction was to put a halt to it, to grab her arm and stop any intention she had of connecting with me, but her touch was soft and determined, grabbing at me with eagerness and addiction, hard enough to grab a proper hold of me yet gentle, as if she was too scared to harm me.

"You're hurt," she observed once her hands moved across my back and through a hole in my shirt, compliments of a stab wound. The realisation woke her from the need for connection and made her detach herself from me, though very reluctantly, I might add. Even though her body made a motion to withdraw from my own, her hands still lingered on my shoulders and she kept them in place while she stepped to my side and then towards my back to observe the wound more carefully.

I instantly heard a gasp and knew the female found the marks. I didn't know how many wounds I had acquired during my rampage through the dark corridors, nor did I have a chance to heal them, since I had either been too busy killing enemies or barred in iron, which incapacitated most of my power.

"Ansgar, your back..." she stopped in place, her palms gently sliding onto my shoulder blades and down my back, touching and discovering the abundance of wounds it must have displayed.

"We need to get you treated immediately, they look terrible. I'm no doctor but I know how dangerous they can be."

Her hands were shaking, as well as her voice, yet she tried to maintain as much of her composure as she mustered. She managed to lift what remained of my clothing and I wordlessly collaborated, raising my hands to allow her to pull the garment off, leaving me shirtless in front of the female. Her eyes summoned a mixture of emotions I struggled to understand. Initially I thought I spotted lust across her face, but the sentiment quickly came replaced with something else. It looked like rage. Or dread. I could not properly place it.

"Who are you?" I asked, unsure of what the answer would be. Of what I wanted it to be. If she told me she was indeed a fireling, then I would have to remove this newly acquired sentiment of peace and dispose of the female as I'd done with the other members of her kind. At the thought, a sharp pain pierced my chest telling me what I already knew. What I dreaded. That I did not want to harm her, that for whatever reason, this creature had settled that need for hatred and bloodshed. That for a sparse moment, she had given me peace.

"Anwen," she answered sweetly, a speck of a smile appearing on her face.

"Anwen," I repeated. "Anwen," I said it again, the sound a balm to my soul. "And why are you here, Anwen?" I could not help myself, I had to find a reason to say it again without making it obvious that I fed on the sound.

"I came to get you out," she immediately replied, then made a grimace, like something truly displeased her and felt the need to add.

"Of this cell," she sighed. "Not sure what we'll do about leaving this kingdom, but we'll figure something out."

I huffed, either she was well trained, repeating those exact words, designed to give me hope and make her look truthworthy, or she actually believed one could leave the firelings like they could leave a training session.

"And why would you do that?" I pushed her on it, keeping my emotion in check and only displaying a plain and slightly disgruntled expression.

"Baby, I had no idea what they were doing to you, I thought you were dead. That bastard Rhylan made me think you died in Evigt and only came to find me because he needs something. We made a deal, for him to bring me here, to you," she started to explain but I silenced her with a hand across her mouth, grabbing both her cheeks to silence her.

"First of all, stop calling me that. And second, when you arrived from *where*?" I frowned, keeping her face trapped, to better analyse her features. One look at her irises and I had all the answers I needed. "You're human," I said, to which she nodded, moving her head feverishly through my hold, and even though I had covered half her face, I spotted the portrait of relief on her features. Why was a human here? And why, no matter what I did, was she not scared of me?

I released her face and Anwen immediately raised both her hands to touch and slowly massage the muscles I'd hurt. I exhaled an abrupt breath, remorse bringing a bitter taste at the back of my throat. Without grabbing a hold of my instincts, I raised my hand to her face, making her remove her own, and continued the soothing caresses across her left cheek, where I had left pink marks. I couldn't see the severity of them very well, since we only had a torch light, but it seemed to be enough to make her relax once more.

She trusted me, I came to understand. Not only with information but with her own body. She must have known what happened in this cell, and if she didn't, the mangled body parts across the iron room must have given the information she needed, yet the woman did not flinch once under my touch, did not move away when I grabbed her and did not struggle to escape. Whatever it was about me, it gave her a feeling of *safety*.

"I won't call you baby anymore," she apologised, "It's what I kept saying in my dreams and memories of you, so it came to me as a habit, but I understand if you don't like it," she tried to smile, her lips curving just slightly as I continued to caress her cheek.

Whatever possessed my face to do so, I did the same, copying her gesture and smiled back, which made her shy grin extend wider and become plastered across her face, while both her hands touched mine, hanging onto me with desperation.

"I apologise for hurting you," I whispered and closed the space between us. I allowed my other hand to reach her cheek and I now found myself grabbing her face fully and dragging it towards my own. I stopped a couple of inches away.

"It's ok, it's not like it's the first time you try to choke me," she giggled. Observing my frown, Anwen added. "That time you almost made me pass out when we had sex in the shower because Vikram told you women like to be choked?" she raised her brows, like it would help to pinpoint the memory in my head. When I maintained my confused expression, her pupils suddenly widened. "Of course, you don't remember that. I'm an idiot, I'm sorry," she shook her head, as much as she could without making me lose the hold on her face.

My eyes widened at the lightness with which she mentioned such things, as though our joining happened as often as taking breath and no regard had to be devoted to it. Yet that smile abruptly faded when her gaze shifted from me and around the cell, scanning, understanding, realising. At once, her pupils shrank, panic mirroring her eyes. Surprisingly, her voice remained sharp enough to continue communicating.

"I know it's wrong of me to ask you for anything right now, but the shock of seeing you alive must have passed and I can't help but start to look around us," she said, grabbing me back from dirty thoughts that had involuntarily penetrated my mind.

"I apologise," I admitted, but removed both my hands from her face, escaping the hold she had on me. I did not want to be too brass and vex the woman, so I released my hold on her and allowed her to escape my touch and retreat if that was what she asked for. She did not. To my surprise and confusion, she stepped even closer to me, her chest so near to mine that every time it drew breath, a union of warmth was created between my bare skin and her breasts.

"I want to say it's okay but I am really freaking out, Ansgar. I feel like I'm gonna be sick soon and I'm very panicky, my hands are starting to shake." She raised both her hands to demonstrate shaking fingers I had not found during her hold. Was it my touch that had held them in place?

"What do you need?"

"For us to get out of here, but that's not gonna happen for hours. And I can't be looking around and seeing all of these parts of...people," she whimpered, tears forming in her eyes and immediately trailing down her cheek. Her muscles started shivering and her eyes moved from place to place, taking in the massacre I had lived through these past few days.

"It was not my intention for you to see this, to create this—it was them or me," I tried to ease her but my words had the opposite effect.

"Oh my god," she wept, her body dropping to the floor as she covered her head with both her hands, shaking uncontrollably. She looked like an injured animal, waiting for whatever beast came first to finish her off.

I dropped to the ground by her side and tried to grab hold of her face again, but her own grip was too strong and all her messy waves entangled with shivering fingers.

Grabbing the shirt she had removed from my back, which remained discarded a few steps away, I tied a sleeve around my wrist and used it as a lash to put off the torch. If seeing the dead bodies caused her to become like this, my reasoning said that darkness could be better. I did not welcome it myself, I'd lived in the darkness and the only source of light came with an attempt on my life, but if that's what would help the woman I had to stick it out.

Once a curtain of blackness draped across the cell, I walked in the direction I had left her in and crouched on the floor, blindly searching for the woman.

I touched part of her leg and felt my way across her body until I found her torso and head, which I grabbed hold of and splayed her across my chest, squeezing her tightly.

She immediately accepted the connection and curled into me, forming a ball with her own body at my side, one hand holding onto my shoulder and the other gripping her knees to her chest. The shaking hadn't stopped, but the sobs became less frequent after a few minutes.

"It's alright, it's just us now. Just you and me. Think about nothing else but this. You and me," I repeated until her brain started to accept the information and allowed her muscles to stop spasming with dreadful intensity. She wasn't completely calm, but it had vastly improved from the trembling mess she had become.

"That door is going to open soon and we'll get out of here," I promised her, deciding to kill whoever came through next time and shove her out.

"I know, it's only a few hours away." She said it more to herself than to me, but it confirmed her words once more. That we would get out of here. Both of us.

I held her for what seemed like hours, gently caressing the sides of her body that I could reach in the darkness in soothing long strokes. I never thought I would feel this lightness again, the uncanny way her fragility and need for protection pierced through me, foregoing hatred and revenge. I did not know how long it would last, but one thing was certain. I knew this woman, and whatever we'd been in the past managed to transform me.

I thought she had fallen asleep a few times, she hadn't said a word and her sobs and shivering visibly calmed, but the trail of constant wetness pouring down my chest told me that she kept crying, only doing so slowly, barely audible.

I did not know when those doors would open if that truly was the case, but I focused all my attention on the female. Even though I could not protect her body from the atrocities she must have seen, I could care for her mind.

"How did we meet?" I asked, a question that would transport her into another world, one that she could feel safe in, one I knew nothing about.

Anwen took a few moments, giving her brain a chance to take in the question and made the jump down the path of memories I had pushed her onto.

A slow exhale, a shadow of a laugh came out of her. "I stabbed you," she said, the voice that sounded raspy with whimpers now a soft clink. "I was attacked in the woods and you came to save me. You took me to your home and cared for me, but I was unconscious so I didn't know who you were. When I woke up, I thought you wanted to rape me so I stabbed you and ran away," she shifted, trying to see my expression through the darkness, but only the direction of her voice and her touch pointed me to where she sat by my side.

"Are you a warrior?" The question made her actually laugh and the sound cut through dark webs in my mind, offering unexpected solace.

"Gods no," Anwen replied, settling on my shoulder in a more

comfortable position. "I still don't know how I managed to do such a cold-blooded thing." She inhaled sharply, realising how the words matched my particular situation. I did not take offence; she spoke the truth. What I had done in this cell, what I had been doing since I woke up in that chamber with the male that kept injecting me, was just that. Cold-blooded attacks.

"Tell me about the woods," I urged, shifting from violent memories.

"Oh, bab...sorry, Ansgar, it's absolutely wonderful," she immediately became excited again. "There's always sunshine, no matter what you do and where you go, the rays will follow you until late evening, and even then, the sunset radiates warmth and wavy hues across the walls until the stars appear. One time, you took me to this plateau on top of a cliff. It was absolutely amazing, the most beautiful thing I'd ever seen, truly a spectacle of light. The plateau is dashed with crystal, which turned smooth from the wind across the years and acts like a mirror to the sky. And we sat right in the middle of it, where the rays of sun connected. I remember being fascinated by it, and I tried to focus on the sunset rather than the way those rays interlocked with your hair. I should've known then," she breathed in, holding something behind. Something she did not want to say just yet.

"It sounds magical," I whispered, grabbing hold of her tighter. I had experienced for myself how cold this cell could become, how the iron bars and columns drew chill from the surrounding ground and became a block of ice. The last thing I wanted for her was to get cold and suffer even more.

"It really is. Honestly, every waking moment I spent by your side felt magical," the woman explained and I sensed a smile in her words.

"Even those choking parts?" I huffed.

"Especially those choking parts," she giggled.

"We must have had some interesting encounters, you and I," I added. From the way she leaned into me, that she did not jerk back at the contact with my injured skin, and the fact that she found solace from this place inside my embrace, I knew we must have been intimate.

"You just focus on getting out of here, and I'll show you interesting," she bumped her shoulder into mine, gently.

We continued to chat and Anwen told me more about the forest, about our first few meetings, and how she cooked for me one day, keeping the information cheery and light. It offered her an escape and as she spoke, a wave of calmness overpowered me at the realisation that I had someone to talk to. Someone who did not want to get information from me or discover my weaknesses so they can attack. Someone who *wanted* to be by my side.

Unknowingly, I let myself float with the sound of her voice, forgetting the pain, the press of the iron against my skin, the wounds, and the dreadful smell of decomposing bodies, and let myself drift into sleep, something I hadn't managed to do in as long as I could remember.

I awoke with voices, approaching at a quick pace. My shaking awake must have done the same to Anwen, because I felt her jerk in the darkness and grab for me, for my face. She placed both her hands on my cheeks and shifted my head towards where she must have been, as though she could see me through the heavy blackness.

"Ansgar, please, I beg you, we need to get out of here," she urged, squeezing my cheeks in between her palms with determination.

"Don't worry, I'll get you out," I said, readying myself for another attack. My pulse started to palpitate, but it did not fill me only with the urge to kill. A new sentiment made way, more powerful than my initial urges had even been. To protect the woman. To do whatever I must to get her to safety.

Anwen sensed it, because she immediately rose alongside me, grabbing me by the arms and squeezing tightly. Or whatever she imagined tight to be.

"No, no, no, you will listen to me," she adopted a motherly voice, explaining things as one would to an inexperienced youth. "I know they've done something to you to make you want to kill people, but the only way I am getting out of here is by your side. If you stay, I stay."

I remained still at her words, a heart-breaking sensation overpowering my senses at the truth she spoke. I knew she would. For whatever reason, the woman would stay here with me.

"I don't want you to do that," I barely said, my voice rasping with emotion.

"That's why both of us need to get out of here. You just have to stop killing people and they'll let us out," she said it like it was the most obvious solution.

I shook my head, even though she could not see it. "You don't know what they've done to me." I stopped. "I don't know what they've done to me," I admitted. "All I want to do is hurt them, destroy them all, until I reach their king and finish him off. There's something inside me that won't let me stop, no matter how much it hurts, no matter how injured I am. Even when I want to stop, give up and let them have me, when I want it all over, it forces me through it, overpowering my wishes. I can't control it, Anwen." I said her name again, the softness of the sound offering temporary relief.

"Oh my god," I heard her say in between sobs, and her body plastered itself across mine in a tight embrace. I returned it eagerly, pleased to feel the connection.

"I'm so sorry, baby," she whimpered as her soft cheeks touched my chest. "We'll get out of here, I swear, we have to." Her determination felt overpowering, pouring some of her hope onto me. It felt as light as a feather, barely perceptible, but it was there. Another new sensation this woman brought into my heart.

The doors opened abruptly and widely as my entire body tensed, readying my muscles for another battle. The light splayed into the cell, illuminating the mangled bodies and gore across the walls and Anwen's face along with it.

Anwen's hazel eyes were wide, scared, and wet, her lower lip trembled and her hands squeezed me tightly.

"I love you," she managed to whisper before soldiers started pouring in.

Anwen

Chapter Twenty-One

Ansgar's face tensed at the sight of the multitude of soldiers making their way inside the cell, an impressive number for the dimensions it held. Splayed along the wall, armed to the teeth and shields high, they formed a barrier. A shower of shivers passed through me at the thought. How many times had they done this before? How many times had they come in huge numbers to attack my mate and how many times did he have to fight them all off to survive?

I barely turned towards them and my instincts screamed to offer Ansgar some kind of protection, so I shoved my back into his chest, trying to cover as much of his body as I could with my own, making myself a human shield. He must have wanted to do the same because he grabbed my shoulders and tried to push me away from him so he could step in front of me, but we both stopped frozen as soon as Rhylan made his way through the iron doors.

Now that light poured through the opening, I had a proper view of the size of the cell and realised that it was entirely made of iron. So last night, when I laid on Ansgar and he rested against the wall, he wasn't actually resting but frying his back against iron just so I could get more comfortable. My heart sank at the realisation and I immediately wanted to check his wounds, remembering how burnt his skin had been when I chained him on the sofa. I didn't even want to think about what had happened to his back at the contact with an iron wall.

I would do whatever it takes to get him out of here.

Rhylan adopted a royal stance as he took a single step through the door, even though most of his body remained outside the cell, and only half of his face and torso had made it through. He looked different, better kept than ever, his dark hair gleaming and determined eyes piercing our minds. He adopted the kingdom's attire, I assumed, a dark velvet tunic and ebony pants, knee-high black boots, and a cloak, adorned at the shoulders with plated ornaments. He truly looked like a king.

"Good morning," he uttered with a wicked grin, shifting his gaze from me towards Ansgar and back. "It's ...nice to find you both alive," he spat. "Apologies if the reunion was not up to standard, here in the Fire Kingdom we strive to offer our visitors the most romantic of prospects," he mocked, distaste splayed across his face.

"Who is he? Do we trust him?" Ansgar whispered into my hair, so soft that I barely heard it.

"Rhylan, what a pleasure to see you," I mocked as well as a reply, loud enough for the entire room to hear me. "It's nice to see how you took out the clothes you wore five hundred years ago; did you fancy a walk down memory lane? Did living in my house for the past three weeks while you blackmailed the living hell out of me just so you could shove me inside a bloodied cell bring out your

284

sense of vintage fashion?" I hoped the short summary would be explanation enough and it told Ansgar that no, we do not trust him. But for some unknown reason, Rhylan fought for my life and defended me several times in those three weeks, so I had to continue to hang onto him if that would get me what I wanted. My mate, freed.

"Tsk, tsk, tsk, you are splayed in brown and amber, princess. You may make proper use of your words but your feelings can't hide how terrified and desperate you are." His adamant eyes locked with mine, reading every emotion I had proved incapable to hide and while he did so, Rhylan's features changed just slightly to relief. But his mask quickly returned, splaying that distasteful smirk across his bronzed cheeks.

"Our deal then?" I demanded. "The prince and I will require a room, lots of gauze and disinfectant, food and drink immediately." And a toilet, my bladder reminded me.

Ansgar remained close, not uttering a word, but I felt his muscles tense and ready at a moment's notice. I knew that if I couldn't convince Rhylan to let us out, he would go crazy at the guards, and judging the way they held their weapons and shields, clenched tightly for dear life, there was a high probability that he would add those men to the pile of rotting corpses.

"You kept your end, it is up to the prince now," Rhylan said, acknowledging Ansgar directly for the first time since the doors had opened.

"What do you need me to do?" Ansgar asked, his voice coming out husky. Only then I realised that he had whispered or spoken in a low voice ever since I entered this godforsaken place and this was the first time he had probably spoken fully out loud for days.

"First of all, I will need that dagger." As soon as Rhylan's words escaped, Ansgar took a step back, his instinct directing him to use the weapon but he struggled to stop and battled the feeling, his entire body shaking from the effort. "Secondly, should you truly wish to leave the cell, you will have to be transported to a room with an iron door and be iron-bound during the journey," Rhylan finished half surprised that Ansgar gave him this long and not attacked yet.

"Wherever he goes, I go," I immediately said, stepping back once again to get myself as close to my mate as I possibly could without shoving him into the wall.

"It never crossed my mind otherwise. Which is why, thirdly, I will need a drop of your blood to enchant the door."

"What? Why?" I immediately tightened my hands over my chest in an attempt to protect them. Some part of me understood the information as if blood would be taken from my hands, maybe a cut of the palm like they did in movies or a prick of my fingers, but then I realised that the bastard could draw blood from wherever he wished.

"I trust him to be incapable of opening the door, even though I must admire how quickly he is building resistance, but nothing would stop you from escaping and wandering around, now would it? Which is why the door must be spelled not to open at your touch."

Rhylan kept his face straight and the same expression tightened across his face, as if he did not care one bit, whatever my choice proved to be.

I turned to Ansgar and looked at him questioningly, but the shivering muscles of his jaw told me what I needed to know. That if I didn't get him out quickly, he would go on a killing rampage and we would have no choice in hell but to remain there, surrounded by dead bodies until we both starved or my heart stopped from panic.

"Fine," I uttered the word and as soon as I did, three soldiers approached with iron chains, walking towards me, towards Ansgar.

"Stop," I immediately shouted, and to my surprise, they did. "No one touches him." I jumped forth and grabbed one of the chain piles from the soldier's hands. Without uttering a word, I carried them back to Ansgar and set them a few inches from his bare feet. I did the same with the second soldier, who dropped the pile of iron into my arms with a disgusted face, and then, with the third one.

Rhylan allowed all this without saying a word, curiously observing me from the door as the light shone on his hardened cheeks. Once I had all of them gathered, I untangled one of the chains with difficulty.

"What do I do?" I asked him once I finished, finally raising my gaze to meet his own. His eyes went wide and savage, but I read trust in them also.

"Do my wrists first, then bind them to my torso and wrap me with the chains. Ignore my legs. I need them to walk and I won't kill them with my bare feet. I'm not that good." he shifted his gaze from me to Rhylan and the soldiers. "Yet," he pressed.

I did exactly as he asked and wrapped iron on his wrists first, while he extended them to help me and then bound them onto his chest, grimacing and asking for forgiveness every time I burnt a new patch of skin.

Once I was done wrapping my beloved in a ton of iron, not understanding how he could still stand with the amount of pain he must be in, I turned to Rhylan and the guard, all of whom remained silent, patiently waiting for me to finish.

"We are ready to be escorted outside," I announced, displaying the most threatening gaze I could muster. They might very well shut the doors on us and leave us abandoned in the darkness, while I struggled to unwrap my mate and possibly hurt him more.

Luckily, Rhylan nodded and my relief must have been evident because I felt my entire body relax, like a hot air balloon that finally released the sandbags and became able to fly away.

The soldiers exchanged looks, probably surprised by their general's decision but I took advantage of the moment and started walking towards the door, making sure to step decidedly and evenly, all the while checking that Ansgar kept the pace. The moment we stepped through the doors and into the wide corridor I felt instant relief, the claustrophobia I kept hidden releasing me from its grasp. It wasn't much improvement, we remained underground within a narrow tunnel, but at least there were people around us and lots of torches illuminating the path.

We all walked silently, Rhylan leading the pace with the black cape waving in his tracks like some kind of faerie version of a mean Batman. Ansgar and I followed after him, me adjusting the pace to my mate whenever necessary. I saw his grimaces while taking the steps and hated myself for making him suffer like this. I guessed that every movement only rattled the chains tighter to him, causing him more suffering. I wanted to cry, to stop and let it all out right there, all the pain and anxiety that had accumulated and burnt through me. I wanted to expose my weakness, to let everyone know that I was a mere human, who had not dealt with such violence, who could not be dealing with it anymore, that this world was too much and all I wanted to do was take Ansgar and go home.

But I could not, I would not. He needed me to be strong for the both of us, needed to get out of there and the only way out would be to play their game. To fake and lie and cheat until we got what we wanted. Freedom.

So I bit my tongue every time the emotion got the best of me and trailed along, trapped in between the two faeries that had changed my life, Rhylan and Ansgar, the darkness and the light of my current existence. Along with a line of about twenty soldiers who marched right behind us, hands clenched on their weapons as though we would suddenly grow strong and organise a surprise attack.

While we stepped through the narrow dark corridors, I tried to gaze encouragingly at my mate every chance I got, and to my surprise, he did the exact same thing. None of us spoke, there was no need for that since our encouraging looks said it all, but also because we did not trust anyone around us and did not want them to have more details than needed.

Finally, just as my feet threatened to start swelling from the uneven ground and all the missteps I took, we reached one of the ornate corridors heading to living quarters, similar to the ones that lead to the king when I first arrived. Two narrow passageways to the left and Rhylan stopped abruptly in front of a, of course, iron door.

"These are the living quarters for the transformed recruits," the old fae explained as he turned to us. "We like to keep them in check for a few months until their transformation is complete. This one incorporates a bedroom and a bathing chamber. You will also have fresh water and food."

"I wasn't expecting a Hilton, so it will do," I kept myself snarky, even though at this point I wanted to jump up and hug Rhylan at the mention of a bed and water.

Without a word, he shifted to me and grabbed my wrist in a movement so fluid, that I did not have time to react until something sharp scratched along my wrist. I looked down to see a ring that Rhylan wore on his pointer finger which looked more like a claw, and it proved to be as sharp, since it immediately drew blood.

I swore but as soon as a full drop filled the inside of the ring, he released me and turned to the door, speaking some ancient language and, I guessed, using my blood to spell it against me opening it.

The entire process took less than a minute and as soon as he finished uttering the words, the fire fae turned to us yet again and adopted a welcoming look and a theatrical smile, opening the door to invite us both inside.

Ansgar was the first to step into the dark room, too used to danger and the unknown by this point and I had no choice but to follow, stepping slowly and wearily behind him.

"Tell the king it is done," Rhylan ordered, dismissing the soldiers who disappeared within an instant, relieved to have avoided conflict and get out of this mission unscathed. Rhylan passed me the torch he had been carrying, then shoved me with such a strength that I flew in and bumped into Ansgar, who had already managed to take a few steps inside.

"You have two days, then we'll talk." With this, he made a gesture to shut the door and lock us inside.

"Rhylan, wait!" My mouth started before I even had a chance to think, before I even considered what I was about to say. He looked as surprised as I was, his eyes widening and a slight crease of his eyebrows revealed his reaction to my unexpected calling. But I knew what needed to be done, I read about it and investigated it over and over, hating myself for the impulsive decision that had bound our fates. One that I was on the verge of repeating, only this time, aware of the stakes. And the repayment.

"I need Cloutie root." I expelled the words quickly, without giving my brain a chance to reconsider, to think through whatever consequences this act might trigger. But one thing was certain, Ansgar needed to heal, and the process had to be quick. Rhylan gave us two days and then only the gods knew what they had in store for us. I had to get my mate in better shape and to do it quickly.

"Now, now princess, there is no need for that, I only made a small cut, it will heal by tomorrow," Rhylan grinned at me, that mask of coldness perfectly moulded to his features.

"I don't think I need to explain that it's not for me," I grunted. My gaze involuntarily shifted towards Ansgar, who took advantage of my stopping in the doorframe, which allowed light in, to scan the room and decide to take a seat on the bed. He must have been exhausted.

"That is a mighty tall order, princess. Even for me." He showed no sign of compassion, only that marble portrayal which made me understand that the man I thought I knew hadn't existed. Rhylan represented everything that was bad with the world, everything I struggled not to feel right now. For Ansgar's sake. One thing was certain, though. I would hate this man till the day I died. The one that pretended to be my friend, the one who cheated me not once, but twice, the one who broke my sister's heart just for fun. The one who had my mate tortured for over a year.

"Considering that I will probably die in here sooner rather than later, I think payment is already made." As soon as I said the words, tears flooded my eyes but I struggled to keep them in check. I was scared out of my mind, but if I only had a few days, I had to make them count and not sit in a corner regretting my life choices. Regretting not hugging my parents harder when I last saw them. Not realising it would be the last time.

Rhylan shook at my words, his eyes glinting in a way that I hadn't seen them do before as his body shifted only slightly, like an impulse had overpowered him but he immediately realised it and kept it in check. Then he nodded, low and slowly, as if he wanted me to follow the gesture fully and give my mind time to understand that my request had been accepted without protest.

"Give me a few hours and I'll have someone bring it to you." Before I had a chance to reply, he added, "It works best in a tea, especially in his condition. I'll send enough to last the two days."

"Thank you," I barely worded, then grabbed a better hold of the torch and turned towards the room, towards Ansgar who watched us

292

talk from the bed. Still in chains.

"Anwen," Rhylan grabbed my arm abruptly from the doorframe. "You will not die here. I swear." His adamant eyes locked with mine in a reassuring contact, but at this point, I knew better than to trust anything coming out of his mouth.

"If you say so," I replied and stepped inside. Two seconds later, I heard the thump of a door shut abruptly and I knew we were locked in.

First things first, I used the torch to light up the room, since I assumed both of us were sick of the cold and damp darkness. There were a few candles on a nightstand by the bed, so I picked them up and lit them one by one, then headed to the hole in the wall which turned out to be some sort of a fireplace, and I made sure to light a few wooden blocks before I threw the torch inside.

The light immediately warmed up the room, which was small but a lot better equipped compared to the cell of rotten bodies both of us had spent the night in. We had a bed, a nightstand, a small table with two chairs, and another door, which I assumed led to the bathing chamber, as they called it.

"Are you alright?" I approached the bed and scanned Ansgar, trying to decide the best way to remove those chains. Because I knew that as soon as I did, parts of skin would fall along with the iron.

"Managing," he replied, but his voice announced the eagerness to be released. I did as directed and started to unwrap him, bit by bit until I reached the last layer of chains, the one I knew would be the most painful.

"Let me stand," he asked in between heavy breaths, "I don't want to get too much blood on the bed."

Like that mattered, I huffed internally. Like I cared the bedsheets were dirty right now, after both of us were covered in blood and remains from sitting on that disgusting floor. But I did as told and stepped aside, helping him rise from bed. Ansgar did so with a grimace, probably the movement pulled the chains tighter onto his skin, but he must have been so used to the pain that no sound escaped his throat.

"You can rip them off, it will hurt the same but at least it will be over quicker," he suggested, stretching his back to give me a better view of the wrapping I had made and allowing me to form a plan as to how to proceed.

"Are you sure?" I asked with a shaky voice, not ready for what was to come, for what I had to do.

He nodded and curved his lower lip just slightly, encouragingly. My insides shook at the sight, at the ghost of the man I loved, now only reduced to a shell.

"Okay," I said quickly, unable to look at him like that, defeated, unable and in pain, so I thought about what I was doing as a simple task, imagining I had to untangle some rope and looked anywhere else but the chains when I started jiggling them across his body. He huffed and grunted, pained sounds escaping his mouth and I knew he was grinding his teeth, but I made quick work of it and within a minute, I found myself removing the last bit of chain, the one tying his wrists while in front of me remained a bloodied, shivering Ansgar.

He looked at me with relief, the weight of the iron releasing its hold on him and the freedom giving him a burst of energy that even I immediately felt. I could not help but smile a bit, even though both of us were surrounded by uncertainty and had no idea what our fates would be after the next forty-eight hours. If we even had that long.

"We'll need to clean your wounds first, I'll go draw a bath," I said, not knowing what to do or how to react and allowing him the space to process the newly acquired freedom. If our situation could even be called as such. Still, I took it as an improvement over the gory cell. Without another word, I headed to the only other door in the room, which I hoped would be a bathroom, and thankfully, it turned out to be just that.

And to my surprise, it proved to be a fully equipped one, with a working bathtub and a toilet, thank god. I turned on the hot water and did my business quickly, hoping that Ansgar wouldn't barge in and saw me peeing half a river. I didn't know if it was a joke directed to me or just a mere coincidence, though I doubted it, but I went to clean my hands in the washing basin and found Odstar soaps. Orange scented Odstar soaps.

My chest pinched at the sight, at the thought of mom and dad and the fear that I might never see them again. That I had been so blinded by the one thing I wanted and trusted the same fae that tricked us in the first place, and did not pay attention to the fact that I directly threw myself into another trap and had only myself to blame.

"I'm sorry," I heard Ansgar's voice from the doorway and jumped with a scare.

"What for?" I turned and grabbed a towel to wash my hands, though my full attention was on him, as he stepped inside the bathing chamber with nothing on. He must have removed his pants in the bedroom and was now fully displaying himself to me.

Savage instincts begged for him, for those touches I had longed for in my dreams, for the memories he stirred in my insides at the thought of all the waves of pleasure he could draw if he wanted to. I had to put a barrier to my mind, so I turned and made myself busy fixing the towels and checking the water temperature, looking anywhere but at him.

"For the suffering I am causing. Please know that the thought of putting you through this is far removed from my mind," he murmured, then stepped closer, his feet stomping on the floor. I felt his closeness, the warmth he brought forth at the close proximity with my skin, the thought that one single movement on my behalf might end up with us touching.

"The water is ready, if you want to get in," I only said, unable to move or look at him. My mind played a conflict on itself. I wanted to jump him then and there, to hug and kiss him and have him inside of me, show him how much I loved him and how much I'd missed him. I had dreamt for so many nights about this moment, the one where we would find each other again, be it in another life or in a parallel universe. Fate had brought us back together and begged me to claim my mate, to make him remember me by covering him in ripples of pleasure.

But we were both trapped in an enemy kingdom, both of us had suffered, albeit in different ways and the last thing he needed was some crazy woman suffocating him with stories of the past while he was obviously tired and wounded, probably famished and lacking strength.

I hadn't truly grasped the extent of his injuries until I watched his wide back arch to get into the bathtub and the hundreds of stab wounds contorting alongside his tired muscles. I came to understand that the wounds he was displaying were not only the effect of the past few days locked in an iron cell but the result of day after day of extensive torture. The cuts looked gaping and intertwined with each other, as though they had fought for space and depth across his muscles and decided to lay one on top of another, old scars forming a shell for newer cuts.

His arms and shoulders were covered in bruises and his chest displayed so many slashes that it looked like someone decided to play board games on his chest and could not settle for only one panel. His hair looked gruffy, the small braids he used to wear now only knots keeping together lumps of dried blood.

The only thing that stayed the same were his eyes, hidden behind his fanning long eyelashes, but even the silvery gray had adopted a more metallic shade, portraying the emptiness of the owner. No regular human being could have survived this, but here my mate was, alive and safe, at least for now. My stomach tightened at the thought, at the uncertainty that followed us. *Live in the present, Anwen,* I encouraged myself and picked up a washing cloth to dampen into the already bloodied water.

Ansgar watched me as he tried to adjust his body to the size of the tub, which proved to be a tad smaller than what he needed, so he bent his knees and allowed his back to soak in the water while displaying his chest and other parts to me. My fingers automatically tightened on the cloth.

"May I?" I asked in a slightly trembling voice, showing him the cloth and what I thought would be my obvious intention to clean his wounds.

"Thank you," he said and changed positions again, turning to display his injured back to me. I guessed that was where the pain lingered most.

I did not respond, for what could I say? Thank *you* for staying alive? For suffering in here, forgotten by the world while I cried in soft bed sheets and drowned myself in expensive champagne? That I hadn't even considered the possibility that you could be alive? That I let myself wait for almost three weeks, stupidly thinking you would be treated right by the same people who killed pregnant women and turned soldiers against their own people?

"Anwen," I heard Ansgar call for me, his hands grabbing mine without hesitation, making me look at him fully for the first time since we'd stepped inside the room. "I'm sorry," he said again, his eyes following mine and the tears I had unwillingly splayed across my cheek.

"No, I'm sorry," I said quickly, dropping the cloth to dry them with the back of my hand, "it seems like the only thing I'm capable of doing is cry," I huffed. "I never used to do it," I explained, "but since Erik died, tears just pop in. For anything, for any reason. Not that your wounds are just anything," I clarified.

Ansgar seemed surprised, his eyes widened slightly and his

298

mouth escaped a breath. "You are crying because of me?" he asked, looking at me like I started to grow horns or something.

"I'm so sorry for what they've done to you," I whimpered, releasing even more tears. By this time I had given up trying to hide them since his face was only a few inches from mine and there was no way he wouldn't see them.

"You have nothing to be sorry about," he said as his wet hands cupped both my cheeks, locking my face in tight closeness to his own. "I am sorry," he repeated. "For causing you reason to come here. I am the one responsible for your suffering."

"Oh baby, you are responsible for returning life back into me," I said, and instinctively, I pressed my lips on his. The kiss was short, only a second or two, our lips barely having enough time to touch, when the sound of a creaking door alerted us into a halt.

Ansgar wanted to rise from the tub but I pressed on his shoulder, a silent offering for me to go. A curt nod showed his agreement, possibly because the warm water started to soak his muscles and he could barely stand as it was.

I opened the bathroom door to find a soldier pushing a trolley of stashed trays through the door.

"The general sent this," he explained as soon as he saw me. "Medicine, food, and water, to last until the agreed time."

I nodded, unable to find it in me to thank the man, a representative of the court who had so swiftly earned my hatred. It seemed to be enough because he nodded in return and stepped outside, locking us in without another word.

Chapter Twenty-Two

By the time I got out of the bath, I felt lighter, the bloodshed and eagerness to hurt had been washed away by those soft, gentle hands along with the infections of my wounds. Anwen, I loved saying her name, washed each small tear of my skin with unimaginable patience, carefully scraping away dry blood or parts of infected muscle until she felt satisfied with the results.

I was unable to stop watching her, following her every movement and the way my skin reacted to her touch, like branches of a tree that had been cut off for years and had finally managed to grow back to their same length, able to reach sunlight.

There was something about her presence. Just by her being there, she managed to shift every feeling I had. There was no more hatred, no unknown feeling that urged me to hurt, to keep fighting, as though through her arrival parts of my mind shifted and started connecting to her, to her kindness and that sheer need to touch me and be next to me, to the new sentiment of protection that she offered. Anwen gave me peace and calmness, both feelings I had thought long forgotten, so I relished in her touch and allowed myself to fully relax under the hot water.

"Anwen?" I mustered enough courage to say her name, risking the chance to pull her from her systematic gentle movements, which became more natural with each wound she found and cleaned.

"Ansgar?" she replied with softness, making me turn to her, chasing the smile I thought I heard in her voice.

"Thank you," I only uttered, though my heart pleaded to say so much more, ask so many questions, and tell her about these new feelings and emotions I'd discovered, that her presence had awoken in me.

"It's okay," she responded, but her voice hid a struggle, she too had more to say. I followed her gaze and admired her long fingers tracing that bloodied cloth on my shoulder, her fingertips touching directly onto my skin and awakening goose bumps in their tracks. The woman noticed the effect of her touch and to my surprise, retracted, eyes shook with realisation.

"Your back is done, and your shoulders, there's only your legs left and your…" she stopped but the understanding made me shift my eyes towards my midsection, covered by the crimson water. I did not know why it bothered her now, since she did not protest or made any displeasing gestures when I undressed and situated myself in the tub, and there was more to see in that instant than right now. Without giving me a chance to reply, she dropped the cloth in the water and retired from the small bathing room, leaving me on my own.

My instinct screamed to jump after her, to chase her and relish in her presence. I could barely contain the thought of being on my own again, but I fought the urge, understanding that even though I needed her company, she may already be sick of mine.

So I stayed back and finished cleaning myself, scraping away days of battle and aversion along with the dried blood, until all of me became cleansed and ready for a new beginning.

By the time I re-entered the room, I found Anwen sitting on a chair by the fire, a kettle of boiling water hanging over the flames emanating a foul smell that immediately reminded me of the cell I had barely broken out of.

"What happened?" I asked, wrapping the only clean towel I had found in the bathroom around my lower parts. I debated whether to leave the room naked and risk causing her discomfort or use the fabric and leave her without a chance of cleaning herself. One look at the bloodied water that was impossible to reuse pushed me for the second option, since I should have been more mannered and offered the clean water to her in the first place. It was obvious I would leave it unusable.

"It smells really bad, I know, but it will make you feel better, I promise," she responded with a slightly apologetic tone. "I know you are in need of fresh air, I'm sorry."

"I shall have the word banned from your lips," I replied and took a small step into the room, unsure if to lay on the bed as I did initially or walk closer to her.

"Huh?" she turned fully to me in search of more details.

"That word, 'sorry'," I explained. "You are not allowed to utter it anymore. Not after you came after me and managed to keep me

302

away from certain death." I took a few more steps in her direction and when she did not shy away or make any gestures of discomfort, I decided that it was safe to close the space between us, so I walked around the bed and sat on the mattress, coming as close as I could to the chair she had found and placed by the fireplace.

"Yeah, I'm not really sure about that," her features adopted a shade of sadness, and her gaze averted from me, shifting unhurriedly towards the flames. "Whatever may come, we still have two more days," Anwen added, as if she had the hope that those forty-eight hours could change the world.

"The hatred is gone," I replied. "I don't feel the calling any longer. Not since your arrival." I don't know why I felt the need to tell her that, since she never showed fear towards me, but I wanted to make sure Anwen knew that she would be safe with me. Even though we were locked away in a room neither of us could escape from.

"Let's hope you won't need to summon it back," Anwen replied, her voice a whisper, afraid to utter the words too loud to avoid waking whatever demons might be summoned back into me.

My reply came replaced by the sound of boiling water, overflowing from the kettle and escaping drops on the open flames, making the woman react and grab a cloth to remove it from the fire. I watched her as she poured the contents into a cup from a trolley that had appeared into the room while I bathed and passed it to me.

"I'll be honest and it's your decision if you want to drink it or not, but if my opinion counts for anything, I am begging you to do it. Payment has already been made." She placed the cup in my hands and let me see the inside, where a root dropped waves of darkness in the water. "It's Cloutie," she said and waited. For what, I did not know but her posture told me she expected some kind of eruption.

I kept quiet and blinked several times, not knowing what to do or what to say.

"Do you know what a Cloutie tree is? Do you remember?"

I felt silly, needing constant guidance with the simplest of actions, but I admitted my fault since she clearly looked affected by the contents of this horrid tea, so I waved no, that I did not know what it was.

Anwen sighed and took a seat next to me, grabbing the cup from my hands and gripping it in her own, squeezing her fingers around the steaming edges.

"How much do you remember?" she asked, her voice shaky and unsure.

"If you were to tell me my name is Cumin and not Ansgar I would believe you," I sighed at the unfortunate attempt of a joke which had absolutely no effect on her. Not even a dash of a smile, so I continued. "I remember the basics, my muscles know what they are doing and clearly, I know how to fight," I said, trying to keep away the memories of the gore she had to witness. "Other than that, there's not much. I know how to speak and how to use the knowledge I acquired, but I cannot recall where it comes from or why I have it. I don't even know who I am or why I am here."

"Because of me," she responded, standing to put the cup away on the tray by the wall, the flashing light of the torch illuminating half her face. "I did something stupid, and you had to pay for it. For my mistake."

I didn't have to look at her face to feel her pain, her raspy voice and body-language let it slip. I didn't reply, not knowing what to say or understanding her grief, so I kept silent, hoping that she would offer more information. To my good fortune, she did.

"A Cloutie tree is the most sacred being in your kingdom, it was left by your goddess after her death. To help you heal, since she could no longer do it. They are spread across the world, but there are very few left and whoever harms one, must pay a debt. One root, one household, one life," she uttered the words slowly, giving the impression that speaking them cut through bleeding flesh.

"I used a Cloutie root, without knowing what it was, to make a tea. To come find you. And you paid with your life," she finally turned, face red and eyes wet, looking at me with a plea for forgiveness.

"I am still alive, they haven't managed to kill me yet," I half-smiled, trying to do my best to alleviate her pain.

She nodded in agreement. "Apparently Rhylan took away your energy, I am not sure how that works, but by taking your power you agreed to become their prisoner. All the while I thought you were dead," she wiped away tears and started walking to me with an embracing gesture, but thought better of it and stopped, afraid to touch me until she shared the entire story.

"This tea is another Cloutie root," Anwen exhaled as she uttered the words, slowly and gently, giving my brain time to adjust to the information. "But payment has already been made, so at least we don't need to worry about that. Of course, it is your choice if you drink it," her lips trembled and she stopped their movement by pressing them together, her eyes the only sign of her wish. She wanted me to drink it, even though she did not say it.

"Do I need it?" I asked, thinking that if the woman showed willingness to sacrifice a life, or an energy as she called it, my state must be more severe than I thought.

She nodded quickly, just as another tear made its way from her cheek onto her chin, quickly crossing the barrier of her neck and I knew. I knew then, that I would do whatever. Whatever she needed, whatever she asked, whatever she wanted me to, as long as it stopped her pain.

"I'll drink it then," I confirmed and she exhaled with visible relief. So long, that I didn't even know how such a large amount of air could have occupied her small chest and immediately brought me back the cup.

"When I drank it, it made me sick, and then I fainted. We also have food, but it's best to drink the tea first and see how it affects you before you eat. Think of it as medicine," Anwen said while placing the cup back into my hands.

I didn't dare check inside the still steaming cup, the smell was enough to announce the foul taste, so I rushed it to my mouth and drank quickly and deeply, holding my breath and swallowing big gulps until the only thing remaining was the dark root.

By the time the liquid reached my stomach, I found myself wrapped in heaviness, my limbs dense and begging me to lie down, so I did just that, unable to situate myself in a more proper position on the bed to allow her space if she needed to sleep. I simply fell on the mattress, feeling like I was flying on clouds while my eyelids opened and closed until I lost all control of my senses, surrendering to the healing liquid.

"Are you crazy?" a female voice gripped me from sleep. I did not know how long it had been since I drank the tea, but even half asleep, I felt no more pain. For the first time in however long I could remember, nothing ached and nothing bled. I dare even say I was comfortable.

"It's the only way, soon you will see the king and you are in no way prepared for what's to come," a male voice replied. I opened my eyes wide enough to spot Anwen at the door, though I could not see the male she was talking to. She held white fabric, possibly clothes, and I had to assume the male brought them for her.

"And how do you think it's gonna go? Oh, hi Ansgar, you know how were been tortured for a year and you are barely able to heal your wounds even after four Cloutie roots? Yeah? Okay, let's fuck now," she replied in an overly sarcastic tone.

"It's up to you, but be advised that the king is angry with the general. For sparing you and releasing him, for giving you this... honeymoon. He knows what your bond can do to him. We all saw it. Even the general took him for dead but a few hours by your side and the prince is whole again."

"And you expect me to trust you?" Anwen huffed, shifting from one hip to another, which led me to think the conversation started some time ago.

"You have no reason to trust me, I agree. But know that I was once Wind Kingdom. If there is an escape for Earth, maybe I can do it too." His voice sounded broken, the same fracture I felt while dominated by the urge for revenge and I knew he spoke true.

I guessed Anwen felt it too because she did not protest or comment, she simply nodded and thanked the male, then took a step back to notify him of the ending of the conversation. The door closed a second later.

With quiet movements, I shifted in bed, faking to wake up just then, and within a second, Anwen was next to me. She placed a gentle hand on my cheek and caressed my skin, whispering, "It's alright, you're safe, rest." She did it with ease, her movements so sure that I could not help but wonder how many times she needed to do just that during the time I slept. How many hours had I rested while she had to care for me? Did she even sleep? Eat?

"How long was I asleep for?" As soon as I said it, I recognised it for the stupid question it was since we had no natural light or clock in sight and had no idea how to measure time.

"I'm not really sure but I made you four cups of tea and we ate twice, so I guess it's more or less been a day," she replied, her fingers still trailing soothingly across my cheek in gentle caresses.

I frowned and stood a bit straighter, though my body begged for more sleep. "I have no memories of that."

"I should think not, you were a bit zombie mode, reminded me of university hangovers," she snickered and that sound was music to my ears.

"Who was that, at the door?" I asked and her eyes went wide, a blush climbing on her cheeks. She looked beautiful.

"Did you hear that?" she pulled her hand away but I caught it in mine, the gesture somehow familiar. I nodded.

"Part of it, about meeting the king and—" I stopped, not knowing how to say it, unsure that I even heard it right, because it sounded to me like the male advised Anwen to bed me.

"Don't even worry about it. Rest up, we still have a day to figure things out," she waved her other hand, the one that wasn't held by my own.

"Why does he think that our... union might help?" I asked, struggling to find the right words.

"He thinks that the mating bond will activate your memory since the effects of whatever they gave you stopped when we reunited," the woman said, the blush overpowering her features and turning her cheeks a deep crimson.

"His logic makes sense," I nodded in agreement, finally able to understand why this woman had such an effect on me and for the first time, she shifted her gaze to mine, our eyes locking.

Anwen blinked a couple of times and I did the same, none of us daring to say it, yet both wanting to. I remembered the way she touched me in the cell, how she connected to me and how her skin felt against mine while a jolt of desire sprang in between my legs. And by the way her fingers interlocked with mine, her skin hot and full of goose bumps at my touch, she seemed like she wanted it too.

"It's fine, we'll think of something else, we don't have to..."

Anwen was the first to speak and as soon as she said the words, her hands abandoned mine. She rose from the bed and stepped away.

I shook awake, immediately reacting. "No, of course. You've done so much for me already, I couldn't possibly ask you for more," I straightened in bed, but realised I was completely naked under the covers and started growing an erection so there weren't very many options of movement in my situation.

"Me?" she responded. "No, I'm, no... I'm worried about you. You've been through so much and the last thing you need is a woman you don't know, demanding things from you." She started pacing across the small room, showing her nervousness. "You haven't seen me in a year and you don't know who I am, and it's probably the last thing you need right now since you are still healing."

It sounded like the arguments were designed more to stop her own thoughts on the matter than my own, so a whiff of courage overpowered me as I spoke.

"I'm...willing," I replied, and feeling the need to show her how ready my body was for her, I removed the cover, giving her an eyeful of my desire.

Anwen

Chapter Twenty-Three

The last thing I expected to see in that moment was Ansgar's dick, but there it was, full-grown, and ready for me. I remained still, not knowing what to say or how to react. Did he really want this? By the looks of it, he did. Oh my gods, and how he did.

A burning sensation in my stomach croaked and urged me to go to him, to jump onto his lap and impale myself into him then and there. If not for his sake, then for my own sanity. I dreamed about our reunion for so many nights, ever since I found out that he was alive and now his body reacted to me, wanting me.

"I don't know if we should do this," I heard myself saying, my brain taking control and winning the battle against my lower parts. He didn't respond, didn't make a single gesture, did not move to cover himself or to step towards me, pushing this on. He simply remained steady, cock hard, watching me, letting me decide the next step. And I knew that one word from me would calm him down and make him forget about this idea without further protest. Just because part of his body reacted to me did not mean that I had to do something about it, that I had to follow the insatiable urge begging in between my legs.

He did not know me, he had absolutely no idea who I was, and in the past two days, I acted like a nurse rather than a girlfriend. Maybe that's why he felt attraction towards me, simply because I was the first person not to try and kill him. No, I couldn't do this.

"I feel like I'm taking advantage of you," I explained, my breath heavy with longing and urge.

"How so?" he asked with equally heavy inhales.

"You are not okay right now. Mentally," I added, the last thing I wanted was for him to think that I felt no attraction towards him.

"You are scared of me," Ansgar sighed and immediately moved to cover himself, but before he could put another word in, I added, "No, Ansgar, I'm not scared at all," I walked to him and took a seat on the bed, dangerously close to him with only that flimsy cotton blanket separating us. "It's not that, it's just— you've been through a lot and me coming here to ask for sex feels...weird, unfair to you. It's not that I don't want it," I shook my head and waved a hand as if to show how much I actually wanted him. "Trust me, I have fantasised about this moment in my head for so long. Obviously not you being injured and not remembering things but us, toghe—"

I did not have time to finish because Ansgar's lips covered mine in a soft caress, making me stop and forget every single excuse I tried to find, to convince myself not to proceed with this. But his lips on mine, his tongue slowly sliding in with delicate movements, making sure I was okay with him continuing the kiss, made me forget about everything else. Everything except wanting him, needing him. So I let myself drift to his lips, finding the heaven I had lost, claiming him once again as mine.

He did not hesitate, his gestures sure and unhurried, tasting every drop of me and feeling every part of my skin, like he was discovering my body for the first time. Which, come to think of it, he was. I allowed my fingers to trace across his shoulders, to reclaim the connection we lost and was surprised to discover smooth skin instead of the hundreds of injuries I had cleaned across his body the day before. Magic, I smiled and felt grateful for this moment, abandoning myself in the present and letting go of worry and fear of whatever may come.

I was here, in his arms. Finally, after so much struggle, after such a long time, I had him again. And by the ravenous way he started devouring my mouth, I knew he wanted to have me too. So I let him. Let him discover, let him chase my lips every time I pulled away to make sure it was not too much, that he did not experience any lingering pain.

"I want you," Ansgar whispered in my ear, his breath brushing against the skin and raising up sensation all across my body. "Goddess, how I want you," he said it again, his tongue building a trail across my neck. "Please, let me have you," he pleaded, his hand cupping my breast over the corset and stained shirt.

"Always," I murmured.

That was it, that was the signal he needed to unleash himself. Within an instant, Ansgar shifted up, pinning me to the bed and climbing on top of me, securing my thighs in place with his own, his length splayed across my lower belly, twitching with eagerness.

I could not contain myself and touched every part of him, relishing in that smooth and soft skin that covered most of his body, replacing the wounds and dread he had been through.

Without a warning, Ansgar pulled on my shirt and ripped it open, just like he did with my dress that first time we'd been together. Involuntarily, I started shaking, with anxiety, with desire and want, with the need to feel him inside of me again.

"Are you alright?" he sensed my trembling and took a halt from kissing the upper part of my breasts, which just then decided to escape from the corset that kept them pressed for so long and enjoy their new freedom.

"Never better," I murmured and kissed him feverishly, devouring his lips like they were some legendary fountain of youth and I was a dying woman. I felt him smirking underneath the kiss and grabbing me tightly, pulling on my jeans and corset with urgent need.

I let him, all the while splaying my hands across his back and drawing lines with my nails, sharp enough to probably leave marks on that newly healed skin.

In the urgency to uncover my full breasts, Ansgar got bored of nibbling at the string of my corset and pulled me up along with it, then gripped the fabric on both sides and ripped it apart while I was still wrapped in it. Gods, how I wanted him, and his eagerness made me unable to contain myself, especially after having another look at his forever growing member.

"What's this?" he stopped, plucking something from the discarded parts of what used to be my corset.

"Oh shit," I exclaimed, everything coming back to me in an instant. The dagger. The dagger his brothers gave me, the one that was supposed to help Ansgar. One that, with everything happening around us, I forgot I had. I must have gotten so used to having it pinching my skin that I grew accustomed to the sensation. And there it was, I noticed, looking down on my ribs, lots of small nips and cuts the weapon formed from the contact with my skin, the constant brushing against it.

"It's yours, I'm supposed to give it to you so it helps you grow your energy back. Your family said you'll know what to do," I explained, but he looked at me with confusion, his lips red and cheeks flushed from what we had been doing.

"I don't," he raised his shoulders slightly and looked at me with innocence.

"Marreth said something when he came to bring us clothes," I started speaking, though I knew how crazy it sounded. But considering that he suggested we had sex and we stopped just in the middle of it, it might not be so far off the bat. "He said that it's best to use something of yours when we...do this," I repeated the commander's words, unsure of what term to use. Have sex, fuck, make love? I knew what it meant for me, but maybe on Ansgar's side I was just a way to enjoy himself for a while, relieve the stress of this wait and whatever would come our way.

"Use it on me?" he asked, shifting closer in bed, so close that I could grab that length of his without changing my position. The length which surprisingly, did not feel the need to release any pressure and remained as hard and wanting as it was at the very beginning of this.

"It's your birthstone, I think it might help…"

"Anwen, if you let me fuck you, you can cut my throat afterward if you wish," he responded in an eager tone, hands ready to explore me yet again.

Well, that answered it.

I nodded and started unbuttoning my jeans and placed the dagger on the pillow, far enough to allow us to continue without any accidents, but close enough for me to reach.

"Do I just cut you while we...?" I didn't want to say it, didn't want to use the term because this meant so much more for me, but I also knew I wasn't in a position to make demands over our relationship status.

"Do whatever you must," he replied, spinning me around and pinning me once again underneath him.

His lips restarted their search, following my breast and trailing down to my lower belly, dangerously close to my pelvis. While one of his hands remained on my left breast, kneading and savouring the sensation, the other one reached my panties and in a brutal gesture, pulled them to the side, leaving my core bare in front of him. Without waiting for approval, he started making small circles on my clit, a proud smirk appearing on his face at the discovery of wetness.

My insides throbbed at the way his thumb played with me, eliciting a small moan I could not contain, and before I knew it, he pierced his finger through me, following the same circles his thumb did, stroking me both from the inside and out.

"Ansgar," I moaned. The sensation was too much, I could not stop myself from moaning and pleading, I wanted him inside of me right then and there, but he enjoyed having me squirm too much to just let me have it.

He added another finger and replaced his thumb with his tongue and oh, my god, did I scream with pleasure. He always enjoyed getting me ready to the point of almost fainting from the excitement, and this time was no exception. Ansgar moved his fingers inside me expertly, yet with surprising gentleness, sending wave after wave of pleasure spinning through my body. I arched my back and lifted my hands above my head, trying to find something to hold onto for dear life while he teased and tantalised me.

"Please," I begged in the end, unable to contain it any longer, unable to wait. I wanted him so damn much and that cock had stayed as straight as a pole all this time, so eager and ready for me that I did not want to find release unless it pierced inside me.

"Alright, alright," he replied with a grin but kept teasing me for another few seconds until he pulled back and stroked himself, trailing my wetness on his length.

I wanted to die right then and there and could not contain my urges anymore, so I pulled my body upwards and grabbed him, spreading my legs around him, and displaying my entrance proudly.

He swallowed and did just that, pierced inside of me like I wanted him to, slowly and surely until most of him filled me, scattering a deep moan from my lips.

"Fuck, that feels good," Ansgar murmured and pulled back just slightly, then pushed into me, starting to build a slow and steady rhythm.

"Harder," I moaned, falling on my back and allowing him to situate himself over me, an arm tightened around my hips.

"I don't want to hurt you," he murmured between pants, though involuntarily his body had started to move deeper inside of me.

"You won't," I moaned my approval when he pushed to the hilt, pistoning deep inside my core, while I reached for his back again and held on for dear life. Because in the next second Ansgar started pumping into me like there was no tomorrow, with so much force that were he not gripping my hips I would be probably flying into the wall.

His mouth found mine and kissed me eagerly, without stopping the penetrating rhythm, drilling so deep that I almost forgot what my name was. I had probably screamed so much that my throat became rasp, the release flushing through me and shattering my entire body, all the while he expelled a few groans to announce how close he was.

I had to do it, I knew I had to do it right then, so I reached for the dagger and raised my hips onto Ansgar, grabbing him by the neck to raise me up so I could have access to his back and made a quick cut down his shoulder, allowing the blade to pierce deep enough to draw a line of blood.

That was all I could do before he pushed me down again and started pumping into me like a possessed man, so hard that the bed hammered into the wall with his every movement.

"Anwen," he groaned, pressing mercilessly into me until he found release, his face taut and brows furrowed with the sensation. "Anwen," he roared my name as he spilled himself into me and finally settled with a last push that almost made me cum again. I knew the exact moment he finished because a wave of sensation came over me, like a blanket of ease that fell on my body, on my spirit. It made me feel weightless like I had become nothing but a whiff of wind, so light and ready to fly away.

"Anwen," he repeated, his eyes opening to find me. As he did, his entire complexion changed, the deep lines on his face turning to surprise and *relief.* He was looking at me like it was the first time, even after burying himself into my body in such a profound way, as though he just then realised he had shared the moment with someone else.

"Anwen?" he asked, voice trembling, eyes scanning me with disbelief.

"I'm okay," I replied. "I'm okay," I repeated, reassuringly. The last thing I wanted him to think was that he hurt me in some way. But he kept staring at me in wonder, blinking repeatedly as if something had been trapped in his eyes and he could not release the image. After every set of blinks, he stared at me again and his gaze continued to go wide at the sight.

"Fahrenor?" Ansgar barely spoke, his eyes wide and wet. I didn't understand why he was looking at me like that, since we had both consented to what happened, yet somehow, it was like I had just dropped in his arms and situated myself underneath him.

Oh, my gods, he *was* seeing me for the first time.

"Ansgar?" I asked in a trembling voice, shifting to him with a motion that released his member from inside of me and a trail of his desire along with it. "Baby?" I cried. Of course I did, was there ever a moment when I did not shed tears?

But this time was different, they were tears of joy because

Ansgar looked at me with recognition and *love*.

"Anwen," he exhaled, pinning me to his chest, my heart resting right above his own. "What...what are you doing here?"

Ansgar looked at me with disbelief, his hands trailing across my skin, like he wanted to make sure I was real. We must have trapped each other in an embrace for hours, caressing and hugging, delighted to be reunited after everything we'd been through. The only times our hands did not wonder was when our mouths did all the work — Ansgar made a point to kiss every inch of my body several times over.

"I don't know how much time we have left," I whispered, playing with a lock of his hair while he rested his head on my lap and stroked my arm lazily.

"There are three guard changes a day and Marreth always takes the morning one if he has to complete a mission. He must have used the excuse to come to you, and that happened a while back, so give or take twelve hours," he replied, brushing his fingers against my cheek.

"I never thought I'll be able to do this again," he admitted, then shifted to give my tummy a kiss. "Or this," he added. "Or this," he lowered his lips, progressing onto my inner thighs. I jumped up at the sensation, his newly formed stubble tickling my skin as I grabbed his face.

"You didn't have facial hair before."

He huffed, then shifted his cheek onto my palm, scratching me with his stubble playfully. It reminded me of a puppy who demanded cuddles. "I'm a full-grown male now, it's been over a year since my coming of age," he explained.

"The wonders of the faerie world," I smiled, calling twenty-six-year-old men teenagers.

"I cannot wait to show you the wonders of the faerie world," he replied, silver eyes pinned on me. I loved seeing him like this, untroubled, free from the shadows that had tortured him, embers of life burning in his eyes.

"What are we going to do tomorrow?" I knew the question would break the spell, wake him back to reality and I wanted nothing more than to give him a few hours of peace, but worry started to crawl inside of me. I could not lose him again, not now that I had him back, that he recognised me, not when we had another chance of being together.

He frowned, like the question had raised physical pain, but he immediately adopted a commanding stance and stood from where he had laid nestled in my lap and took the three necessary steps to reach the cart that still held several trays of food.

If one thing, Rhylan showed generosity with our meals, the cart arrived stacked full of trays with packaged food and drink, from sandwiches to ready-made meals that we could heat up by the fire, butter, soft bread buns and lots of water bottles.

Ansgar picked a few things on a tray and when he felt satisfied with the food haul, he returned to bed. Instead of eating, however, he started picking the food and organising it into, what minutes later, looked like some sort of map made out of lettuce leaves, cut bread, and butter containers.

"The entrance is somewhere in the tunnels down below, and the king and court must be situated at the centre, with the corridors spinning downwards," he explained, positioning a bun at the very centre of his creation. "When they took us out, we made seven left turns and two right, which brings us somewhere here," he gestured to where the small butter container sat, "close to the court but not inside it."

I was surprised at the amount of detail he had gathered during that walk, especially since he looked on the verge of fainting from the chains I wrapped him in.

"Okay," I replied, trying my best to squeeze any useful information from my brain.

"It means that all this side," he moved his fingers across several lettuce leaves, "is part of the court, therefore it will be well guarded and protected, possibly the deepest part of the kingdom. And I believe the prisoners are held in this area," Ansgar gestured to where he had created various lines of rolled bread to mimic the tunnels. "They would have to be the furthest away from the entrance on this side, the last thing they want is to give their prisoners a chance to escape." He showed an area that contained almost half of the court.

"So how do we find out where it is?"

"Do you remember anything from when you were brought here? Anything might help, even the smallest detail," he asked hopefully, looking at me with calm and reassuring eyes, trying to jiggle my memories.

"I don't know, Rhylan jumped me in. We were on a beach in India and he bought me sugar, so I wouldn't faint. Then we walked the same corridors until we reached the ones with carpets and got into the throne room," I explained. I wanted nothing more than to point that entrance on the map, but I had to be honest with both myself and him, I had no idea where I'd come in through and at that moment, the last thing I cared about was to sightsee.

"How long was the walk?"

"About an hour?"

"Did you leave the throne room through the same door?"

I tried to calm my nerves, forcing myself to remember. Ansgar grabbed one of my hands in his and caressed the inside of my palm slowly, with reassuring gestures.

"It's alright," he whispered, "take your time." Even though he wanted to calm me down, his words had the opposite effect, raising the tension in me. I wanted to help so much, but I hadn't even thought about remembering details, I had blindly followed Rhylan across the halls.

"Someone else brought me to see you, there were guards around me and I walked with him, with Marreth," I explained, closing my eyes to get a better grasp of my memories. "They had to hold Rhylan down, he wanted to come after me...through the doors!" I jolted. "Yes, there were the same doors!" I replied with excitement, happy to contribute.

Ansgar smiled encouragingly. "That's great fahrenor, stay with the memory. Tell me everything that happened," he said, continuing to massage my wrist with his thumb.

"I walked with Marreth, and he told me about you, about what they had done to you. It didn't take as long as the first time. Maybe twenty minutes?"

"Did you go into any other room?"

"No," I quickly said. "As soon as I learnt they were keeping you away, I asked the king to take me to you."

He nodded several times and his eyes lowered to the makeshift map he created, gazing over details, his eyes scanning visuals I did not understand. I could only look at him and admire my mate, the sheer determination he possessed to get us out of there, to fight for us.

"There are two options," he announced in the end, grabbing me back from the daydreaming state to pay attention. I was decided to inhale every detail and help as much as I could.

"The entrance must be around here somewhere, and it must, of course, be well guarded. It needs to be close to the soldier's quarters so they can be ready to attack at immediate notice," Ansgar advised, thinking like the prince he was. Trained in strategy and battle.

"The soldiers must be close to the king and their court, which means that their quarters are in close proximity, maybe the same distance as this room."

"So what are the options?" I asked, not understanding where he was going with this.

"I can either become the soldier they want me to be, play my part just like Marreth does and fool everyone into accepting my loyalty, I get assigned to the quarters and search for the entrance."

"Or?" I asked, hoping that the other alternative was much quicker. It could take months for Ansgar to gain their trust again, years maybe, if it would ever happen at all, after the killing spree he had been on these past days.

"Or we become part of the court."

"What?" I jumped up, trying to rearrange the sounds he had just released into a sentence that made more sense.

"They still need information from me, I could negotiate for shelter and safety."

"What makes you think they will believe it? They tried to gain information from you since they brought you here, why would they think you want to negotiate now?"

"Your presence here changes everything and they know you are my mate. Any male would give up his all to protect his better energy."

My heart fluttered at the words, *his better energy*. His starlight. Gods, how I loved this man!

"From inside the court, we can get information. Speak to Marreth. And Rhylan." He pressed the words, waiting for a reaction on my end. And it came quicker than expected.

"Rhylan? I don't want to speak to that son of a bitch ever again. That bastard kept you here, tortured you, and let me believe you were dead. Also, he fucked Cressida and played with her heart. I hate him!" I raised my voice, finding the most adamant tone I probably ever had.

"He doesn't hate you, though," Ansgar murmured, his words soft and barely audible, the opposite of my immediate burst. His tone sounded calm and calculated. "For some reason, Rhylan cares about your safety. You said it yourself, he made sure you don't faint, he confronted the king in front of the court, he came to stop you from entering my cell, worried that I would hurt you, and now he gave us two days of recovery, food, shelter, and safety. Don't make the mistake of thinking any of this is for my benefit. Were it not for the fact that I am your mate, he would have probably killed me by now."

I shook at the words, at the realisation, understanding how close Ansgar had been to real death. I remembered Rhylan telling me about the change of plans, changing the date of our trip. He must have done it so I could find Ansgar before anything happened to him.

"What does Rhylan want with me?"

"That's something we need to find out, fahrenor," my prince gripped my fingers in his own and lifted them to his mouth, placing a small kiss on my shaking hands.

Ansgar

Chapter Twenty-Four

The best sleep of my life happened with Anwen in my arms. I could hardly believe that the goddess returned her to me, yet here she was, her wavy hair curling on my arm while her hands grabbed my chest, like a cub holding on.

We took it in turns, she cared for me that first day and let me sleep, cleaned my wounds, and guarded me throughout what seemed like a very delirious healing state. According to her words, I drank four Cloutie tees, but I could only remember having a few sips from the very first one and falling into a deep sleep. Her version of the events turned out to be quite different though. Anwen said I twitched and twisted in bed, woke up shouting several times, haunted by whatever dreams weighed heavy on me, and had to be spoon-fed like a babe, because I could barely swallow the food, let alone take it to my mouth. I apologised several times for the state she must have seen me in, but she waved it off like it was nothing.

"After being in a room full of dead bodies with you the night before, it felt like a blessing, honestly," she said, eyes averting from mine. I hated myself for being in that state, for letting her see me like that and suffer the consequences of my demons, knowing that I would spend the rest of my life if I had to, trying to make it up to her.

The fact that she still wanted me after all she'd seen was a miracle in itself, I couldn't even imagine how all of this would be perceived through the eyes of a human female, untrained for battle, who probably never experienced bloodshed. I was surprised and proud of her resilience, the strength she had displayed during these days, and the determination with which she wanted to fight for us, for our escape. *My mate.*

I caressed her soft skin and admired the features that for once looked tranquil, no hidden emotion haunting her thoughts. I let her sleep for the rest of the night, or until the guards decided to barge in on us and fulfil whatever command they had to execute, while I squeezed my mind for every bit of strategy and planning advice I could recall from my years of training.

"Come to bed," Anwen murmured, probably awoken by the movement of my fingers down her neck.

"I am in bed," I whispered back to her, placing my hand in her hair and stroking her scalp the way I knew she liked. My lips curled in satisfaction at her sleepy moan, enjoying the new sensation. In the span of a few minutes, she fell back to sleep, turning to the side to give me better access to her wild hair.

I had to get her out of here. My instinct urged me to break down the door, to do whatever necessary to get her free, set fire to this place if I had to, whatever to keep my mate safe. But the startled expression on her face, the rasp pants caused by her panic in the cell told me that even though she proved to be strong, Anwen could not endure more of this. That I had to find another way, as peaceful as possible and that she would need time to heal after all this.

My brothers and I had suffered through many anatomy and human society lessons to know that their emotions remained as frail as their bodies. The tutor compared them to a shaken bottle of mead, the tap could contain the liquid for a while, but in the end, it had to burst out, making more mess than if released slowly in the first place.

I feared this happening to Anwen, all the fear she kept hidden, masqued by the bravado my mate struggled to portray. I did not know how much longer she could do it for, but one thing was certain, I had to be there and make sure that whatever way the liquid burst, the bottle would not break.

I grabbed her tighter in my arms and squeezed her tenderly, feeling all the longing and yearning dissipate as she rested in my arms, reclaiming her rightful place. I breathed her in, the soft aroma of her hair, which even after days of captivity still managed to keep a pleasant scent, the way her fingers moved from time to time, twitching lightly in her sleep. Goddess, how I loved her. I let myself drift away in the embrace, craving that union, that bond that exploded between us.

A knock on the door made Anwen jump in my arms, and I jolted along with her.

"You have a minute to get dressed," a cold voice announced from behind the iron door, which I immediately recognised as

Rhylan. Anwen watched me through sleepy eyes, blinked a few times, and settled herself back on my shoulder to fall asleep again. I always loved that about her, how she could fall asleep in an instant, sometimes walking up and not remembering what happened during the minutes she was awake.

"Anwen," I shook her slowly, devastated that I could not provide more of the peace and rest she obviously needed. Her eyes forced open again, watching me with intensity. "They're here," I said gently, uttering the words to her to make her react.

My mate inhaled quickly and jumped awake, looking at the door and throwing herself from the sheets in search of something.

"The dagger," she exhaled, wording the sentence with barely any sounds at all, showing me the weapon.

"We can't take it with us, they'll perform a search," I grabbed it from her, casting it into the fire. I threw some more logs on top of it, disguising it between the flames and hoping that once they burnt through, it would be covered enough.

As soon as I finished, the door screeched open, finding Anwen and I on either side of the bed, standing. I wanted to jump in front of her, wanted to be the first one they saw should there be an attack, but part of me calmed at the sight of Rhylan. I knew he would not hurt her. Hoped so, at least.

We must have been a sight to behold, I wore an old yellowed shirt and some pants that barely stayed over my hips, clothing I suspected came from Marreth's old wardrobe. And Anwen had just woken from sleep, wearing another stained shirt and nothing more, her thighs on display along with her bare feet.

One look at her and Fear Gorta grimaced, then he theatrically waved a hand in the air while covering his nose with the other.

"It reeks of bad sex in here," he said, eyes not leaving my mate.

"It reeks of your stupid face," she immediately retorted, gaining a proud grin from him.

"I always liked sprouts that bite," Rhylan replied, then turned his head to the other side of the room to find me, his movement regal. "Makes everything more interesting, doesn't it?"

"Indeed," I replied, piercing him with a sharp gaze, communicating that he better stayed away from her.

"So, did you two have fun?" he forced a smile and took a step closer to Anwen. "By the look of...all this," he moved his wrist in an upwards, then downward motion to display her body, "one would assume so." He then grabbed a lock of her hair and curled it around his pointer finger. "Very wild fun."

I wanted nothing more than to twist that damned wrist that dared touch her, but I breathed in, filling my lungs with as much air as they could grasp, before I said, "I would appreciate it if you took your hand off *my mate*," accentuating the last words.

"And he's back," Rhylan pouted, redirecting his attention to me and instantly removing his hand from Anwen's hair. "I hoped we'd have a little more fun, a duel even," the fire fae inclined his head to the side in a playful motion, a cat playing with its food. "I can see earthlings still remain dominated by their females. Does mommy not let you play anymore?" he ridiculed me in a tantalising tone.

"If it is a duel you seek, Fear Gorta, I would be more than inclined to accept," I replied but before he had a chance to show that stupid smirk of his, I added, "as long as my lady is escorted safely out of here."

That seemed to bring a shudder through him, because his shoulders involuntarily relaxed, like he had received pleasing news and all the tension dissipated.

"Of course," he replied drily, his playful tone evaporating into a formal one. Rhylan looked back at Anwen when he said, "Please follow me and I will escort you to your new lodgings."

She did not move, even though Fear Gorta stepped away and waited for her to exit, so I inched towards her and grabbed her hand in mine, turning her to face me.

"It's going to be alright," I whispered and my mate nodded, grabbing my arm with her other hand and wrapping it around my biceps.

"Whenever you're ready," Rhylan announced from the corridor, the door wide open to step through. I thought I read concern on his face at the sight of Anwen, terrified to leave this dreadful place from fear that the next one could be a worse version, but he regained his composure immediately.

"As the prince is ready to come peacefully, there should be no need for that," he spoke to the guards, whom I just spotted in the corridor. They carried more sets of iron chains.

"Let's go," I kissed Anwen's brow and stepped under the door frame, urging her to do the same. Reluctantly, she followed me out, not once letting go of my arm. I felt her shaking, hands gripping my skin with more desperation with each new step we took.

"Count the turns," I whispered into her hair, low enough for no one else to hear. I didn't even know if she heard me herself, but after the second turn her fingernails stopped piercing my skin and I knew the distraction had worked.

We followed Rhylan wordlessly, stepping slowly through the narrow corridors, all of them ornate with chandeliers and carpets. I must have been right because the deeper we went into the halls, the more rooms and soldiers wandered around. At one turn, there were even court members who gasped at the sight of me and surrounded themselves with soldiers for protection, should I decide to listen to my urges once more.

Even the old fae pressed his steps, unsure of my reaction, but my attention was only on Anwen and focused on gathering as many details as I could. I didn't even pay attention to the court members, didn't deign them with more than one look as we passed the hall and headed forwards.

Three left turns and we reached another hall with various doors, Rhylan stopping in front of the second one on the right. I exhaled in relief when I didn't spot any iron covering the entrance.

"These will be your chambers during your stay," he announced, and on cue, one of the guards opened the door.

Anwen loosened her grip on me, stepping closer to Rhylan and extending her hand, expecting him to draw blood again.

The fireling smiled. "There is no need for that," he announced. "These are my private guest chambers, I will occupy the one opposite," Rhylan gestured to an identical door, situated on the left side, mirroring the one they had opened for us. "The entire corridor is connected to my energy, so I will know when you leave."

My face must have dropped ten inches because he gazed at me with satisfaction. "Please, enjoy," he grinned at Anwen this time and left us there, heading out with the guards. "The king and queen expect you to be present at dinner tonight," we heard the announcement just before he turned the corner, his robe forming an ebony curling wave as he moved.

It meant we had another few hours and a new room to live in. Silently, I followed Anwen inside and closed the door, only to find her stunned and unmoving, looking around the room.

"What is it?" I immediately asked and went to her, but she did not reply, only shifted to me and grabbed my jaw to turn my face towards the closet wall. It looked familiar, though I did not know how to place the memory, so I took her silent advice and looked across the room, where I immediately recognised the sofa. And the small table with the wooden chair. And the ficus in the corner. We were standing in a perfect replica of Anwen's sitting room back in the Evigt forest, the place where we shared so much, where we liked to stay up late at night and watch stories on her device. To the right, white doors announced what I guessed would be the kitchen and when I pushed them open, I spotted many similarities to the one from the mansion. Even the sink was onyx coloured and some boxes of cereal rested by the right side, just like Anwen had them back then.

"This is creepy as fuck," it was my mate who uttered what we both thought, as she stepped towards the part where the stairs would have been situated to open another door. By her gasp, I didn't have to look inside to know it would mimic her own bedroom back in the queen's mansion.

I didn't know what kind of games Rhylan was playing, but one thing was certain. If he had put so much effort into recreating the home we shared together in the forest, it couldn't be for nothing, which meant that our stay could turn out longer than either of us hoped for.

"There's a clock on the wall in the kitchen, so at least we can keep track of time," I announced, adopting a positive tone and hoping she did not realise the same thing I had.

"Urgh, this guy is obsessed with Boss," her voice echoed from the bedroom. "At least we have clothes, lots of them." After a few more seconds I heard her say, "And there's a TV and lots of DVDs, some are not half bad."

I didn't know what a DVD meant but I felt glad that she was focusing on discovering things and did not share my concern regarding our new living arrangement. Maybe that's what Rhylan intended, to give her a safe space and keep her occupied with mundane things. Was all this for her?

"How's the kitchen?" she popped her head out from the bedroom door, biting her lips.

I smiled, understanding what she was asking. "I'll go prepare something for you."

"Do you mind if I take a shower in the meanwhile? There's an actual shower installed in here and running hot water," she said with excitement.

"Of course," I replied, feeling guilty for sullying the water that first night, forcing her to wash with cold water from the tap.

335

Thoughts of my naked and very wet mate kept me distracted in the kitchen, but I managed to create some sort of sandwich with the cut meats and cheeses I found in the fridge, yet another word Anwen had taught me. I cut it in two triangles, the way I saw her do hundreds of times before and grabbed a cold juice, then headed to the bedroom with the plate.

By the sound coming from the bathroom, she was still in the shower. My heart started thumping in my chest, prompting me to go in, to help her wash and caress every part of that body. *Calm the fuck down,* I hushed myself and the growing thing between my legs. She needs to rest and she needs quiet, the least important thing right now is your wants.

Fuck it, I urged myself as I shifted from bed, abandoning the sandwich and the drink on the cover, and opened the bathroom door to be invaded by a hurricane of hot steam.

"Anwen?"

"Wash my back?" I heard her voice through the pouring water and immediately leaped at the opportunity, sliding the flimsy curtain that did absolutely nothing to disguise her body in its transparency.

She passed a sponge so full of foam that looked like a cloud and turned, displaying her backside to me. So I did as requested and washed her back in temperate strokes, containing as much self-restraint as I could but her round ass invited me for a squeeze so I lowered the sponge, extending my caresses onto her lower back until I reached the area I so craved to touch.

Anwen giggled, and by all the goddesses, it was the sweetest sound I heard in my existence. I kneeled to her, a goddess in herself, begging to be allowed to taste her, my hands not abandoning the claimed territory.

I slid my palm to her centre to show my intention and a slight moan announced her permission. I lunged at her core, drinking from her like from a fountain after hours of hard training, my lips and tongue fighting for possession, claiming more and more of that sweetness.

Anwen spread her legs wider to allow my chin to pierce through and I pushed her onto me, making it feel like she was taking a seat on a very blessed chair, which became my mouth.

I binged at her centre, feasting until I could not feel my mouth, and even then I wasn't ready to let go, having Anwen's depths hammered onto me, while my head sustained her weight, with only her hands gripping at the shower curtain.

I did not stop until she called for me over and over in between moans, pants, and screams, each time shattering onto me a bit more, until she said my name so many times I was sure it had become impossible to forget. When my mate started begging for me, I listened, grabbing her thighs and spreading them wider, while splaying her front to the wet wall, the hot stream of the shower covering us as I thrust deep and hard, pushing my entire length inside of her with that first movement.

"I love it when you are so ready for me, fahrenor," I groaned and started to move with sheer force, my testicles slapping onto her womanhood from the velocity of the movement. Anwen shattered again, making her pleasure known to the entire court but I did not care. I only wanted to be inside my woman, lose myself into her, abandon every last shred of me.

She felt exquisite around my body, the missing piece I had longed for my entire life, and every thrust made me discover a forgotten part of myself. I pumped into her mercilessly, enjoying how deep she was receiving me, every inch begging to reach further. I let myself go, be abandoned into the sensation while my throat escaped sounds of pleasure that I had never in my life, uttered before then. Only with her, only with my mate. With the way her body was contorting onto mine to reach the deepest connection, the way she turned her head in that hazy state between pleasure and madness to find my lips. To show me that even then, even when she was losing herself in the deepest pleasure, she still craved for more of me.

When I found my release, Anwen's body relaxed, turning into a trembling mess in my arms, her legs shaking so hard that I knew they could not sustain her weight.

I grabbed her in my arms and walked her to the bedroom, spreading my mate's wet body on the bed, then ran back to grab a few towels and wrapped her in them, using a large one for her hair. I tried and miserably failed to do that twist all females magically knew how to do, but at least I made her giggle with my useless attempts.

"I love you," I whispered before kissing her lips and she threw me a giddish smile.

"I know," Anwen turned to me and grinned pleased, "You give me food and orgasms," my mate barely managed to speak through her hazy state.

"I'll give you anything you ask for, my love," I smiled and

kissed her lips one more time, bringing the plate of food closer and placing it on her lap.

"Eat while I wash quickly?" I suggested.

"Okay," she replied with an endearing gaze. By the time I reached the bathroom door, she had opened the drink and taken a big bite out of her sandwich.

I stood still as a marble pillar while Anwen scanned me up and down, her lips puckered in what I feared was discontent. She had spent the better part of an hour choosing our clothing for dinner and picked a stunning black dress for herself which stopped just below the knee. She paired the garment that she called a 'cocktail dress' with metallic high heels which made her calves tense and look sexy as hell.

As for me, she picked one of the black suits and three different shirts, which I had to try on first so she can decide about styling my hair.

I did not comment or object, if putting her attention in clothing helped her keep the nervousness in place until dinner, I would be happy to oblige, so I did everything she told me to. I also tried on several pairs of shoes which surprisingly fit me perfectly.

"Is it going to be hot in there?" Anwen asked, scratching her ear, careful not to touch the curls she had placed perfectly on that side of her face.

"I'm not sure," I admitted, but she did not seem satisfied with my answer, taking a few more seconds to scan me, her attention mostly on my upper body.

"This shirt makes you look too muscly, but the other one highlights your eyes too much."

I honestly did not care what I wore, but it clearly meant a lot to her. After a couple more seconds she reached a decision. "No, go for all black," my mate pointed at a fourth shirt she had laid on the bed, 'in case of emergency.

"It will piss off Rhylan and disguise your arms," she nodded in confirmation.

"Disguise my arms?" I repeated, confused.

"Yup," Anwen replied, turning to the mirror to check on the long lines she had drawn on her eyelids for a fourth time.

"Why would I need to disguise my arms?"

"So your muscles don't show too much," Anwen replied like it was the most obvious thing.

"And why do I need to disguise my muscles?" I came from behind her and wrapped my arms around her waist, pressing her back on my chest, her ass fitting perfectly into my midsection. "You used to love them if I remember correctly." I placed a kiss on her neck.

"And I do," she giggled, the sound releasing tension from my body, "a lot. But it may come across as a threat. Plus, you said something about the queen might have a thing for you?" she turned to me with a frown.

"That never came to be, I was too offensive and got sent back to the cell," I pointed out. I had told her fragments of what happened to me since we'd last seen each other, mostly about the royal family, who were beings we had to deal with again and kept most of the hard memories away, not wanting to cause her more harm.

"And it never will, nobody is getting their hands on my man," she turned in my arms and placed her lips on mine possessively.

"Fahrenor," I groaned a warning. "Your *man* can barely contain himself with you in that dress, don't make it more difficult," I pleaded. She smiled, obviously pleased with herself, then ordered me to change. I stole another kiss and released her from my arms to do as commanded.

At seven o'clock sharp a knock on the door announced the time for dinner and Anwen hurried to open.

"My, my, what a deliciously looking sprout," I heard Rhylan's voice from behind the door and blood boiled in my veins. I did not doubt Anwen's love for a second, but if Fear Gorta attempted something with my mate, we would have an exceedingly big problem.

"Rhylan," she replied, her tone even and uncaring.

"How are you finding your rooms?" his dark voice vibrated through the walls, taking over the surroundings.

"A bit creepy," Anwen replied to my delight, as I made my way to the door.

"Rhylan," I stepped behind Anwen and announced my presence.

"Prince," he grumbled at the sight of me. "A word of advice for future," he said, shifting his gaze from Anwen to me so slowly, timed to finish his next phrase as he locked his gaze with mine. "Next time you fuck her in the shower, cover her mouth or something. Some of us are trying to catch our beauty sleep."

I felt Anwen tense but I adopted Rhylan's tone and replied with the same cold cadence. "Noted," then turned my attention to her and said, "Shall we go to dinner, my love?" extending my arm for her to grab.

Rhylan's eyes narrowed with distaste but seeing how his words did not have the desired effect, he moved aside in the corridor to make room for us to exit. Anwen stepped first, holding my hand the whole time and I followed right behind, sealing the door shut.

We stepped behind the old fae through the narrow corridors, both Anwen and I taking in as many details as we could until we reached a set of plated doors, smaller than the main entrance in the throne room.

Two soldiers on each side pulled them open for us to enter, with Rhylan only a few steps ahead, not renouncing the cloak over his black tunic. Anwen and I pressed our steps, entering together through the set of doors that closed behind us as soon as we reached the room. Not the throne room, I realised, this was a smaller version of the massive dining table overlooking the court which the king had first invited me to sit at.

Only six chairs and sets of plates had been arranged at the table, along with a grand feast of meats, fruit, cheeses, and every garnish imaginable.

"My guests will arrive shortly, please take a seat," Rhylan announced and situated himself head of the table, without waiting for either of us to approach.

A million thoughts ran through my head in that second. I knew Anwen had to sit next to me but with Rhylan already occupying a chair, the situation had complicated. I debated whether to take the chair next to Rhylan and have her to my left, but I did not know who would sit at the other end of the table and the last thing I wanted was for her to be uncomfortable or even worse, in danger. Or I could have her sit next to Rhylan, but who knew what disgusting things the fireling might say to her.

I did not have to make a choice however, because Anwen, to both mine and Rhylan's surprise, pulled the chair at the other end of the table and placed her sexy bottom comfortably in there, situating herself like a queen. My mouth dropped while Rhylan threw her a proud and satisfied grin.

"Ansgar," she addressed me and moved her hand elegantly to the chair to her right, a silent invitation for me to occupy, which I did without protest.

"Making ourselves at home, are we, sprout?" Fear Gorta grinned again, resting his chin on his knuckles.

"I will never call this home," she responded dryly. "And don't act like you are better than me just because you can claim your place at an empty table," she snarled at him.

"I would never dream of it," Rhylan smirked again. Even though I sat next to Anwen, I felt out of place, a stranger in such a dense connection which I hadn't realised they shared. My mate could openly admonish Fear Gorta and get away with it, while others would be turned to shreds just for looking at him the wrong way and he was ... playful, enjoying this battle of retorts, teasing her openly.

Even the way they looked at each other, interacted, showed familiarity, making me question how often their interactions were in the past few weeks for them to become like this, comfortable in each other's presence. Anwen kept saying how much she hated him but every time he appeared the tension in her shoulders relieved, and the bleakness from Rhylan's eyes dissipated at the sight of my mate.

"What is your intention, Rhylan?" I heard myself spurting out the question, unable to convey my feelings any longer.

He raised his brows, surprised and offended by my speech, by the fact that I'd said anything at all.

"Meaning?"

"What business have you with *my mate*?" I pressed the last words, claiming her in a way I knew it was wrong to do.

He blatantly ignored my question, turning his attention back to Anwen, who poured herself a glass of wine. "Hear that, sprout? Fuckboy is jealous," he smiled, pleased with the effect he had on my temper.

"Suck it, Rhylan," Anwen replied, focusing her attention on filling my glass with the same kind of wine she had taken a sip from.

"Don't you want us to be alone for that?" he threw her a seductive smirk which, fortunately, my mate ignored. "Or do you care for your mate to join us?"

She did not reply and I had to grab the chair not to erupt. "Thank you," I inclined my head to Anwen as I grabbed the wine, trying to

344

copy her and completely ignore Rhylan, but he immediately realised our plan and continued, his next announcement making me splinter the armrest of my wooden chair.

"After all, those tiny sounds in the bathroom were nothing compared to the screams I drew from you last time."

Anwen jerked away at the flying splinters that covered our side of the table, but my mate kept her calm, looking at me as though she had to offer the most rational explanation.

"He's being a jerk, and that is nothing like it was," she explained quickly.

"How was it?" I barely pressed the words from behind clenched teeth. With the corner of my eye, I spotted Rhylan, resting his chin on his knuckles again, watching us, pleased at what he created. That's what the bastard wanted, for me to lose control before the king arrived.

Struggling to turn my full attention back to Anwen in between deep pants, I asked again, barely controlling my trembling voice. "How was it?"

"Rhylan entered my mind and created the illusion that you were there. I felt you, touched you, you were speaking to me. Apparently, he used my memories of you to create new ones, or something."

I felt a drop of air escaping me. Then another, making it easier for me to breathe. Anwen continued, "It's not like Rhylan was physically there, even though I hate the son of —" she stopped a moment, then added, "for what he did. But it was you whom I'd imagined to be with. I don't know if the disgusting bastard saw what we did or not."

Rhylan opened his mouth to speak, but Anwen lifted a finger, silencing him. "And I do not want to know." She then turned to me again, pressing her fingers over mine on the table. "Hie vaedrum teim," she whispered, eyes wide and sincere, completely shattering the heaviness in my chest.

"Hie vaedrum teim aldig," I replied, then turned towards our host. "Even though I appreciate keeping my lady entertained while I was away, I will take it from here."

Rhylan's jaw became rigid and his fingers squeezed the glass so tightly that his fingertips became white.

"The king is coming," he announced.

Anwen

Chapter Twenty-Five

This was it, our only chance to escape. During the few hours we spent alone in the creepy copy of our first home, apart from devouring every part of my body and forcing me to take another shower, Ansgar also took the time to talk me through the customs and cordialities of the court.

Which is why I knew that we all had to stand as the royals entered or left a room and could only turn our backs to them after being excused. Also, the word 'no' did not enter their vocabularies, so the best option for us to get into their good graces was to always be polite, approving, and agreeing with them. "Flattery can't hurt," I remembered Ansgar's words.

Ansgar, who panted like he'd just ran ten miles next to me, was still shaken by what Rhylan had announced. As soon as the doors opened, I rose from my seat and hurried behind my prince, occupying the empty chair between him and Rhylan. Wanting to piss off the fire faerie aside, I knew occupying the king's rightful place at the table before his arrival would not prove to be a very wise decision on my end.

I grabbed Ansgar's arm and squeezed a little, letting my eyes tell him what my words could not. Within a heartbeat, his brain must have translated my intention because the shadows in his eyes immediately dissipated, leaving only grey clearness and a dash of light. Hope.

"Welcome, your Royal Highnesses," Rhylan spoke and my eyes turned to his direction just enough to see that he also stood, showing the same respect to the king and queen.

"General," the queen exclaimed in delight, her voice a scraping of metal against my senses. She was a tall woman, slender and... old. Apart from Ansgar's parents, I couldn't recall seeing an old fae, even though my mate had told me they did not live for hundreds of years. But even so, the Earth Kingdom's king looked vigorous and strong, like a fifty-year-old bodybuilder. This woman, however, struggled to drag her step and I knew her long black velvet dress had been designed to hide her difficulty in walking.

Wrinkles interlocked on her face, hardening her expression. Even her smile looked tired and exhausted.

"My beautiful queen," Rhylan exclaimed and took two steps towards her, bowing even lower, his right knee hitting the ground, then grabbed her hand, adorned by lavish jewellery, and kissed it.

"It is a pleasure to have you back, Rhylan," she spoke, her voice protruding through the carved stone of the walls, so thick and lashing.

"The pleasure will be all mine, my queen," he replied, maintaining his kneeling position in front of her. I had never seen Rhylan like this, so humble and obeying, it shocked me.

"Let's hope not," she let out what I believed wanted to be a giggle but sounded more like a low bark.

"Rhylan," the king was the next to greet him, and only then, he rose from in front of the queen, but still kept her hand in his.

"My king," Rhylan nodded. Only nodded. None of the cordiality and obedience he had displayed with his wife.

So much tension accumulated that even the queen sensed it, having to act as a mediator between them. I could not grasp what happened, but I remembered how the king previously received Rhylan when he brought me in front of him the first time. They looked friendly, happy to see each other. What changed? I made a note to tell Ansgar about this when we returned to our room. When we *hopefully* returned to our room.

"Rhylan, we haven't received an invitation to your quarters in decades, this must be an important event," the Queen shifted the attention back to him, forcing the general to react and shift his gaze from the king, back to her.

"Please," he pointed to the seat on his right, the one opposite my own, and pulled it aside, allowing the queen to situate herself in it before he gently pushed it back to help her reach the table.

"My King, if you would be so kind," he then pointed to the chair at the head of the table, the one I occupied for a short while, which still had the glass of wine I had poured and a few wooden splinters from Ansgar's anger just then.

The King inclined his head, obviously displeased with the situation but did not protest when he realised he would be sitting next to Ansgar, who tensed in his chair. I immediately extended my hand to grab his under the table, our fingers interlocking tightly.

The Queen started scanning me with curiosity, observing my

every move and gesture, but her attention was snatched back to the door. When it opened again, a cheerful Marreth appeared in the room.

"Rhylan," he nodded to the host, "My King and Queen," he acknowledged the royals, and then his eyes shifted to Ansgar and I. "Other guests," the commander politely said and occupied the seat in between the royal couple without awaiting an invitation.

"Will there ever be a day when you are on time?" Rhylan sighed as if admonishing a son.

"Forgive me for taking another minute for grooming, I wouldn't want my general to be displeased by my rough appearance," Marreth smiled, talking to a friend.

"Please Rhylan, explain this invitation," the King interrupted the conversation, which the Queen was obviously enjoying and passed to abruptly serious matters. I stopped sipping from the glass of wine I'd been nursing through the round of appetisers, we all wanted to know what he planned.

"Of course, my king," Rhylan smiled and placed his own glass to the side. "I cordially invited you tonight to introduce the newest member of our court, Anwen Odstar." I choked with my own saliva. What? Without even acknowledging me, he continued, "Anwen is my personal guest and will be sharing my territory, I also demand a title for her status. I know how much she likes to be called a princess."

He grinned, cold as ice, and only then his attention turned to me in such a slow-motion, that his eyes took a long while to find mine. Long enough for me to have enough time to paint all the confusion and surprise across my face.

"Unfortunately, she arrives with an inconvenience," his eyes transferred to Ansgar for a mere second before coming back to mine, "though I have been assured he is aware of what will happen if he continues to adopt his old ways of aggression and violence."

"We shall measure the prince's capabilities for self-restraint then," the King agreed. "Is this a consort petition, general?"

What? My eyes gouged out of my head and by the way Ansgar squeezed my hand and his face turned as red as his boiling blood, I knew he was as surprised and angry as I was.

"It is, my king," Rhylan inclined his head in approval and my jaw dropped.

"Excuse me?" I said, forgetting all about our plan and where we were. "What do you mean your consort?" My voice trembled, unsure and unready for the words I already expected to come out of his mouth.

"Let me handle the details, princess," he accentuated the words, that damned title he had asked for me. Rhylan wanted me to be his fiancée and become a princess? My brain could not wrap around the new information, my chest became heavy and knotted with what felt like stones inside my lungs and I wanted to be sick.

I did not know what Ansgar's reaction was, I could not look at him, because I barely focused on my own breathing and consciousness. Rhylan continued to speak but I did not hear the words, my mind unable to grasp their meaning until Ansgar's fingers wrapped around my own again under the table. I didn't even realise I had let him go.

"Do not trouble yourself, prince, I like to share," was the only thing I heard before Ansgar erupted, crashing his fist on the wooden table, making it shake violently.

"Before you get any ideas, *prince*," Rhylan accentuated his title mockingly, "remember our deal. One misstep and you go back to that quaint little cell you like decorating in crimson so much. This time, your mate will stay with me, however," the old fae grinned wickedly, enjoying the torture he was putting us under. And we had no choice but to play his game, like senseless little puppets he manoeuvred to his own whim.

Ansgar swallowed deeply and retook his seat without saying another word. He didn't even look at me, hands shaking with ire.

"We will have to organise a suitable trousseau for the new princess," the Queen said excitedly. "Though I hope you will not be too busy with your new toy that you'll forget your previous arrangements," she purred and traced a finger along his arm playfully. My gaze automatically switched to the king, who kept himself occupied with a steak and threw a question from time to time in Marreth's direction.

"Of course, my queen. Plus, I don't want to take my betrothed's pet just yet," he grinned at her and they started engaging in a hushed conversation, giggling from time to time.

Only Ansgar and I remained unmoving, looking at each other helplessly. We were left without an option, the royals wanted nothing to do with us, considering us 'Rhylan's toy and her pet,' as the Queen so delicately put it when talking about us.

Throughout the rest of the dinner, we hardly spoke, only

answering some yes or no questions that either of the royals addressed from time to time, out of cordiality more than anything. I couldn't eat, only focusing on the wine, which I had three glasses of already and planned to get some more, while Ansgar's jaw remained so tight I thought his teeth would shatter and fall out of his mouth.

"Well, my dear," the queen turned to me for what was about the fourth time in the entire evening, "I shall have my best seamstress prepared for a fitting tomorrow, we need to get you measured and organised as soon as possible," she smiled and I recognised the same wickedness pouring through Rhylan. These two deserved each other and I hoped they would both burn in hell.

"As for the prince, he would do well in training the new members. Under constant supervision, of course," the King spoke, with Marreth nodding at his every word. "After all, we do not want his talents gone to waste, now that we managed to tighten the leash."

Ansgar didn't even turn to acknowledge the king, his eyes gazing forward somewhere into the wall, probably focusing on keeping that anger in place.

It was the commander who replied, "I'll see to it, my king."

"Shall we, dear?" King Drahden announced his intention and the Queen nodded and rose, forcing us all to do the same. We kept our heads bowed, tracking each step they took and nodding when they acknowledged each of us by name, then departed through the doors the soldiers opened for them.

In the following moment, everything that Ansgar had kept in place for what seemed to be the longest hour of my life expelled wrath from him, erupting towards Rhylan. His fists slammed into the fire faerie's face, smashing hard and deep, with sharp and repeated movements until Rhylan's features became a blur of blood and crimson shades.

I screamed for him, begging him to stop, but my reaction caused deeper ire, so much that Marreth had to take me further away from the scene. To my surprise, the commander placed himself in front of me, ready to receive the blow of their fight, should it reach us.

Rhylan did not take long to defend himself, allowing Ansgar a few more fists before tapping into his energy, making dark swirls of smoke appear and push my mate away, slamming him into the nearby wall with a thumping sound.

"That is enough," Rhylan yelled, a sound that penetrated my bones, sending another wave of power into Ansgar, making him growl in pain.

"Stop it!" I jumped from behind Marreth, ready to throw myself in between them. The commander caught me in a brisk movement and grabbed both my arms, tightening them to my chest and keeping me locked in what could have been called a bear hug. No matter how hard I tried to wiggle away, to escape him, his grip proved effective, so I appealed to the next best thing I had. Shouting and pleading at Rhylan to stop hurting my prince.

"You are a miserable bastard," Ansgar's voice barely pierced through the wave of energy slamming into him, sounding raspy. "Can't even fight like a male." Blood started pouring down his nose and was slowly making its way to his lips, ready to cover the delicate softness I had kissed so many times.

"Rhylan, please!" I cried out. I didn't know if my words or my desperation proved effective to his ears, but it made him turn to me, if only for a moment. Enough to take my presence in, to see Marreth struggling to hold me.

"Why would I do that, prince?" the general spat. "You may be stronger, but my power has no limits. Why would I waste my time being honourable in a situation where you attacked me?" he grinned wickedly and slammed another wave of that darkness into Ansgar, forcing his muscles into a tremble.

I went mad, terrified of what would come if another ripple pushed more of his power, colliding into Marreth as hard as I could and forcing my entire body to push out of his grasp. Maybe I managed to do it, maybe he let me go of his own volition, carrying the same concern for my mate's life as me. Either way, I found myself jumping on Rhylan's back and clawing at his face, knees squeezing his waist while my fingers tried to grab at his cheeks, scraping skin underneath my fingernails.

"God damn it sprout, get away from me," he screeched, waving his hands in an attempt to catch my own and make my attack stop. With the corner of my eye, I spotted Ansgar, falling to the ground, his wide back heaving with deep pants.

"For fuck's sake," Rhylan growled again and threw himself into a wall, taking me along with him. As soon as my back bumped into the hard surface, my body jerked in self-defence, forcing me to push against the wall to lessen the impact. It only took a second, enough for Rhylan to recover and escape me.

The fire fae stood and looked at me, blood pouring from the two deep scratches I had managed to forge, one across his cheek and one on his forehead, cutting his brow. Rhylan's eyes confessed disbelief at the sight of me, and surprise at the realisation that I was preparing to jump him again.

"This is ridiculous," he exclaimed, taking a step back, looking at my battled self and then at Ansgar, both of us panting against opposite walls, with Rhylan in the middle of the mess. Marreth only stood to the side and watched us all, an amused look on his face.

"Commander, take the prince back to their room," our captor ordered with a long sigh, but before Marreth could move, Ansgar shifted, trying to stand up for another round of attacks. Tried, and failed.

"I will not leave her with you, you disgusting piece of —"

"Yeah, yeah, you've said it already," Rhylan looked unphased, but he crouched next to my prince and gripped something from his belt. I hadn't even noticed he wore one during dinner. A small silvery dagger appeared in his hand and with no effort at all, he gripped Ansgar's neck, raising him in the air as if he were a puppet.

"One cut is all you need, prince. Piss me off some more and I'll end that pathetic miserable life of yours." Hatred rippled through him, exhaustion from the entire situation and I knew we had pushed Rhylan to the limit of his indulgence.

"Please, no! Oh gods, please," I shook and started begging. I did not know if I was on my knees or still a fallen pile of mess by the wall, but I sensed my hands joining together, like in a prayer. I was shaking and crying, snot mixing with tears across my face.

"Shut the fuck up and sit at the table," he addressed me with a look that lasted less than a second, enough to bark the order at me, so I forced my body to obey and crawled to the table, struggling to take my seat with shaking limbs.

"As for this one," Rhylan turned back to Ansgar, "either take him to the room or kill him on the way there," he ordered, placing what I supposed was an iron dagger into the commander's hand, who dragged Ansgar away and left the room without giving me a chance to speak or protest. I remained quiet, barely sitting on the chair, my hands clasped on the tablecloth in a continual shaking motion.

"Relax, you know I'm not gonna hurt you," Rhylan sounded tired, frustrated when he retook the same seat he had occupied during dinner, right next to my own. He looked around, scanning the table then sighed heavily, "that fuckboy of yours destroyed my favourite set of crystal glasses," he exhaled, then grabbed the only remaining undamaged glass and found an untouched bottle of wine, pouring himself a drink.

"It's time to talk, sprout," his adamant eyes fixated on me as he relaxed in his chair, taking a sip from his drink and closing his eyes to enjoy a silent melody only he could hear. Resting after a tiring day's work.

Ansgar

Chapter Twenty-Six

Marreth dragged me out, while I screamed for Anwen, every part of me fighting to be released, so I could return to that room and break that bastard into pieces.

"Calm down," the commander ordered my shaking self. I was still tied to him, my limbs unable to take control and overpower him. "The more you struggle, the more it will hurt," he advised, stopping for a mere moment to better position my body across his back and make it more comfortable to carry me.

He spoke true, I realised when I once again tried to shake free from his hold, muscles trembling in pain and unable to connect with the commands I sent onto them.

"What is happening to me?" I asked in between wheezing breaths. One or two broken ribs would require mending and the sooner the better.

"The general took your powers, you brought him great offence attacking him like that," Marreth explained while continuing to drag me down the dark corridors. Understanding my lack of knowledge regarding Rhylan's powers, he did not wait for me to ask and started offering more details, I assumed in the hope to create a distraction.

"Rhylan is the oldest remaining fireling, at least in this part of the kingdom, he has power over all of us, even the king. He can take away a faerie's energy and incapacitate them temporarily as long as they share a bond."

"I don't share a bond with that bastard," I grumbled.

"*You* may not, but your mate does. And you are bonded to her. So..." he stopped, realising the subject hurt more than helped. "You'll be fine; he'll probably release you as soon as he returns her. She'll be fine as well, I've never seen the general so attentive with a female before."

I clenched my muscles, my entire body, my bones, forcing all of them to take hold and let me escape, but the more I struggled, the worse it got. Pain shot through me, every nerve ending screamed in ache and my bones felt as though shattered glass ran through them.

"Calm down," the commander urged again, "It's a good thing. It means he'll keep her safe. After all, that is what you both want, yes?"

I nodded, not knowing or caring if he accepted that as a response and let myself be carried away from my mate, hating the poor excuse of a male I had become.

"Here we are," I felt my body being released as Marreth crouched low enough to allow me finally to stand. Barely. I immediately gripped the door handle to sustain my own weight, but even with the extra support, it proved difficult to stand.

"You should lie down, I'll come get you tomorrow for training. We start at seven," he announced and turned to walk away.

"Commander," I stopped him and Marreth quickly turned back, concern on his face.

"Thank you," I nodded, "for it all." I didn't need to offer further explanation; he knew what I meant. He had been the only one who cared about the miserable life I had lived under these lands.

"Of course, prince," he nodded and bowed to me just slightly, reverently. I returned the gesture and extended my hand for him to grab. He did so eagerly, his palm grabbing onto the midsection of my arm and wrapping tightly, while I did the same.

A salute amongst soldiers.

Two hours passed, Anwen had not returned to me and my legs remained as limp as when I was brought to the room. Even so, I tried to escape, to go after her, but as soon as I opened the door I was met by several guards, all armed to the teeth and waiting for a misstep.

So I appealed to the next best thing to calm my anger, destruction. I went to the kitchen and ripped apart the fake curtains that wanted to create the illusion of a window. I grabbed the knives and threw them towards every object I found, ripping things apart with my bare hands.

When I felt satisfied with the chaos I created, I proceeded onto the next room, the sitting room, ripping apart everything I could get my hands on, paintings, fake plants, the table and chairs, the pillows on the sofa, and even furniture itself. Every single object that remained in smithereens offered me another drop of satisfaction. If I could not hurt Rhylan, I would at least break everything that reminded me of him.

I was on my way to kick the sofa when the door opened and Anwen appeared in the room. I did not give her a chance to react to what I had done, I lunged for my mate and grabbed her close to me, slamming her body against the door she had just arrived through, kicking it shut.

Anwen gasped at the force of my movement, even I was surprised by the velocity of my motion. The bastard must have released me. But it didn't matter right now, not when Anwen was returned in my arms. Possession overtook my senses, forcing me to jolt towards her, to have her then and there, to feel that connection and the bond we forged when she cut me during the mating process. The dagger must have enhanced my energy and bound Anwen onto me, allowing our connection to finally take place. Making Anwen a part of me. And I needed to feel whole again.

Without thinking, without caring, I lifted Anwen's legs and spread them wide, forcing the seams of her dress to fracture and break apart. I pushed her body into the door, her legs across my waist, and pressed my lips against hers in urgency and desperation.

She barely made a sound, just a slight moan, probably with surprise more than desire. But I did not care. Damn all the goddesses, I did not care. I wanted her, then and there. To feel her again, to make sure she was still mine.

Without breaking the kiss, I slid her panties to one side and cupped her womanhood, rubbing the palm of my hand aggressively against it until I felt wetness and without a warning, I pushed myself inside her in two abrupt movements.

Anwen's lips released a scream but I covered them with my own and started moving, rough and hard until my entire member was sheathed inside her. Her tightness overpowered me, making every one of my senses lose control. All I wanted was to be with her, melt my body to hers for no one to ever take us apart.

"Ansgar," she moaned while I continued to slam into her like a savage beast devouring its prey, unable to stop, crazy with desire.

"Ansgar," her hands managed to release my hold and pulled onto me, onto my hair. "Ansgar!" she insisted again, forcing me to look at her. "Stop!" she demanded, her voice rough, eyes damp and surprised.

I continued to press into her, decreasing the rhythm just slightly, her body still moving up and down against mine, her entrance still squeezing the soul out of me.

I wanted to kiss her again, wanted to devour her lips but she shifted her head, denying me the gift. Anwen's face became taut and a broken voice uttered, "Stop, you're hurting me!"

I froze, halting abruptly at the request, my gaze following her lips, trying to catch the words from thin air to put them back together and understand if they had spoken true.

Her expression told me yes, that they were. Her furrowed brows and disappointed expression broke the remaining pieces of my heart.

I immediately removed myself from inside of her and allowed her body to descend to the ground, carefully placing her legs back on the floor. When I removed my hands, she pushed me and escaped, walking away quickly and into the bedroom.

"I'm sorry," I murmured and followed after her, struggling to pull my pants up. Before I could place a step, the bedroom door was slammed in my face.

I stopped in shock, not knowing how to react. I had taken her so many times, a lot harder than this and she always enjoyed it. Sometimes when I thought I couldn't fit more of myself inside of her she screamed and begged. What made it different now?

"Anwen?" I knocked on the door but received no response, so I decided to enter, and may the goddess damn me if it turned out to be the wrong move.

"Anwen?" I called her name again and spotted her already in bed, hugging her knees to her chest, a pillow squeezed in between her legs.

I hurried to her and fell on my knees on the floor, next to where she sat. "I am so sorry, fahrenor. I am so, so sorry," I cried out, dread carving its way into my chest at the sight of her.

"I just thought…" I stopped, not knowing what to say.

She lifted her gaze to me, tears covering hazel eyes.

"What? That after everything I've been through, I would need a good fuck to calm down?" she accused with hatred. Hatred. For *me*.

"Anwen, please forgive me, I didn't mean to hurt you," I said again, a hand reaching for her, but she quickly moved away so I retracted, respecting her space.

"I wasn't ready," she replied, focusing her attention on a random spot on the wall. "What were you thinking? Well, this girl has just been slammed into a wall, what would be the next best thing? Hm... let's see. Let's slam her into a door and fuck her," she mocked, animosity piercing through her tone. For a moment, she reminded me of Rhylan.

"I'm sorry, I went crazy, I didn't know—"

"Where I was? If I was safe?" she replied in my stead. "Do you think Rhylan tagged your location on the map and let me follow you by GPS to make sure you were safe?"

I stopped, not understanding what she meant. "I'm sorry," I repeated. "I'm sorry I am not GPS," I said honestly, not understanding her words but sharing the sentiment.

She looked at me for the first time, her lips curving just slightly to sketch the faintest of smiles, then anger overpowered her features again. "Don't you dare be cute right now, not when you shoved your dick in my stomach."

"I thought you were ready, I found wetness and—"

"Yeah, well Ansgar, that's what happens to a vagina when you rub the hell out of it. It becomes wet. It's a physical response. That doesn't mean I am ready," she snapped.

"Sometimes you are ready before I do anything," I frowned, remembering times when she would pull down my pants early in the morning and jump on me without a warning. "Is your attraction for me gone?" I asked. We had so many more important matters to discuss, to plan, to understand, but I could not stop the silly question from escaping my mouth.

"I..." she waved her head in frustration. "It's not that, of course, it's not that," she replied quickly. "You just jumped me, thinking you know best," Anwen huffed.

"I became enraged when Marreth took me away, I couldn't control my anger, I had guards at the door and my powers were shut. I couldn't do anything but wait for you," I explained. "And when I saw you, I needed to feel you again. To feel us. I am sorry I overstepped, causing you displeasure was the last thing I wanted to do. Please believe me," I begged, my hands barely containing their urge to trap her inside a hug, but I understood that it may be the last thing she needed.

"And you think I wasn't? Do you think I enjoy depending on Rhylan's moods, not knowing if he is ever going to let us go? That I have to pretend to be engaged to him and help him with whatever sick plans he has?" she accused.

Involuntarily I sighed in relief at her words. She had to *pretend.* Which meant that as usual, Rhylan had a bigger plan and Anwen was a means to an end. That he didn't truly want to take my mate as consort.

"I'm gonna go to bed," Anwen pulled the cover over her body, wrapping herself in the massive blanket.

"Okay," I said, "let's go to bed."

"I'd rather sleep alone tonight," her voice sounded from underneath the covers. "You can take the sofa."

"I tore the sofa apart," I murmured, now regretting my decision.

"You can sleep on what's left of the sofa," she replied dryly and turned away, leaving a trail of her undulated hair where her face used to be.

I understood the request and motivation. I was not dignified to share her bed that evening and had to respect her decision. So I stood and withdrew slowly until I reached the door.

"Do I have your permission to leave the bedroom door open?" I asked. She may very well have the bed but I wasn't prepared to abandon her for the night completely.

"Uh-huh, "Anwen replied from underneath the covers.

After slamming myself with every insult I remembered, cursing myself for my stupidity and idiotic urges, I went into what remained of the kitchen. Trying to redeem myself, I opened the fridge and prepared a mixture of ice which I put into one of those bags that closed with a seal at the top and wrapped it in a clean towel.

I didn't dare enter the bedroom without permission, so I knocked again.

"What?" Anwen asked. She hadn't changed position.

"I brought ice," I explained. "For the wound I caused." I remembered that nothing felt better than an ice bath after long hours of training, it had a pleasing effect on bruises and cuts and left the body refreshed for the next session.

"What?" she half stood from bed, finding me in the darkness.

"From when I took you against the door. For when I hurt you." May the goddess kill me on the spot, I hated myself for saying those words, for being such a brute with the person I loved most.

She sighed. "You didn't hurt me, it was just...bad timing," clearly finding it difficult to explain herself. "I wasn't ready," Anwen repeated.

"Ice is good for wounds," I tried to explain.

"Ansgar, I don't have a wound. It just felt uncomfortable so I needed to stop. I'm fine." She turned slightly, raising her eyes from under the cover to spot me by the door, nervous and unmoving. "I'm fine," she dragged the words to make me understand. "Plus, I can't really shove ice into my vag, can I?" she half grinned at my lack of sense.

I looked at her, not knowing what to say, apart from how sorry I was. Which she heard a hundred times over and had ordered me to shut up.

"Good night," she filled the silence.

"Good night," I repeated and withdrew from the room.

I couldn't shut an eye, so for the remainder of the night, I listened to her breathing and shifting in bed, stepping inside the bedroom every half of the hour to make sure she was alright.

A soft knock announced the arrival of the morning and though we did not have a clock any longer, due to my rage fit the night before, I assumed the time for training had arrived.

"One sec," I whispered and stood from the nook I created during the night. Luckily, one of the sofa pillows hadn't been shattered like the rest of them so I used that and some of the filling from the rest of the pillows to make some sort of laying place. I used it to comfort my back against the outside bedroom wall, just by the door, all the while checking on Anwen with rhythmic precision.

I hurried to the door and opened it quickly, preventing Marreth from having to knock a second time and wake my lady.

"Morning," he greeted me with excitement but at the sight of my face and the shattered background around me, his eyes went wide.

367

"Care to explain?" he asked with a raise of his eyebrows.

"Maybe on the way there, my mate is still sleeping and I don't want to wake her," I communicated in a hushed tone. I hurried back to the bedroom, tiptoeing around the bed, and found Anwen resting, wrapped in the duvet just the way she liked it. Unable to contain myself, I pressed a small kiss on her cheek, soft enough to let her continue her sleep undisturbed. There were no words in the world to express my apologies, so I referred to the next best thing and used whatever energy I had in me to grow her a bouquet of white roses with the biggest petals I had probably ever created and left them on the unoccupied side of the bed, then stepped away and returned to the commander.

He grinned and shifted to the side, allowing me room to exit. I did so reluctantly, part of me wanting to make sure Anwen was feeling better before I left, but I assumed rest would do her more good than seeing my face right now, so I closed the door behind me slowly and followed the commander through the halls.

His smirk permeated for so long that I had to ask. "You look satisfied," I posed the question as an observation.

"Me?" he grinned wider. "You're wearing the same clothes as last night, or well...what's left of them," he replied with amusement. "The room is destroyed and you are very concerned with giving your lady time to rest."

"And?" I huffed, turning to the right just after he did and following the commander into deeper terrain.

"Someone had a busy night," he observed with delight.

My lips pursed. "You can say that."

Marreth immediately caught my tone and stopped. "What's wrong?"

"Apart from Rhylan wanting to take my mate, us being trapped in a horrid kingdom with no escape and receiving life threats every single day?" I responded sarcastically, but he ignored my comment.

"Apart from that." Marreth pushed, searching beyond the obvious.

"I was a prick last night," I admitted, and seeing how he still looked concerned, I decided to confess the whole thing to the only half-friendly face I could find around here. "After you let me inside I went ballistic and destroyed everything in the room and by the time she returned I felt possessive, desperate so I..." I took a moment to find my words, "I behaved like a jerk. Long story short, she doesn't want me touching her."

Marreth's face crumpled in understanding and had the good sense to fake a grimace if only to imitate the state of my feelings.

"She'll forgive you after she finds those flowers," he encouraged, placing a hand on my shoulder. "That's a nice trick," he admitted, "It would have saved me so much trouble in my old life if I could do something like that," the commander admitted and squeezed my shoulder, a gesture to help me regain my stance and brighten up.

"I doubt it, seeing how I'm not even allowed in bed," I huffed under my teeth but nodded as a thank you for his encouragement and pointed my hand out, a silent request for Marreth to continue walking.

"I heard that about human females. Apparently, they take

comfort away from males as a means of repercussion. Never tested it though," Marreth lifted his brows in surprise, but did as advised and continued walking. "I guess you tested that theory for the both of us," he added, laughter in his voice.

"Is there someone in need of flowers on your behalf?" I took the opportunity to ask, seeing how he was chatty this morning, and for the first time, the male had a chance to treat me as a companion soldier, rather than a hostage.

"Prince, are you sure you have time for all my love stories?" he turned his head only slightly and grinned proudly at me.

"Anything to distract me, even if it has to do with your hideous self," I grinned back, teasing him, just like I used to do with my brothers.

On the way to the training field, Marreth told me about his life and love, about the females he had been with in the Fire Kingdom and back in his own, his words trailing along at the mention of a particular lady, way above his status, whom he had loved deeply, always from afar.

The rest of the day was spent training, long hours flying by just like they did back at home when the sun-scorched our backs and blades tore our skin. To my relief, I did not recognise any soldiers from the Earth Kingdom, but felt a dash of happiness to be returned into the ring, able to touch real blades and feel the heaviness of the steel.

It took a while for my muscles to regain their balance, but after the mid-morning breakfast, I felt refreshed and challenged the higher ranks into the ring, claiming victory in each and every field.

Even Marreth confessed his surprise at my abilities, especially after the time I had been submerged in iron, but none of that seemed to matter when blades connected to my arms. I felt them as a part of myself, reminding me of better days and normalcy back at home, so I enjoyed every moment of holding them and cutting through armour after armour, always careful not to deeply wound or break any limbs.

"If you don't stop soon, prince, the single ladies in the kingdom will form a queue to your room," a voice made me stop in place, my battle partner seizing the moment and striking right into my teeth, making me tumble to the ground.

"Rhylan," I greeted him after spitting the accumulation of blood from my mouth. "We need to talk," I uttered, exiting the ring and abandoning my partner in the middle of combat, an un-soldier-like thing to do. I would explain my actions at a later date, I told myself.

"Indeed we do," Rhylan nodded and left the ring with long steps, allowing me enough time to return the weapon and trail after him through the dark corridor.

"I assume Anwen will be the first subject matter," Fear Gorta started speaking again when he sensed my steps approaching his own.

"You assume correctly," I quickened my pace enough to grab hold of his arm and twist it, forcing him to stop and face me. A dangerous move, I was well aware but I would not take a stroll while having an extremely important conversation regarding my mate.

"We are not going to converse until we reach a place where I feel comfortable discussing," Rhylan shook his hand away to let me

371

know I had sullied it with my touch. He scanned my body, the sweat trailing along my naked torso, and rose his lip in disgust, then turned once again and started walking.

I sighed and followed him through the narrow corridors, trying to count my way up from the training field and focus my attention and anger towards something else, knowing that I was one wrong move away from attacking Fear Gorta right then and there.

"Here will be fine," he announced and opened a door that led us to a small chamber containing a round table, a fireplace, and two chairs. I entered and followed after him, taking a seat without being told to and grabbing the bottle placed on the table and a glass to serve myself a drink.

"What happened last night?" Rhylan turned to me, preferring to stand by the fireplace and watch my dirty self lean against the velvet chair, sullying it with my sweat and grime.

"Apart from you announcing to take my mate as consort and removing me from your way to be alone with her?" I pressed my words from between gritted teeth.

"What happened after?" Rhylan pressed and addressed me as one would an insolent youth. "What did you do?"

My breath stopped, eyes going wide. "Is she alright?"

Rhylan scanned me for a long moment, leaving me to boil in a cauldron of wrath of my own making until he deigned me with a reply. "Physically, yes. Otherwise, she is hurt. I assume you are to blame for that, she was perfectly fine when I brought her yesterday," the fireling explained, pressing his accusation.

"I need to speak to her," I immediately said and tried to rise, but

Rhylan pressed his energy around me, forcing me to keep my place on the chair. It felt like an invisible cliff had dropped on me, allowing my blood to flow freely but keeping everything else immobile.

"You will do no such thing. As a matter of fact, it suits my purposes in a much better way since she is willing to spend more time away from you."

"That is exactly what I need to prevent, you miserable bastard," I accused, trying to shift and escape.

Rhylan rolled his eyes, finally taking the seat in front of me. "Such dramatics," he sighed. "Honestly, you two act like the next best thing since Romeo and Juliet," he waved his head in disapproval. "And of course, I cannot hurt one without hurting the other, so I am stuck in a fairly unpleasant situation." He grabbed the bottle to serve himself a glass and after he took a long shot, Fear Gorta started scratching his ear, caught in deep thought.

"What is your plan, Rhylan?" I demanded, analysing his every move.

"I mean to kill the queen," his voice sounded inside my head, through whatever new connection he had forged against my will. I remained silent to the confession, watching him take another sip of his drink. My eyes went wide, I expected him to say anything else but this.

Fear Gorta remarked on my reaction, this time aloud.

"Yes, it is rather complicated indeed, and a far longer story than what I plan to tell you. And not because of lack of time," he pointed out, "but because I simply do not care for you enough to waste my precious breath."

I ground my teeth but said nothing, only scanned him, his features, trying to read his lies.

"To do that," he continued as if nothing, "I need Anwen. For various purposes, but the most important at the time being is to distract my target," Rhylan confessed, uttering the words carefully.

"And what makes you think she will help you?" I pressed my words.

"You," he admitted. "The fact that whatever you did yesterday, made her docile enough to engage in my plan and play her part. So I am to ask you to continue doing whatever it is until Autumn Solstice." Rhylan stopped and took another drink, awaiting my reply.

"You had your males torture me for four solstices to get information about the tear and now you change your mind and want to keep me alive to help you. What changed?"

Rhylan knew or must have guessed that he did have to waste enough breath to explain this, because he responded with a fair amount of tension, enough to allow me to see the truth in his words.

"I finally have someone to take her place."

Seeing, or maybe realising that I did not possess enough background information on the queen to help me reveal the meaning of his words, he continued, "They are a direct descendent of the god, same as me. And there is a certain amount of energy that I can hold, so even if I have craved this disappearance for the past two centuries, I didn't have a place to store all that energy she will leave behind when she fades. Not until now."

Rhylan served himself another drink and chugged its contents before speaking again, this time back into my mind. "I need the queen dead, prince. I can't take it any longer, and I have the perfect replacement."

"What about her husband?" I did not dignify him with the title, especially not in front of Rhylan. And not in a kingdom that kept me and my mate prisoners.

"He's a small creature, easy to dispose of once she is no more. Cut the connection loose and he is doomed," Fear Gorta waved a hand as though to reassure me killing his own leader was child's play. I wanted to spit in his face, not because I was affected by his plans, but because I felt disgusted by his lack of loyalty. Appalled by a general who had no honour, or innate need to protect his leader.

"So what, you expect me to help you kill her so you can then have free rein to keep torturing me until I die or spill the information? Information that no longer takes priority for you? I've been trained better than this, Fear Gorta," I scanned him up and down, freely showing my distrust.

"All you need to know, my liege," he replied with his usual mocking tone, "is that I recently received information, which places the conversation we've been having for the past year as a second priority, due to some very fortunate turns of events," he replied with delight.

"And what makes you think I will help you?"

"I assume a male in love, such as yourself, would do anything to gain his lady's freedom, would you not?" he asked as though it was the most obvious question.

"You will free her?" My heart-pumped desperately in my chest. This was it, this could be my chance to get Anwen out of this misery.

"I will, on the account that you work with me and do as I require." As soon as he spoke the words, the invisible cliff released me, allowing my chest to inhale deeper, my arms automatically moving to rest on the table, towards Rhylan.

"When will she go free?" My gaze pierced to his, drilling into that immortal blackness of his soul.

"Autumn solstice. As soon as my plan is fulfilled, she will be returned to her world," he promised.

I knew better than to hope for myself, for my own freedom. The fact that he offered to return Anwen to her family was more than I could have hoped.

"I need a blood oath." I knew better than to blindly trust Rhylan, especially after all the lies and tricks he had played on us.

"I expected no less of you," he smirked wickedly and used a sharp ring that looked like a claw, the same one he had cut Anwen with to rip a slit in his palm and allow dark red liquid to escape.

"I, Fear Gorta of the Fire Kingdom, swear onto you, Prince Ansgar of the Earth Kingdom, the safe return of your mate, Anwen Odstar back into the human realm on the date of Autumn Solstice of the current year, untroubled and unharmed, upon completion of my plan to defeat and kill the Queen of the Fire Kingdom and in exchange for your help and cooperation with all that I require."

He stopped and extended his hand, so I offered my palm for him to make the same cut. As soon as my blood appeared, I started uttering my vow.

"I, Prince Ansgar of the Earth Kingdom, swear onto you, Fear Gorta of the Fire Kingdom, that I will help and cooperate to achieve your plan of defeating and killing the Queen of the Fire Kingdom with the oath of safe release of my mate, Anwen Odstar, into the Human Territory. This oath will only remain valid as long as my mate is unharmed in every way during and after her stay within the Fire Kingdom and especially during her release."

I would not take any chances with Rhylan, but he nodded in acceptance and stood, allowing his blood to continue dripping until he placed his hand over the fire. I followed suit and did the same, allowing my blood to drip into the flames, bonding the oath between us.

"Very well, now that we have such things sorted, you are free to return to training," Rhylan smiled and pointed a dismissive hand. "You can eat with the soldiers, your mate will dine with me and the royals for the remainder of her stay."

I nodded, though I hated his terms, which meant I wouldn't be able to see Anwen at all throughout the day, and now the bastard made it even worse.

"You are, of course, not allowed into the throne room or dining hall and since my future consort," he pressed the words to spite me, will be otherwise engaged, your presence will not be needed until late in the evening, if at all," he grinned wickedly.

I nodded and turned to leave.

"And Ansgar?" His voice called me and forced me to look at him yet again.

"I have replaced the items you destroyed. And the couch," he grinned.

"Son of a bitch," I barked, but Rhylan only laughed with delight.

Anwen

Chapter Twenty-Seven

Ansgar hadn't arrived by the time Rhylan walked me to the room. When I found the roses on the pillow this morning, I jumped from bed and ran to the sitting room to find him, to apologise for the night before and explain myself.

I spent a terrible night without him, without my heat finding his, unable to cuddle into him or splay myself on his chest, just like I loved to do. I sensed him awake a few times and had an internal battle on whether to wake up and talk to him, but some part of me needed the space, the quiet of the night.

My thoughts had been all over the place and I hadn't had a few hours to myself, to think things through, to analyse and understand what happened, what was still happening. To me, to him, to us. Nothing I ever imagined could have prepared me for what I found in this dreadful kingdom, the time I'd spent surrounded by dead bodies. I could not deny it, part of me despised that. Even though I was in favour of self-defence, seeing how easily Ansgar erupted with every chance he got gave me the shivers.

I was never afraid of him, but his attitude had begun to be more and more volatile, and last night, his anger turned into possession. I loved him, with all my heart, with everything I was, and I couldn't even imagine what he had been through during the time we'd been apart, what kind of trauma he gathered.

My sweet soft prince, now reduced to a brutal soldier.

I wanted to allow us that night. To be apart, to think, to try and repair our wounds before becoming one again. I knew I snapped at him and regretted my poor choice of words, but the last thing I needed was to be treated with possession again.

Not after Rhylan had… I forced the memories from my mind, struggling to keep them in check. The last thing I wanted now was to feel like the stupid silly girl Rhylan had accused me to be.

"I am so sick of your spoiled brat bullshit," he had said. "All you do is cry and beg, squirm like a powerless worm. It's disgusting."

"What do you expect me to do?" I had cried out in a fickle attempt to preserve my dignity last night.

"Fight, in the name of the god. I told you, I warned you about this place, but you were willing to give up everything to save him. So I trusted you, I believed you, I put my hopes in you. Only for your true self to resurface at the slightest sign of trouble. You are ruining everything, you silly brat," his anger had pierced through his expression, tiny specks of his spit covering my face from the wrath of his words.

"And what do you expect me to do?" I still felt my voice tremble at the memory.

"To do as you're told," he sighed. "I wish your brother was here. I needed someone strong." He stopped and looked at me, up and down, twice. "Instead I got you," his tone drilled into my brain with disgust. The last person I wanted to see that morning was, of course, the one to come pick me up at nine o'clock sharp, while I still nestled in the sheets, hugging the flowers Ansgar had left for me.

"I'm not in the mood for more fighting," I announced when I spotted Rhylan through the open door of the bedroom.

"Clearly. You had a busy evening," he stated the obvious, scanning the broken pieces across the room, with a single pillow nestled against the wall, which is where I assumed Ansgar had slept. I felt a clench in my stomach at the sight of it, my muscles trembled with the need to wrap him in my arms.

"Are you going to be more cooperative today?" Rhylan stopped right at the bedroom door frame and leaned his shoulder against it.

"I see your modern outfit is back," I observed the return of his Boss obsession, a perfectly tailored suit with black leather shoes and an open collar black shirt made him look stunning.

He grinned proudly. "I am adopting my future bride's style. Fits me like a glove, won't you say?" The fae had the audacity to rotate slowly, parading himself to me, then turned and displayed his best smile. Where I in another situation, were I not already in love, I would have laid myself at his feet and told him to do whatever with me.

I never understood this obsession with Rhylan, the fact that even though I absolutely despised the bastard, something inside of me squealed for his contact at a primordial level. I would never understand it and wanted to stay as far away from that feeling.

"Yes, the lady likes," he shimmied by the door with a proud

expression.

"Stop reading my emotions," I accused and placed a pillow over my head like it would hide whatever colours he said he saw.

"Be glad I am not talking about the fact that you are all pale yellow. That dash of lilac is a positive improvement," he remarked.

"I have no idea what that means. I feel you stole all of this from chakras and stuff," I admitted.

"Or they stole it from me." Would this man ever stop grinning? "Yellow means you are sad, judging by the mixing shades you are also regretful, sorrowful, and needy," Rhylan waved a hand in the air as though chasing away a fly that came too close to him.

"Okay mister fortune teller, it's not like you couldn't read the fight I had with Ansgar last night from all the broken pieces of furniture behind you, but I'll give you that."

He turned to observe everything with a fresh eye, the fact that Ansgar had done this due to a fight seemed to brighten his morning.

"The lovely prince is so passionate, is he not?" Rhylan returned to that wicked smirk of his and I wanted nothing more than to slap that joy away from his face.

"Where is he?" I asked, scanning Rhylan's expression in hope to read the truth on his features.

"Training with the commander and new recruits. They'll be at it all day," he explained.

"I'd like to go to him." Before I gave him the opportunity to say no, I added. "Please."

He stopped for a beat, analysing my request, but replied dryly. "You will have enough time to see him tonight. The day is reserved for your trousseau and you are already late."

I wanted to protest, to fight him, but I kept myself in check. I would not give him the satisfaction, not after last night. "What is your plan, Rhylan?"

"Oh princess, you know very well I can't tell you that," he replied like it was obvious. I scanned him, looking at me from the doorframe, without taking a single step inside the bedroom, not even by accident and said, "Then why should I help you?"

He tsked, the displeased sound of his tongue pulsating into my eardrums. "Princess, how do I explain this to you so your little brain finally understands?" he changed his tone of voice to make it like talking to a little kid. "If you do not cooperate, your little fuck boy goes bye-bye. Forever this time."

By the slithering darkness in his gaze, I knew he meant it.

"So what is it that you need from me?" I swallowed my urge to regurgitate in fear at his threat.

"I need you to act like in that movie humans love so much, with the door," he pointed.

"Huh?" I replied with a frown.

"They are on a ship and they die?"

"Titanic?" I asked, surprised.

"That's the one," Rhylan replied happily. "For two hours, they distract you from death, showing you happy pictures of a couple. I need you to do that for me, only for two weeks. Until Autumn Solstice."

"So I am a distraction from death?" I asked with a trembling voice, terrified that he would point another threat at my prince.

"Exactly. I need you to smile, be polite, take strolls with me through the kingdom, and act like you are in love and happy, or at least semi-excited about becoming a princess to the Fire Kingdom," he extended his arms at the mention of the kingdom, yet another one of his theatrical gestures I had come to recognise. They came in some of his most sincere moments, even though he struggled to show otherwise.

"And how can I do that? How can I pretend to be happy and excited for a wedding I do not want?"

Rhylan pursed his lips, thinking for a short while. "Imagine it is all planning for your prince. Think of it as though you are marrying him and all of this is training for what it's to come. I'm sure the first thing once you get out of here will be to take you home and marry the hell out of you."

My stomach contorted. I didn't know if that was his intention, but he gave me unimaginable reassurance with his words, the fact that he had expressed a possibility for both Ansgar and I to leave this place.

"You will help us?" I asked, hope accumulated in my veins.

"If you behave," he sharpened the words and turned his back to me. "Now be a good sprout and get dressed, we shall discuss more at breakfast."

And we did just that. Rhylan and I had breakfast together and he told me about what was expected of me as his future consort, the laws of the kingdom, and how it would be acceptable from today for me to stroll unaccompanied through the court halls and share a table with the royals.

It ended up with me spending a very long day standing in front of a mirror with various females spinning me around and measuring me, having only a few minutes allowance to eat a quick sandwich. The result of the day's work was a long dress that was brought to me with a dinner invitation.

With Rhylan. And the royal family.

I allowed the females to comb and arrange my hair into some sort of crown, just like the queen wore hers, and dress me the way they wanted to, in the hope that I would finally see Ansgar. I wanted nothing more than to be returned into his embrace and apologise for the night before. I wanted him to trap me in those big arms of his and never let me go.

Unfortunately, it became clear that my wishes had been in vain when there were only four chairs at the table this time, inside a huge hall overlooking other sets of tables, where I assumed other members of the court took their dinner.

Rhylan stood at the sight of me and offered me his hand, which I half-heartedly took and allowed him to arrange an escaped lock of my hair and serve me a glass of blood-red wine. He must have read the question in my eyes because he explained, "The commander and rest of the soldiers have other dining arrangements." And that was that.

I allowed an inaudible sigh before I continued the charade and took my allocated seat at the table. It felt weird dining like that, having a view of everyone and everything, almost like the king and queen had to supervise their subjects constantly and demonstrate their supremacy over the others.

Even the air around us was flooded with tension. The king looked at me like I was a bug who all of a sudden gained merits to sit at his table while the queen inspected me with the same disgust, but also a dash of something else, a feeling I could not place.

She was the first to address me, breaking the long-settled silence.

"Tell me, girl, do you realise how lucky you are?" She turned her head to me regally, with an elegance that had clearly accompanied her for centuries, acting like she was a precious work of art. She looked beautiful, I had to admit and even though old age had settled around her features, flashes of youth still kept a good fight across her cheeks, making her look decades younger than her partner. A partner who, I had to respect above everyone, I had been told. No one could do anything, even move or breathe the wrong way, until the king settled himself at the table and no drink or food could be touched until he had tried it first or allowed us to do it in his stead.

"I am not sure I could call myself that," I responded cordially, keeping my tone even, focusing the tension on a big gulp I eagerly swallowed from the wine Rhylan had poured for me.

"A mortal betrothed to Fear Gorta? Out of the billion beings he could have chosen? No one could even dream of such a lucky strike of chance," the Queen immediately jumped to contradict me. And there it was, the feeling I couldn't place before. Jealousy. Suddenly everything clicked into place. The smiles, the delighted looks, the way Rhylan lived for her attention, and the way she purred like a cat while he was her canary. In front of the entire court and the king, who seemed very used to this, as though it was a daily occurrence.

I turned to face Rhylan, who bowed his head, showing how grateful he was for the compliment and I knew I had found my way in. Something to engage the queen with and keep her entertained, just like I was supposed to.

"You are right, your majesty," I responded. "Not in my wildest dreams had I seen this happening." To make my point, and to prove my theory, I extended my hand and reached my wannabe fiancé, grabbing his fingers into mine and squeezing slightly, while I made sure to throw him my most dashing smile.

Rhylan almost choked on the half-chewed piece of steak, but surprisingly, lifted my hand and placed a thirsty kiss on my fingers, after which he threw me a genuinely happy smile.

"Well, since you too are so eager to consummate your vows, there is much to do and much to plan. We can have a feast right in this room, can't we, Drahden?" the queen turned abruptly towards the king like she wanted to block the image of us from her mind. Bingo.

"Oh Anwen, there is so much planning to do," she seemed to change her mind and turned her full attention back to me and the hand I was still touching Rhylan with, which she snatched from his hold and made a grand gesture of squeezing my fingers across the table, as though we were some kind of sorority planning the ball of the season. We all read it for what it was, her inability to see me touching Rhylan, but I played along. That was what I was supposed to do there, after all.

I allowed my mind to drift away as I ate whatever was served on my plate while engaging in small talk with the queen, the conversation solely concerning dresses and underwear, Rhylan's favourite colours, and how my hair would look better in a bun. I acted like I was supposed to, treating it like any other business meeting where I had to nod and smile, make myself pleasant, and engage on a satisfactory level, without overpowering the conversation.

After dessert, 'my future husband' invited me for a walk which I, of course, accepted with a smile and we asked for permission to retreat. The queen excused us with fake excitement while the king nodded, concerning himself with more walnut pie.

"You did a marvellous job," Rhylan said while walking me back through the corridors I had started to recognise.

"And we didn't even get to the Irish party bit," I huffed and when it came his turn to frown, I explained further. "Jack and Rose, they go to the third class party to drink and dance?"

He smiled, pointing to the right, advising me to follow the path he had shown. "Cressida loves that movie." His words surprised me, especially since I had been so overwhelmed with everything, I hadn't even had a chance to think about home. Nor did I want to, because that would be a subject matter where my tears would not be contained any longer.

"I miss her," he continued, making my stomach twitch at the thought of my friend. Of how I wished I could talk to her and receive one of her friendly smiles. Or one of those tight hugs she always was so generous with.

"I miss her too," I admitted, just as we reached the door to our room.

"I have some unexpected duties to take care of after that dinner, so I must leave you. Good night, sprout. I'll pick you up tomorrow at the same time."

"Good night," I nodded and pushed the door to open our new room. To find everything intact, every single piece of broken furniture had been replaced, not one hair out of place, it all looked impeccable. I swallowed hard, expecting to find Ansgar already in the bedroom. I had no sign of him throughout the day.

Since he hadn't arrived yet, I decided to bring back memories from the mansion, where our only worries were caring for the plants and enjoying each other, and headed to the kitchen. After hunting down the ingredients I thought I might need, I had enough on the table to hopefully be able to make muffins. Something about the easiness of the action, the normalcy of it all calmed me down enough to even turn on the radio. I didn't know how it worked or if it was just a recording, but hearing a Maroon 5 song almost brought me to tears.

Here I was, after everything we'd been through, baking for my man. I chuckled at the thought and started mixing things together, eye measuring rather than struggling to find a recipe and follow it. I figured not much could go wrong if I added flour, baking powder, sugar, eggs, and cocoa. I even found some vanilla extract and chocolate chips and mixed them together, then carefully separated the contents into blue polka dot cupcake holders and baked everything until I was satisfied with the result. Thank goodness for Rhylan having electricity in his quarters.

About half an hour later, I finished baking muffins in a place that could easily be described as the underworld and felt very proud of myself. The clock in the kitchen announced ten o'clock and I hoped Ansgar would be back soon. After all, how many hours of training could a person take?

I hurried in the shower to scrub away remains of flour and forced conversations from dinner and washed my hair quickly, then applied body lotion — thank you Rhylan for thinking about the small details — and wrapped myself in a cosy bathrobe I found hanging on the door, my hair twisted in a towel.

"Hello," Ansgar's voice surprised me. He was in the bedroom, searching through the closet, and my mouth automatically watered at the sight of him. My prince had adopted his 'uniform' if I could ever call it that from back in the forest, which meant pants hanging low and bare torso. All of him was smudged with dirt and a few bruises pinched here and there, but the sweat pouring down his body and messy hair made him all the more remarkable. He looked like melting ice cream and I felt the need to do the honours and eat him whole.

"Hi," I said, readying to unwrap myself from the bath robe and get dirty all over again, rubbing onto every single muscle of his

390

body, but to my surprise, he turned and avoided my touch, walking decidedly towards the bathroom.

"Would it be alright if I took a few minutes to wash or do you need the water?" he asked, barely looking in my direction and tugging a clean pair of pants to his waist.

"All yours," I murmured, surprised by his attitude. Had he not missed me as much? Was he still upset? I needed to clarify things between us, I wouldn't be able to take another night like this, with the two of us separated, unable to touch each other. It felt weird, heavy, as though something was missing from me and I really wanted it back. Wanted him.

I waited until the sound of the shower stopped, steadying myself onto the bed and waiting for him to return in a more forgiving mood. He came out a few minutes later, hair wet and only a towel wrapped around his waist, catching whatever drips of water remained on his body. I swallowed hard. "Did you have a nice day?" I tried to be as normal as I could.

"I did," he half-smiled. "I missed training," Ansgar confessed with excitement, the soldier in him striking out and regaining his position. His muscles looked even more defined than usual if that could even be possible, and his shoulders, tense with effort.

"I expect your day was not too tiring?" he replied. I frowned at his coldness, the cordial conversation he held with me.

"I made muffins," I announced, the only thing coming to mind that had no reason to upset him. I didn't think that telling him how I'd spent most of the day getting dolled up for Rhylan and spending long hours in his company would have a positive effect.

"They smell delicious," he agreed and left the bedroom. I followed his steps until he went into the kitchen and I assumed it was to try one of them out. This was not going as planned, normally Ansgar would be more than happy to eat *me* first, but now his attention focused on the food.

When I spotted him leaving the kitchen, chewing on something and two more muffins in hand, I wanted to go to him and hug the hell out of the man, take him right there on the floor, and confess how sorry I felt for keeping him away. But he stopped and took a seat. On the sofa.

"What are you doing?" I immediately asked, jumping from bed.

"Going to sleep," Ansgar answered while grabbing one of the pillows to settle it under his head.

My eyes went wide. Was he punishing me for not wanting to have sex with him last night? No, he wasn't that kind of man, I told myself. Yet here he was, denying his closeness.

"On the sofa?" I asked with panic in my voice, ready to drag him back into bed.

"Uh-huh," he only responded, lashes dragging him to sleep.

"Ansgar?" I called, but by the time I had circled the sofa and spotted him, his eyes were already closed and shoulders relaxed, an arm resting laxly across his stomach. "Are you asleep?" I whispered in another attempt, but he did not reply. So I stayed there, watching him for a long while, following his breathing, calm for once and even though I wanted nothing more than to drag him into bed with me, I did not want to deprive him of rest. At midnight, I placed a few more kisses on his lips and cheeks and went back to bed, sad and alone.

"Morning, princess," Rhylan's voice gave me a fright, forcing me to jump in bed.

"What are you doing here?" I reprimanded him, grabbing the sheets to cover myself until I realised I had fallen asleep in my bathrobe.

"I knocked for about two minutes and you didn't answer. I got worried," Rhylan said but a grin appeared on his face as he continued. "I can see you had a busy night and needed your beauty sleep."

"What?" I frowned, not understanding his meaning, but he pointed to the empty side of the bed, where Ansgar should have been and I turned to see about two dozen red roses with the biggest petals in existence, arranged in a bouquet right next to the pillow.

I had an urge to hug them to my chest and cry, but I would no longer do that in front of Rhylan, I promised myself.

"Give me a minute to get dressed," I said and he nodded, walking towards the sitting room and the sofa.

"Don't," I immediately stopped him when he wanted to take a seat.

Rhylan looked at me in surprise, then his eyes thinned, scanning me from head to toe, preparing himself to make a remark. But at the sight of my sorry ass, he nodded and announced, "I'll wait outside."

After breakfast, I was forced to do the whole thing over again, get measured, learn etiquette and rules, have a quick lunch, and dine with the king and queen, who seemed to get more used to my presence and engaged more in conversation, which meant that I couldn't just sit there and had to interact.

The only thing keeping me from not losing my mind was Rhylan's plan, that we would both get out of here. So I did as advised and found joy in my voice, imagining Queen Bathysia asking me questions and Ansgar by my side rather than Rhylan, all the while counting the seconds to be back into my mate's arms.

But I was once again the first to arrive in our room and waited for my prince for hours, until I fell asleep once again, alone, in the bed. During the following nights, he started to make a habit of arriving extremely late, sometimes at two or three in the morning and crashing directly on the sofa. By the time I got out of bed to go to him, I found him already asleep or just about to, the only exchanges between us courteous questions about my day.

Although it broke my heart, I allowed him the time he needed, hoping that he would soon enough want to talk to me again. The only sign that he still cared was the varying coloured roses, which seemed to multiply on my bed with each passing day, so much so that I had filled half of the room with vases, those roses the only companions in my lonely nights.

"Are you planning to open a flower shop?" The sound of Rhylan's giggles woke me up. He had made a custom of this in the past week, acting like my alarm clock with whatever silly remark he came up with that particular morning.

"It will probably be more successful than your silly grins," I groaned at him and started rising from bed.

"I should think so, most of these beings haven't seen a flower in their entire lives. Yet here you are, accumulating half a planet's rose stock. Fuck boy must be content," he smirked and shifted to the doorframe, his usual place to wait for me.

I groaned again but said nothing. In the past week, I had barely spoken to Ansgar for more than four or five minutes in total, let alone engaging in the activities Rhylan suggested. That would be something I kept to myself though, and even if he may have remarked on whatever colour this separation torture painted on me, he never said a word.

"More dresses today?" I asked with a sigh, wondering how many clothes did they think I would need, especially since, as far as they were aware, I would stay here with Rhylan and could have a dress ready for me whenever I needed to.

"I thought you would be happy with a new wardrobe, sprout.

Isn't that what you used to do all day back at home? Get dressed and be shiny?"

"Do you miss it?" I cut him off. For whatever reason, I did not feel the need to listen to his impertinence today. I missed having a proper conversation with someone, one that didn't involve lying or pretending and even though Rhylan wasn't a fine example of either situation, he was the only one I had. The only constant presence in this past week.

"I have my days," he confessed, and watching the expression on my face, the dire need for conversation, he continued. "As you may have realised by now, I am one of the few who can come and go as they please, so I have enjoyed the benefit for the past two centuries. I love the technological advancements, it's wondrous to see how humans turned the world," he confessed and I was surprised to read excitement in his voice.

"Of course, that leads to their destruction since they prove unable to abstain themselves," he paused and lingered, wanting to reveal something else, something more. I guess I wasn't deserving of the confession, because he continued, "It is still surprising to discover how every time I resurface, there is something new to be obtained, some new toy for me to play with," he added with a smile.

"How is it?" I asked with curiosity, absorbing his every word, "To be there every time the world changes?"

"Terrifying," he stopped. "Thrilling." Another moment. "Scary. One day you humans will manage to make me feel old," he said sweetly, and both he and I knew that wasn't true.

"I doubt someone as dashing as yourself will have difficulties,"

I confessed with a grin and Rhylan's eyes went wide.

"Well, well, sprout, keep behaving like this, and I will have to marry you for real," he smiled back and I didn't know if he meant it as a joke or not, but my need to be attached to someone, to have someone in those lonely moments, made me escape a perky reply.

"Keep smiling like that and I might say yes." As soon as I said it, as soon as I heard myself pronouncing the words, I realised my mistake and hated my tongue for uttering them. Although I promised, I swore not to do it again, not in front of him, tears flooded my eyes.

I lowered my head quickly to hide them, to disguise my feelings somehow, but he was by my side in an instant. Stepping that self-imposed barrier into the bedroom.

I felt his hands around me, tugging me to his chest where a whiff of expensive perfume tickled my nostrils. Was there ever a time when this man did not look and felt impeccable?

"I'm sorry," I tried to drag myself away from the embrace and wipe my nose with the back of my hand but his arms wrapped around me tighter and I let go. Let myself be lost in an embrace I needed so badly.

"What is it, sprout?" His hands caressed my head in such a way that they removed most of the hair from my cheek, leaving my face bare and extremely close to his own.

"Nothing, silly girl problems," I said, remembering his accusations from the very first night, after dinner.

"Tell me," he pleaded and his voice sounded understanding, concern flickering in his tone.

"I'm with people all day, but I never felt so alone. Not even in Evigt…" I cried out, allowing my face to rest on his chest. I felt like a traitor, that was not the man I wanted, not the chest I wanted to cry on, but I felt so desperate that it didn't matter. All I wanted was someone. Anyone. To talk to. To hold.

"Isn't your prince caring for you?" he asked with both surprise and concern.

"I barely spoke to him all week," I admitted. "He's always late, avoiding me, angry with me," I panted, new tears forming in my eyes. "It's like staying away is his new mission or something."

Rhylan's jaw clenched. "That's not what…" he stopped and breathed deeply, as though to calm himself, eyes closed only for a moment, some sort of realisation striking him.

"Get through today, and I'll have something waiting for you at dinner," he caressed my hair once again. That was my cue to separate from his touch and stand, taking a step back. Away.

Away from him.

"Don't you dare hurt Ansgar," I threatened, though my voice sounded raspy and defeated.

"It may not seem like it, princess, but I am also capable of kindness," he pierced me with a disappointed gaze, then stood from the bed himself and walked back to the door, without saying another word.

I got ready quicker than ever and followed after him in the hallway, unable to shake the impression that I might have hurt him with my words. As if Rhylan cared enough to listen.

After another long day of dress fitting — this time they were preparing my engagement gown, a dark, almost crimson velvet dress designed in a very puffy and strange A-line— Rhylan came to escort me to dinner.

Or so I thought, because he did not accompany me through the usual corridors leading to the throne room, which I had learnt by heart. Instead, we walked to the right and back towards mine and Ansgar's room. I assumed, for the surprise he had mentioned.

My heart started trepidating, terrified of Rhylan's view of a surprise and whatever he planned, but curiosity led me forward so I followed after him like a lost puppy until we reached the corridor with our rooms.

Instinctively, I walked to my door, just like I did every night after dinner, but Rhylan stopped me by grabbing my wrist.

"That one," he pointed to the door opposite our own. Where he had mentioned his rooms would be.

I swallowed hard but did as told and shifted to open the other door, which cracked with a noise. I waited for him to enter first but he pointed towards the entrance, a silent invitation for me to go ahead. Again, I did as told.

I don't know what I expected but it was not this. A modest sitting room displayed a table and a desk, large curtains, and a fireplace. A simple and modern design with illuminating shades of grey to create the illusion of space. And small. A lot smaller than the sitting room Ansgar and I had occupied in the past week. If I were to guess, I would say the bedroom would be smaller too, judging by what I could spy through the cracked door.

"I expected more," I confessed and took a few steps in, enough to allow him to close the door behind us.

Rhylan chuckled at my reaction. "It used to be bigger," he admitted with a smirk.

"What happened?" I frowned, taking a spin so I could get all the details from the small room of such an imposing figure.

"I had to give my room up. I'm hosting," he kept smiling as he walked towards the bedroom, allowing me time to analyse his personal space.

"Us?" I asked, stunned. "You gave up your room for...us?" I couldn't believe it, couldn't understand why he would do such a thing.

"To say I gave it up for you *both* is an overstatement," his voice pierced from the bedroom. I deepened my frown, extreme confusion and realisation hitting me at once. Rhylan kept confessing how much he despised Ansgar, kept insulting my mate every chance he got, so it would be unwise to think he had given up his personal space for him. Which could only mean, he had done it for me. And for the love of all the gods, I could not understand why.

"Please, take a seat," he invited again, voice echoing interrupted from the bedroom, struggling to reach something, but by the time I made myself comfortable in the black leather chair, I saw him arrive with three gift boxes, all shoe-sized.

"Is your surprise going to be more high heels?" I scoffed, hating the constant ache in my feet from the amount of time having to stand during long fitting hours in said heels.

He ignored me and placed two of the boxes on the table, leaving one on the floor, next to him. "Pick one," he invited, excitement gleaming on his features.

I took a minute to look at him, scan him for wickedness. With Rhylan one could never be sure, but he looked as excited as a kid in a candy shop, so I assumed nothing too bad could come out of this.

"The left one," I said, not having a reason for my choice. Just instinct, I guessed.

"Open it," the fae encouraged and I swear he held his breath while I slowly removed the cover of the gift box. And immediately started laughing.

"No way!" I exclaimed cheerfully, laughter inundating my chest and I wondered how long had it been since I truly laughed. Truly found joy in something so small.

"I thought we could have a different kind of dinner tonight since my sprout needed cheering up," he confessed and grabbed a kit kat from the dozen packages laying in the box.

I didn't miss his words, but followed suit and grabbed a bar of chocolate.

"How did you know I would survive?" I heard myself asking the question that was lingering at the back of my mind every time I found myself in Rhylan's presence.

He didn't need further explanation, understanding my question to its exact extent. "Have you not seen sprouts piercing through rocks to get their way?" he asked, a dash of admiration in his gaze. "You guys are resilient," Rhylan half smiled and shoved two full bars of kit kat in his mouth.

"Not a princess anymore then?" I questioned as I bit from my bar, the chocolate melting on my lips, a bliss I had not hoped to relive so soon.

"Anwen, you can be whatever you wish to be," he said, then lowered his gaze to the second box and invited me to open it.

I shivered at the sound of my name falling out of his mouth like a waterfall unleashed but focused all my attention on the second box, which managed to draw another smile from me.

"Kit kat and coke," I chuckled, grabbing a can of perfectly cold coke and popping it open, the sound magic to my ears.

We spent about an hour laughing, drinking fizz, and eating chocolate, just like the good old times in Evigt, when I thought of him as a friend. I felt unsure about the present, about his intentions, and could not, for the life of me, understand Rhylan's reasoning. Sometimes, especially when we were alone, he looked sincere and relaxed, as though he enjoyed the time spent together, but other times he turned into a vile monstrosity of a being, only caring about himself and his own purposes.

"Ready for box number three?" he asked as he bent in his seat to reach for the third box, one that had remained resting at his feet.

"I hope it's not ice cream," I chuckled but he placed it on the table and pointed at me to open it. I did so quickly, ready for another surprise.

"What is this?" I frowned again, finding a plastic box inside the gift wrapper.

"Open it," Rhylan invited me again, breathing heavily like *he* was nervous.

I opened the plastic box, struggling to do so and nipping two fingernails in the process when..." Oh my god!" I burst out, my trembling palms reaching to cup my cheeks and settle on my face while tears dripped freely, inundating my eyes.

"I assumed you don't know numbers by heart, so there is a list. I got your father's mobile, your mother's, their house number and the office," Rhylan reached inside the box to find a small card containing all the numbers.

"Oh my god," I said again, unable to believe he had thought of this. That he had done something like this for me.

"Although it's a satellite phone, signal is almost impossible to reach here, as you can imagine, so I doubt the battery will last more than ten minutes. My advice would be to calm down first, so you can converse with your family freely, without worrying them. If that is what you choose, of course," he said and shifted in his seat with an intention to stand.

I grabbed his hand over the table, squeezing it tightly. "Thank you," I said, struggling to see his face through the mess of tears.

The fae didn't respond, his only reply an encouraging squeeze of a hand.

"I'll give you privacy," he said and stood, walking to the door.

"Rhylan?" I called after him and he immediately turned. "Stay with me?"

My heart thumped in my chest and I didn't trust my fingers, didn't want to do this by myself, so I figured that if I focused my attention on him, I could at least try and go through a few minutes without crying.

"Of course," he replied and returned to his seat, giving me a moment to calm down. When I signalled I was ready, he typed in the first number and passed it to me at the second ring.

"Jason Odstar." I could recognise that voice anywhere. I started smiling and crying at the same time.

"Daddy?"

"Anwen, baby, is that you?" The joy in my father's voice resounded through the entire room. We spoke for long minutes, my parents passing the phone between them, sometimes asking me the same question, but I did not mind, the joy of hearing them overpowering everything. I assured them I was fine, that I would be home soon and business went great, telling them how I met new people every day and how I had to wear amazing dresses for daily events. Not a lie in its entirety.

Aware of the time and not wanting to let them go abruptly, I said my goodbyes and told both of them how much I loved them before I passed the phone back to Rhylan with shivering hands, watching how he pressed the red button to end the call.

"You will see them again soon, I promise," Rhylan grabbed my hand in his, reassuringly, and I smiled. I truly smiled back at him with no prejudice or judgement, seeing him as the companion I needed at that moment.

"Come, I'll walk you back," he said after I had fully calmed down, passing me the two remaining chocolate bars. "For your prince," he groaned, more as a joke, which made me chuckle.

"Thank you," I replied and headed to the door, which he opened for me, both of us leaving his place with a wide smile splayed on our faces.

"I see the new couple had a pleasant evening," Ansgar's voice echoed from the corridor and I turned to see him only a few steps away from us.

Watching me leave Rhylan's room. With a smile on my face.

Oh. My. God.

Chapter Twenty-Eight

"Please excuse me," I only said and skittered past them into the corridor. I heard Anwen's voice calling after me with desperation, but I hurried through the dark hallways, wanting to leave the image behind. Unable to believe what I had seen.

My mate. *My* mate leaving Rhylan's room with a satisfied smile on her face. Even the bastard looked different, pleased. I didn't have to think too hard to find a reason for such gratification, not in an officially courting couple.

How had I been such an imbecile? Rhylan had stated his intention with Anwen in front of the royal family and played with me, yet again, to keep me out of the way. To keep Anwen displeased and alone, so he could swoop in and offer her the consolation I would not. And I took the bait like an idiot.

I couldn't remember how long I ran for or where my feet took me, even though I was probably late to meet Marreth. I looked around like a dimwit, my eyes burning and unable to focus on their surroundings after the image I had witnessed.

"Ansgar!" A voice called after me, so far away and distant, coming from another world. Yet judging by the grip on my shoulders, it had come from the person standing right next to me. The commander.

It didn't take him long to study the dread on my face, to see my shaking body, filled with perturbation and remorse.

"Ansgar, what's wrong?" he shook my shoulder, my body so frail that it moved along, unable to steady my bones.

Bile rose in my stomach and I had no other choice but expulse it, vomiting the remainder of my dinner right at Marreth's feet. My stomach took a few turns and even after everything was released, it still tightened, forcing my belly to constrict yet again. Unfortunately, the hurt could not be vomited away.

Poor Marreth stood by me, crouching at my side and gripping my hair. It reminded me a lot of Vikram and the way we used to hold each other's hair when we drank ourselves close to death at festivities, hiding away in one of the servant's quarters to avoid our mother's wrath.

When I calmed down enough to let myself fall to the ground, he directed me towards the wall and away from my sick, allowing me to gasp new air.

"What happened?" he asked, concern formatting his face while he scanned my broken self.

"Anwen..." I mumbled, the rest of my words inaudible, protruding only my brain.

"What's wrong with her? Is she safe?" Marreth asked, pulling my face enough to point my gaze to him.

"Yeah...she's safe," I grunted. "In Rhylan's fucking arms." My entire body shook, my face, my tendons, and everything that held me together at the thought and I wanted to be sick again, but there was nothing left for my stomach to release.

My new friend frowned in confusion, waiting for me to explain. "I saw her leaving your general's room," I panted.

"And?" he pushed.

"And she looked happy," I struggled to breathe as I said it but with all my pain, all my concern and ache, Marreth started grinning at me like I was the last idiot in the world.

"Is that it?" he chuckled, relaxing enough to take a seat on the floor next to me.

"Do I need more?" I snapped at him, my eyes wide with the nerve he had to mock my feelings.

"I swear, newly mated couples are the worst. It's like your brain stops working for some reason," he waved his head in disapproval.

I frowned and wanted to protest, to explain to him what I felt but Marreth raised a hand to silence me.

"So you are telling me that you are this upset because Rhylan is keeping your woman happy before setting her free? And keeping her away from the royals too, it seems?" His eyes scanned mine in disbelief.

"They were together; they were—" I stopped, unable to say the words, unable to think then and praying to all the goddesses to be wrong.

"Oh," Marreth stopped, understanding where my thoughts lead. "You think that a human who came to their version of hell for you, and defied everyone in sight to release you from chains will have a change of heart in a week and seek comfort with the person who did all of this to you?"

I didn't respond, I couldn't find the words. Did I really think Anwen would discard me so easily? Had I really let my jealousy overcome my mind in such a way that I started thinking the worst?

"I can assure you that Rhylan hasn't had sex in at least two days. He may be the strongest of us but even he suffers the effects of the queen's hunger. And he is scheduled for tonight, so I guarantee he won't be wasting power with your woman. When my turn comes, I don't touch anyone for a week and spend my time eating as much as I can and doing minimum effort," he confessed, a shiver shattering his entire body at the thought.

"Does Rhylan have to partake in it as well?" I asked, surprised. I had heard about it from the soldiers during training. It was an ancient tradition, one that sirens still practiced from time to time during important rituals, but apparently, it was a regular occurrence in the Fire Kingdom. The Queen invited the mightiest warriors to her bed and fed off their energy during the joining, which is why sometimes she looked younger and brighter.

"Oh yes," the commander responded quickly, "he most of all since he is the strongest being this end of the kingdom. The other two commanders as well, though she never cared much for Crypto. You might have been invited too, had it not been for your outburst during dinner that time."

I didn't know which option was worse, becoming a sex slave to a female I did not want to join with or being poked with needles and turned into someone who could kill without hesitation.

"Regardless," Marreth continued, "Your woman is safe from Rhylan's advancements, which is the important message here. So let's get you cleaned and back to her, the poor girl must be going crazy with worry."

He urged me to stand and led me through different corridors until we arrived inside what I supposed was his room. Lots of weapons decorated the walls, reminding me, yet again, of Vikram. He had a small room, a double bed, a desk, a table, two chairs, and a fireplace, all crammed in one room and a single door which I guessed led to the bathing chamber.

Luckily, he also had a shower so I shoved myself inside of the small doors and turned the tap, allowing cold water to wash away my thoughts and the remainder of my stomach spillage, cleansing my body and mind.

I must have stayed there for a while because Marreth waited long enough until he decided to come in and bring me a pair of pants and a shirt, making a joke about how he wants it cladded in mating smells when I returned it to him.

I smiled and thanked the male for what seemed like the millionth time, then headed back to the corridors, in a desperate attempt to find my room and get back to Anwen, decided to fall to my knees in front of her and apologise a thousand times if I had to.

Unfortunately, the direction my feet led me towards didn't turn out to be the one I originally planned because a wrong turn brought me face to face with none other than the Queen. She was wearing a black silk cloak and the way her form-fitted the garment made me realise it was the only thing she wore. Marreth hadn't lied then.

I wanted to withdraw immediately, but she spotted me and stopped me with a greeting, which I had no choice but to return.

"Good evening, prince. What brings you here so late?" her voice sounded playful, her tone relaxed for once.

"On my way to bed, Your Majesty," I responded with a deep bow, hating myself for the reverence she did not dignify.

As soon as I said it, I realised my poor choice of words, because her eyes sparkled, most certainly considering it an invitation.

"Is that so?" the Queen snickered, signalling her guards to part so that she could step closer to me. I tensed when her finger touched my clavicle and started moving downwards, to my chest.

"You look like you could enjoy some company," she purred deeply, like a female in the heat of the act. This time her full hand replaced the original finger that traced my torso, setting her attention on my abdomen. "It's been a while since I tasted prince," the female whispered. "I can guarantee you will have fun."

Her lips travelled to my neck and, oh my goddess, she sank her teeth in, right below my earlobe. I felt her pinch hard, while the hand that caressed my abdomen progressed to in between my legs, squeezing me in her palm. She stopped biting abruptly and shifted her gaze to find my eyes, wide with surprise and panic.

"This feels like it would be loads of fun," the ruler licked her lips, clenching my manhood with a sharp squeeze that made me tense every single muscle in my being.

The queen grinned in satisfaction. "You are lucky I have plans for the night, but I will send for you soon," she promised, her tongue licking her lips and then heading towards my face, where she planted it on my cheek and licked her way up to my lips. I did my best to keep them shut, but I felt her saliva lingering over my mouth.

Without another word, she signalled her guards, who started walking and guiding her, leaving me on my own in the corridor. Running is a poor word for what I did next, my legs sprinting so quickly I thought they might fall off my body, only stopping when I reached the door that I hoped led me to Anwen.

I opened it abruptly and ran inside, closing it with a sharp thump and allowing myself to fall against it, drawing breath for the first time in minutes.

"Ansgar!" Anwen rushed to me from the bedroom, skittering around the sofa and allowing herself to fall on the floor, on her knees, right in front of me. Her arms wrapped around my body and she splayed herself on my chest, grabbing as much of me as she could reach.

"Anwen," I sighed and hugged her tightly, enjoying the feel of her against my skin. "Anwen," I said again, shivers running through me, her smell filling my nostrils and hair tickling my jaw.

"I'm sorry. Nothing happened, I swear," she explained with muffled words because I hugged her so tightly her breath stopped on my shoulder. I was decided to never let her go ever again, whatever may come. "He brought me a phone so I can talk to my family, that's why I was happy," she continued to explain and I swore at myself for my idiocy. Of course she had a perfectly good reason and at that moment, I felt gratitude towards Fear Gorta for offering that dash of happiness to my mate.

"I am sorry too, fahrenor, I don't know what possessed me to think ill of you," I tried to excuse myself, knowing perfectly well I shouldn't have had a doubt. Anwen squeezed me tighter, nestling her head onto my shoulder, basking in my scent just like I did with her. We remained like that, hugging on the floor, reconnecting with each other for a long while, recuperating that missing part the other had become.

"What happened here?" I felt Anwen suddenly tensing, her hand travelling to my clavicle and then upwards on my neck.

"Where?" I asked, half-drunk from her presence, continuing to place small kisses on her arm.

"On your neck, it looks like a... bite mark."

That was enough to wake me up. "The Queen," I responded with honesty but as soon as the words escaped my mouth I realised I could have uttered them with better preparation because Anwen jumped up as if electrified, her face red with ire.

"Excuse me?" she accused, her hands adopting a threatening pose on her hips. "The Queen *bit* you?" She turned her face slightly, displaying only part of it to me and moving her head in such a way that her ear took priority in my field of vision like she wanted to make sure my words will travel straight there, with no interruption.

"We met in the corridor and she stopped me." I didn't say more, afraid that our reconciliation would abruptly end, but my mate looked possessed, her entire face crimson, fiery wrath overpowering her gaze.

"Tell me exactly, frame by frame, what happened," she commanded, scanning me from head to toe, awaiting an explanation.

I frowned and took a moment, unable to think the events through and how to better portray what happened, but Anwen's words pierced my chest, making it impossible for me to contain a proud grin.

"Ansgar, tell me exactly what that bitch did to you!" her fingers wrapped in fists as if she prepared herself to go outside and challenge the queen to a fight over territory. Anwen was jealous, I realised with pleasing joy. My mate was jealous because another female had touched me. Marked me.

I took the moment to rise from the floor, situating myself against the door, just in case. "I'll tell you, but I want something in return," I replied, the grin now permanent on my face.

"What?" she answered angrily.

"A kiss," I smirked, enjoying this state of her. Was this the most adequate situation to take advantage? Probably not. Did I feel like a jerk? A bit. But was I enjoying the possessiveness my mate felt over me? Definitely.

Anwen huffed, but her shoulders immediately relaxed, her body taking the step that separated us and allowed herself to rest against me, hands cupping my face with affection.

"Are you okay?" she asked, worry in her expression.

"I am now," I smiled and placed my lips on hers, a gesture I dreamt of doing for the past week. Every time I watched her sleep alone, every time I heard news of her or spotted her in the corridors, surrounded by soldiers and maids, every single morning when I wanted nothing more but to throw myself in that bed and wrap her in my arms.

The kiss only lasted a few seconds, Anwen too concerned with the answer. "Tell me," she demanded, so I listened and confessed.

"I was coming back to you but missed a turn and found her in a nightgown, surrounded by soldiers. She touched me and bit my neck, then left." I didn't feel the need to add the queen's desire to add me to her damned energy-eating schedule.

"I will kill that bitch when I see her," Anwen repeated the insult to my wicked delight. "No one touches my man!" she uttered with conviction.

"No one?" I prodded playfully at the spectacular décolletage the dress she was wearing created around her breasts.

"No one but me," she allowed herself to smile.

"Show me," I barely murmured, "show me how you touch your man." I swallowed hard with anticipation and she must have heard it because a lustful gaze replaced the wrath in her eyes. And she did just that.

Her hands tugged onto me, pulling up the borrowed shirt with eagerness to reach my skin and when she did, her palms splayed on my chest, caressing my pecs. I breathed hard, accustoming myself yet again with the feeling of her, a sensation that pierced so differently from the Queen's old and abrupt hands.

Anwen's heart drummed inside her chest, with desperation and longing, the same sentiments that reflect in my entire body. How did we stay separated for so long? Why did I even think it would be a good option when Anwen's soft skin connected to mine like old tree roots into new soil after a rainy day.

"I love you," she whispered just as she reached to kiss my clavicle, and oh my goddess, that was my undoing. I grabbed her hips and lifted her onto me, splaying her legs on each side of my hips, grabbing her entire body to mine and enjoying the full sensation of warmth she propagated.

I kissed her deeply, profusely, with desperation and yearning, my tongue sweeping inside her mouth with possession and deep strokes, claiming the taste of her, the flavour I had missed during long sleepless nights.

Luckily I didn't have to struggle too much to uncover my mate because the dress quickly slid downwards, allowing the silk to shimmy across her body until it fell on the floor, leaving her bare to me, with only some lace covering the inside of her thighs, designed to attract rather than protect.

I went to her like a bee to a blooming flower, my mouth eager to taste her, but Anwen's hands stopped me right as my teeth prepared to rip into the black lace.

"We don't have time for this," she whispered, her voice roughened with desire, urging me to take her. Instinctively, I cupped her core with the palm of my hand and felt wetness, but after the last time we had done this, I wasn't willing to take any chances, so I pushed my head towards the inside of her thighs yet again, biting the area I had originally planned to.

She moaned and grabbed me by the hair, holding on for dear life. I bit the lace and pushed it to the side with my mouth, unwrapping her like a long-awaited present, and started devouring her with teeth and tongue, playing with her folds and feeding on her until she melted in my arms, falling into complete relaxation.

I gently placed her on the sofa and spread her legs wider, enough for my head to be able to reach every single side of her, but I did not have time to continue with my plan of adding fingers and rubbing her from the inside, because she wiggled away from under me, her hands raised for me to join her, to take my allocated seat on top of her body. I wanted to ignore this request and take extra time to prepare my mate for what we were about to do, but her soft voice stopped me in my tracks.

"Ansgar, please," she moaned, a female in heat demanding attention. *My* female.

"Fahrenor, I want to—" I needed to explain but her eyes went wide and demanded, "Please!" she said again, the urgency in her tone telling me all I needed to know. I immediately took off my pants, her hands helping to pull them down, and as soon as I shimmied out of them, showing my readiness, Anwen grabbed me and pulled me on the sofa next to her.

I let myself fall at her side and in the next instant, she jumped on me, her hands stroking my desire with tight and mind-bending movements until she situated her core in the perfect position to take me in.

She slit me inside of her, slowly and carefully, allowing me to feel her body stretching while her closed eyes communicated the pleasant sensation she enveloped herself in. My mate started moving onto me with feline satisfaction, up and down, up and down in a rhythm that had me lose my mind in no time. I wanted to slide myself inside of her fully, desperation overpowering my senses.

Instead, I grabbed her hips and focused my attention on her breasts, licking and nipping at them until my mate's exhales started to be released more abruptly.

Only then I allowed myself to take control, to push her harder onto me, shoving myself inside of her as deep as I could, her throat escaping a moan when I filled her up to the hilt. I took a minute to kiss her, remaining fully sheathed to give her enough time to adjust until I started moving her onto me, her hips listening to my every command.

Within minutes, I had her body pistoning into my own, Anwen opening up for me wider, her body fitting perfectly onto mine. I pumped into my mate with desperation, abandoning my worries and troubles. The only thing that mattered was our joining, that perfect place where our bodies became one and I let myself float into the sensation, taking her along with me.

Anwen shouted her own pleasure, claiming my body, wrapping herself against me as she rode the last waves of her release and then began to move faster, slamming into me abruptly, while her hips started rolling with me inside of her.

I had never felt anything like this before, my eyes going wide with the discovery of the new sensation, but Anwen threw me a wicked smile. One that said she knew perfectly well that she kept this talent hidden from me and only now, did I do something deserving to unlock it. She continued pushing her hips around my hardness, taking me along with her and moving me inside of her core in such a way that unknown parts of her body opened for me to reveal pleasure and sensations I had not felt before. It felt like a possession dance, her core leading the way into madness and I blindly followed, being pushed and squeezed and torn inside of her with every abrupt movement, her folds squeezing me and undulating savagely.

"Woman, you will be the death of me," I grunted, my abdomen shaking with the growing waves of pleasure she was creating. To my shame, it took me only two or three minutes to reach ecstasy and spill into her, panting deeply and abruptly, my mind still berserk with the feeling she had summoned.

I did compensate for my lack of resistance later that evening when Anwen went into the kitchen to prepare a snack and I followed her, unable to contain my desire at the sight of her bare ass bouncing as she moved. I splayed my mate on the kitchen counter and took her from behind, slow and profound, making her moan and rasp, scratching the surface until her fingernails started aching and until wave after wave of release flooded her.

We did not stop there, for the remainder of the night we licked, tasted, and devoured each other with raw passion and possession, until we washed away those cold nights we'd spent apart. Until every part of my body had become reacquainted with hers and I left my scent all over her skin. Along with a few bite marks. For good luck.

"Are you two ever going to wake up?"

The sound of a bored male voice made me tense for a second until I realised Anwen was in my arms and immediately found calmness. Her hair splayed across the pillow and her head rested on my shoulder, while my arms lingered around her torso. I didn't know when we went to sleep last night, because every time we settled into bed, one of us started caressing the other until it transformed into kissing and that increased our desire, which lead to shameless sex. A lot of it. The last memory I had was being inside Anwen and did not know when I had fallen asleep.

"Huh?" The voice pierced through my dreams again and made me shift in place. I turned to the side, finding the annoying little tone that dared disturb me, especially when my body had given out and needed the rest. I supposed my lady felt the same.

I blinked a few times until my lashes found the origin of said voice.

"What the..." I leaped awake, sliding Anwen off me in the abrupt movement.

She grunted, barely able to control her own body. "What is it?" her voice sounded roughened by sex and sleep.

"Are you two ever going to wake up?" Rhylan repeated the question, and by the exasperation in his tone, I assumed he had to utter these very same words a few times over.

"Urgh...go away," Anwen shimmied closer to me and wrapped the bed sheet around her body, to cover herself, though by Rhylan's attitude, he already saw everything there was to see.

"It's past lunch and you two idiots are still in bed?" Fear Gorta called for us with irritation, his hands crossed around his torso.

My eyes widened enough to take the fireling in for the first time. He looked pale, sickly, drops of sweat piling on his forehead, not at all his usual self, the male who loved parading his beauty across kingdoms, the one who always had to look perfect.

Suddenly, the puzzle connected in my mind. If this is what the queen was doing to him, to them all, then he had all the reason to want her death. My stomach turned at the thought of Marreth having to do this and the toll it would take on him.

I placed a gentle kiss on Anwen's forehead and rose from the bed, finding the closest pair of pants, which turned out to be the one my friend had lent to me. Since I missed half a day of training, I didn't think taking a shower would greatly benefit me anyway, so he would have his wish. I would wear his clothes and sully them with mating scent.

"Hie vaedrum teim, fahrenor," I placed another kiss on Anwen's sleepy cheek and hurried out the room, having to pass Rhylan who had politely positioned himself in the bedroom door frame. I couldn't help but appreciate the space.

"One week," I told him, a form of promise and encouragement, letting him know that I would honour the oath.

"One week," Rhylan nodded and extended his hand towards me. It was trembling slightly and felt clammy at the touch, but I granted his wish, offering the salute amongst soldiers.

Before I got out of the room, I heard him bossing my mate around. "Come on sprout, you have dresses to try on. And for the god's sake, take a shower, you reek of sex."

I chuckled, imagining the day these two would have. If there was one thing my mate needed above all else, that was her precious sleep, and I had chased away most of it last night.

"Have fun, Rhylan," I smirked as I walked the corridors towards the training grounds.

The following week fell heavy over all of us. Marreth and I partook in long training sessions which lasted until late at night and left both of us, along with the new soldiers, completely shattered. Rhylan paid us a single visit during this time, supervising the planning and making us repeat back to him our actions, step by step, over and over, his eyes scanning the possible outcomes until we ended up devising four different strategies, all pointing to the same result.

It took a few days for his skin to return to its original soft tan and for his eyes to glint with wickedness once more. Even Anwen noticed the changes and started asking questions. I hated leaving her in the dark with our plan and what the queen wanted to do to me, should Rhylan not find success, but I clinged to every moment I could spend by her side.

As soon as we finished training, I skipped dinner and ran to our room to find my mate. Sometimes she was already there, waiting for me eagerly, other times I was the one who had to wait for her arrival.

I spent long hours worshipping her body. Sleep be damned, if I only had a few days left with this woman, I would not lose a second.

She taught me how to massage her feet, the soles tired and aching after long hours of strolling around the kingdom in high heels, and sometimes we watched stories on the television in the sitting room.

Started watching would fit the description better, since every time our bodies touched for more than a minute, our impulses rushed and we allowed ourselves to be compelled by them, joining together a million times in a million ways.

Anwen's body moulded perfectly into mine in every situation, during every position and I could not help but curse everything and everyone around for making us have to part each morning. Every approaching day made it harder to let her go, knowing that the end came near, and that particular morning, the last one we possibly ever shared together, came like a hurricane over a forest of young firs, scraping everything away to leave destruction.

"Good morning," I kissed her forehead, locking with her soft skin, a bead of sweat protruding in between my lips. I licked it eagerly, tasting her scent.

"I don't want it to be morning yet," she whispered my exact thoughts and nestled into me, seeking comfort and quiet. As though she could magic the world away and make it so that just the two of us and this bed remained in the world.

"Me neither," I agreed and planted another kiss, this time taking a moment to smell her hair. "I love you," I whispered, hoping that my breath would invade through her memories and remain locked in her mind.

"Love you too baby," she slightly giggled and looked at me with those beautiful hazel eyes, sleep still curling onto her lashes.

"I'll see you tonight," I promised and moved to stand from bed, but her arm remained draped across my waist, pulling me closer to her. "I need to go, fahrenor," I tried to reason, though I wanted nothing more than to stay with her in that bed until time dripped from the world.

"I love you," I whispered again and bent to kiss her shoulder, making her giggle slightly. Loving her reaction, I did the same to her arm, then passed to her elbow and then to her wrist, finishing planting sweet kisses on each of her fingers.

That seemed to settle her enough to go back to sleep, unaware of what was to come.

Marreth and I spent the entire day preparing the new recruits, polishing their weapons and uniforms, and getting them ready for the evening celebration. We had rehearsed this moment, making sure that every soldier knew their place and what position to adopt while entering court.

The males were becoming restless and fidgeting, counting the hours until they had a chance to enter through the halls and meet the royals.

"Weapons ready!" Marreth ordered to keep them in check, rehearsing their entrance for what must have been the tenth or eleventh time. But they listened, eager to fight for their chance of freedom, the only one they would get, ready to die rather than live as slaves, serving a kingdom that branded them traitors and only spared them to use their bodies as weapons.

"Tighten the right flank," I ordered alongside my friend, rehearsing the battle formations I had poured my heart and soul into making the soldiers learn, ones that gave them the best fighting chance once we reached the halls, perfect for crowded places with no escape or chance to fall back.

As the late hours of the afternoon came upon us, we let the men indulge in food and relaxation, allowing them to linger amongst their friends for what could be the last time for some.

Maybe even for Marreth and I, who preferred to stay away from the fighting ring and occupied one of the farther benches to eat our meal undisturbed and away from the singing of the soldiers.

"Ready for tonight?" he asked the obvious question while biting avidly into a rack of lamb.

"As ready as I can be," I confessed and sighed, focusing my attention on an apple. My stomach felt queasy so the last thing it needed was heavy food. It wasn't the battle that kept me on edge, I had fought many firelings before this day and lived to tell the story.

Anwen. She was the only thing on my mind, her safety the main reason for all my purpose in this attack. One that, I hoped, would help her regain freedom.

"Does she know what to do?" he asked, probably deciphering the concern on my face. Marreth was present for various conversations with Rhylan and had developed the plan alongside the general, so he was no stranger to what would happen tonight or my reasoning.

"Rhylan made an oath to keep her safe and release her," I told him what I knew, the only part of the plan that truly mattered. I would break rank and keep her safe until Rhylan killed the queen. Until he got his revenge and while the soldiers pushed the attack, I would re-join them to help gain territory while Fear Gorta took my mate back home.

Basically, I had agreed to remain and vanish in his kingdom while he ran away into the sunset with the love of my life

Anwen

Chapter Twenty-Nine

Today felt weird, wrong somehow. The entire mood weighed in a specific way, even though I could not place it. From Ansgar's troubled gaze, which he tried so hard to disguise in the morning, to Rhylan's constant fidgeting and him coming to check on me every hour.

Normally, I spent the day with the ladies, learning court etiquette or being fitted for more dreadful dresses, and only saw Rhylan in the afternoon, when he came to escort me to dinner.

Today, however, he watched me like a hawk. He constantly came into the fitting room finding some poor excuse to be there and supervise me. His eyes scanned me up and down and questioned everything, everyone around me and their motives, up to the point where the ladies who dressed me had to show and explain to him the reason for using a needle in that particular area of the silk. Even though I ushered him away, he kept coming back or if he didn't, I heard him outside, ordering the soldiers around.

It was only in the evening, when all the efforts to finish the engagement dress had paid out and I was dolled up and ready to go, in an amber dress with orange satin elements, made to showcase a connection between fire and autumn, with a bronze veil woven into my locks that he finally settled. Surprisingly, today of all days, after being tortured for two weeks by wearing impossibly high heels, they chose boots to go with my outfit. Once he had me by his side, ready to lead me into court and present me as his official betrothed, Rhylan gleamed.

"Excited much?" I wanted to mock him but his roughened features and tight jaw told me it may not be the best of moments.

"Have you talked to Ansgar?" he turned and questioned, scanning not my face but the air around me. To see if I lied, I came to understand.

"Only this morning," I admitted, surprised at the fact that Rhylan didn't use one of his pet names and took the trouble to pronounce my prince's name.

His eyes slithered over me again, as though to make sure, then nodded. "Trust your senses tonight, sprout," he advised and adopted his usual regal demeanour, forcing me to do the same. I had so much training on how to act in court and how to walk alongside Rhylan that I felt like I was back in drama class and had somehow become the star of the show.

When the doors opened to let us in, I took a moment to admire the decorations. All autumnal colours, thousands of ornaments, and candles adorning the grand hall, but missing the most autumnal thing of all, amber leaves. Even though the firelings managed to grow roots and potatoes, they didn't benefit from sunlight, so displaying trees or the changing of seasons was out of the question.

Everyone remained quiet during our entrance, gazes scanning us, me, from head to toe and even though Rhylan and I had travelled that same path to get to the main dinner table and accompany the King and Queen, this day was different. This was the day when Rhylan had to make the announcement in court and even though I suspected everyone already knew, something about having me dressed as a seasonal offering and his hand tight around mine, gave me the shivers.

We walked in silence, keeping our heads high and looking straight ahead until we reached the three stairs separating us from the dais, where the royal family waited. Rhylan bowed, bending at the middle in front of the royals, who nodded and ordered him to rise. Once he did, the general extended his hand towards me, to introduce me to them yet again. I did what I had been trained to do, curtsied low, grabbing my dress at the sides until my head was as low as Rhylan's hips.

The king smiled, pleased, and gestured to me to rise, which I did as slowly as I originally bowed, my gaze not rising from the ground. *Never look the king in the eyes*, they had told me, unless he directly addresses you.

I felt more than saw Rhylan smile, his hand catching mine, helping me up, his fingers tightening with anticipation.

"King Drahden, Queen Shayeet, beloved court, I am beyond joyous to introduce to you, Anwen Odstar, my future bride and your princess." His voice echoed through the grand hall, and I could almost see it travelling around the room when realisation settled on the faces of the various members of the court. That a human would become a princess.

Shock, rage, and disappointment primed through their features, yet none of them displayed a protest. Their eyes scanned the crowd, the people around them, to make sure they heard correctly, whispers making way across the hall. Until someone started clapping.

It sounded faded, probably the person was situated at the farthest tables, but the sound pierced sharp and silenced the whispers, making everyone shift in search of the disturbance.

I found myself doing the same, but, as opposed to the other members, I was able to instantly find its source. I could recognise those golden locks anywhere. Ansgar.

Not a second later he stood from his allocated seat and I spotted my prince, dressed in armour to the teeth, eyes filled with rage as he continued slapping his hands together to make that dreadful sound.

Clap. Clap. Clap.

I felt it crawling under my skin, filling my own blood with dirt, the expression on his face, the way he looked at us, at *me,* making my stomach revolt.

"Ansgar," I breathed out, probably an attempt of my mind to understand the truth, but there he was, no doubt about it, clapping at us with disgust and slowly approaching.

"I do not believe you were to receive an invitation to the celebration, soldier," the king spoke, his voice tense and demanding.

"But your Highness," Ansgar spat in a mocking tone, "how could I miss the occasion?"

He stopped then, tilting his head just slightly to take us all in. And what a gathering he must have seen, how I must have looked through his eyes. A traitor.

"Escort him out," the king pointed to the guards behind the dais, who hurried past us and made their way to the centre of the hall, where Ansgar stood.

"No," I protested and immediately wanted to sprint to his side, were it not for Rhylan to grab my arm. "Trust your senses," he whispered in my ear yet again, just like he had done before, like it was supposed to mean something to me.

"I am, you jerk," I tried to escape his hold but only managed to get his fingers to tighten around me.

I had no other choice but to watch in terror as five guards hurried towards my prince, ready to attack him, their swords already out. I did not expect to see Ansgar break free of them in less than two minutes, striking each one with precision. Not to kill, but enough to injure or knock out.

He rested on his sword, his elbow on the hilt while his jaw situated itself over his knuckles, a curious look on his features.

"Is that all you have for me, king?" he spat, daring the royal. I tried to escape Rhylan yet again, terrified of what would happen, decided to put myself in front of him and be used as a human shield if necessary, everything in my power to protect him from the wrath of the king.

"If you want your mate to taste your blood at her engagement party, I can do nothing but oblige," the King retorted, clicking his fingers.

Suddenly, an entire army appeared from behind the dais, as armed as Ansgar was, ready to strike.

"No!" I heard myself shout with desperation. "No, please!" I screamed at the top of my lungs until a hand covered my mouth, muffling my panic. "Shut the fuck up!" Rhylan ordered and grabbed my chin, and my entire face along with it, slaying me tighter onto him.

I couldn't watch this, couldn't let this happen, but no matter how hard I tried to escape, the fireling's force stopped me in my tracks.

"You may have many things, king," Ansgar replied while the guards moved to circle around him, "but the loyalty of your court is not one of them." His voice echoed rough, scarred even, as if he too understood how dangerous the situation had become.

I turned to the king, ready to beg, ready to do anything he asked for to stop this, but the challenge I observed in his eyes told me that this was it. Ansgar had touched a nerve and no matter what I did, no matter what I said, there was no turning back.

I turned my attention to my prince, and Rhylan surprisingly let me, positioning me in such a way that I had a perfect view of my mate. And the circle of soldiers around him.

Ansgar turned and looked at me. Smiling. His eyes glinted and he *smiled*.

"No!" A muffled cry escaped my lips, but before I could do anything else, a whistle silenced me. A whistle coming from Ansgar's lips, a calling of some sort, and not a second later the doors to the grand hall shuddered as a multitude of soldiers came rushing through. Marreth, one of them. I took a sharp breath as I watched a hoard of soldiers shoving their way inside ... and fighting the king's guard. Fighting alongside Ansgar.

After that everything turned blurry, there were screams and

blood, people running to save themselves or running into battle, I did not know. I found myself on the ground, by the dais and only turned enough to spot Rhylan running away with the queen, covering her with his own body as they made their way out of the room.

I started shaking, not knowing what to do, where to go, unable to stand. I was covered in blood. Why was I covered in blood? I couldn't do anything but look around, even my gaze trembled at the surrounding gore.

"Fahrenor, come," a voice called for me, grabbing me from behind and shoving me against a hard chest.

"Ansgar…" I turned to see him, blood running down his face. He smiled. He smiled at me and oh my god, how my heart fluttered at the sight of him. He was alive and had come for me.

"Come, my love, hurry," my prince said as he grabbed me, dragging me along to get me out of the hall, just like Rhylan had done with the queen. I was nestled tightly against his torso, his left arm covering my head and as much of me as he could while the other swung a sword to make way for us to leave, stopping and throwing blows from time to time. I did not want to think, did not want to understand beyond that protective hold of his, and especially, did not want to see what was happening around.

I followed him blindly, focusing on him, on his orange and rain scent that even now, perceived underneath the metallic tang of the blood he was covered in. We were both covered in. I could only focus on him, at the closeness and his heart, still breathing inside his chest. As we took hurried steps through the corridors. I needed to understand that he was alive, that his heart kept beating and this was truly real, so I started counting them, my mind unable to think beyond anything else. He was alive. And he was here.

His heartbeat.

I could sense it.

Every breath, every heartbeat, meant that my mate remained by my side and since I could not control anything happening around me, I focused on that one thing, the most important of them all. The beating of his heart. Nothing else mattered as I started counting every single thump.

Thirty-six.... thirty-seven... Someone found us, a soldier, and rushed to attack. Ansgar's torso moved and I heard muffled cries. I closed my eyes and continued to count. His heart beat stronger, overwhelmed by the effort. It bothered me, that he was moving. I was afraid I'd miss some of his beats. How could I continue counting if I missed them?

Seventy-three.... we were moving and his arm tightened around me again, allowing me to bask in his warmth. I couldn't see him for some reason. I didn't know if my eyes were closed or if there was no light in the corridors.

Where are we going? Did I ask him that? I really wanted to ask him that. One hundred thirty...one hundred thirty-one... he shifted again and stopped. Why was he stopping? I did not understand.

One hundred fifty-eight...

"Is it done?" Ansgar's chest moved, the vibrations making me think he was the one speaking.

"Yes, prince, it is done," another voice answered far away.

One hundred eighty-three… Ansgar was pushing me away from him, leaving me bare to the darkness, away from his warmth. From his chest.

"No, I have to count," I shivered. "I have to keep counting," I said, my trembling hands struggling to retake my place.

"Fahrenor, listen," he moved my head so I could see him. I blinked. He looked beautiful. Even with the blood and the cuts across his face, he looked beautiful.

"Anwen?" he asked, unsure, but I smiled at him. I smiled at his beauty. He returned the gesture, though his eyes looked sad. "You need to go with Rhylan now, okay baby?"

Baby? He never called me that. I frowned, not understanding.

"No, I'll stay with you," I barely protested. My face felt numb, lips hardly able to pronounce the words.

He kissed my forehead eagerly, then my face, both of my cheeks, and finally, my mouth. I pressed my lips to prepare for the kiss but by the time I positioned them accordingly, it had already ended.

"Hie vaedrum teim, fahrenor," Ansgar said and pressed me closer to him, embracing me tightly. My hands grabbed onto his shoulders, my heart and all of my body happy to be enjoying his warmth once again. I realised I had forgotten my count so I started again, placing a hand over his chest and finding his heart beating.

Three...four...five...

Suddenly he was separating from me again, another set of arms grabbing hold on me. What? No!

"No!" I don't know if I said the words or shouted them, but

Ansgar's trembling hands did not listen, shoving me into another set of arms, ones that clamped around me.

"No, I don't wanna go, I'll stay with you, please," I cried, struggling to escape, to go back to my prince.

"I'll see you soon, my love," he took one of my hands in his and kissed it reverently, but by the shiver, in his voice, I knew. I knew he was lying.

"No, please," I begged, I implored, trying to escape and go back to him, every muscle in my body begging for reconnection. Begging for him.

"Come, Anwen," another voice, Rhylan, ordered and started dragging me away from Ansgar, even though I screamed and shouted and fought to escape. I called after my prince, over and over, but only managed to make him take a step away from me.

And another.

And another, while I myself was being dragged in the opposite direction. This happened on a loop, none of them caring about my cries and supplications until Ansgar disappeared into the darkness and away from my sight.

"No, please!" I begged yet again, hauled by Rhylan's unrelenting grip, pulling me further and further away.

"I made an oath, sprout. To take you to safety," he tried to explain but I did not care and only fought him harder. We did this back and forth, over and over, corridor after corridor, where I tried to fight him and escape and he kept dragging me and positioning me better into his arms.

"Please," I said it again, probably for the millionth time, after

436

my body had probably given out because Rhylan started to carry me rather than drag my body like a sack of potatoes. A sack of potatoes that was fighting back.

"I need to keep counting." I tried to explain, placing my hand over his chest, finding his heart. "I need to keep counting to make sure he is alive," I said in between tears, or blood, I did not know what was dripping on my face at this point. I tapped over his chest, rhythmically, imitating a beating heart.

Rhylan's gaze turned to me, compassionate for once. "You really love him, don't you?" His voice sounded raspy, hurt somehow.

I nodded, unable to say it. Unable to find my words and explain how much.

Boom.

I heard a sharp noise before I started flying. Or falling. When I looked around, pieces of rock surrounded me, swishing the air around with anger. My body contorted awkwardly before being pushed away, slammed into a hard surface. My hands fell over my face and chest, a sharp pain pricking my fingers. And my back. Luckily my legs didn't hurt. I couldn't feel them. There was blood around. Lots of it and... Rhylan. His body had fallen too, now laying splayed on the rocky surface.

Laughter echoed through the tunnel. Vengeful and merciless, sounding psychotic and enraged. I turned my head enough to see the king stepping closer to us before everything went blurry.

By the time I woke up, hazy breaths escaped with difficulty from my chest as I struggled to regain full use of my limbs.

Everything looked destroyed around me, the remains of broken columns aligned with what used to be a hallway, now covered by dust and destruction. I tilted my head to the side, trying to find Rhylan, but his screams were the only thing left of him. Coming from somewhere far and piercing through stone to reach me.

"Rhylan?" I cried, not knowing where he was or what had happened. I rose to my feet with difficulty, struggling to keep my body upright long enough to grab the remaining part of a wall and lean against it.

There he was, on the other side of the ruins, whaling in pain as his body flew across what remained of the room and splattered into the wall, forcing his body to expulse a fresh gush of blood.

"Rhylan…" I shouted, struggling to see through the darkness and flames spilling on the ground from the massive chandeliers. Or what remained of them. Someone small, crippled even, crouched low to the ground and hugged something. Someone. The queen, I realised after a few blinks. The queen's body, now a husk with no life inside of it.

"You will pay for this!" The king's ire flew through the ground, forming a small earthquake as his echoes continued to spill punishment. With that, Rhylan's body flew yet again, squashing everything in sight, the sound of cracking bones the only thing I could focus on beyond Rhylan's screams of pain.

"Stop!" I cried out, long enough to summon the royal's attention. As soon as those blood-red eyes shifted to me, I knew it was the worst possible decision I could have made. He grinned, suddenly forgetting his hold on the general, and started moving towards my direction with determination and all the hatred compiled within the earth.

I winced at the pain in my legs when I wanted to draw back and looked down at my ankle to realise the bone arrangement wasn't in its rightful position.

I only managed to take about three steps back until the king was upon me, gripping my hair with a rough pull and forcing my body to lean forward, towards Rhylan. Since I couldn't really walk, my hair supported the weight and forced my body to drag across with him. I wasn't sure how my scalp didn't just rip from my skin because the pain was excruciating, piercing through my head, my neck, and most of my back while bones contorted and followed the King's lead without my approval.

Rhylan's eyes locked with mine, emanating pain and disdain as I was dragged closer to him, my hands shifting in the air and blindly trying to catch the King's wrist and better support my weight.

"Release her," Rhylan threatened, a gulp of dark blood escaping from his mouth as he said the words. Pleaded them. For my safety.

"Ha!" the king mocked, his rage suddenly focusing solely on me. "Why would I do that?" As he said the words he dropped me on the rocky floor, right where Rhylan struggled to pull himself off the ground and grabbed me by the neck, resting a cold object at my throat. I started shaking, feeling the sharpness of the steel against my skin, my entire body trembling with the realisation. This is where I die.

"Don't..." I tried to speak but the words forced my throat into the knife, making a small cut.

"Let her go, she has nothing to do with this," Rhylan pleaded on my behalf, his upper half now fully upright.

"Nothing?" the king's voice trembled and I could sense it more than hear it because his every syllable shook his hand just enough to make the blade jiggle against my throat. "Do you take me for a fool, Fear Gorta?" I tensed, it was the first time the king addressed Rhylan per his faerie title.

"She has nothing to do with this. The revenge was solely mine," Rhylan expelled the words slowly, quietly, wanting to arrange them in front of the king and help him fully realise their meaning.

"Do you not think that I kept my eyes on you long enough to recognise who she is? What she means? That she is the only reason you could take away my Shay? She may have had her flaws, but she was mine! My partner for centuries!"

The king's voice broke at the mention of his queen or better said the loss of her. Which made me realise that somehow Rhylan had everything to do with it. Drahden pulled my hair tighter, forcing my neck upright, the pressure so taut that I knew the finest movement would easily break my neck. "Do you not think I recognise your kin?" he spat, gripping my hair tighter. But I couldn't move, couldn't do anything but stay there and try not to shake, trying to keep my neck from being either broken or severed.

"Let her go," Rhylan's voice accentuated, a promise for revenge lingering in the words. With whatever force he could muster he stood, towering against the king. Against me.

With a single movement of his hand, the tiniest gesture, the king's arms went rigid, their tightness slowly dissolving around the hold he had on me. Rhylan's eyes turned into flames, raw energy pulsating with the command, deep pants portraying the effort his body was going through at the execution of the order.

"Anwen," Rhylan spoke my name but kept his full focus on the king, "very carefully, lift your right arm and drag your hair from his hand." I did as told, fingers trembling as I found the king's hand wrapped around my hair. I had to pull a few times and I was sure that half of my hair remained on his statuesque hand, but that was the very last thing I cared about right now.

"Perfect," he said. "Now slide your neck to the left, very slowly, push yourself against him if you have to but whatever you do, do not lean forward."

With shaky movements I did as told, feeling how the King struggled to escape the hold of whatever magic Rhylan poured onto him, whom, judging by the blood dripping from his nose, wouldn't be able to do for much longer. So I released myself from the blade as quickly as I could and skittered towards Rhylan's legs, crawling my way out from the king's side.

As soon as he saw that I was safe, Rhylan bent to lift me just enough so I could be able to lean against him and then guided me backward, taking slow and steady steps back.

"I can't fight him, I am bound to the ruler's protection," he explained, answering a question I might have asked. Or thought about asking. "We have minutes to do this," he added as he kept pushing me, pushing us further and further away, his jaw tightening with each passing second.

I tried to hold onto him, to help sustain his weight when his muscles started trembling from the effort, but it was all in vain, my body so tired and fickle that I knew I was hurting more than helping.

"When I give the signal, run to the cave to your right," Rhylan gestured in the direction he wanted me to go to by tilting his head, wanting to make sure I understood what right meant and what a cave was.

I nodded and he must have felt me, because his shoulders relaxed only for the slightest of moments, until he took a deep breath, preparing for his next step. "Now!" he said and even before the words were out of his mouth, I started running, or crawling, towards where he pointed.

I didn't look back but heard the earthquake, the destruction of the ceiling, and all the rubble that pushed into me, sliding into my back, my arms, my legs. Rhylan was by my side moments later, shoving me inside the cave, which I initially thought wouldn't be big enough for the both of us, but after a few metres of darkness, it turned into an impressive conglomerate of columns piled together. Some kind of decor storage room.

"Are you alright?" he grabbed my face to check my response, touched my chest in search of wounds and draped his hands over my arms and legs.

"Yes. You?" I asked, not knowing what else to say, what to do.

"For now," Rhylan groaned and took a few breaths to calm himself. I'd never seen him injured, never seen him bleeding except for that one evening when Ansgar attacked him but now, he looked terrible. Like his body had been run over by a train and then thrown out of a plane without a parachute. Every single part of him was either a cut, bleeding or a forming bruise and I could not, for the life of me, understand how he'd managed to keep himself alive.

"Anwen, we only have minutes until he gets through and I don't have time for your snarky remarks right now, okay?" Rhylan's bloodshot eyes pierced through mine, forcing me to nod.

"You need to survive, need to get out of here," he stated like it was the most obvious fact.

I nodded. "As soon as I get Ansgar," I said, trying to reason even now, with the man that had tricked us and used us for his own purposes over and over again.

"For the god's sake! I do not have time for this. I need to save you; don't you get that? Don't you finally understand?" Rage pulsated through his veins as he spat the words, shaking reason into me.

"Why do you care so much?" I asked but the king's words immediately echoed in my mind. *Your kin.* "Rhylan?" I said his name, my voice shaking with the impossibility of it all. "Why do you care so much?"

His fingers traced a line along my jaw, eyes wishful and glazy. "You are mine, Anwen. You are of me," Rhylan said, voice hushed and trembling.

"What?" I frowned. "What do you mean?" I shook my head but my neck was stiff and didn't allow much movement.

He quickly added, "You have my powers. You are my kin, I made you," Rhylan's eyes scanned over me with pride.

Before I could say anything, before the panic started roaring through my body, he sent a pulse of energy through me. I guessed it was something similar to what he had done to the king because I couldn't really move and any feeling I had inside my chest had been put to a halt. Even breathing seemed weird like my lungs weren't really my own.

"Like I said, we do not have time for this, so I will have to be blunt. And I will be doing all the talking. This energy, the connection you and I share allows me to control your body, so do not freak out or cry as you always do, and for once in your life, listen and trust what I say."

I wanted to protest, to scream, to shout, but my mouth didn't utter a single word. That energy, that thing I had always felt towards Rhylan had suddenly multiplied and overpowered everything else as if my very blood was listening to him.

"Remember when I told you about the Swedish Queen's faerie lover, back in Evigt? It was true, all of it. *I* was her lover." He settled back, keeping his position close to me, able to see and read my reactions, but enough for him to have space and get comfortable. "We had a boy and as you can imagine, a youth outside wedlock wasn't good news, so he was sent away. By the time I returned for them the forest was destroyed. The king's revenge. The news didn't go too well with him."

I took in more air, still not understanding what all of this had to do with me. My eyes must have been filled with a thousand questions because he gave me the answer I needed.

"Years later I found that the youth, my son, had been sent to America, but it turned impossible to trace him, no matter how hard I tried. So I had to wait. One hundred and fifty years to be exact.

Seven generations. That's when the power manifests, every seven generations. That's how I found Erik," he took a reverent pause.

I shook my head in disbelief, refusing to understand, to listen to him. Unable to do so. No, I couldn't be connected to Rhylan, couldn't be related to him. It made no sense at all.

"For the god's sake Anwen, didn't you wonder why your father is so proud of his Swedish origin? How he always brags about his favours with the royal family? Don't you find it surprising that no one can access Evigt, but one phone call from your daddy makes it possible?"

I did wonder about that, many times over and even I found it hard to believe how easy it had been, considering that scientists and more important people than me, people that could change the world with their knowledge, weren't granted access.

"And you know what's the funniest thing of all?" he said with a sad huff. "That you turned out to be the princeling's mate." He rested his forehead over his fingers and started massaging the area lightly, circling the skin around his temples. "Fuck me if I ever expected that to happen. For my blood to be connected to theirs..."

I wasn't sure if he wanted to cry or laugh because he was on the verge of doing both. Of course, it made sense. Because if I was part of Rhylan, I had an energy of my own. Which could connect to a fae. For whatever game of fate, I must have been the seventh generation of Rhylan's heir.

A chain of explosions rattled the walls around us, making the surroundings shiver. Rhylan sighed and shot back to his feet, grabbing me along with him. "Listen, sprout, whatever happens next, you are the part of me that survives this day. You have to," his wide eyes scanned mine to assure me of the truth in his words.

Then he grabbed my arm and dragged his fingers along it, sharp and unyielding, drawing blood in many places from the brutality of his touch. I screamed in pain and had no choice but to observe how he did the same to his own skin.

"Say *I accept your blood as mine, your life as mine, your energy as my own. For we are one and the same*," he ordered, but I sucked in my lips, refusing to utter a single word. He may have released the hold of our connection and he might have been who he said he was, but I didn't owe him anything. Didn't want this from him. He remained the same bastard faerie who tortured my mate, used us for his tricks, and lied to us repeatedly.

"Do you want to die?" he shouted at me and I saw wetness in his eyes. Desperation. He was scared, I came to understand.

For the both of us.

"Do. You. Want. To. Die?" he rasped the words at me again, shoving me against the wall and protecting me with his own body as another explosion ripped through the entrance of the cave. The king's silhouette started forming between the rubble and smoke, stepping closer to us.

Rhylan's eyes went wide, locking with mine in a final pleading gaze.

"I accept your blood as mine, your life as mine, your energy as my own. For we are one and the same," I whispered, tears pouring down my face, knowing that this was our last moment. That we would both soon die.

Rhylan released a breath and immediately, fire roared through him after the last word dropped from my lips, surrounding him, then me, sealing our union. Our connection.

"Once I get out of this, I will come find you and will explain it all. I promise." His hand was locked with mine, pressing our arms together and allowing the blood from our wounds to connect, each pouring drop creating wave after wave of fire until we were both surrounded by a sphere of flames.

Rhylan smiled at me with relief, then severed our connection, the joining of our hands, and pushed me back, making the ball of flame withdraw from him and take my body further back until I was pressed against a wall. The flames surrounded me, becoming part of me and while my brain zapped with so many unknown facts, I knew I could control it. Because it was mine. It was of me. Of us. The sphere I was trapped in made me fly, lifting my body and transporting it further away from Rhylan, just as I saw the king approaching him.

Even though the energy protected me and lifted me off the ground, I couldn't move, couldn't do anything but let myself be taken away by those unharming flames that pressed me against the wall and... through it?

I struggled to see, to move, even to breathe because my body was becoming one with the stone, taking me through it while everything around turned to embers. The last thing I remember seeing was the king's sword slashing towards Rhylan's chest.

I shouted his name until everything turned dark.

Someone shook me gently and I winced in pain. Everything hurt. It felt like rivers of blood had been passing through my brain. I struggled to open my eyes and find someone through the foggy images.

Ansgar.

"You're safe," he whispered. "You are safe," he placed his lips on mine, leaving specks of blood on my mouth, his entire face caked with it.

"Rhylan…" I forced my head towards the massive rubble from which I have been spared during the collapse.

"There's nothing we can do for him," Ansgar's words whispered softly. It was a miracle he could still hold me, his arms and torso were covered in deep cuts and bruises and I didn't even want to think about the injuries below his armour.

I blinked a few times, struggling to move a hand to his face, to make sure he was real. His chin leaned in and kissed the palm of my hand. Softly. Carefully. As if I could break any second.

"Let's go home, fahrenor," he murmured, a yearning for freedom in his shadowed eyes.

Follow the journey in Tales of Forever and Now

For a new author, reviews are everything, so if you enjoyed this book, please give it some stars!

If you enjoyed this book, you'll love the FREE bonus story *Tales of War and Fire*. Subscribe to my newsletter and get your copy, along with bonus chapters and fun content.

www. xandranoel.com

THANK YOU

I would like to place a special thank you to my beta readers and booktok community, to all the wonderful and supportive accounts I found online and the indie authors I became friends with.

Jessika (Jessikadarkstar) you truly are a star and the best beta anyone could ask for. I cannot wait to read your work and I'm sure it will be fabulous!

Mia (itsmiaregine) you are the funniest beta reader and girl, your comments crack me up every single time!

A very special thank you to christinagizzi, scout.ticklequeen, toricameron, pc0208, bettyrodz11 and feline_fatalistic as well for your wonderful input.

And to everyone who took a chance and read my debut novel, to everyone who took the time to review or to message me and share your thoughts, THANK YOU!

My dream grows a little bigger each day because of you and I am beyond thankful.

Printed in Great Britain
by Amazon

22528134R00255